ties that bind

A SHELBY NICHOLS ADVENTURE

Colleen Helme

MB

www.colleenhelme.com

Publisher's Note: This is a work of fiction. Names, characters, places, and incidents are a product of the author's imagination. Locales and public names are sometimes used for atmospheric purposes. Any resemblance to actual people, living or dead, or to businesses, companies, events, institutions, or locales is completely coincidental.

Ties That Bind/Colleen Helme. -- 1st ed.
ISBN 9798355386139

Dedication

To Tom and our cruising friends
Good times and great memories!

Gary and Colleen
Jamie and Anne
Ed and Tammy

ACKNOWLEDGEMENTS

I'd like to begin by thanking Paul Knoop for his amazing help with my understanding of cryptocurrency. I knew nothing about crypto, so it was a huge learning curve for me, and his help was awesome! Any mistakes about crypto are definitely my own and not his. He even came up with some great crypto names!! Thank you Paul! You rock!

I'm so grateful for all of you who love Shelby as much as I do! Thanks for your support, encouragement, friendship, and great reviews. You keep me writing.

As always, I need to give a big shout-out and thanks to my daughter, Melissa. You are always willing to listen to my crazy ideas and keep me going.

Once again, I'd like to give a huge thanks to Kristin Monson for editing this book and making it better. Thanks for your great insights and enthusiasm! You're the best!

I am so grateful to the talented Wendy Tremont King for bringing Shelby and the gang to life on audio. Thanks for sticking with me through sixteen books! YOP Forever!

Last but not least, thanks to my wonderful husband, Tom, for believing in my dreams. Thanks to my awesome family for your continued encouragement and support.

I love you all!

~Colleen

Shelby Nichols Adventure Series

Carrots
Fast Money
Lie or Die
Secrets that Kill
Trapped by Revenge
Deep in Death
Crossing Danger
Devious Minds
Hidden Deception
Laced in Lies
Deadly Escape
Marked for Murder
Ghostly Serenade
Dying Wishes
High Stakes Crime
Ties That Bind

Devil in a Black Suit ~ A Ramos Story
A Midsummer Night's Murder ~ A Shelby Nichols Novella

Sand and Shadow Series

Angel Falls
Desert Devil

NEWSLETTER SIGNUP

For news, updates, and special offers, please sign up for my newsletter at www.colleenhelme.com. To thank you for subscribing you will receive a **FREE** ebook: *Behind Blue Eyes: A Shelby Nichols Novella.*

Contents

Chapter 1

The warehouse sat empty and dark except for the light shining from a window in the far corner of the building. My knees began to ache, and I adjusted the car's seat to give me a little more room. I'd been watching this building for nearly two hours, and I'd just about reached my limits. I'd give Ramos ten more minutes. If he didn't show up by then, I was going in without him.

I didn't usually work for Uncle Joey and my husband, Chris, at the same time. But, since Chris was Uncle Joey's lawyer, it was bound to happen. The man I'd been following all night, Max Huszar, was Chris's client, as well as a business associate of Uncle Joey's.

From what I understood, Uncle Joey had invested heavily in Max's company, MantaTira, and he suspected that Max was keeping secrets from him. Since I was Uncle Joey's truth-o-meter, it was up to me to find out what was going on.

As his lawyer, Chris was helping Max with some legal work involving his company. My job tonight had begun after they'd finished their meeting in Chris's office.

I'd followed Max to a bank, and after that, to a bar. Since he'd never met me, I was pretty sure I could follow him inside the bar without attracting his attention.

My luck held out since the lights were low. Max sat at the bar, and I'd managed to duck around it, and find a booth in the back, where I could still see him.

In his late thirties, Max had the sophisticated look of an up-and-coming business executive. He'd worn a dark suit over a white shirt, and there wasn't a single hair out of place on his dark head.

After Max had ordered a drink, I'd listened to his thoughts, picking up that he was waiting for someone, and that someone was late.

In the meantime, a server came to take my order, so I'd asked for a Diet Coke with lime. I tried to pick up who Max was waiting for, but it was hard to get the details with all the thoughts going on around me.

After the server brought my drink, I drank it down pretty fast, since I had a good idea that Max might not stay long enough for me to finish.

At that point, Max was thinking about the risk he'd taken and hoped this ended his—

"Hello beautiful. Mind if I join you?"

That threw me, and I totally lost Max's thoughts. An attractive thirty-something man slid into the booth across from me. He wore a suit and began loosening his tie like he was ready to stay a while. "I haven't seen you here before. Do you work somewhere nearby?"

I knew I should be flattered that he was hitting on me, but he was ruining everything. "Oh... I'm sorry, but that seat's taken."

His gaze narrowed. "Really? I thought you were alone." It annoyed him that I was lying. He'd watched me come in by myself, and I hadn't looked at my phone once. In fact... I'd been staring at the man at the bar since I'd arrived. Tilting his head toward Max, he said, "You shouldn't be wasting your time on that guy. He hasn't even noticed you."

"Oh... he's not... it's not him. I'm waiting for someone else. But thanks anyway."

He did that chin-lift thing before raising a brow. "Right. Maybe next time?"

I smiled brightly, like that was the best thing I'd heard all day. "Of course."

That seemed to satisfy him and he left. Relaxing my smile, I sighed and glanced Max's way, hoping I hadn't missed too much. He held his phone in front of him and was sending a text. Finished, he took a few more sips of his drink and checked his phone every few seconds.

Tapping his fingers on the bar, his agitation grew. He was thinking *where is he*? He couldn't believe the guy wasn't there yet, and this had better not derail his plans. After several minutes of this, he shook his head, thinking he couldn't wait any longer. Frowning, he laid a couple of bills on the bar and got up to leave.

I grabbed a ten-dollar bill from my purse and put it on the table. Watching him walk toward the exit, I took a few more gulps of my drink before scurrying after him.

Back in his car, Max put a call through to someone who must have answered, because he made wild gestures with his hands, like he was angry. Finished with the call, he put his phone away and drove straight to the warehouse.

I'd parked on the street and watched him unlock the outside door and disappear inside. I'd wanted to follow him in so I could get this over with and go home. Unfortunately, I'd been told by both Uncle Joey and Chris that I had to wait for Ramos before I did anything dangerous. But they'd really been thinking before I did anything stupid. It sort of hurt my feelings, but, based on past experience, I couldn't blame them too much.

That was two hours ago. Now I was beginning to wonder if Ramos would ever show up. Unease filled me that something had happened to him. He wasn't answering his phone, and I couldn't imagine why he'd leave me hanging.

My cell phone beeped with a text message, and I quickly pulled it out. Instead of Ramos, like I'd hoped, it was Chris asking me what was taking so long. I explained that Max was still in the warehouse and I was waiting for Ramos. Chris texted me back, telling me to give it another ten minutes and then head home. He assured me that I could talk to Max another time.

I let out a breath. Uncle Joey or Chris should have just let me come to one of their meetings with Max. Then I wouldn't have had to follow him all over the place. But Uncle Joey had wanted to know who Max was meeting with before he did that. Too bad the person had never showed up.

After ten minutes, I checked my messages one more time for anything from Ramos. Sighing, I put my phone away. It didn't look like he was going to make it, so I might as well leave. I cast one last glance at the building just as the light in the corner office blinked out. I straightened. Was Max leaving? What should I do now?

I watched the building's exit for a glimpse of him and slipped out of my car, grateful I'd worn black clothes. Taking my stun flashlight with me, I gently closed the car door and hurried toward the building. If I could get close enough to hear his thoughts as he left, it might give me something to tell Uncle Joey. It wasn't as good as talking to him, but it was better than nothing.

The security light above the door was broken, leaving the exit in darkness, so I crept to the bushes a few feet from the door, and hunkered down to wait. From my spot, he'd have to walk right past me to get to his car, so this should work as long as he couldn't see me.

If Ramos had been here like he was supposed to, I wouldn't have any qualms about rushing into the building and confronting Max. Now I was reduced to hiding in the bushes.

I caught a flicker of movement off to the side of the building and froze. Nothing moved in the dark shadows, and I waited several long seconds before relaxing. It must have been my imagination. Shaking my head, I glanced back at the door.

Minutes passed and still nothing happened. My knees were getting stiff again, so I shifted to rest against the wall. More time passed, and my patience was wearing thin. Was there another way out? Maybe he'd already left, and I'd missed him? His car was parked around the corner, so I hurried as fast as my stiff legs could take me to the other side of the building.

Max's car was still there, so he had to be inside. Creeping back to the door, I plastered my back against the wall and reached down to pull on the handle to see if it was unlocked, but it didn't budge. Coming to a decision, I reached into the pocket of my cargo pants, and pulled out my lock-pick set. It was time to do some sleuthing.

Ramos had showed me how to do this a while ago, but I'd just completed my hours of training with a private investigator for my PI license, so I'd had a little more practice. Hopefully it would pay off.

It was hard to see what I was doing in the dark, so I ran my fingers over the keyhole and fit my picks inside by feel. I wiggled them around a bit before closing my eyes and concentrating on my task.

"Need some help?"

"Gah!" I jerked back and fell on my butt, dropping my tools and landing in a heap.

"Whoa. Are you okay?" Ramos reached out to help me up.

"Ramos!" I batted his hand away, barely keeping my voice above a whisper. "What the hell. You scared me to death."

"Sorry, I thought you were expecting me. Didn't you get my text?"

"No."

"Oh. That's too bad."

Was that sarcasm in his tone? He reached for me again, but this time, I let him help me up. "Where have you been? I've been waiting for nearly two hours!"

"I explained it all in my text."

I heaved a sigh. "Yeah... right... the one I didn't get."

He shook his head. "Let's figure that out later. Right now I need to know what's going on. Why are you trying to break in?"

"Max turned out the light a while ago, but he never came out. His car's still here, so I thought I'd go in and check on him. As you can see, the stupid door's locked."

"Uh... would you like me to help?" He moved to take the tools from me, but I jerked my hands away.

I wasn't sure why I did it, but it might have had something to do with the fact that he'd scared me to death. He'd obviously blocked his thoughts from me, which didn't seem like a nice thing to do.

In the shadows, I could barely make out the look on his face. His right brow had risen, and his lips had parted with a hint of surprise.

"I can do it myself," I huffed, knowing I sounded surly.

"Sure. Go ahead. But make it fast. We don't want to get caught in the act."

I knew it would only take him a couple of seconds to get the door open, lots faster than me, but I hated giving in. Irritated, I handed the tools over. "No. You do it. You're faster."

He took them without arguing and bent to the task. A couple of seconds later, he had the door open, and we both slipped inside. "You know where we're going?"

"Mostly. The light was in the corner of the building, off to the right. So we need to go in that direction."

He pulled a penlight from his pocket and flicked it on. The soft glow lit the darkness, and he sent a quick flash around the room. The light showed us an office desk stacked with cluttered papers, along with a phone and a computer. Beyond that, a hallway led toward the right side of the building, and we started in that direction.

As we crept forward, my heart began to pound, and I tried to keep my breathing steady. As much as I hated to admit it, having Ramos lead the way was a game-changer. Why did I ever think I could do this without him?

We reached the office door, and Ramos twisted the door knob. It turned in his hand and he glanced my way. "Get down."

After crouching down, he pushed the door open. I expected to hear shouts of surprise, or even a gunshot, but it was quiet. Waiting for a couple of heartbeats, Ramos straightened and stepped inside.

He panned the light over the office before bringing it to a stop on the chair behind the desk. Someone sat in the chair. The man's head listed to the side at an awkward angle, and blood soaked his shirt from a gash across his neck. I gasped and tried not to gag.

"That doesn't look like him," Ramos said. "What do you think?"

I swallowed back the bile in my throat and took a good look at the man's features. "No... it's not Max. I don't know who that is, do you?"

"No." Ramos froze. "Did you hear that?"

With my heart pounding so loud, I couldn't hear anything else. "No. What?"

"Come on... we've got to get out of here."

Listening closely, I heard a beeping sound, but lost it as Ramos grabbed my arm and began to drag me out of the office. It took a moment for it to sink in, but I'd heard that sound before, and it sent shards of fear down my spine.

I couldn't get my legs moving fast enough, and nearly fell before getting my feet under me. Ramos continued to drag me toward the door, and I thought each second that passed might be my last.

The adrenaline kicked in, and we sprinted out of the building and kept on going. Just as hope filled my heart that we'd outrun it, a blast of heat, along with a concussive roar, threw me forward. I tumbled onto my stomach, and my chin scraped against the pavement. Ramos landed half on top of me, pushing the breath from my lungs.

Debris rained down beside us, and Ramos flinched from something landing on him. He got to his hands and knees, relieving the pressure on my chest, and I sucked in a breath.

"Come on." He tugged at my arm to get me moving. Gasping, I crawled beside him through a field of burning wood and papers.

We finally made it to the outer edge of the parking lot and Ramos collapsed onto his stomach. Worried he'd been injured, I got to my knees and glanced over his prone form. His shirt was smoking in a few spots, so I pounded my hands against his back to get the fire out.

Ramos groaned and managed to jerk away from my touch. "What the hell are you doing?"

"You're on fire."

With a huff, he sat up and yanked off his shirt, giving me an eyeful of his well-muscled chest. Swallowing, I glanced at his back, finding red spots and bruises beginning to form. Otherwise, he looked pretty good.

Who was I kidding? He looked freaking amazing. "Uh... I don't see any blood. But there's some bruising and a few burn marks."

Unable to resist, I raised my hand to brush some of the dirt from his back. My fingers skimmed over his warm skin, and his muscles rippled beneath my touch. A tattoo on his shoulder caught my attention, and I couldn't help running my fingers over the black ink. I'd seen glimpses of it before, but I'd never had the chance to study it up close.

All at once the shape made sense, and I gasped. "The ace of spades? That's what it is... a spade with a stylized A running through it."

He huffed out a breath, and I heard *Duh* in his mind.

I ignored him. "You must have gotten that while you lived in Florida." Ramos had belonged to a gang in his younger days, and he'd gone by Ace back then.

In a quick move, Ramos twisted toward me, with his face close to mine. "That's right." His lips were close enough that I could feel his hot breath on my cheek. Turning my head slightly was all it would take for our lips to touch. Mesmerized, my lips parted, and I could barely keep from running my tongue over them.

The corner of Ramos's mouth tilted up, and my gaze flew to his. A wicked gleam flashed in his dark eyes, reflecting the orange fire burning behind us. My eyes widened, but I couldn't seem to move.

His gaze moved to my mouth, and his lips parted. "If you're done, I think we need to leave before the police get here."

That broke the spell, and I pulled back, chagrined to find my hands still caressing his bare skin. I jerked them away and climbed to my feet. "Uh… I'm not sure we should leave. I mean… there was a dead body in there. We should probably explain what we found."

Ramos stood beside me. "Babe… I don't want to get involved with the police. We broke in, remember? We're here because of Manetto. How would you explain that?"

"But… it's not just Uncle Joey. Max is one of Chris's clients, too. I could tell them I was investigating him for Chris's law firm, and you were helping me. It's the truth, and, since I'm a private investigator, that should explain everything."

Ramos slipped his shirt over his head, and I held back a sigh. He was thinking that might work for me, since I worked with the police, but he couldn't risk it. "You can stay if you want, but I'm out of here."

Resigned, I nodded. "You're right… you should go."

He sighed. "You sure you can't come?" He was thinking it might be nice to have someone with my light touch dab ointment on his burns. Didn't I know he'd gotten them protecting me? He couldn't reach them, and it was the least I could do after he'd saved my life… again.

My breath hitched. "Hey… stop that. Now I feel guilty."

His lips twitched. "That's the idea. Ready to go?"

I let out a deep sigh and shook my head. "You sure know how to play dirty."

His smile got even bigger, and I stifled a groan. He was thinking that was the best way to play… and I could learn a thing or two from him.

"That's enough. You'd better get going, or it really will be too late."

"I guess, but I think you're making a mistake."

"I'm sure you do, but you'll get over it."

"I might, but what about you?" He stepped closer, his dark eyes flashing with a challenge.

I held my ground and met his gaze. He might be intimidating, but there was a competitive streak in me, too. The sound of sirens reached us, and I let out a breath before stepping back and shaking my head. "Maybe not, but now you'll never know." The surprise in his eyes made me smile. "See you tomorrow."

He huffed out a breath, thinking I was getting cocky, but two could play that game. He stepped away before meeting my gaze. "Since you're staying, make sure you keep Manetto out of it."

"I can't guarantee that."

Ramos froze and his right brow rose. "What?"

"I mean... yes, I won't say anything about Uncle Joey, but that doesn't mean his name won't come up."

"As long as it's not by you, it'll be fine." With a shake of his head, he hurried away, and I spotted his motorcycle parked halfway down the block. As the sirens drew closer, he picked up the pace. A few seconds later, he was gone.

Feeling a sudden chill, I jumped into my car to wait for the police. I'd probably enjoyed bantering with Ramos way too much, but at least it had kept my mind off the murdered man and how close we'd both come to getting blown up.

All the small scrapes on my hands, knees, and chin began to burn, and I knew it was just the beginning of my aches and pains. At least Ramos had saved me from the brunt of the blast, and I tried not to feel too guilty. On the other hand, he was a brawny, tough man, so it was no big deal for him, right?

The firetrucks got there first and began pumping water into the blazing building. I stayed in my car until the police arrived. A small crowd had gathered as well, drawn by the sound of the explosion and the burning building.

An unmarked police car with a couple of detectives drove up. After conferring with the firefighters, they turned their attention to questioning the crowd. Relief filled me to recognize Clue and her partner, Williams. We'd worked a case together, so I knew I was safe with them.

I climbed out of my car and stepped across the debris toward Clue. She glanced my way, then did a double-take. Excusing herself from an onlooker, she hurried to my side, taking in my scraped chin and disheveled appearance. "Shelby... what are you doing here?"

"I'm a witness to the explosion. There was a bomb inside."

She gasped. "How do you know that?"

"I went inside and saw it. I barely got out in time."

"What? You were in there?" At my nod, she continued, "Why?"

I shrugged. "I'm investigating someone, and this is where he ended up."

"Investigating?"

"Yeah... I have my PI license, so I do work on the side." I ignored her shock and told her I'd been following Max all evening, and that he'd ended up here at the warehouse. Naturally, I left out the part about Ramos, as well as the part where the door had been locked.

As I told her about the dead body, her eyes widened, and she held up a hand. "Wait. I think Williams will want to hear this." She called him over, and I told him I'd followed Max to the building, mentioning that when he didn't come out, I'd gone inside, only to find both the body and the bomb.

By the time I got done, the aftereffects of the adrenalin rush had set in, leaving me shaky and exhausted.

"Wait a minute," Williams said. "Did you say his car was still here?" At my nod, he continued. "Then where is it?"

"It's in the back, on the other side of the building. I'll show you." We passed the firetrucks and continued around the corner of the blown-up building to the back parking lot. My breath froze to find it empty. "It's gone. It was right here before the blast."

Williams shook his head. "I need the guy's name again. Maybe we can get the license plate number of his car and track it."

Dazed, I nodded. "Sure. It's Max Huszar."

"Can you spell that for me?" I did, and he continued. "Okay. Got it. Maybe you'd better come down to the station so we can get your statement."

I picked up that he wanted me to go to the station now. Since that was the last thing I wanted to do, I tried to look more pathetic than normal. "Why don't I come first thing in the morning?" I glanced at my watch. "It's really late and I nearly died from the blast, so I'm a little shook up. Besides, I don't know what more I can add."

He took a breath to argue with me, but Clue put her hand on his arm. "She's right, it's late." She glanced at me. "You'll come in first thing?"

"Yes. Of course."

"That should work. Maybe you'll remember something you may have forgotten by then." She was thinking it wouldn't hurt to give me some time to think things through, mostly because I wasn't telling them the important things, like why I was following Max, and where he had been throughout the evening. If he'd killed the man inside the building, they needed to know.

"Sure. I'll see you then." I sent her a quick nod and hurried to my car. She didn't miss much, and I was grateful for the reprieve. I picked up her hope that, by cutting me some slack, I'd be more open to passing along my information. Since I wasn't sure what to tell her without talking to Chris first, I knew I'd just had a lucky escape.

I made it home in one piece and found Chris asleep in bed with the bedroom lamp on. He must have fallen asleep right after my text telling him I was on my way home.

I sat down on the side of the bed and pulled off my boots. He stirred and opened his eyes. "You made it." His gaze roamed over my face, and his brows drew together. Taking in my scraped chin and disheveled appearance, he sat up straight. "What happened?"

"I ran into a snag." I picked up his alarm and quickly explained the events of the night. The murdered man took him off-guard, and he wouldn't let me continue until I explained that I had no idea who he was.

"But how did your chin get scraped up?"

"That's the part you're not going to like, but just remember that I'm here now, and I'm okay, so it's not so bad."

His eyes widened. "Shelby—"

"There was a bomb." That shut him up, and gave me the chance to tell him everything without interruption. "Ramos left, but I waited for the police. I had to tell the detectives about Max and the dead body. I agreed to go to the station in the morning to give them my statement, but what am I supposed to say? After I got done explaining things to them, Max's car was gone, so he must have left between the time Ramos and I went inside the building and the explosion. Do you think he killed that guy and planted the bomb?"

Chris shook his head. "Damn. I don't know. We met to go over what it would take to legally change his tech firm from a small business into a corporation. That doesn't sound like someone who'd plant a bomb and murder a man." He rubbed the back of his neck. "But this is only the first time I've met with him, so I don't know him very well."

"Don't forget he stopped at a bank. If he withdrew a lot of money, it could have been to pay someone off. Maybe the bomb was a backup plan to cover up the murder? If we hadn't seen the body, no one would have suspected anyone was inside."

"They would have found evidence of the body eventually, but not for a few days. Still, setting off a bomb takes a lot of planning. It's not something you do on a whim."

"That's true."

Chris rubbed his hand over his face. "There's obviously a lot more going on with this than any of us know."

He got out of bed and I sank into his arms, grateful for his warmth. "I never would have wanted you to follow him if I'd known he was so dangerous." He was thinking it was just my luck that a simple surveillance job could get so deadly. Why did these things always happen to me?

"I'm fine. Just a little stiff. I think I'll take a hot shower and get ready for bed."

"Sure. I'd better see if Max or Manetto left me any messages."

A few minutes later, I stepped out of the bathroom. Chris was gone, so I quickly put on my pajamas and hurried downstairs. I found him talking on the phone in the study and joined him inside.

"—no, I don't think so, but I'd sure like to know how much money he took out of the bank. Yeah... I'll let you know if he contacts me." Chris disconnected and shook his head. "That was Manetto. He wants you to be careful about what you tell the police."

"Careful, how?"

"He doesn't want his name involved."

I rolled my eyes. "As if I would."

"I know... sorry, but this case just took a turn for the worse, and I have no idea what's going on."

"I told the police I was investigating him for you, but nothing more. They'll want to know why I was tracking him."

"You don't have to explain anything to them. All you have to tell them is what you saw, not where Max had been or who he spoke to. The rest is protected by client-attorney privilege, which applies to you, since you're working for me."

"Oh... okay. So, does that mean I should leave out the details of where he went before he stopped at the warehouse?"

"Yes. If they push you, tell them they'll have to take it up with me."

"I don't think they'll like that much."

He huffed out a breath. "Too bad."

"Okay." I rubbed Chris's back, surprised at how tense he'd become. "We can't solve this tonight. Let's go to bed. We can figure it out tomorrow."

Chris sighed and shook his head. "You go ahead. I've got to check on a couple of things." I caught that Chris wanted to look over the paperwork he'd drawn up for Max in case he'd missed something. He thought it was too bad that I hadn't been able to talk to Max, since that would have made all the difference.

"Okay... well, don't be too long."

"I won't."

I shambled up the stairs to bed. If I were to guess, I'd say that Max blew up the warehouse to hide something, but the thing that kept me from going to sleep was wondering if Max knew that Ramos and I were in the building.

Had he spotted me following him? He probably knew Ramos on sight, but I'd never met him before, so he wouldn't be suspicious of me. But if he knew we'd followed him inside, he should have warned us about the bomb... unless he meant for us to die. But why would he do that? As I understood it, Uncle Joey was a big contributor to Max's business, so killing us didn't make a lot of sense.

But what if I wasn't the only one following Max tonight? What if the dead man had been following Max and found another way in, only to have Max kill him? Was he the person Max was waiting to meet at the bar? Had Max planned to kill him all along? If I'd gone inside the warehouse earlier, would he have killed me too?

Chapter 2

I slept in until seven-thirty the next morning and had to rush to get the kids off to school. Chris left right after them, reminding me not to tell the police anything about Uncle Joey. "And come by my office after you're done. I want to know everything the police have on the case."

He didn't wait for a response before he dashed out the door; otherwise he would have seen my frown. In that moment, he'd sounded just like Uncle Joey, and it was a little disconcerting.

Still, as much as I didn't like it, I had to remember that my ability was a tool everyone wanted to use for themselves, even if it did cause a moral dilemma for me. I was sure that telling Chris or Uncle Joey all the details about an ongoing police investigation could get me into a lot of hot water, but what did I expect? I should be used to it by now.

If it wasn't for that fateful day when I'd stopped at the grocery store for carrots, who knew what my life would be like? Instead of reading minds and working for both the police and the mob, my life would probably be boring as hell. So maybe this part wasn't so bad.

Sighing, I turned to find Coco sitting on his haunches in front of me. He met my gaze and let out a low yip. I heard *go walk*. He was a trained search-and-rescue dog who'd saved my life more than once, and, because of my mind-reading skills, I understood him perfectly.

There was no way I could turn him down, and he seemed to know it. "Sure. Just let me get my shoes."

He barked triumphantly and dashed off to get his leash. I shook my head and quickly got ready. It might make me late to the police station, but I treasured these walks with my dog. A few minutes later, we left the house, finding the autumn morning air crisp, but not cold. The leaves were beginning to fall around us, and I enjoyed crunching them underfoot.

As we walked to the park, I turned my attention to all the good things that I had going for me. Besides Coco, I had a great husband, two awesome kids, who were sometimes a pain in the butt, and my extended family, which included Uncle Joey and all the Manettos.

Who would have thought a mob boss and his family would become so dear to me? That included his hitman, Ramos. We had a special bond that went beyond the physical attraction, and I knew I could count on him for anything.

Our relationship tended to hinge on the edge of propriety, but somehow, we made it work, probably because we cared enough about each other not to go over the edge. If that ever happened, I'd have to make a choice. Him or my family, and I'd have to let him go. I'd choose the balancing act over that every time.

Thoughts of him reminded me that I still didn't know where he'd been last night. Had he been lying to me about the text he'd sent? I'd checked a dozen times and it hadn't come through. At least he'd shown up, even if he was late.

But where had he been? Once I got through talking to the police and Chris, I intended to find out. Besides, Uncle Joey would need to know what was going on with the police investigation, so it only made sense to stop by.

We got home from our walk and I got ready for the day, throwing on a clean pair of black jeans, and a sea-green, scoop-necked tee, which went nicely with my black motorcycle jacket. I loved my jacket. It had character and hardly showed the dirt and scrapes from nearly getting blown up. Plus, I figured it never hurt to be prepared to go for a ride on a motorcycle, and looking hot would increase my chances.

After parking my car at the police station, I slipped the lanyard with my ID badge over my head and hurried inside. Stepping into the detectives' offices, I hoped to spot Dimples so I could talk to him first. He was my partner with the police, and I needed to fill him in on last night before the others did.

He sat at his desk, and I quickly stepped toward him. He spotted me and his lips tilted into a grin before they flattened. He was thinking I was working a case for Manetto, and now I was in big trouble.

How did he know that? Clue or Williams didn't know, so it didn't come from them. Did that mean the police had some kind of information linking Uncle Joey to the warehouse? I sure hoped they didn't. It would put me in a difficult bind, and I hated lying.

Since he was the only person in the police department who knew I could read minds, I answered his thoughts. "I was working for Chris's law firm last night. There's nothing wrong with that."

His lips flattened even more. Did I really think he didn't know when I was lying?

"I'm not lying."

"Isn't leaving information out the same thing?"

That took the wind out of my sails, and I sat down in the chair beside his desk. I glanced around and lowered my voice. "Not always, especially if you're me. I know stuff most people don't, so I have to lie. That doesn't mean it's a bad thing to do, or make me a bad person."

"You're not a bad person." He hated that I always said that. It distracted him from the real problem. "Wait. Is that why you always say that? To distract me?"

I drew in a breath. "What? No." His eyes narrowed, and my lips turned down. "I don't know... maybe. But it's totally subconscious if I am. I mean... I don't want to be a bad person, and I know bad people lie all the time... so I guess it's something I worry about."

Dimples shook his head, a little amazed at how my mind worked. He tried to hold back a grin, but couldn't do it. I'd done it again... and now he wasn't even angry with me. How could he be angry when I was so earnest about my badness, or was it my bad-ass-ness? There wasn't a single person in the world like me, so he had to roll with the punches.

"Was that a compliment?"

His grin widened, making his dimples whirl around in his cheeks like little tornadoes. The sight of them always lightened my heart and made me smile. I still didn't know why I reacted that way. Maybe it was a question for Bob Spicer, my therapist.

I hadn't seen Bob for over a month, so it was probably time to stop by. He was the therapist for the whole police department, and I'd been ordered to talk to him by internal affairs after I'd killed a man in the line of duty.

Talking to Bob had been touch and go at first, since he'd wanted to know all about my 'premonitions' and how they worked. That was another lie I'd told, but telling people I had premonitions was a lot better than telling them I could read minds.

I glanced at Dimples. At least he knew the truth. We didn't just work cases together; we were friends, so I tried my best not to lie to him. "Okay... here's the truth. Uncle Joey has an interest in the man I was following last night, but I don't know more than that."

Dimples's eyes widened. He hadn't expected that. "Oh... okay."

"Why did you think he was involved anyway?"

"Because of—"

"Shelby. There you are," Clue said, stepping beside me. "I don't mean to interrupt, but we're ready for your statement."

"Oh... sure." I stood to leave and glanced at Dimples. "I'll come back after I'm done, and we can finish our conversation."

He nodded, thinking that they were sure to press the issue about my ties to Manetto, and I needed to be careful about what I said. He didn't want to lose his partner over this.

I sent him a quick nod of thanks and tried to quell the sudden unease in the pit of my stomach. To make matters worse, Clue led me into an interrogation room, and my anxiety spiked. Now, instead of making a simple statement, I had to worry that they would be recording what I said as well.

I sat down at the table across from Clue, and she smiled to put me at ease. "The team is still going over the blast site, but they did find some human remains. We're hoping to get a DNA match once we have more."

Nodding, I squelched thoughts of flying body parts and changed the subject. "What about Max? Did you track him down?"

"We're still looking." She didn't want to tell me that they'd already checked his home and office, but there was no sign of him anywhere.

"What about his car? Did you find it?"

She blinked a few times. "We're still trying to track that down too." She didn't want to tell me they'd come to a dead end, and the car was missing as well. It was like he'd disappeared off the face of the earth.

"Oh... that's too bad."

"Do you have any ideas about where he might have gone?"

"Me? No. My only contact with him was yesterday when I followed him to the warehouse."

Her eyes brightened. "So where was he when you started following him?"

"Uh... I'm not sure I can tell you. Attorney-client privilege and all that." I leaned forward, like I was letting her in on a secret. "He made a couple of stops before ending up at the warehouse, but nothing that would help the investigation, or I'd tell you."

She stared at me, wondering if she could take me at my word. I was probably more loyal to my husband than I was to the police, but she'd try to give me the benefit of the doubt.

"Do you know what Max's connection to the warehouse was?" She'd checked to see who owned the building, but found that the warehouse was a recent acquisition of a corporation who claimed to want to develop the property.

She'd looked into the previous owners, but all she'd been able to come up with was another corporation. That sort of thing made it look suspicious, like someone was hiding something. She knew Chris had a connection to the mob, and if this was tied to them, she hoped I might have something to add.

I shook my head. "Honestly, I have no idea."

She nodded, but wasn't convinced. "Let's go over everything one more time." She was hoping I'd remember something I'd left out last night. Not wanting to tell her more than I already had, I listened real close to her thoughts and stayed with what she remembered that I'd told her.

By the time we got done, I was grateful the whole process was over. Reading minds and saying the right things at the right time could be exhausting.

Clue sat back in her chair. "I just want to be clear about something. You were working for your husband's law firm, correct?"

"Yes."

"And Max is a client of his, and the firm wanted you to follow him because..."

I shrugged. "I have no idea. I guess you could ask them."

She pursed her lips, knowing that with attorney-client privilege she'd never find out unless I offered the information, and it didn't look like I would do that. "Okay. Thanks Shelby. I'd consider it a favor if you let me know what turns up on your end of things. Maybe we could help each other."

She was hoping I'd be willing to tell her what I knew in exchange for keeping me in the loop with the police investigation. It was a nice thought, although I didn't need to agree, since I could just pick up what I needed from her mind.

"Sure. I can do that. And I'm more than willing to help with the police investigation if you'd like." I threw that in, just to be on the safe side.

"So you can tell your husband?"

"What? No. Of course not. I just want to help solve the case."

She wasn't buying it, but what could she say? "Sure. I'll let you know."

"Okay." Disappointed that she thought the worst of me, I hurried out of the room and straight to the detectives' offices.

Dimples wasn't at his desk anymore. I glanced toward the break room, but hesitated, not sure I wanted to talk to him. He may be my friend, but when it came to this case, he questioned my ethics as well. It might be better to stay away from the police and figure this out on my own. That way, they couldn't accuse me of anything.

I glanced at my desk and the computer, knowing the research I could do with police resources would come in handy. But that was unethical too. Since I really didn't want to go to hell, I turned to leave and barreled into Dimples.

"Whoa," he said, grabbing my arms to steady me. "I'm surprised you didn't know I was there."

"Sorry. My mind was on something else."

He nodded. "Oh... right. Hey... I know this is short notice, but there was a homicide this morning that several of us are working on. We identified the victim, and I just got the search warrant for his apartment. Can you ride along with me? You might pick something up... like..." He lowered his voice. "His ghost."

I checked my watch. I still had to meet with Chris before heading to Thrasher, but, since it was only ten in the morning, I could probably spare an hour or so. "Sure, I'll ride along."

"Thanks. I'll fill you in on the way."

Clue watched us leave the office with a frown on her face, and I tried to block out her thoughts of distrust. Dimples noticed and glanced my way. "How'd the interview go?"

"Fine. They just don't have a lot to go on yet. I told Clue I'd be happy to help, but she doesn't seem to trust that I won't tell Chris."

"I don't blame her." Dimples smiled to soften the blow. "But you might be able to work something out." His dimples worked their magic, and I smiled back, liking his positive attitude.

"That would be nice." I followed him out of the precinct and to his car. "So tell me about the case."

"A jogger was found early this morning on one of the trails in Lincoln Park. He was stabbed, and died at the scene. A woman walking her dog called it in, but there were no other witnesses.

"His wallet was in his pocket, and we identified him as Kai Nisogi. There was also a business card." He didn't know how much time I had, but he thought it would be great if I'd visit Kai's office with him as well. "Uh... you probably heard that... so what do you think?"

"I think I can... but it all depends on how long it takes. I've got somewhere I need to be in a couple of hours."

"Right." His thoughts went straight to Uncle Joey, and he tried not to frown. "Okay... well, let's play it by ear. The good news is that his apartment and his office are within walking distance of each other, so we won't have much travel time."

"Sounds good. So... you don't think it was a mugging because he still had his wallet full of credit cards and money, right?"

"That's right. Now, the question is, how much of that did you pick up from my mind, and how much did you figure out on your own?"

I chuckled. "I'll never tell."

We arrived at the apartment complex, and Dimples found the manager pretty quick. After we showed him the warrant and explained that Kai had been found murdered, the manager took us straight up to the apartment.

On the elevator ride, Dimples asked him what he knew about Kai, and he told us he'd been there for a couple of years. "He's a... he *was* a successful engineer of some sort. I know he has a sister. I think her name's Mikiko... yeah... that's it."

"Does she live around here?" Dimples asked.

"No... but I see her a lot because she works close by."

The elevator came to a stop on the eighth floor, and we followed the manager to Kai's apartment. As he reached for the door knob, he realized it was ajar and stopped.

"Stand back," Dimples said, pulling out his gun. With his shoulder, he pushed the door open and stepped inside. "Police! Come out with your hands up."

There was no response, and Dimples continued inside the apartment. I stayed back in the hall with the manager who was trying not to snicker, thinking, *do the police really say that?*

I caught his gaze and nodded. His brows drew together, but luckily Dimples came back. "The apartment is clear, but I need to call in a team because it's been vandalized, and it could have been the killer."

After making the call, he handed me some gloves and we went inside. The place was a mess. Cushions had been pulled from the couches and chairs and a book case lay overturned on the floor.

I stepped through to the kitchen and found several drawers open with their contents on the floor. On the other side of the kitchen were two rooms, one a study, and the other a bedroom.

In the study, I found papers strewn all over and pictures ripped off the walls. The desk drawers stood open, with several on the floor, and littering the carpet. The place where a computer should have been was empty, leaving only an outline of dust. I spent a few minutes looking through the papers and books, but there wasn't anything that stood out.

Next, I stepped into the bedroom. Clothes had been dumped from the drawers, and it was hard to pick my way through the mess without disturbing anything. The closet doors were opened as well. Most of the clothes were still hanging up, but had been shoved to the side, and the shoes had been scattered, leaving the closet floor empty.

Finding nothing, I turned to study the room, hoping to pick up a remnant of anything that might remain of Kai. A couple of framed photos were broken and lying on the ground. I picked them up. One showed Kai smiling with his arm around a woman. The other photo was the same woman standing beside Kai, and an older couple next to them.

I realized how closely they resembled each other and figured the woman in both photos was Kai's sister, Mikiko, and the older couple had to be his parents. They looked like a close-knit family, and sorrow washed over me to know their lives were about to change in a terrible way.

As I placed the photos back on Kai's dresser, the scent of eucalyptus washed over me. A few other dead people had communicated with me, using a special scent, and now a shiver ran down my spine.

Glancing down at the electrical outlets, I spotted a Wallflower scent container and bent to get a better whiff. The eucalyptus scent was stronger at the source and had a nice touch of mint to it. That meant it wasn't coming from Kai's ghost, and I frowned with disappointment. On the other hand, maybe I could get one of those for my room since it smelled so good.

It struck me as kind of funny that, in some cases, a smell would lead me in the right direction, exactly like it worked with my dog. Maybe that was another reason I got along so well with dogs. Of course, I'd never tried to read a cat's mind. Would I be able to do that? For some reason, I didn't think so. Cats were on a whole different level than dogs, and I doubted they'd be so willing to help me find a killer. But who knew? Maybe someday I'd find out.

After one last look around, I stepped into the master bathroom. This room hadn't been disturbed, and a small hope that I might find something of value crept over me. Several minutes later, my hope vanished. I'd even tested the shaving cream can, in case it was one of those fake containers, but it was real.

I heard voices in the other room and realized the team had arrived. I doubted the killer would have been stupid enough to leave prints on anything, but they still had to try to find some.

Dimples filled them in and made a quick call to Detective Bates, who was working the case with him. Dimples shared what we'd found and told Bates the news that Mikiko Nisogi was Kai's sister. "She must work close by, so let me know if you find her address, and we can notify her of Kai's death after we visit his office."

He disconnected, hoping that Bates would be successful so I'd have time to help him with that, too. He glanced my way, taking in my frown. "Hey... you're a valuable asset to the department, and I've got to use you when I can."

I wanted to tell him to take a number, but shook my head instead. "If that's the case, then we'd better get going."

"Sure thing, boss." He tried to sound like an underling and totally failed. I rolled my eyes, but had to admit that it lightened my mood.

Since Kai's office was only a block away, we decided to walk. Within minutes, we were inside the building and talking to the receptionist. She called the manager's office for Kai's department and told us to head up to the third floor to see Preston Mitchell.

His office was close to the elevator and overlooked the cubicles on this section of the floor. As we entered his office, he stood to greet us, concern etching a deep crease into his brow. "Hello detectives. Please have a seat." He motioned to the chairs in front of his desk. "What's this about?"

"I'm sorry to tell you this," Dimples began. "But one of your engineers, Kai Nisogi, was found murdered this morning."

"Oh my God!" Preston's shock came through loud and clear. "What happened?"

Dimples explained a few of the details, adding that we hoped to talk to anyone in the office who was close to Kai.

"Of course." Preston stood, glancing out at the cubicles. "Dane and Tina were the closest to him. I'll go get them."

A few minutes later, a man and woman close to Kai's age joined us. As they entered, curiosity flowed from both of them, and I hated to be the bearer of bad news. Once again, Dimples related the news of Kai's death, and it shook them up.

Once their initial shock wore off, Dimples asked them about Kai. "Did either of you know Kai well? Did you socialize with him outside of work?"

They both shook their heads, thinking that he had other friends he spent time with.

"Did you notice a change in his behavior recently?" I asked.

"Not really." Tina shook her head. She was thinking he'd been quiet lately, and it wasn't like him. She should have asked him if something was wrong. Now it was too late. This was terrible.

"What about his work?" Dimples asked. "Was there a project or a person he didn't get along with? Did he have disagreements with anyone?"

Dane let out a breath and nodded. "Yeah... there was a project he was working on that he wasn't happy about. But that was nearly a month ago. I know he talked to the project manager, so I thought they'd worked it out, but I don't know any more than that."

"What project was it?" I asked.

He shrugged. "I'd have to look at his files, but I think he was working with a construction firm, something like a father-and-son thing. Let me take a look at his desk."

We all followed him to Kai's cubicle, where a few papers and plans were scattered over the desktop. "Here it is... Walker and Sons. I think this is the job."

"So it's not with your company?" I asked Preston.

He shook his head. "Kai manages environmental risk factors on site, and deals with applications for environmental-related permits. We were sub-contracted by..." He glanced at the work flow sheet. "Yeah... MRP Capital Development. We do a lot of sub-contracting work for them." He was thinking MRP was their biggest client, so he hoped it had nothing to do with them, since he didn't want to mess up a good thing.

"Okay. Then who is this other construction group, Walker and Sons?"

"They're another sub-contractor group, probably involved in the construction part of the project. Kai would have been interfacing with them about the plans and permits for the main project."

I glanced at Dane. "So you think that's who he had a disagreement with?"

Dane nodded. "I think so... he mentioned talking to Eli Walker, so that's the one."

"Did he give you any details about his interaction with Eli?"

"Not specifically; just that he'd found something on site that may have been overlooked. He's kind of a stickler for keeping things safe, so if he saw something that was wrong, he may have wanted it fixed."

I glanced down at his desk, noticing that there were two other projects he was working on. "What about these? Were they going okay?"

"He just got those jobs this week, so I have no idea. The MRP Capital job was his latest job, and it looks like he'd finished it up a few days ago. See this green dot on the corner? That means it's ready to be filed."

I shuffled through the plans, finding green dots on all the corners but one. I stopped to look it over, but of course, it made no sense to me. "This page isn't dotted. What does that mean?"

Preston stepped in and glanced over the sheet. He was thinking that the permits on this page would have been completed months ago, so it must have been a mistake. "He must have missed it."

"Okay," I said. "I guess that means we need to talk to both of the other companies. Can you think of anything else? Any reason someone would want Kai dead?"

"No," Tina said, her voice a little loud. "He was a great guy. Everyone liked him. It must have been some random attack."

I nodded to placate her. "I'm sure this is hard for you..." I glanced at the others. "For all of you. If you think of anything that might help us find Kai's killer, will you let us know?"

"Of course," Tina said. "You need to find the person who did this."

"We will." I knew that was a lot to promise, but I'd solved all my cases so far, so it wasn't too much of a stretch to make the promise.

Dimples pulled a few business cards from his wallet and handed them around. "Thanks again for your time. If you remember anything, call me."

As we left the office building, Dimples put a call through to Bates. "Did you find the sister?" He listened for a few seconds and nodded. "That's great. We'll head over there now."

He glanced my way. "She's not far. Let's go."

"Sure thing, boss." I tried to use the same accent that he had, but it wasn't any better than his. He smiled real big and pointed me in the right direction.

As we walked, he glanced my way. "So was there anything Kai's co-workers didn't say that will help us?"

I shook my head. "No. Sorry. They were all shocked and upset that Kai was dead, but that's about it."

"Okay. At least we have a lead with those construction firms. Maybe we can chat with them tomorrow?"

"I'll see if I can fit it into my tight schedule."

He smirked. "Please do."

We found Mikiko's office building and told the receptionist we were police detectives and needed to speak privately with her. The receptionist asked us to sit down while she put the call through. After hanging up, she told us we could speak with Mikiko in her office.

This was the part of the job I hated, but at least Dimples would take the lead, and all I'd have to do was hear her scream and rage in her mind while she sat in disbelief and pain. I decided to put up my shields once it got to that point, and I hoped that would keep her despair from choking me.

We followed the receptionist down a long hall past a conference room to a door with 'Mikiko Nisogi' on the name plate. She knocked before opening the door and announcing our arrival. A beautiful Asian woman with long, dark hair stood to greet us. Her brows dipped with worry. "Hello Detectives. Please have a seat." She motioned to the chairs in front of her desk and sat down. "How can I help you?"

"I'm Detective Harris, and this is my partner, Shelby Nichols," Dimples began. "I'm sorry to have to tell you this, but we found your brother, Kai, in the park this morning. We think he was out jogging and someone attacked him. I'm sorry, but he died. A woman walking her dog found his body."

Disbelief washed over her, and she glanced between us, wondering if we could possibly be telling her the truth. "But... I just saw him yesterday. Are you sure it was him?"

"Yes. We're certain it was him. I'm sorry for your loss."

Mikiko glanced between us, looking for any sign that this was all a bad joke. How could her brother be dead? "Oh my God." She crumpled into herself. "This can't be happening." But she was thinking, *this is all my fault.*

"Please don't blame yourself," I said, hoping to get her to explain.

Tears began to stream down her face. "But I was supposed to go jogging with him this morning. If I'd been there, this might not have happened."

"I'm not sure you could have stopped what happened," Dimples said. "And whoever killed him might have killed you too."

She shook her head, still stuck on the fact that she didn't get up this morning to go with him. Now she'd never talk to him again... never see him again. Her parents would be devastated.

"Do you know anyone who might have wanted to harm him?" Dimples asked. "A co-worker, or someone with a grudge? Was he having trouble at work or with a friend?"

She sniffed and wiped at the tears on her face. "No... I don't think so." She knew he'd mentioned a work argument he'd had with someone, but that had been days ago, and she thought he'd handled it. "You might want to talk to his co-workers, just to make sure."

"Of course. Anyone else?"

She took a deep breath and closed her eyes, thinking of her ex-boyfriend. "Maybe. I broke up with my boyfriend a couple of weeks ago. He's had a hard time accepting it, and he's been bothering me. I think Kai may have told him to back off."

"What's his name?"

"Kase Navarro. I've got his information on my phone." She took out her phone and gave us his name and number. Finished, she began crying again, and I knew that was all we'd get from her today.

"Is there someone we can call?" Dimples asked.

She shook her head. "Will you tell Jenny? She's the receptionist. She'll know what to do."

"I'll go get her," I said, leaving Dimples to stay with Mikiko.

Ten minutes later, we were on our way back to the station, both of us subdued by the experience of relating such bad news. "That was rough," I said, unable to shrug it off.

"I know. It's the worst." Dimples sighed and focused his thoughts on the case. "Did you pick up anything she didn't say?"

"Just that he'd had an argument with someone for his job, basically what we'd picked up at his work. At least we have a good lead with the ex-boyfriend."

"That's right. I'll see if I can track him down." He was thinking it would sure be nice if it was the ex and we could put this case behind us.

"I agree."

We made it back to the precinct, and Dimples thanked me for my help. "I'll see about getting the ex-boyfriend in for questioning. Want to come listen in?"

"Yes. In the meantime, keep me posted."

"Will do."

As he hurried inside the station, I went straight to my car. It was almost one o'clock, and I hoped Chris wasn't wondering where I was. Still, since I didn't have much to tell him about the police investigation, it didn't matter what time I got there.

I just hoped nothing else had happened this morning that needed my attention. Between last night's explosion, Max's disappearance, and now this murder case, I was starting to feel overwhelmed.

Chapter 3

Arriving at Chris's office building, I hurried inside. Elise, Chris's executive secretary, sat at her desk and stopped me from entering his office. "Hey Shelby. I'm sorry, but Chris is with a client."

"He is?" I glanced through the glass and did a double-take. "It's okay." I told her. "That's my brother." I quickly opened the door and stepped in. "Justin! I didn't expect to see you here."

Justin was a couple of years older than me, and it was a surprise to see him. He lived out of state and had recently made the decision to move his family back home, but I didn't know he'd be here today.

He got to his feet and gave me a quick hug. "I got in last night. Chris is looking over the contract with my new business partner."

"That's great. So do you have a date when you'll be moving back?" They lived in Riverside, and Justin was in the process of relocating his dental practice here. He had a colleague who'd made him a great offer, and he seemed eager to take it. Right now, Justin's wife, Lindsay, and their three kids, were still back in California.

He shook his head. "There's still a lot to do, and once we get the legal side taken care of, we'll need to find a house. I'll have a better idea of the timing once everything's finalized."

"Great. I can't wait. It'll be nice to have you closer."

"Yeah. We're excited to move back home."

Chris and Justin were old school buddies. In fact, it was because of Justin that I'd met Chris in the first place. When Justin was a junior in college, his girlfriend dumped him right before a big frat party he'd been planning to attend.

Wanting to save face, he'd coerced me into going with him. I was a high school senior at the time and only a couple of months away from graduation. I had acted like I was doing him a big favor, but, secretly, I was thrilled to get a taste of college life a little early.

Justin made me promise not to tell a single soul that I was his sister, or still in high school, which I considered a no-brainer. Once we got to the party, he basically left me to fend for myself. That's when I met Chris. The attraction between us was off the charts, and I fell pretty hard for him. Of course, he didn't know I was in high school when he got my number, and I didn't want to spoil things by telling him the truth.

I should have, but at the time, I didn't think it mattered. What's that saying? Hindsight is twenty-twenty? Naturally, Chris found out after our first date. I mean... he was Justin's friend, and I should have known better. Needless to say, he wasn't too happy about my deceit. Thinking on my toes, I blamed it all on Justin, and that seemed to help. Still, Chris took a step back, and it kind of broke my heart.

I didn't see him for several months until I was in college myself. We bumped into each other one day, and the fire burning between us burst into a roaring flame. I may have discretely planned the bumping-into-each-other part, but what can I say? A girl's gotta do what a girl's gotta do.

Chris couldn't resist me a second time, and we started up right where we left off, only on better footing. When Chris went off to law school a year later, I went with him, and now, here we were, an old married couple with two kids. Of course, it hadn't always been a bed of roses, but I couldn't imagine my life without him.

"I'll bet Mom and Dad are glad you're here. How long are you staying?"

"Just a few days. Once things with the practice are settled, I want to look at some houses before I head home." He was thinking that the housing market around here sucked, but the prices were less than where he lived now. His kids hated the idea of moving away, but it was the only way to get a fresh start. Regret slithered over him like a living thing, and I knew something was wrong.

"Yeah," I agreed. "The housing market isn't the best right now, but I'll bet you can still find something you'll like." What did he mean by a fresh start? Was something going on with Lindsay? Or the kids?

His brows drew together. He hadn't said anything about the housing market. "That's true, but I'm sure we can."

Sensing trouble, Chris popped up from his chair and handed me a file. "Here's the file I made for you about my client. Why don't you look it over? You might want to show it to Manetto. Then, if you have any questions, you can give me a call." He was thinking that there were some things he needed to help Justin with in private, and I should probably go.

"Oh... okay... sure. I'll get going."

Justin had no idea what we were talking about, so I quickly explained. "I'm a private investigator these days, and right now, I'm helping Chris with a client."

Justin nodded like it made more sense than it did. "That's right. Mom told me you got your PI license." Since we weren't the best at keeping in touch, most everything he knew about me had come from our mother. Still, it was enough to make him think I'd gone a little overboard trying to prove myself. It wasn't like I needed the money with Chris's prominent lawyer job, so it must be a mid-life crisis type of thing.

He glanced at Chris, surprised that he was so supportive of my independent streak. From the few things Mom had told him, I'd even come close to being killed once or twice. Why would Chris let me do something so dangerous? It boggled his mind.

Let me? I drew in a breath to argue, but clamped my lips shut. Now wasn't the time to pick a fight, especially when he hadn't said anything out loud. Still, I hoped I'd get a chance to let him have it in the future. What was he anyway? Neanderthal man?

"Shelby?" Chris said. "If you want to see Manetto today, you should probably get going."

"Oh. Sure. Right." I stepped to the door and pulled it open. "I'll uh... see you later." I glanced at Justin. "Let's get together before you head home. Maybe tomorrow night?"

"Oh... sure." He was thinking he'd have to make up an excuse since he had no intention of spending more time with me. He knew I'd want answers, and he didn't want me prying into his business. "Let's figure something out."

My lips turned down. "Okay. But you're not leaving until you explain to me the real reason you're moving here. And don't give me that crap about this being a great idea. Call it intuition, or whatever you like, but I know there's more to it."

His eyes nearly popped out of his head. "I'm not sure what you're talking about. There's nothing going on. Lindsay and I just want to be closer to family, that's all."

If he was this defensive, I knew I'd struck a nerve. But confronting him about it wasn't the way to go. I'd get it out of him a lot easier if he thought I wasn't prying. "Okay... if you say so. But don't leave until we've had a chance to talk."

"I won't." He was lying, and I vowed that he wouldn't get away with it. Something he'd pushed out of his mind came to the surface before he shoved it down again. It was shadowy and dark and sent a chill down my spine. I wanted to shake him into confessing, but now wasn't the time. I'd pry it out of him, no matter what it took.

"All right. See you later." I shut the door behind me and absently waved to Chris's executive assistant. On my way to the car, I kept thinking over what I'd picked up from Justin. He was in trouble, but how or why, I didn't know.

In my car, I took a minute to look over the file on Max that Chris had compiled. There were papers showing Max's credit rating, along with business applications and bank account statements. It looked like they had something to do with taxes and payroll accounts.

The papers showed a bunch of financial transactions between Max's bank and a couple of other accounts, but I had no idea what they meant. Several were circled in red, and they stood out because the amount was just under ten thousand dollars each and appeared at two-to-three-week intervals.

I knew that Max had claimed he'd been set up for something, and maybe these transactions were the proof? Had someone deposited money in his account to make him look guilty of embezzling or something? I still didn't know what it meant, but I hoped Uncle Joey or Ramos could explain it to me.

With that in mind, I drove to Thrasher Development.

Ten minutes later, I pulled into the underground parking garage and found a good parking space close to the elevator. As I headed in that direction, I made a quick detour to see if Ramos's motorcycle was there.

Disappointment washed over me to find it gone, and I let out a sigh. It still bugged me that I didn't know where he'd been last night. I knew he wouldn't lie to me about sending the text explaining things, but if he'd sent it, then why didn't I get it?

As I stood there, a low rumble came from the garage entrance, and my heart quickened. It got louder, filling me with anticipation. A second later, Ramos drove up on his Harley in his black leather jacket, black helmet, black gloves, and black boots.

He pulled beside me and cut the engine, then unclasped his helmet and tugged it away from his chiseled face. It was like unveiling a live, breathtaking work of art, and I tried not to drool or stare.

"Babe. You waiting for me?" His low tone sent a tingle down my spine.

"Uh... no. I just got here myself." His brow quirked up, so I rushed to explain. "I mean, I just looked to see if you were here, and then you showed up. Good timing, right?"

"Yeah." He got off his bike and popped the trunk to his car before stowing his helmet and gloves inside. While the trunk was open, I leaned in to see if my helmet was still there. Yup. Warmth filled my heart, and a happy grin curved my lips.

Ramos turned to see my grin and closed the trunk. He was thinking that, with the cooler weather coming on, there wouldn't be many days left to ride the bike before winter set in. Maybe we could fit in a ride in the next day or two?

"Oh... I sure hope so."

"Me too."

He stepped closer to me and my breath hitched. I let it out and backed toward the elevator before doing something stupid, like sniff him. "So, how's your back? I've got quite a few bruises on my knees, and scrapes on my hands. That was some blast, wasn't it? Which reminds me… where were you? Why didn't I get your text?"

His brows dipped and he held out his hand. "Give me your phone."

I reached into my purse and pulled it out.

"No. Not that one. The one Manetto gave you."

"Oh… shoot. I left it charging the other day and forgot all about it." Nearly two months ago, Uncle Joey had given me a special work phone that the police wouldn't be able to trace. He'd done that because we'd been worried they could request my cell phone information and have evidence of all the times I'd told Uncle Joey about the police cases involving him. As necessary as it was, it reminded me that I wasn't the upstanding citizen I liked to believe I was.

Ramos shook his head. "Well, at least you know why you didn't get my text."

"Yeah… I feel like an idiot. So would you mind telling me what happened?"

Ramos pushed the call button and the elevator doors opened. We stepped inside and he began. "I was helping my neighbor with a problem, and it took longer than I expected." He'd also said a few things in the text he wished he could take back, but it was too late now.

My eyes widened. "What? What did you say?"

He shook his head. "I guess you'll just have to read it and find out." The elevator doors opened, and he stepped out, leaving me hanging. I followed him into Thrasher and stopped to say hello to Jackie while Ramos continued to Uncle Joey's office.

After exchanging pleasantries, I stepped down the hall to my office. I wanted to put my purse away, and it was always nice to admire the poker trophy I'd won a few weeks ago.

It sat beside the photo of Chris and my kids, along with all the Manettos, taken at the New Amsterdam Theater in New York City. Uncle Joey, Jackie, and Miguel, along with Uncle Joey's sister, Maggie, and his cousins, had all become just as dear to me as my own family.

It wasn't long ago that I'd thought I'd never see any of them again. After falling into a deep, dark hole in the ground, I was lucky to be alive, and all the gold down there meant nothing compared to my life and the people I loved.

That's why it had been easy to turn my back on it when I had the chance to escape. Plus, I'm pretty sure the cave was haunted, or maybe even cursed, and I didn't want to tempt fate. Maybe someday I'd go back, but that wasn't going to happen for a while.

I slipped my purse into the bottom drawer of my desk and took the file Chris had given me to Uncle Joey's office. He and Ramos were chatting, but they broke off when I entered the room.

Uncle Joey stood from behind his desk and beckoned me inside. "Shelby, come on in and sit down. From what Ramos was telling me, you're both lucky to be alive."

"We're alive thanks to Ramos and his quick thinking." I met Ramos's gaze. "I'm really glad you showed up."

"Yeah, me too." He was thinking that he'd cut it close last night, and he vowed never to do that again. When it came to me, all hell could break loose in a matter of seconds, and if he wasn't there to save the day, who knew what would happen? Trouble followed me everywhere, and I wasn't always as vigilant as I needed to be.

I sucked in a breath. He was right, but did he have to make it sound like I was incompetent? Sure, I'd done some stupid things that I shouldn't have, but I was learning. Although, going inside that building without him could have ended my life, so maybe he had a point. But how was I supposed to know there was a bomb inside just waiting to explode?

"Shelby?" Uncle Joey said.

"Huh?"

He and Ramos exchanged glances. Ramos was thinking I'd gone quiet and wondered if it was his fault. He didn't think he'd thought anything bad, but sometimes it was hard to know.

Uncle Joey wondered if I was having second thoughts. I'd nearly died last night, and it was partly his fault, although, if anyone was to blame it was Chris, not him. Chris was the one who'd sent me after Max, so I should remember that.

I shook my head. Picking up all those thoughts made me forget what I was doing there in the first place. "We're talking about Max, right? What did I miss?"

Uncle Joey's eyes narrowed. "We weren't sure until now, but we think Max was running a con."

"Oh no. What did he do?"

"It looks like he conned me out of a hundred million dollars' worth of cryptocurrency."

"Holy hell! That much?"

He nodded. "Yeah."

I glanced at Ramos, then back at Uncle Joey. "What is cryptocurrency anyway? I mean... of course I've heard of it... but... isn't it like play-money? It's not real, right?"

Ramos's lips twitched, and I caught a glimpse of satisfaction that I'd pretty much nailed what was wrong with crypto. "It depends. In its simplest form, it's digital money designed to be used on the Internet. That seems pretty harmless, but it's not reliant on a bank or government to tie it to real money, or even fiat money, so there's a lot of risk involved."

"What kind of risk?"

Uncle Joey took up the narrative. "Digital money is susceptible to numerous problems because it isn't backed by any type of governmental regulations. That means you have no recourse to get it back if you get hacked, or if your storage data is stolen. It just disappears. And, once you buy something, you can't return it or reverse a payment.

"But there are some positives. Since you don't supply personal information to a merchant, there's little risk of your identity being stolen. Paying with crypto can also be useful because certain currencies are hard to trace, making it easy to use on the black market, as well as for money laundering and tax evasion." He shrugged. "The government can't seize your crypto assets because they have no means to do so."

"Oh... yeah. I can see how that could be useful to some people." Oops. Since Uncle Joey was one of them, I had to tread lightly. But now I knew why he'd be interested in using it. "So... uh... what's going on with Max? How did he steal that much money?"

Uncle Joey shook his head, mentally kicking himself for getting caught up in Max's scam. "I met Max through a business acquaintance who deals with cryptocurrency. My acquaintance works for a crypto-coin commerce company and handled some transactions for me. I was impressed with how much money he made for me, so when he told me about Max and his startup ICO, CryptaCoin, I decided to invest. Getting in on the ground floor had the potential to make me a lot of money, and I figured, why not?"

"What's an ICO?" I asked.

"It's a new type of cryptocurrency. It means initial coin offering. Some turn out to be worthless, but others, like

Bitcoin, are huge. My initial investment wasn't much, and the beginning was a little rocky, but things took off pretty quick after that. The ICO doubled, then tripled in value, along with my investment. I wouldn't have worried except that my friend told me to start pulling my currency out while we were ahead. Then he told me that Max's payout had skyrocketed, and it looked suspicious.

"I confronted Max, and he told me that he had taken the funds from another source and planned to grow the business with the goal of creating an exchange." Uncle Joey shook his head. "A goal like that is unheard of unless you're a genius. But I pretended to go along with it. He wanted more of my money to invest, so I told him I'd be happy to give him more as long as he spoke to Chris about setting up a corporation.

"He agreed to meet with Chris, which he did last night, and then talk it over with his silent partner." He glanced at Ramos before continuing. "Ramos began looking for this so-called silent partner, but he didn't have any luck. We hoped last night that Max would lead you to him, and you'd find out what's really going on. But that turned into a disaster in more ways than one."

"You mean because he nearly killed us?"

"Yes... of course... but it was the explosion that ruined everything." He shook his head. "That's where my server stored the key codes for my cryptocurrency. Now it's all gone... over a hundred million dollars."

He shook his head. "For Max to profit, he'd have to hack into the server and use the key codes to take the crypto. I don't know if he could have done that, but he could have easily taken the hard drive out before blowing up the warehouse so there'd be no trace of his meddling. Now he just needs the codes to download the crypto. I don't know how he plans to do that, but there must be a way or he wouldn't have gone to all the trouble."

His eyes took on a gleam that held no mercy. As far as he was concerned, Max was a dead man. No one scammed Uncle Joey out of that much money and lived to tell about it. No one. Uncle Joey glanced at the file I'd handed him and tossed it aside, knowing it was worthless. "So what did you tell the police last night? Are they trying to find Max?"

"Yes. They're looking into him as a person of interest, but only because I told them he was there."

"What exactly did you tell them?" Uncle Joey was thinking that I should have left instead of speaking with the police, but it was too late now. Because I worked with the police so much, he worried that there was a chance I had more allegiance to them than I did to him. I was a good person, after all, and working for him wasn't exactly honorable. Still, he hoped I wouldn't give him up that easily.

I pursed my lips, hating the suspicion in his tone. "I told them that I'd been following Max, and he'd ended up at the warehouse. I did say that I'd gone inside and found the body, but I left Ramos out of it. Of course, they wanted to know more, but Chris told me that it was attorney-client privilege and all that, and I needed to stick with what I saw at the warehouse, so that's what I did."

Uncle Joey let out a breath. "Thanks Shelby... I'm sorry if I came across a little strong, but this whole thing has me upset."

I nodded and sent him a half-smile. "I totally understand. I'd be upset too if I'd lost a hundred million dollars."

Uncle Joey narrowed his eyes. The way I'd said that made him sound gullible or stupid.

My eyes widened. "I didn't mean it that way."

"I'm sure you didn't. But, just so you know... I pulled my initial investment, plus several million out, so I didn't lose anything. Still, it's the principle of the thing. Max scammed me and probably a lot of other people, and I'm sure he'll do it again if he's not stopped. I doubt that we can count on the police to find him, so it's up to us. What do the police know about him anyway?"

"They're looking into Max's background, but there's no physical evidence that he was ever there, so I'm not sure how far they'll take it."

"What about his car?" Ramos asked.

I pursed my lips, knowing he wasn't going to like what I had to say. "After I told the detectives at the scene what had happened, we walked to the parking lot to go through Max's car for clues. It was gone. He must have left after we went inside the building, before the explosion."

Uncle Joey's eyes narrowed. "So he knew you'd gone inside, and he didn't try to stop you?"

"I don't know, but that's what it looks like."

Uncle Joey huffed out a breath. "So where did he go before the warehouse?"

"He went to a bank and then a bar. I think he was supposed to meet someone at the bar, but the person never showed up. After that, he went straight to the warehouse."

Uncle Joey nodded, but he was disappointed that we didn't know more about Max. And now he was gone. How were we supposed to make him pay if we couldn't find him?

"There's something else you should know." I hesitated, knowing Uncle Joey wouldn't like it, but he needed to hear it anyway.

Uncle Joey's brows rose, so I quickly continued. "The police are looking into the warehouse. They want to know why Max was there and who owns the building. So far, they haven't found anything, but I thought you should know."

Uncle Joey shrugged it off. "They won't find a connection to me."

"Oh… that's good." I tried to sound cheerful and glanced between Uncle Joey and Ramos. "So… what about the dead guy? Do you think he was Max's silent partner?"

"That makes the most sense," Ramos said. "But I'm having a hard time believing the partner was a real person. Based on what I could find, he seemed like a figment of Max's imagination." He shrugged. "But who knows?"

"Maybe finding out who he was would help us find Max."

Ramos cocked his head in my direction. "That's what I was thinking. Did you just—"

"No! I came up with that all on my own."

A slow grin spread over his face. "Hmm… you're getting better at this."

Uncle Joey rolled his eyes. "Tell her what you found."

Ramos nodded, but kept his gaze on mine. "I just came from Max's office. I guess he used the space as a front, because there was nothing of real value there. I checked with some of the other businesses in the building, but they didn't seem to know him. There was a design company next door, and the woman running it said she didn't know him, but I think she was lying. If she knows something that could help us, you'd have more luck with that."

"Yeah… I should go talk to her. She might know who his partner is… or maybe she's seen him and I could pick up if it's the dead guy."

"That's a possibility."

"I'd like to know who the dead guy is before the police figure it out."

"Why's that?"

I shrugged. "I don't know. I just have a feeling that he's the key to this whole thing."

"You mean like a premonition?" Ramos asked, a playful smirk on his lips.

I raised my brows. "Exactly."

Ramos smiled back, and my heart warmed.

"So what did the dead guy look like?" Uncle Joey asked, shattering the moment. "You never told me."

"That's hard to say," I answered. "I mean… his throat was slit, and there was blood everywhere." Just thinking about all that blood made me woozy.

"He had short, dark hair, and I'd put him at mid-thirties," Ramos said. "But no beard. He wore a dark suit and tie, which reminded me of some kind of federal agent."

My eyes widened. "You mean like the FBI?"

"Yeah."

"Oh no. What if he was tracking Max like I was?"

"If that's the case, wouldn't you have seen him?" Ramos was thinking that if I'd apprenticed to a better PI than Dirk Steele, I wouldn't have missed it. Too bad he couldn't have trained me.

Imagining being trained by Ramos, and how much better that would have been, momentarily sidetracked me. "Uh… I don't remember seeing the dead guy before. I wasn't even thinking about watching for someone who might be following Max."

"It's okay, Shelby," Uncle Joey said. "You did good."

I nodded and swallowed, wishing I could get the picture of his dead body—and all the blood—out of my mind. "Well… what do we do now?"

"I'm headed to Max's house to do a little breaking and entering," Ramos said. "I'm taking the bike. Ready to ride?"

Before I could stop myself, I nodded. "Yes, especially if it will help with my training."

His lips twisted. "Sure. After that we can stop by his office, and you can see what the next-door neighbor is hiding."

"Sounds good to me."

"Great. Let's go."

Uncle Joey sighed, thinking that, for a good person, I was easily persuaded to break the law these days. I didn't used to be like that. The first time he'd sent me with Ramos to break into someone's house, I'd been horrified. Now it didn't seem to faze me.

Of course, that was probably because a motorcycle ride with Ramos was involved. Too bad he didn't know about my weakness back then. He could have mentioned Ramos and a motorcycle ride, and I would have jumped at the chance to do anything he wanted.

My mouth dropped open. "That's not true."

Uncle Joey grunted, but hid a smile. "I take it the police aren't on their way to Max's house?"

I shrugged. "They've already been to his house, but he wasn't home, and they couldn't go inside since they'd need a search warrant. I'm not sure they have enough of a case to get one anytime soon, so we're probably safe if we go now."

"Then you'd better get going." As I stood to leave, Uncle Joey raised his hand. "Oh... one more thing. Miguel's coming home for a few days, and I thought we could get together."

"He is? That's wonderful. Yes, we'd love to."

"Good. Maggie's coming with him, and she'd like to see all of you too."

"That's great. When will they be here?"

"On Thursday. So we thought Friday night?"

"Sure. I'll see what's going on, but that should work." I didn't say we'd make it work, but I was pretty sure that if the kids had plans, they'd drop them to see Miguel. At least

I was sure Savannah would. She may only be thirteen, but she had the biggest crush on Miguel I'd ever seen.

Five years older than her, Miguel was more on the 'friend' side of the equation than she was. Still, I knew he cared about her, so that was good. But did I want the two of them to have something more? Nope, not even a little. Sure, I wanted Savannah to be happy, but being Uncle Joey's daughter-in-law was too mind-blowing to even consider. Still, I knew Savannah would be thrilled to see him again.

A few months ago, we'd been to New York to see Miguel play the lead in *Aladdin*. Before that, Miguel had always thought we were related since I'd called his father Uncle Joey. We'd all been in on the lie, so when Savannah spilled the beans, it had been a shock to Miguel. Even Maggie, Uncle Joey's sister, had been in on it.

Because this was the first time Miguel had come home since then, I'd wondered if he'd been upset with Uncle Joey, and that's what had kept him away. So the fact that he was coming home was great news. After a quick wave to Jackie, I hurried out the door to find Ramos waiting for me in front of the elevator.

The elevator had already arrived, and he held the doors open for me to step in beside him. He stepped closer to push the button for the parking garage, and I leaned in to get a whiff of his clean, woodsy scent without him knowing.

I didn't know why I was so completely drawn to the way he smelled, but it seemed like I had no control over the urge. It had to be more than his complete hotness, because I could totally resist him if he didn't smell so darn good.

Ramos straightened, and I jerked my head back before his shoulder hit me in the nose. I quickly turned away and folded my arms. "So... you seem to know a lot about cryptocurrency. Do you have some hidden away somewhere too?"

"I've dabbled, but I don't have half the funds to play with as Manetto does." He was thinking how much he liked my play-money analogy for crypto, since it fit so well.

I smiled. "Thanks."

"You're welcome."

His low voice sent tingles down my spine, and I scrambled to think of something else to talk about. "Uh… so, did you know Max?"

"Not really. I met him a couple of times, so he definitely knows me. Since it looks like he was willing to blow both of us up, he should be very worried."

My eyes widened. "Yeah… that's for sure, unless it was a fluke that we showed up when we did, and he had no control over it. I mean… if he'd already set the bomb to go off, he risked getting blown up to go back inside, so it kind of makes sense that he didn't warn us. And don't forget that he may not have even known we were there in the first place."

"We'll see." He was thinking that my positivity was working overtime to come up with all those excuses. Sometimes I was just too damn nice, and it grated on him. Of course, I'd always thought he was worth something more than a hired thug, so how could he complain?

The elevator doors opened, and I lost my chance to thank him for the compliment, which was probably for the best, since that would have been awkward.

After pulling our helmets from the trunk, we donned them and straddled the bike. With a big grin on my face, I wrapped my arms around Ramos and held on tight. The thrill of riding behind him never got old, and I picked up that he liked it too, which just made my enjoyment that much better.

We stayed on the side streets and wended our way to the neighborhood where Max owned his house. It was in a nice area, just south of the city, and the streets were lined with sidewalks and large trees.

This might be a great place for Justin to look for a house. I made a mental note of it while Ramos came to a stop in front of a quaint, ranch-style home with a wide porch and inviting walkway.

After a quick glance, Ramos continued down the street a few houses and parked there, not wanting to be obvious. I climbed off the bike like a veteran. Pulling off my helmet, I secured it to the bike and hurried to join Ramos on the porch. While he got to work, I blocked him from view and fluffed up my flat, helmet hair. Ramos appreciated the distraction, and hoped anyone watching would be focused on me and my hair fluffing instead of him and his lock-picking skills. I smiled, happy to know that we made such a good team.

He opened the door and slipped inside. I followed, quietly shutting the door behind me. As I glanced around, my eyes widened. For the second time today, I found another house trashed, with slashed cushions, papers, and books scattered across the floor.

Ramos froze, listening for any sounds that would indicate someone was still inside. Hearing nothing, we cautiously stepped through the living room and into the kitchen. After checking the halls and bedrooms, we found ourselves alone, and relaxed.

I shook my head. "Max didn't make this mess, right?"

"Right."

"Then who would do this?"

"I don't know."

"At least that means there's not another bomb ready to go off, or it would have blown up when the first guy trashed the place. Right?"

His lips twitched. "Maybe."

I elbowed him, and he grinned down at me before stepping across the hall to the master bedroom. As he opened the closet door, I held my breath, just in case. Nothing happened. Inside, only a few shirts were left on the hangers, but otherwise, it was empty.

"It looks like he left in a hurry." Ramos examined the room, then moved on to the next one. After a thorough search of the house, we came up empty. "There's nothing here."

"I guess we might as well go then."

He nodded, and I followed him to the living room. Entering the room, Ramos froze, and I ran into his back. He reached around and grabbed me before I fell. Pressing his lips against my ear, he whispered. "Someone's outside."

A key turned the lock, and Ramos pulled me into the hallway, just as the door opened.

I held my breath.

"What the hell?"

Something about that voice sounded familiar. With a growing sense of dread, I stepped around the corner.

Justin took one look at me and screamed. Startled, I flinched back and knocked into Ramos, who caught me by the elbows and pushed me behind him. Ramos stepped toward Justin, ready to knock him down.

"Wait!" I yelled, grabbing Ramos's arm. "Don't hurt him."

Ramos stood his ground, not taking take his eyes off Justin. "Why?"

"He's my brother." I managed to step around Ramos and faced Justin. "What's going on? What are you doing here?"

Coming to grips with the situation, Justin let out a deep breath and shoved his fingers through his hair. "What the hell, Shelby? You about gave me a heart attack."

"Seriously? That's all you can say? How do you think I felt? And you still didn't answer my question. Why are you here?"

"I could ask you the same thing." He glanced at Ramos and swallowed. "Is he with you?"

"Yes."

A whole contingent of thoughts went through Justin's mind. Why was I here? Was I mixed up in the same mess he was? His gaze shifted to Ramos. How did I know this brute? He looked like a criminal. How could I be mixed up with someone like him? Was it because of my PI business? His eyes widened. Did Chris know? Was I cheating on my husband?

"Justin, calm down. I'm sure there's a rational explanation for everything. First, you need to tell me what's going on."

His shoulders sagged, but his defiant gaze met mine before he glanced at Ramos. "Who's your friend?"

Ramos leaned back against the door jamb and folded his arms, showing the bulge of his muscles through his leather jacket. His lips twisted into a sardonic smile, and he was thinking *oh this is going to be good.*

I wanted to smack him, but shook my head instead. "Ramos is helping me with a case. He's like my partner, but more. I mean... more because we work together... and he's training me... so you can trust him."

Justin's brows rose with shock. Was I serious? This Ramos person looked like an assassin for hire, not partner material. Why would I ever think he was someone I could trust? It had to be his good looks. I'd obviously lost my mind over a handsome face. Typical.

I wanted to scream. "Justin... focus. What are you doing here?"

His brows dipped, and he rubbed his forehead. He wasn't sure how much he could say in front of my partner, so he tried to be vague.

"This place belongs to a friend of mine. I was supposed to meet him here." He checked his watch. "I'm a little early, but I didn't think he'd mind."

A chill ran down my spine. "Who are you meeting?"

"Max Fielding. He's a field agent for the FBI."

Ramos straightened. "We've got to go."

"Why? What's wrong?" I asked.

Ramos caught Justin's gaze. "I don't know what he told you, but Max is no field agent. This is a trap."

Ramos ushered both of us to the front door, but Justin pulled away. "Wait. I'm not going without my money."

"Justin." I grabbed his arm. "Trust me. If Ramos says this is a trap, it's a trap. Whatever you're doing, it isn't worth your life. Come on. We'll figure this out somewhere else."

"But—"

"No! Let's go!"

Justin's mouth snapped shut. With a frustrated groan, he followed us out of the house. We sprinted to the driveway, and Justin jumped into his car.

"Meet me at The Tower," I said. With a quick nod, Justin backed out of the driveway and zipped up the street.

Seconds later, we took off after him. Justin made it through the light at the next intersection, but we were too late to follow. As we waited for it to turn green, a van came around the corner. It had Pest Control in big letters across the side, and the man driving had his window down.

He slowed to admire the Harley, and he was thinking that the money he made from this job would give him enough to get out of debt and still buy the motorcycle he wanted. Maybe then, he'd have a pretty girl riding behind him just like that guy did.

Normally, hearing a man admire the bike wouldn't have alarmed me, but hearing the amount of fifty grand for a pest control job sent shivers down my spine. Before the light turned green and we drove away, I watched the van turn down the street we'd just come from, and I knew we'd just dodged a bullet.

Chapter 4

With Justin out of sight, Ramos pulled off the road into the nearest parking lot to ask me where "The Tower" was. I gave him the address to a park with an old clock tower where Justin and I had spent a lot of time when we were kids.

Twenty minutes later, we pulled into the parking lot next to Justin's car. He wasn't inside, but I spotted him sitting on a bench under a tree beside a tiny stream.

"You want me to wait here?" Ramos asked, thinking my brother might be more forthcoming if he wasn't there.

I nodded. "He's a little intimidated by you, so it might be for the best."

"Sure. While you're talking to him, I'll check his car to see if there's a tracker on it."

"Oh... that's a good idea. Thanks." I squeezed his arm and hurried to Justin's side. As I sat beside Justin, he ignored me, so I gave him a minute to unwind and waited for him to start.

"Remember when we used to play tag down there?" He pointed to a small gully full of trees. His gaze wandered over the park. "We used to play baseball over there, and I remember having soccer practice out on the field."

"Yeah, I remember. Most everything's the same except for the new pickleball courts. Have you ever played pickleball?"

He nodded. "Yeah. A couple of times. It's fun."

I waited for him to continue, feeling the cool breeze tussle my hair. Several minutes passed before he let out a sigh and began.

"I made a stupid mistake, and now I'm trying to fix it, but it looks like I'm doing a terrible job."

"What happened?"

"You've heard of cryptocurrency, right?"

My eyes widened and I shook my head. "Seriously?"

Justin's brows drew together. "What?"

"Nothing. Just tell me what happened."

"About eight months ago, I had a new patient who needed a lot of work done on his teeth. It ended up being quite expensive, so I worked out a payment plan for him. He's one of those tech-savvy guys, and he talked me into accepting cryptocurrency instead of money for his payment."

Justin shook his head. "I thought, why not, you know? Plus, Landon showed me his portfolio and how much money he was making. He told me he could make the same for me, and he'd use a substantial amount of his own cryptocurrency for the initial investment. Since I wasn't out a dime, I agreed.

"He showed me the basics and opened an account for me. After the first few weeks, he diversified my account into six different currencies, and, by the third month, I was making over twenty grand a day. It was insane."

Justin shoved his hands through his hair. "At that point, Landon recommended that I invest more money into the account so I could get higher returns. It was doing so well that I didn't think I could lose, so I borrowed money from the bank, using the house and my dental practice as collateral."

Seeing my widened eyes, he shook his head. "I know it was stupid, but I thought twenty grand a day was worth it. Just a couple of months later, my profits had grown even more, and I had amassed over three million dollars."

"Whoa... that's amazing."

"Yeah. In another few months it grew so fast that it nearly doubled. That's when Landon suggested I start cashing out the account. I'd made a ton of money, and he told me it was time to get it out of there before things went south.

"Part of me didn't want to, but since I needed to start paying back my loans, I agreed. Everything would have been fine except that all the cryptocurrency I downloaded into my wallet disappeared."

"What? How did that happen?"

Justin closed his eyes and rubbed his hand over his face. "Landon had set everything up on my work computer, and, at some point, he must have installed a malware app that sent the crypto to his wallet instead of mine. After I'd made the final exchange, I checked my crypto wallet, and it was completely empty.

"At first I thought there was a mistake. For days I tried to get a hold of Landon, but I couldn't find him anywhere. That's when I realized he'd scammed me. I lost it all, and Landon had disappeared."

"Oh no."

Ramos joined us, and I picked up that he'd heard most everything, including all the money Justin had poured into the account and that he'd lost it all.

Justin scratched his head. "I called the feds and everyone I could think of, but no one had any hope that I'd ever get it back. That's when Max contacted me. He told me he was an agent working with a federal task force, and he could use my help tracking Landon down.

"I gave him all the information I had on Landon, including everything from my computer, and we kept in touch. Max was grateful for my help, and he told me that once we found Landon, it was possible that I could get most of my money back. It gave me hope that I could get out of this mess."

Justin shook his head. "I kept in touch with Max, hoping he'd find something, but weeks passed with no news. In the meantime, I had to pay back my loans. The only way out was to sell both my practice and the house. Luckily, a friend put me in touch with the practice here, and I had just enough money left to buy into it, but that means we have to move in with Lindsay's parents and live there until we can save up enough money to buy a house of our own."

"Oh wow, I'm so sorry."

He blew out a breath and shook his head. "You know the worst part? It's looking Lindsay in the eyes and seeing her disappointment in me. It's affected her, the kids, and every part of our lives. All because I was a fool. I should have known better. If something seems too good to be true, that's because it usually is."

I patted his back. "So why were you at Max's house today?"

"He finally called with the news I'd been waiting for. He said he'd tracked Landon down and he needed my help. I was supposed to meet with Max last night, but my flight got delayed, so he told me to come to his house today. That's why I was there."

Ramos met my gaze, thinking that my brother may have just missed getting his throat slashed. "What kind of help did he expect from you?"

Justin pursed his lips. "He wanted me to help him persuade Landon to give me back my money."

"How did he plan to do that?" Ramos wondered if Justin had known it could get violent, and if he was okay with using force to get what he wanted.

I thought that was a good question and met Justin's gaze. He flinched with guilt and dropped his head. I picked up that he'd been desperate and hadn't wanted to think too hard about how Max planned to persuade Landon.

"He never told me, but I was worried about the money, so I didn't think it through," Justin said.

He was thinking that the main reason Max had wanted his help was because he'd discovered a link to a group that was dubbed The Crypto-Knights by a cyber vigilante.

The vigilante had made a detailed report of the exact scam that had happened to Justin, along with several others, including SIM hacking, ICO fraud, and fake cryptocurrency investments.

I had no idea what any of those scams were, but it made sense that Landon might be on a few hit-lists.

I gave Justin a moment to explain all the things I'd picked up from his mind, but he kept his mouth shut, and I couldn't hide my disappointment. "Is there something else you want to tell us?" I arched my brow, giving him that pointed look I reserved for my kids when I knew they were lying.

He shrugged, not about to say any more than he had to, so I continued. "What about all the other schemes Landon was involved with? Were you going to tell us about those?"

Justin's eyes widened. "Huh? Where did you hear that?"

Since I wasn't about to let him in on my little secret, I had to come up with something fast. "It doesn't matter. What matters is why Max would want you dead."

Justin sucked in a breath. "What? No he wouldn't. He's helping me get my money back. In fact, I should probably call him and see if he's all right."

I shook my head. "No. Don't. He's not who you think he is."

"You don't know what you're talking about. He's been helping me. I lost everything, so there's nothing in it for him. There's no reason he'd want me dead."

"That's where you'd be wrong," Ramos said. "Like I said before, he's not a federal agent."

Justin wasn't buying it. "Why do you keep saying that? Of course he is."

"No he's not," Ramos answered.

"What makes you so sure? Huh? Maybe you've got it wrong."

Uh-oh. He wasn't backing down, and from the thunder in Ramos's eyes, I knew Justin was in trouble. Ramos turned to me. "Shelby. Your brother is an idiot."

Justin drew in a quick breath, and his eyes flamed with fury. He stood up to his full six-foot height and puffed out his chest. He was still four inches shorter than Ramos, and no matter how hard he tried to pull it off, it was easy to see that Ramos could beat him to a pulp. Still, Justin was desperate and angry enough to pick a fight.

"Justin! What the hell?" I jumped to my feet and pushed against his chest. "Don't be an idiot... I mean... a worse idiot. We're trying to help you. Now sit down, and let's talk about this without all the drama."

Justin's chest heaved with pent-up frustration. He stood completely still for a good ten seconds before his shoulders sagged and all the fight went out of him. He sank onto the bench and buried his face in his hands.

His shoulders moved with each deep breath he took until he got under control. A few moments later, he sat up straight and faced us. His voice steady, he glanced between us. "Okay. What's going on? You obviously know more about Max than I do. What is it?"

"We're pretty sure he stole about a hundred million dollars in cryptocurrency last night," I began.

Justin blinked. "What?"

"Yeah... and he nearly killed us too."

Justin's eyes bulged. Before he could ask another question, Ramos spoke. "What does your friend Landon look like?"

"Uh... he's not that remarkable. I mean... he's got short dark hair and a beard... at least he did the last time I saw him."

That could be just about anyone. I needed more detail to know if it was the murdered man in the warehouse. "I know this might sound a little strange, but could you just picture him in your mind for a minute?"

Justin's face twisted. "What kind of a crazy question is that?"

"Just humor me."

He shook his head, ready to tell me I was nuts. His gaze moved to Ramos, and Ramos's hard, unbending stare changed his mind. "Fine." Letting out a breath, Justin closed his eyes and concentrated on the image.

I focused on his mind and picked up a shadowy image that coalesced into a face. My gaze flew to Ramos. "It's him. The murdered man."

"What are you talking about?" Justin asked.

I filled him in on the events of the night before, telling him I was following Max because he was Chris's client, and ending with the dead body and the explosion. Justin's eyes widened with each sentence I spoke. Then his brows drew together and he shook his head. "But how do you know that was Landon?"

"I have premonitions, remember? Didn't Mom tell you about that?"

"Oh... yeah, she did, but I didn't think it was real."

I grimaced. "Believe me. It's real."

"But that doesn't make sense. You were never like that before."

"It's a relatively new development. Didn't Mom tell you about the robbery at the grocery store?"

"Well... yeah. She told me about that, but I didn't exactly believe her."

"And now?"

His mouth opened, but nothing came out.

Ramos was ready to move on. "I don't understand why Max would want to kill Justin. There's got to be more to it than that."

I nodded. "There is." I turned to Justin. "Tell Ramos about the Crypto-Knights."

"The Crypto-Knights?" A laugh burst out of Ramos and he shook his head.

Justin sucked in a breath, completely ignoring Ramos. "How did you—" He blinked several times. "Never mind." Justin spent the next several minutes explaining his research on the dark web and the link he'd discovered between Landon and the Crypto-Knights.

"And you told Max?" Ramos asked.

"Yes."

"That must be it," Ramos said, his brow arching. "He and Landon must have been working together. Maybe Landon double-crossed him, so Max used Justin's personal information to track Landon down. There is a way to track crypto if you're smart enough."

"But that doesn't explain why Max would want me dead," Justin said.

Ramos nodded. "That's true, unless it's because you can link Max and Landon together with this group you found."

"That hardly seems like enough for murder."

"I agree," I said. "There must be something we're missing. Did you tell anyone else about this?"

Justin's thoughts went to the anonymous hacker who'd helped him, but, since he'd promised to keep him out of it, he wasn't sure he should tell us. On the other hand, his life was in danger, so maybe it didn't matter.

While Justin debated the matter, I decided to hurry things along. "How did you find out about this Crypto-Knight group anyway? I didn't know you knew so much about computer hacking or navigating the dark web. You must have had some help. Who was it?"

Justin's eyes widened. If he'd had doubts about my psychic ability before, he didn't now. "I did, but I don't know anything about the hacker, so I doubt it will be any help."

"No name?"

"No. And since I thought Max was with the feds, I didn't pursue it with him."

"So Max didn't know about this guy?"

Justin ducked his head. "Not exactly... I may have led him to believe that I was the hacker. It seemed like the best way to keep the guy anonymous."

"Yeah... okay." Too bad it had painted a target on his back, but I didn't tell him that since he'd already figured it out.

"What now?" Justin asked.

Ramos caught my gaze, thinking Justin was in over his head. Did this sort of thing run in our family?

My mouth dropped open, and I wanted to smack him, but, since that would seem strange, I just shook my head. "Uh... I think Max might still want you dead. Maybe we can use that to draw him out?"

"That's a great idea," Ramos agreed.

"Hey," Justin said. "Don't I have a say in this?"

"No," Ramos and I said in unison. Our gazes met and his lips quirked. I tried to hold back my smile and glanced Justin's way. "It's too late for that."

"Yeah," Ramos agreed. "Max has got to know by now that you're not dead. I think you'd better call him. You could tell him that you went to the house like he said, but it was all torn up inside, so you panicked and left. That way he'll still think he's got you fooled and might set up another time to meet."

I nodded. "That's a great idea." I turned to Justin. "Why don't you give him a call and see what he has to say?"

Justin's lips turned down, and he shook his head. He was thinking this was a terrible idea. He wasn't good at lying, and talking to Max like he didn't know what was going on would be hard.

"It won't be so bad," I said. "Just call him and tell him you got out of there as fast as you could. Ask him if he wants you to call the police. That should get him talking. You could agree to meet up with him somewhere, and it would give Ramos and me a chance to catch him."

"I like that idea," Ramos said, nodding with approval.

"Well, I don't," Justin chimed in. He didn't like that we were talking about him like he was expendable.

I shrugged. "Hey... it's not our fault you got into this mess. You should be relieved we're here to help you out of it." I didn't add that he would be dead by now if we hadn't been at Max's house. He should count his blessings.

Justin closed his eyes and pinched the bridge of his nose. "Fine. I'll call him."

"Put it on speaker."

After a couple of deep breaths, he pulled his cell phone from his pocket and made the call.

It clicked. "Hello?"

"Max? This is Justin. Are you okay?"

"Yeah... barely. Where are you?"

"I went to your house like you said, but it was trashed and I panicked, so I got out of there. What's going on? Did you find Landon?"

He sighed. "Yeah... I did, but he was dead. Listen, I think they might be onto me. I'm going to drop off the grid for a while. Don't pursue anything until I tell you the coast is clear. Okay? These guys are killers, so just leave it alone until you hear from me. I'll be in touch."

The line went dead and we all stood frozen in silence.

"That didn't sound like someone who was behind all this," I said. "Could we be wrong, and Max really is a federal agent?"

"No way," Ramos said. "He's just playing his part. If he thinks Justin is the hacker, it makes sense that he'd tell Justin to back off while he regroups. Once he's got things figured out, he'll get in contact with Justin and set him up. Right now, he's backed into a corner and figuring out his next move."

Justin shook his head. "I don't know... he sounded convincing to me. He even admitted that Landon was dead."

"I know," Ramos agreed. "But we can't trust anything he says. Don't forget that he tried to kill Shelby and me last night."

I nodded. Ramos was right. "Now what?"

"Justin should lay low for a while." Ramos met Justin's gaze. "Where are you staying?"

"At my parent's house."

"Does he know that?"

"No."

Ramos nodded. "Good. Then go to their place and wait until we know more."

Justin sighed. "Okay, but what about you guys? Where are you going?"

"Shelby and I have another errand to run." Ramos was thinking that it wouldn't hurt to visit the woman at Max's office and see what she was hiding.

"That's a good idea." I turned to pat Justin's arm. "Don't go anywhere else until I call you. We should know more by this afternoon, or tonight at the latest."

"Sure. But you'll call me as soon as you know anything, right?"

"I will."

Justin could hardly believe I was involved with this whole thing. It also raised a red flag that Ramos had convinced me that Max was the bad guy. If anything, Ramos was the bad guy in all this. Maybe I was the one who'd been blinded? Had I lost my head over him?

Justin sighed, knowing he needed more information. Maybe he should call Chris. Of course, hadn't I told him that Max was Chris's client, and that's why I'd been following him? So what the hell was going on? I must trust Ramos if he was my partner, still, it seemed like there was a lot more to it.

As we walked back to Justin's car and the motorcycle, I tried to block out the rest of Justin's thoughts about me and Ramos. It was hard when Justin got his first good look at the Harley and salivated a little.

He was thinking that Ramos sure fit the mold of a gangster. How did Chris put up with it? Maybe Chris didn't know? On the other hand, Justin didn't want to get in the middle of anything. Still, if he were Chris, he'd want to know. But... maybe he already did. He had seemed okay with my PI business.

Justin's lips flattened, it was too much. For now, he might as well concentrate on staying alive long enough to figure it out. Until then, he'd keep his mouth shut.

I let out my own breath, knowing how mixed up this whole situation was. How could Justin be involved with the exact same people as Uncle Joey? It boggled my mind.

With a quick wave, I told Justin I'd be in touch, and climbed behind Ramos on his motorcycle. I tried not to look like I enjoyed it, but I had to admit that it made my coolness factor go up at least a hundred percent. Once we were out of Justin's sight, I tightened my grip around Ramos's waist.

I caught his amusement at my predicament and picked up that he hoped he remembered to ask me what my brother thought about him, and, more specifically, what he thought about me and him. That could be highly entertaining, and he didn't want to miss it.

I rolled my eyes, but, of course, Ramos couldn't see it, so I tightened my hold around him instead. He chuffed out a breath, but otherwise ignored me. All too soon, we pulled up to a rectangular office building, and parked in the lot.

Inside, we walked through a small lobby with a listing of the businesses in the building on the wall, and continued to the elevator. We exited on the third floor and continued toward a door at the end of the hall. Passing another office with a glass door on the way, I caught a glimpse of a woman sitting at her desk. She had to be the neighbor Ramos had mentioned earlier.

Ramos had no trouble picking the lock on Max's door, and we soon stepped inside, finding the office trashed, just like his house.

"I didn't do this," Ramos said. "So someone else must have come after I left, looking for something."

"I thought you said there was nothing here."

"There wasn't that I could see, but someone else must have thought otherwise."

"Should we still look through this mess?"

"Might as well." We took a few minutes opening drawers and looking for notes or papers that would tell us more about Max and his activities.

Most everything was already on the floor, but I took a minute to look through his garbage can. I found a receipt for Chinese takeout, but nothing else.

"Let's see if his office neighbor knows more than she did this morning," Ramos said.

After locking Max's office, we stepped down the hall to the glass door with 'Homespun Living' across the front. Ramos pulled the door open for me, and I stepped inside. The contemporary office was painted in shades of teal, with a navy couch, accented by colorful pillows along the back. A framed conglomeration of color in the form of paint swatches covered one wall, and, from the name, I figured the woman must be an interior decorator.

She was about my age, with thick, long, dark hair. She wore a colorful, hot pink blazer, over a low-cut, v-neck, black cami. As she glanced up from her seat behind a dark wooden desk, her brows rose in surprise. I picked up that she wasn't expecting anyone.

Since her business was by appointment only, she wasn't pleased to be interrupted so close to the end of the day. Then she spotted Ramos coming in behind me, and recognition flooded over her. He was the hot guy who'd been there earlier looking for Max. As much as she didn't like the interruption, she couldn't help the flicker of excitement to see him again.

"Hi," Ramos said, stepping forward and offering his hand. "I don't know if you remember me. I was here this morning. Alejandro Ramos?" At that moment I was glad that Ramos had taken charge, since she wouldn't have given me the time of day.

"Oh... yes, of course." As a red blush stained her chest and crept up her neck, she lurched to her feet and reached over the desk to shake his hand, sending him a huge smile and giving him a clear view of her biggest assets. "What can I do for you?" She straightened her spine to show off the rest of her toned figure, and hoped he liked what he saw.

Ramos's lips curved up in that sexy half-smile of his that made all women everywhere swoon, and I was surprised she didn't start fanning herself.

"I'm just wondering if you've seen any sign of Max since I was here earlier."

"Oh... right." Some of the sparkle in her eyes left, but a small hope lingered that Ramos had come back because she interested him. Maybe he was using Max as an excuse to see her? She could always dream. "I'm afraid not. Like I said earlier, the last time I saw him was yesterday morning."

She sank back into her chair. "Is Max in some kind of trouble?" She wouldn't mind having some answers, especially since it was like a three-ring circus around here. Not only was Ramos back, but the police, and that other guy she'd barely glimpsed had shown up as well. What was going on?

My ears perked up. Maybe the other guy was the same one who'd trashed Max's house? "I take it you've been asked that question a lot today?" At her nod, I continued. "Did someone else show up besides us and the police? Someone in a... blue blazer, perhaps?"

Her eyes rounded. "Yes. Do you know who he is? He was the most secretive of all... in fact, I didn't get a good look at his face, so I can't tell you what he looked like, but I noticed he walked by my door toward Max's office, and I didn't see him again until about ten minutes later. I was watching for him to leave, but he walked by so fast that, by the time I got to the door, he was gone." She shook her head. "So what's going on?"

Sensing her genuine concern for Max, I capitalized on it. "We're trying to find Max because he's in trouble with some... people, and we'd like to help him out. Anything you could tell us about him would be great."

She shrugged, thinking they'd become friends since he'd moved in. They'd even exchanged keys to their offices in case anything came up, but he'd been too focused on his work for more than that. "I don't know him that well. I mean... we shared lunch a few times, and we looked out for each other, but that's about it. He seemed to be doing okay as far as I know. In fact, he had a lot more people visiting him in the last few weeks, and I know he was pretty happy about that."

She glanced over at the plant he'd given her a few days ago, and her brow creased. "I hope he's okay."

Since that was all she knew, I met Ramos's gaze and tilted my head toward the door. He got the message and stepped toward her desk. "Thanks for your time. Sorry we interrupted you."

"Oh... it's no problem."

He leaned slightly closer. "Do you have a card I could have? In case I need to get in touch?"

"Uh... sure." She scrambled to find the stack of business cards inside the top drawer of her desk. "Here you go."

Ramos took it and smiled. "Celeste... I like that." He caught her gaze. "Thanks."

She nodded, but couldn't seem to form the words to reply.

Rolling my eyes, I started toward the door and stepped into the hall with Ramos following behind. As he shut the door, the spike of her passionate thoughts abruptly ended, and I let out a breath. Whoa. She had it bad. And Ramos had enjoyed it. Wait a minute. Did that mean he was interested in her? He *had* gone out of his way to get her card, right?

As we exited the elevator into the lobby, I couldn't hold it in any longer. "Why did you get her number?" Oops. That didn't sound as disinterested as I was going for.

Pulling the outside door open, he shrugged. "We might need it." He glanced my way and lifted his brow. "Why? You think I want to ask her out?"

My mouth dropped open. "I... I don't know."

He held back a smile. "Babe... if I didn't know better I'd think you were jealous." Before I could protest, he continued. "But don't worry. She's not exactly my type."

"You have a type?" As soon as I said it, I knew I shouldn't have. "Wait... don't answer that."

Nearly to his motorcycle, he chuckled, thinking that, since women threw themselves at him all the time, he'd learned to be picky. But, just to make things clear, he did happen to like the ones who loved riding behind him on his motorcycle the most.

My breath whooshed out of me, and I nearly choked. Still, I couldn't help the grin that spread over my face. Of course, he noticed, so I shook my head. "You're..." I took a deep breath, but couldn't find the right words.

"Amazing? The best?"

I scoffed. "Such a tease..."

His phone began to ring, and, for once, I was grateful for the interruption. "Yes?" He listened before nodding his head. "We're not far. We'll be there in a few minutes." He slipped his phone away. "That was Manetto. He wants us in his office ASAP."

"Did he say why?"

"No, but it must be important. Ready to ride?"

That was the second time he'd said that today, and I knew I'd never get tired of hearing it. With a sassy gleam in my eyes, I met his gaze. "You know it."

His answering chuckle made me laugh.

Chapter 5

We arrived at Thrasher just fifteen minutes later. As we entered the office, Jackie motioned toward Uncle Joey's door. "There's someone in his office he wants you to meet. Go on down, they're waiting for you."

I listened real close to her thoughts for a clue to the stranger's identity, but she didn't know who the guy was. I picked up that she was grateful we were there, and she hoped it wasn't someone with more bad news. Losing all that cryptocurrency had put Joe in a bad mood, and, so far, nothing had managed to change it.

I stepped down the hall, feeling a sense of impending doom. Now what? A sudden worry that it could be my brother nearly stopped me in my tracks, but I shook it off. Justin didn't know about Uncle Joey, so it was stupid to think it could be him.

The door stood ajar, so I knocked once and pushed it open. A man with dark hair and wearing a blue blazer sat in front of Uncle Joey's desk. He glanced my way, and his eyes widened. Then a pleased grin broke out over his handsome face.

My breath caught. What the heck? The guy from the bar? What was he doing here?

"Well... hello there." The man's eyes sparkled with curiosity, and he stood to greet me. Tall and slender, a lock of dark hair fell over his left brow, giving him a certain allure. "It's nice to see you again. Allow me to introduce myself. I'm Forrest Slater."

"Again?" Uncle Joey asked. "What do you mean?"

Forrest glanced between me and Uncle Joey, and his lips twisted into a small smile. "Do you want to tell him, or shall I?" Speaking with a low, deep voice, he made it sound like we were keeping secrets.

Flustered, I huffed out a breath. "He was at the bar last night." I glanced at Uncle Joey. "He hit on me. I thought he was just... you know... someone at the bar."

Forrest ducked his head, managing to look a little sheepish. "That's true." His gaze landed on Ramos and he quickly continued. "She turned me down flat."

Ramos's eyes narrowed and his lips thinned.

I glanced back at Forrest. "So what are you doing here?"

Uncle Joey waved his hand. "Forrest, this is my niece, Shelby, and my colleague, Ramos. They work for me." He gestured toward the chairs in front of his desk. "I think we're all on the same side, so come in and sit down so we can get to the bottom of this."

Forrest moved into the next chair over and motioned for me to take his place, which left Ramos to pull another chair over from the table. He placed it beside mine and sat down, not liking the smooth friendliness coming from Forrest.

I might have enjoyed sitting between two handsome men if not for the uncomfortable dislike between them. They were like two opposites. Ramos had the whole bad-boy, dangerous vibe coming off him in waves, and Forrest's clean-shaven jaw and quick smile lent him an easy-going, boy-next-door charm.

"I think I'd better start," Forrest began. "I've been looking into Max Huszar and his business practices for several months now. I invested in one of his decentralized finance companies a while back and lost my investment when he and his group pulled out the rug. It's taken me some time to dig up his trail, but I managed to track him down last night at the bar.

"Finding him was a real breakthrough for me, and I was planning my next move when Shelby showed up." He glanced my way and smiled, thinking that I was the most interesting part of the night... at least until the warehouse blew up. "I followed both of you to the warehouse and waited to see what would happen next."

"You did? So you saw the explosion?" At his nod, I continued. "Do you think Max knew I was following him?"

"Not that I could tell." He shrugged. "But I could be wrong. I parked on the other side of the building so I could watch his car. He was in there for a long time."

"Did you see anyone else go inside?" I asked.

"No. Why? Was someone else there?"

I glanced at Ramos. "Yeah... when we went inside, we found a body."

Forrest inhaled sharply. "Do you know who it was?"

"We think it was one of his business partners, Landon. Does that name ring a bell?"

"Landon Woods? Yeah... I believe he's the one who went by Lancelot."

Surprise washed over me. "Oh my gosh! That totally fits. Their group name. They're called the Crypto-Knights."

A huge smile broke out over Forrest's face. "That's right. How did you know?"

"I just found out that they scammed my brother."

"Oh... that's too bad."

"Yeah... he's having a rough time of it."

"How did they scam him?" Forrest had helped several people who'd been scammed by the group. Could my brother be one of them?

"Oh my gosh! Are you the anonymous hacker? Justin told me someone helped him."

"Your brother's name is Justin? Justin Davis?"

"Yeah."

He nodded. "I did help him. He's one of the reasons I made it this far."

I sucked in a breath. "Then you're the reason he almost died."

"What?"

"Well... not directly, but in a way. Max told Justin he was a federal agent and would help him find Landon and get his money back. Justin made the stupid mistake of telling Max that he was the cyber-vigilante who found the Crypto-Knights on the dark web."

I shook my head. "Justin was supposed to meet with Max last night to confront Landon and get his money back, but then his flight was delayed and he didn't make it."

Forrest's brows rose. "So not only did Max kill Landon, but he wanted Justin dead, too? Why?"

"I guess he thought he was you."

As realization dawned, Forrest sucked in a breath. Max was a much deadlier foe than he'd thought. "Is Justin okay now?"

"Yeah. Up until we spoke with him, he still thought Max was a federal agent. Now at least he knows Max lied and wanted him dead. He's staying at my parents' house, so he should be safe there."

"That's good."

"Yeah... no kidding."

"But why did Max kill Landon?"

I opened my mouth to tell him that Justin had actually spoken with Max, but a nudge from Ramos cautioned me not to. He was thinking that we didn't know this guy, or how he'd known to come here.

Ramos made a good point, so I shrugged and said, "that's a good question. Maybe they had a falling out or something?"

"Maybe." Forrest could hardly believe that Max would kill a member of his own group. From what he knew, they were as tight as thieves. Landon must have done something pretty bad to deserve that. Maybe he'd taken more than his share of the crypto? Or maybe he'd wanted out and Max couldn't risk it? That only left Max and Galahad, the other member of his group.

I rubbed my chin. Forrest's reasoning made sense, and it didn't sound like something he'd be thinking if he was in on it. While I appreciated Ramos's warning, I wasn't sure it was warranted. Still, I'd keep Justin's information to myself until we'd explained it all to Uncle Joey.

"I'm sorry about your brother, Shelby," Uncle Joey said. "But I'd like to hear the rest of Forrest's story, if you don't mind."

Forrest glanced his way and nodded. "Oh... sure. Where was I?"

Ramos huffed out a breath. "Did you see anything while you were watching the warehouse?"

"Oh... yes. I saw Max climb out from a back office window, with a large box." He glanced at Uncle Joey. "He put it in the trunk of his car at about the same time Shelby and Ramos were breaking in."

Uncle Joey narrowed his eyes. "Did Max know they were there?"

"I don't think so. He'd already come out and was fiddling with something while he stood next to his car. I wasn't sure what he was doing, but I guess he was setting the timer for the bomb. Then he jumped into his car and sped off. I was just about to follow when I saw Shelby and Ramos come running out of the building. I was confused until the building blew up.

"I have to tell you, that was some blast. It totally shocked me." He glanced my way. "I got out of my car to see if you guys were okay, but you both got up and managed to get out of the blast range. By then, I'd missed my chance to follow Max, but I hoped to pick up his trail, so I left. Unfortunately, I didn't have any luck."

"So how did you end up here?" I asked.

He glanced down at his hands. "Since I'd lost Max, I came back to the warehouse. After you spoke to the police, I followed you home. I've been tailing you ever since. But it wasn't until you came here earlier, and I caught a glimpse of you and Ramos in the parking garage, that I knew this was the right place. I did some research on Thrasher Development and put two and two together."

He met Uncle Joey's gaze. "You're the one with the most capital to invest, so I thought I'd come and introduce myself. I'm hoping we can help each other."

"And why would we do that?"

"Because, from what I picked up this morning, the Crypto-Knights struck again last night with another rug pull. I take it you were an investor?"

Uncle Joey hated to admit it, and his lips turned down. "That's right."

"How much did he make off with this time?"

"One hundred million."

"Shit." Forrest glanced my way. "Sorry."

"That's okay," I answered. "It's a lot of money. But at least Uncle Joey didn't lose his initial investment." I glanced Uncle Joey's way. "Right?"

"Yes Shelby." Uncle Joey said, wishing I'd be quiet and let him take control of the conversation.

"That's good," Forrest answered, totally missing Uncle Joey's annoyed tone. "But it doesn't make it any easier. I'm sure you'd all like to get your money back, including your brother." He glanced at Uncle Joey and squinted. "Uh... I guess that makes him your nephew?"

Uncle Joey hadn't even thought of that. "Uh... yes, of course. But I don't know how we do that other than tracking Max down and using force to persuade him." He glanced my way. "But now that he's after Shelby's... my nephew... we might have a chance."

I tried to keep a straight face and nodded. "Maybe we can get Justin to call him and play dumb, or Max might try to contact Justin, so that's a possibility."

"I can help track him down," Forrest said. "I've been following this group for a while now, and I'm close. If there's any hope of getting your money back, I think I can do it."

Uncle Joey leaned forward and studied Forrest with narrowed eyes. He seemed so eager to help that it made him uneasy. What would Forrest get out of the arrangement? A finder's fee? That made the most sense. Most people would do anything for money, and he was grateful I was there to get to the truth of the matter.

I glanced at Forrest, taking in the sudden paleness of his face. I picked up that he knew he had to be careful, or his days were numbered.

"As much as I like the sound of that," Uncle Joey began. "I need to know if you're working with someone."

Wow... Uncle Joey was really good at asking the right questions.

Forrest quickly shook his head. "No sir."

"How about the police or the FBI?"

"No. I'm a private citizen. I work alone."

"And do you plan to involve them?"

Forrest swallowed, knowing he had to answer as truthfully as possible. "I might, but only so these guys can be arrested."

Uncle Joey sat back in his chair. "I'm not interested in arresting anyone. If we were to join forces, I wouldn't want the authorities involved."

"Right." Forrest nodded, thinking that Uncle Joey was probably using crypto for things like money laundering or tax evasion, so it made sense that he would be averse to going to the authorities. "I understand. Frankly, I don't see the need to involve them. There's not much they could do anyway."

"So tell me," Uncle Joey said. "Why should I accept your help over a crypto recovery service?"

"You mean like ProHackers or CryptoKey?"

"Exactly."

Forrest shrugged. "For the simple reason that I'm more invested in finding these guys. They stole a big chunk of money from me. I'm planning on getting my money back, and I'm willing to help you get yours."

His lips turned up in a friendly smile, and he spread his hands for emphasis. "I know I can't guarantee anything, but, if it makes you feel better, I'd be willing to consider a finder's fee. But only if you're satisfied with my work. I'm still going after them whether you pay me or not, but this arrangement might ease any concerns you may have about me." Satisfaction rolled over him that his plan to offer a small fee for his services had worked out so smoothly.

"So, if I agreed to a finder's fee, you'd be more amenable to finding my money as well as your own?"

Forrest's lips tilted in a small smile. "I think that about covers it."

Uncle Joey glanced my way. "What do you think, Shelby? Is he trustworthy enough to hold up his end of the bargain?" He didn't want to trade one scammer for another.

I caught Forrest's gaze. "Is there anything else we need to know?" I couldn't pick up that there was, but I did get a fleeting insight that Forrest knew better than to scam a mob boss.

"Not about my sincerity to help," he answered truthfully. "I'm dead serious." He was telling the truth, but there was more to it, and I picked up that it was personal because of Max. They'd met in an online forum, and he'd given Max some pointers on crypto. It still rubbed him the wrong way that Max had used their connection to double-cross him.

It was a bonus that they'd never met in person, and it was even better that he'd done a little hacking into Max's code to examine it before he'd invested. Unfortunately he'd missed a few things that would have raised some red flags, and he'd gone ahead with his investment. But at least that had given him a starting point to track Max down.

In the back of his mind, he knew that coming to Uncle Joey raised the possibility that Max might not come out of this alive... especially if the danger coming from Ramos was any indication. It dawned on him that he wasn't bothered by that. In fact, Max was scum, and it would serve him right to pay a price for his schemes. Working outside the law with a mob boss could make that happen.

"I think it's a win-win for both of us," Forrest said. "If you agree, of course."

Uncle Joey was still waiting for my assessment, so I sent him a quick nod. "I believe he makes a good point."

"All right," Uncle Joey said. "Then I'll agree. How does a two percent finder's fee sound?"

Forrest's brow lifted, and he wondered how far he could push the issue. He was in the driver's seat, but he didn't want to appear greedy. "Make it three, and you've got my undivided attention."

Uncle Joey thought that, to get back a hundred million, three million was pocket change. He would have gone up to five, but Forrest didn't need to know that. He waited a beat before responding so that Forrest would know who was in charge. "You drive a tough bargain, but all right. Three it is. Where do we start?"

Forrest held back a smile of victory, thinking that, with the three he'd earn from Uncle Joey, along with the seven Max had stolen, he'd make out with a cool ten million... with the opportunity to grab the crypto they'd stolen from anyone else. Now he just needed to put his hacking skills to the test.

"I have a few questions, and I'll want to look at anything pertaining to your crypto account. Which ICO did you invest in?"

"CryptaCoin."

"And the DeFi?"

"It's called MantaTira."

Forrest nodded. "Do you think Max got your key codes before he blew the warehouse up? That means he would have to know your passwords to get into the computer. Did he have access to them?"

"No," Uncle Joey said, upset that Forrest thought he would be so stupid. "Of course not."

"Sorry, but I had to ask." Forrest knew he'd hit a nerve, but it couldn't be helped. Uncle Joey was a little older than most of the people currently investing in crypto, but he wouldn't underestimate him again.

"I'm just trying to figure out if Max had time to hack into your accounts and get your codes before he took off. If not, he may have just taken the hard drive from your computer with the idea of hacking into it later. When I saw him last night, he was carrying a large box to his car. Was there anything else in the warehouse he might want to steal besides the hard drive?"

Uncle Joey hadn't considered that possibility. Besides the key codes to his crypto, he did have some other files on the hard drive he wouldn't want anyone getting their hands on. Would Max take the time to look into the other information stored there? He hadn't even thought about that. "I do have a few files on the hard drive I wouldn't want him to have. But, unless Max does some real digging, they wouldn't make much sense to him."

"I see. Did you store anything else at the warehouse?"

Uncle Joey shrugged. "Sure. I kept hard copies of some of my old business dealings there. I don't consider them worth stealing, unless I had some information on someone Max thought was relevant. I guess I shouldn't rule it out, but most of those people are dead, so it shouldn't matter now."

Forrest perked up, thinking it made sense that, by blowing up the warehouse, Max was destroying more than just the computer. Of course, covering up the murder was probably reason enough to blow the place up. Still... there might be more to it than that.

"Got it, but I wouldn't rule anything out at the moment. You might have had a file on someone that Max was interested in, and blowing up the place would be a good way to make you think it was destroyed, rather than stolen."

Uncle Joey huffed out a breath. "I suppose that's a possibility. I'll try and remember what was in those files, or at least the families involved. But it would surprise me if there was a connection to Max there."

Forrest shrugged. "You never know."

Uncle Joey nodded, realizing this might be a lot more complicated than he thought. Still, the crypto was his most valuable asset. "How long do you think it will take Max to hack into the hard drive and take my money?"

"I don't know. You didn't use a system he set up did you?" Forrest thought that was the best way for Max to take advantage of the situation.

"No."

"That's good. Then it might take him a couple of days to hack in, which gives us more time to find him. Do you mind if I hook up to your computer files here and see if I can find a code he may have planted?"

That Max had infiltrated his computer system had never crossed Uncle Joey's mind. He remembered Max coming to the office a few times, so it was a definite possibility. "Yes. As long as I can trust you not to do the same thing you're accusing Max of doing."

Forrest blanched. "I think I know better than to cross a mob boss."

Uncle Joey's smile didn't reach his eyes. "That's good to hear. But you should know... if I have even the smallest inkling that you're taking advantage of me, you're a dead man." His eyes darkened. "That's not a threat. It's a promise. Understand?"

Forrest swallowed with the realization that his life was on the line. Maybe working with a mob boss wasn't the best idea, but it was too late now. "Yes sir."

Uncle Joey kept his stare fixed on Forrest before he glanced my way and raised his brow. I gave him a quick nod to let him know Forrest wasn't about to double-cross him.

He nodded before turning back to Forrest. "Why don't you get set up in Shelby's office?"

Uncle Joey glanced my way, thinking that my office was about the only private office space he had. "Do you mind?"

"No. That's fine." I turned to Forrest. "I'll show you where it is and help you get set up."

Forrest nodded, sufficiently scared out of his mind. "Sure... if it's not too much trouble."

"Not at all."

"Okay. Thanks."

Ramos wasn't pleased that Forrest was moving in, but since he looked scared enough to piss his pants, he didn't mind too much. He stood and moved his chair back to the table so we could leave.

Managing to keep from smiling, I led Forrest to my office and opened the door. "This is it. Come on in. I guess you have your own computer?"

Relieved to be away from both Uncle Joey and Ramos, Forrest held up the briefcase. "I never leave home without it, but I'll need to use yours as well." He was thinking my computer would be the easiest way into Uncle Joey's files.

"Uh... sure. Let me just move a few things out of the way, and you can get started." I pushed my photos and my stapler and pen case closer to the corner of my desktop, but in reality, there wasn't much I needed to do. Sure, I had my own office space and computer, but there was very little that I used it for.

I stepped out of the way, and Forrest took my place, setting his laptop next to my computer monitor. While he got it plugged in, he wondered what I did for the mob boss. Manetto had introduced me as his niece, so that was one connection.

But it seemed like there was more to it. Manetto had asked for my opinion about his trustworthiness. Why would he do that unless I was more important? Maybe I was his second in command? Then what about Ramos? Whatever the reason, it intrigued him, and he hoped he stayed long enough to find out.

He booted up his computer and noticed the family photo and the other things on my desk. He smiled at the block of wood that read '*No good deed goes unpunished,*' and figured there was a story behind that. Maybe he'd get a chance to hear about it?

"Is that your family?" he asked, pointing to the photo.

"Yes. That's my husband, Chris, and my kids, Joshua and Savannah, along with Uncle Joey's branch of the family from New York."

He wrinkled his brow, unsure why I'd call them 'Uncle Joey's branch.' Weren't they my family too? "Nice looking bunch."

"Thanks."

He pulled the chair closer and sat down, taking in the paperweight from the newspaper and the poker tournament trophy beside it. His eyes widened. "Is that your name on the trophy?"

"Yup. I won a ten-million-dollar poker tournament a little over a month ago in Las Vegas."

"Shut up! You must be one helluva poker player."

"You might say that. Is there anything I can get you?"

More than a little impressed, he glanced sideways at me. "Yeah… I'll need to sign onto your Internet connection. Do you have the password somewhere?" He opened his computer browser to access the Internet and found the WiFi connection for Thrasher Development.

"Yeah… I'll need to get into the top drawer." He scooted back while I rummaged through my sticky notes and found it under a tin of mints.

He successfully logged on and sent me a grateful smile. "Thanks."

"Sure."

"So how's your brother doing? As I understood it, he lost a few million."

"Yeah... it sounded more like four or five million. Now he's losing his house and his dental practice."

"Ouch."

"That's why he's moving back here. I guess he and his family will be living with his wife's parents until they can save enough money for a down-payment on a house."

Forrest shook his head. "There's a definite downside to investing in crypto. You should never invest more than you're willing to lose."

"But Justin didn't lose it. That's the worst part. He was taking it out but, instead of ending up in his wallet, it went into Landon's. Landon tricked him. It's so maddening, and there's nothing Justin can do about it."

"Yeah... well... don't lose hope. There's still a chance we can find Max, especially if we move fast. Let's hope he hasn't hacked your Uncle's software yet."

I watched him get to work, and my brows drew together. "So tell me how this works. Once Max gets into the computer, he can take the crypto, right? But I don't get how that happens. You don't store crypto on your computer, do you?"

"No. To put it simply, if you own any form of crypto, what you actually own is a private key that's made up of a bunch of numbers and letters. You could think of this key as an actual key, because it grants you the opportunity to spend your crypto. So whoever owns that key—by having access to it—is the owner of the cryptocurrency associated with that specific key."

"Okay. That makes sense." It mostly made sense, but it was still beyond me to know how Forrest could track Max down.

At least it was something I didn't have to know, and I was grateful for that. Forrest had already gone deep into the computer software, and I picked up his thoughts that Uncle Joey had pretty good security in place. He'd found a couple of vulnerabilities, though, and was eager to show Uncle Joey how he could fix that.

I shook my head and stepped toward the door. "I'll talk to you later, okay?"

He nodded without looking up, and I left him to it.

It had been a long day, so I wasn't surprised to find it close to four-thirty. But before I could go home, I needed to tell Uncle Joey about Justin's call to Max, so I headed back to his office.

I knocked before opening the door and headed inside. I picked up that Ramos had already told Uncle Joey about Justin's phone call with Max, and they were discussing it. "Come in and shut the door," Uncle Joey said. "What do you think about all this? Is Forrest who he says he is?"

"I believe so... at least, I didn't hear anything to say he wasn't. Still... I wish I could have talked to Max. That story he told Justin is pretty convincing. I wish there was a way to make sure he's not working for the FBI."

"There is a way to know," Uncle Joey said. "I could give Blake Beauchaine a call." Blake was an old friend of his, but he was in the CIA, not the FBI.

Just hearing the man's name curdled my stomach. "No."

Uncle Joey nodded. He'd known I'd hate that idea, but he had to ask. "What was that other guy's name? The one who went after Leo Tedesco?"

"Oh... you mean Deputy Gerard? He was a US Marshall, so probably not."

"Right."

"I know a guy," Ramos said. "I'll ask him to look into it."

I listened real close to Ramos's thoughts, but he'd shut them up tight, so I just nodded.

"Thanks, Ramos," Uncle Joey said.

"I've got to go," Ramos said. "Is there anything else you need?" He was thinking of his neighbor, and the text he'd just gotten from her asking him if he could finish the job tonight.

"No. I'll call you if something comes up."

Ramos nodded and glanced my way, knowing I'd picked up all that about his neighbor. He scowled, thinking it was hard to keep anything from me, and he hoped it didn't tarnish his image too much that he was helping someone.

That brought a smile to my lips, and he winked as he hurried out the door.

"Is Forrest all set up then?" Uncle Joey asked.

"Yes. He's looking into your files, but I couldn't pick up anything you need to worry about. From what I could tell, he's not going to do anything to jeopardize getting the money back."

Uncle Joey snorted. "That's good to know. It's hard to let a hacker have access to my files."

"Yeah... I totally get that. But he was thinking he'd patch up some of your security for you, so letting him help was a good call."

Uncle Joey sat back in his chair. "So... your brother's in trouble? I guess I'm surprised. I didn't even know you had a brother." He was thinking that he hardly knew anything about my family other than Chris and my kids.

"Yeah... it's kind of crazy to think he's involved with the same people as you. I mean... with his crypto problem."

"Yes," Uncle Joey agreed. "I think we need him in order to find Max. It might be dangerous for him, but..." he shrugged. "He's already involved."

"Yeah... I agree. I think he'd probably do just about anything to get his money back, since he's losing his home and his dental practice. But I don't want him to get killed."

"Of course not." Uncle Joey was thinking that if it wasn't for Ramos and me, he'd probably be dead already, so it was a little late to back out now.

"You have a point," I said, answering his thoughts. "But that means involving him with you and... the business you're in."

"He doesn't know your secret, does he?"

"No... just the premonition part."

"Then he'll have to deal with it." Uncle Joey shrugged. "I guess he's part of the family now, so I'm afraid you'll have to clue him in on the whole situation. If he has a problem with it, I'm sure I can straighten him out. Besides, I've learned that family ties are more binding than any other kind. In fact, it eases my mind about involving him because he's your brother."

"But you don't even know if we have a good relationship."

"It doesn't matter. He's family. That's all I need to know. Let's meet tomorrow. Say nine?"

"Uh... sure. I guess I'd better get going. If anything comes up in the meantime, let me know."

We said our goodbyes, and I hurried down the hall, stopping beside Jackie's desk. "Forrest Slater is in my office. He's a hacker, and he's agreed to help Uncle Joey get his crypto back. That should put Uncle Joey in a better mood, right?"

Jackie smiled. "That's good to know. I swear, there's nothing worse than a disgruntled man."

"That's for sure." I glanced down the hall toward Ramos's apartment, and let out a sigh. "Well. I'm going home. I'll see you tomorrow."

She nodded. "If you're looking for Ramos, he left for the day. He said something about needing to help his neighbor." Her brows drew together. "Do you know what that's about?" She was thinking that he'd been helping this neighbor a lot, and she wondered if there was more to it. Ramos was so tight-lipped about his personal life that it was hard to know.

"Uh... not really. I mean... he said something about helping her out with a problem."

Jackie's brows rose. A damsel in distress? That was a sure fire way to get Ramos's attention, since he seemed to thrive on helping women out... well... mostly me... but it could apply to his neighbor as well. Maybe she was a beautiful woman who'd made some bad mistakes. He could certainly relate to someone like that.

Damn. "Uh... well... I'd better get going."

Jackie said goodbye, and I hurried to the elevators, not liking where Jackie's thoughts had taken her. The last thing I wanted to hear about was Ramos's personal life. If he liked his neighbor, that was his business.

On the way to my car, a spike of jealousy stabbed me in the heart. I shook my head in disgust. What was wrong with me? I had no claim on him. If he found happiness with someone, I'd be happy for him. As long as she was a good person, and treated him right, and loved him with all of her heart... I'd be totally fine.

Inside my car, I pulled out my phone and called Justin. "I have a plan, but there's some things we need to talk about. Can you come over later... like around ten or ten-thirty?"

"I guess. But why don't you just come over here? It would be easier."

I rolled my eyes. "Do Mom and Dad know you've lost everything?"

He huffed out a breath. "No."

"Then talking over here's better. Besides, Chris will want to be in on it."

"Okay. I'll be there at ten-thirty."

Chapter 6

On the way home, I tried to figure out what to make for dinner, which only partially took my mind off Ramos and what he might be doing at this moment. That reminded me of the text message he'd sent last night to my other phone. Since he'd seemed embarrassed about something it said, I could hardly wait to read it.

As I stepped into the house, Coco greeted me with happy kisses and excited tail-wagging, which always brightened my day. I searched for my kids and found Josh playing a video game.

"Hey Josh. I'm home." He mumbled something and continued playing his game, so I left him alone, knowing he'd come out for food, but that was about it.

I went upstairs and knocked on Savannah's door, opening it to find her lying on her bed and talking on her phone. I picked up that she was talking about a new boy in school, and they were discussing how cute he was. Before I caught much more than that, she pulled the phone away from her ear. "Mom. I'm on the phone."

"Okay. I just wanted to say hi."

"Hi." But she was thinking *you can go now*. She widened her eyes and frowned so I'd get the message to leave her alone.

It reminded me of Uncle Joey's news that Miguel and Maggie were coming for a visit over the weekend. I opened my mouth to tell her, but caught her thinking *just go already*. So I closed my mouth, backed out of her room, and shut the door.

This was the first time I'd caught her thinking of anyone else besides Miguel, and it gave me hope that maybe she could move on. But if she saw him this weekend, would it mess that up and send her back to forgetting about everyone else? Crap.

I turned to find Coco waiting for me. He sat on his haunches and gazed at me with his big, adoring eyes. My heart melted a little. At least someone was happy to see me. He woofed. *I here. Outside? Treat?*

"Sure. I just need to get my phone." He took off down the stairs. I hurried into my room to find my phone still plugged into the charger and grabbed it. After stopping in the kitchen for a Diet Coke and a treat for Coco, I took everything outside to the deck.

Coco followed me out and, with a happy yip, he took the doggy bone I offered him. He sprawled out on the deck by my feet, while I sat down on the swing and popped open my soda. I took a nice, long swig before tapping the text message app.

Finding the text I'd missed from Ramos, I opened it up. The first message read: *Something came up but I'll be there soon. Wait for me*. Twenty minutes later, it was followed by: *Taking longer than I thought. Don't do anything without me*. The next one said: *You'd better not be in trouble*. It was followed by: *Since you're not answering you must be in trouble. What part of wait for me did you not understand? You drive me crazy. I don't like it. You'd better be okay when I get there, or you'll pay for this.*

His worry was evident in the angry tone he'd taken, and I knew that, even though he'd been helping his neighbor, he was still thinking about me. It showed he cared, and my heart warmed.

With a contented sigh, I finished off my soda and enjoyed the moment outside with my dog. Sure, Ramos might like this neighbor of his, and maybe there was something to it, but he still cared about me. How could I feel bad about that?

I stayed outside as long as I could, but, with my own stomach grumbling, I knew it was time to start dinner. Back inside, I slipped the burner phone into my purse where it belonged, and, with a small smile on my face, began fixing dinner.

Just as I finished up, Chris came through the door. "Hey beautiful." He gave me hug, grateful to see me, and even more grateful to smell dinner cooking. He'd missed lunch and was starving. "What's for dinner?"

"Spaghetti and meatballs."

"It smells great. I'll go get changed and then we can eat."

"Sure."

As he left the kitchen, he slowed his step. "How did the rest of your day go?" He kept walking, and I knew I'd have to yell or follow him to answer. Since I didn't want to do either of those things, I mumbled that it was fine, and began to set the table.

A second later, he popped back into the kitchen and wrapped his arms around me from behind, pulling me back against his chest. "Sorry... that was rude." He kissed the nape of my neck, sending a tingle down my spine. "I'll change out of my suit and be right back to help you set the table."

Mollified, I let him off the hook. "Okay. Go on then."

After another quick kiss, he hurried away. He returned in short order and finished setting the table while I worked on the salad.

"So what happened after you left my office?" he asked.

"Plenty. You're not going to believe it, but Justin nearly got himself killed."

"What?"

"Yeah." I quickly caught him up on the rest of my afternoon, including the visit of the real cyber-vigilante to Uncle Joey's office. "Uncle Joey wants to use Justin to draw Max out, so I arranged for Justin to come over later tonight so I can explain what's going on."

"You really want to involve Justin with Manetto?"

I shrugged. "What choice do I have?"

He pursed his lips. "Yeah… you're right. Okay… but you're not telling him about your secret."

"Definitely not."

"Okay, good."

"What secret?" Josh asked, coming into the kitchen. "The one about Uncle Joey being a mob boss?"

"Yeah… that's the one."

"What's going on with Uncle Justin?" Josh had heard enough to think that Justin must have really screwed up to need a mob boss.

I knew I had to tell him some of the story, but at least he'd get an education about the pitfalls of investing in cryptocurrency. I gave him the shortened version, leaving out the part about the dead body and the warehouse explosion.

By the time I got done, Savannah had joined us, and I had to explain it all over again. Once we'd finished dinner, they knew the significance of the problem without all the details. Still, it was more than I liked them knowing. But…

on the bright side, at least Josh had mistaken my 'secret' as working for a mob boss instead of reading minds. That had been a close call, so any day that happened was a good day.

The rest of the evening passed by quickly. Before I knew it, ten-thirty arrived, and so did Justin. The kids had gone to bed, so we could talk without them overhearing anything, which was why I'd asked him to come so late in the first place.

After offering him something to drink, we sat down in the living room to talk.

"I guess Shelby told you everything?" Justin asked Chris.

"Yeah. But at least now it all makes sense. You could have told me about the scam. I would have understood."

"I know... but it's hard to admit making a mistake as big as that one." He glanced my way. "Do you think he'll forget all about me now that he's laying low?"

"Not a chance."

He thought I sounded so convincing that it was hard not to believe me. Is that how my premonitions worked? He shook his head. None of this made sense. How had he ended up running for his life?

Sympathy for his predicament washed over me. If he thought this was bad, he was in for a shock. "There's more we need to tell you. Normally, you wouldn't need to know all the details, but now I have no choice. Just promise me that this stays between us. You can't tell Lindsay, your kids, or Mom and Dad."

Justin's eyes rounded. Were Chris and I getting a divorce? Was that why I was so chummy with Ramos? He was right... we were having an affair. But how could Chris be so calm about it?

I wanted to smack him upside the head. Instead, I took a deep breath and let it out slowly. "I told you that I was following Max because he was Chris's client, right?"

"Yeah... that's right. But you didn't say what it was about. And I still don't get why you and... well... why you were at Max's house, either." He almost said *you and your hunky boyfriend Ramos*, but he held off at the last second.

"That's what I need to talk to you about. You see... I... well... actually both Chris and I work for someone who is... well..." I huffed out a breath. "We work for a mob boss."

Justin's brows disappeared into his hairline. "What?"

"Yeah... he found out my secret... you know... that I have premonitions? And, to make a long story short, I ended up working for him. At first it was against my will, but now it's a little different. Uncle Joey's not such a bad guy after all. Well... that's not entirely true. He was pretty bad, but now he's not so bad.

"He's actually changed his ways. Well... not all of them of course, but, for the most part, he's mostly gone legit and does most things on the legal side. So he's not like the regular type of mob boss you see in the movies.

"I mean... sure, he has rules, and he expects people to follow them, but he doesn't just kill anybody he feels like killing, you know? He likes to give people second chances, and he's even helped the police a few times. I mean... what kind of mob boss does that?"

Justin's eyes glazed over, and he was wondering if I could hear how I sounded. It was like I was making excuses for the guy. Had he brainwashed me? Was it that Stockholm Syndrome he'd heard about? Where the captive actually joined the bad guys and thought they were good?

He glanced at Chris. "Wait... so you work for him too?"

Chris blew out a breath. Listening to me explain things had made him realize how crazy this whole situation was. How had it come to this? We were both defending a mob boss. No matter what kind of a person he was, he was still a bad guy. "Yes. I'm his lawyer. In fact, he's my biggest client."

"Damn. And here I thought I had problems. You guys are so screwed."

I sucked in a breath. "No we're not."

Justin didn't believe me, but he didn't want to argue either. "No wonder you didn't want to talk about this at Mom and Dad's house. If they found out, it would kill them."

I let out a heavy sigh. Of course I didn't want them to know, but I didn't think it would be that bad. Sure, they would be disappointed in me, but they'd get over it. Well... except for the part where Uncle Joey had claimed us as part of his family. Mom would hate that. She'd probably hate that I'd pretended I was adopted, too.

I shook my head. "It doesn't matter. They're not going to find out, okay?"

Justin straightened, and raised his hands in surrender. "Okay... sure. Of course not."

"Good."

He glanced between us before speaking. "So... I couldn't help noticing that you called him Uncle Joey. What's up with that?"

"It's a long story."

"Honey... I think you'd better tell him what happened," Chris said. "I think it would help him understand the situation a little better."

"Fine." I took a deep breath and sat back against the couch. "You know that time I went to the grocery store for carrots and got shot in the head? That's when I got my... premonitions." At his nod, I continued with how I met Uncle Joey, and it made me feel a little better to blame Chris for most of it, since it was because of him that I got involved with Kate and met Uncle Joey in the first place.

I left a lot of the details out, but, by the time I got done, Justin could definitely see what had happened. Then his eyes widened. "Crap. What about Josh and Savannah? Do they know? You haven't told them, have you?"

"Yes... they know. But they're good. We've worked it all out. In fact, Uncle Joey's kind of... made us all part of the family."

Justin's eyes got big. "Oh... uh... okay. I guess that's good. Maybe it means he's less likely to kill you. Uh... listen, I promise I won't tell anyone, but now I think we'd better get back to why I'm here. You know... the thing with Max and the cryptocurrency problem? Do you have any ideas about how to solve that?"

Frustrated, I huffed out a breath and tried not to yell at him. "Yes. That's why I told you about Uncle Joey. Max stole Uncle Joey's crypto. That's why we were at Max's house, and why I was following him. I told Uncle Joey that Max was trying to kill you, so now Uncle Joey wants your help to lure Max out so you can both get your money back."

"Wait, what? You want me to work with a mob boss? Shelby, what the hell? Are you out of your freakin' mind?"

"Justin," Chris said, his voice low with warning. "Don't talk to Shelby like that. She's just trying to help you."

Justin swallowed. "Well, yeah... sure... but getting involved with a mob boss could get me a lifetime prison sentence. I don't want anything to do with him."

I closed my eyes and counted to ten. "Not even to get your money back?"

His mouth opened and closed a few times, then his shoulders slumped, and he put his head in his hands. After shaking his head, he looked up. "Okay... maybe for that, but nothing else. I don't want his claws in me, and I don't want him anywhere near my family."

He was thinking I might be stupid enough to fall for that, but he wasn't. He'd do whatever it took to stay out of the mob boss's clutches. "Besides that, I'm not positive that Max isn't who he says he is."

"We're looking into that, but there's something else I haven't told you yet. Uncle Joey had a visitor this afternoon, and we found out he knew all about the Crypto-Knights and Max. Does the name Forrest Slater mean anything to you?"

"No. Why should it?"

"Because he's the cyber-vigilante who helped you out."

"But... are you sure? That's not the name he gave me."

"What name was that?"

"He goes by Viper. When I told Max I was Viper, he finally took me seriously and offered to help me track Landon down."

I shook my head. What was up with these crazy names? Viper sounded so much like Cypher, that I got an instant stomachache. Cypher was a terrorist who had nearly killed me, and just thinking about him sent dread down my spine. "He never said that was his hacker name."

"Are you sure he's the same guy?" Justin asked. "Can you trust him? If Max was telling the truth, this guy might be the bad guy."

"No he's not. At least... I don't think so." But was I sure? My stomach tightened, and I got a little dizzy. On my say-so, we'd set him up in my office and given him access to Uncle Joey's files. What if he wasn't the real deal? What if he was in on it with Max?

"I'd better call Uncle Joey." I found my phone and put the call through. After five rings, he finally picked up.

"Shelby? What is it?"

"Uh... sorry to call you so late, but I was just talking to my brother and I got a little worried."

"What for?"

I swallowed. "Did Forrest Slater ever tell you his hacker name?"

"I thought you said he was legit. What's going on?"

"My brother just told me his hacker name is Viper, and I got a little freaked out because he didn't mention that. It's probably nothing, but I just needed to check."

Uncle Joey huffed out a breath. "Shelby... you would have known if he had bad intentions. You didn't pick up anything like that did you?"

"No... not at all."

"Then it's all good. You shouldn't second-guess yourself. If it will help, Forrest gave me his number. Why don't you call him and find out?"

"Okay... that sounds great. Let me get a piece of paper." Uncle Joey rattled off the number, and I wrote it down. "Thanks. I'll call him."

"Good... and Shelby... I expect to see you and your brother in my office first thing in the morning. He needs to know where he stands."

"Uh... sure... see you then."

Uncle Joey hung up, and I knew I hadn't done Justin any favors by freaking out. What was wrong with me? Why did Justin make me question everything? He was my older brother, but that didn't mean he knew better than I did.

"What did he say?" Chris asked, worried that I may have overstepped my bounds by calling Uncle Joey so late.

"Yeah... I forgot it was this late, but he gave me Forrest's number. I'll just call him real quick."

I put the call through, and Forrest picked right up. "Hello?"

"Hi Forrest, it's Shelby Nichols. I'm here with my brother, and he mentioned that you have a hacker name. Would you mind telling me what it is... just so I can confirm you're the person he worked with?"

He let out a sigh. "Sure. It's Viper."

"Okay great. Thanks so much. I'm sorry I called you so late. Will I see you at the office tomorrow?"

"Yeah... I'll be there."

"Okay... thanks so much. See you tomorrow." I disconnected and turned my attention to Justin. "Okay. It's him. He's Viper. We're all good."

Justin nodded. "That's a relief. If he's helping your Uncle Joey out, then you won't need me. He's really good. He'll have Max flushed out in no time."

My eyes widened, and I stared him down. "You can't be serious. You're part of this now, and you're not getting out of it. Uncle Joey wants to see you in his office first thing in the morning. I'll pick you up at eight-thirty."

"But—"

"No! No buts. You're coming with me, and that's final."

He blinked a few times before letting out a breath. "All right. I'll be ready." He was thinking that I'd backed him into a corner, and he didn't have a choice. As his sister, shouldn't I be trying to keep him out of danger? Instead, I was siding with my fake uncle over him.

"Justin... this is the best way to get your money back. I'm helping you, not trying to hurt you."

He knew I was right, even though he could hardly believe how far he'd just gone down the rabbit hole. "Sure Sis. I get it. Hey... I'll see you tomorrow." As he walked toward the door, he glanced over his shoulder and gave Chris a head nod. "See ya."

He closed the door behind him, and I let out a breath. I picked up that he was resigned to his fate, even though he wasn't happy about it. Still, it didn't relieve me like it should. In fact, I almost felt guilty.

Chris's arms slid around me, and I leaned against him. "He'll be fine, Shelby. He's just going through a lot all at once. Don't be too hard on yourself."

"Yeah... I know. I just don't get it. I thought he'd be relieved to have help, you know?"

"Yeah. But I think the whole mob-boss thing was more than he could handle. After he sleeps on it, he'll see the benefits."

"I sure hope so."

The next morning, I arrived at my parents' house ten minutes early. Since Justin would be coming with me to work, the possibility of a motorcycle ride with Ramos was slim to none. Knowing that, I'd decided to wear my cute denim skirt and black top with my black ankle boots. It was fun to show a little leg and wear something different from my jeans-and-tee combo. Plus, I looked pretty good for a middle-aged woman, so why not?

After pulling up in the driveway, I knew I couldn't just honk for Justin, so I went around to the back porch and rang the doorbell. Opening the door, I stepped into the kitchen. "Hello. I'm here."

"Hey Shelby." My mom came into the kitchen wearing yoga pants and a t-shirt that said, *I've got it all together, but I forgot where I put it.* "Justin said he was going house hunting with you this morning. Isn't it great they're moving back?"

"Yeah... it sure is. Is he ready? I don't want to be late."

"Justin!" She yelled, sounding just like she did when we were kids, and I couldn't hold back my smile. We didn't hear anything, and she shook her head. "I'll go see what's taking him."

I nodded as she hurried away. She knocked loudly on his door. "Shelby's here. Are you coming?" He mumbled something and, a few seconds later, she came back with him following behind. As he joined me, she told us to have a good time.

"We will," I answered. On the way to the car, I glanced his way. "She's happy about your move back."

"Yeah. At least somebody is."

Okay... I guess he wasn't in a good mood. "Are you nervous about meeting Uncle Joey?"

He thought that was a stupid question. He was more than worried; he was terrified. "I guess so."

Ignoring his thoughts, I tried to put a positive spin on it. "I think that's a good thing, since it will keep you on your best behavior. He wasn't real happy about losing his crypto, or my late phone call, so I have to warn you to be ready for anything."

Justin shook his head, thinking it was just one more nail in his coffin, so what did it matter? "I will." His phone call to Lindsay last night popped into his mind. She'd told him she'd spoken with a lawyer about declaring bankruptcy. Bankruptcy. Him. That was about the worst thing he could ever do.

He'd told her not to give up yet, and that he had a plan. So now, here he was on his way to meet with a mob boss. Still, he had his doubts that it was the right thing to do. But which was worse? Working with a mob boss or declaring bankruptcy? Neither of them sounded good, but now it was too late, and he supposed he'd know soon enough.

As we got closer to Thrasher, Justin began thinking that he had no idea how he was supposed to help find Max, but, since this was the path he was on, he'd do whatever he could and hope it worked out.

"What should I call him? I don't want to call him Uncle Joey... you know that, right?"

"Yes, of course not. Call him Mr. Manetto. He's really not that bad. You just need to stay on his good side. He doesn't like people who grovel, lie, or double-cross him, so I think you'll get along just fine." I sent him a cheeky grin, but he was too busy feeling sorry for himself to think it was funny.

"Sure."

We spent the rest of the drive in silence, and I tried to block Justin's depressing thoughts from my mind. After parking the car, we took the elevator to Thrasher Development, and some of Justin's apprehension leaked through to me.

I didn't like it one bit, since it reminded me of my own anxious feelings the first time I met with a mob boss. "Justin. It's going to work out. Stop feeling so sorry for yourself. And, just for the record, this is the best way to go. It's lots better than declaring bankruptcy. And look on the bright side; if things work out, you'll get your money back... and maybe even all the profit you made, too."

His jaw dropped open, and he didn't know what to say. How had I known? Being with me was starting to creep him out. The doors slid open, and he snapped his jaw shut before we stepped out. I led him into Thrasher and found Jackie sitting at her desk.

Her eyes sparkled with interest to meet my brother. "Hi Jackie, this is my brother, Justin Davis. Justin, Jackie. She runs the show around here, and she's Uncle Joey's wife, so be sure to stay on her good side, all right?"

Justin's eyes widened, but he smiled and shook her hand. "I'll be sure to do that. Nice to meet you, Jackie."

"You too. Joe's expecting you. Go on down." Even though Justin's hair was much darker than mine, she could see the resemblance between us. With his dark brows, he reminded her of that guy who played a vampire in a movie, but, for the life of her, she couldn't think of his name.

A vampire? Hmm... now I was curious, and I vowed to look up vampire movies for Justin's look-a-like.

We passed by my office, and I was tempted to see if Forrest was there, but, since Uncle Joey was waiting, I kept going. I glanced at Justin and gave him a head nod before knocking and then pushing the door open.

Uncle Joey sat behind his desk in all his mob-boss splendor, looking regal and commanding. To my delight, Ramos sat in front of him. He stood as we entered, dressed in his black hit-man attire and giving Justin a hard stare.

Justin hadn't expected to see Ramos, and he stiffened slightly, but followed me inside. He wondered what Ramos was doing there. Then it clicked, and he realized his instincts had been spot on that Ramos was part of the mob.

I wanted to correct him, since he'd thought *gangster*, not *mobster*, but I let it go. "Hey Uncle Joey, this is my brother, Justin. Justin, Uncle Joey."

"It's nice to meet you, sir," Justin said, shaking his hand. "Shelby's told me a lot about you."

His eyes twinkled. "She has? All good, I hope."

"Uh... yes. Definitely."

"And you met Ramos yesterday," I said. "Ramos is Uncle Joey's right-hand man."

"Right." Justin offered Ramos his hand. "Thanks for coming to my rescue yesterday. I owe you." As soon as he said that, he could have kicked himself. He didn't want to owe Ramos anything, but now it was too late.

Ramos lifted a brow. "Sure. Next time I need my teeth cleaned, I'll know where to go."

"Please," Uncle Joey said, motioning to the chairs in front of his desk. "Have a seat."

As we moved to the chairs, I caught Ramos thinking that I looked hot in my short skirt. It wasn't my usual style, but, since it gave him a nice view of my legs, he wouldn't complain.

My gaze flew to his, and I tried not to blush or smile, but failed miserably. Ramos sent me his sexy smirk, and I pursed my lips to keep from telling him to knock it off, but inwardly, I couldn't help the pleased warmth that spread through me.

Then he ruined it by thinking he'd hoped to take me out on the bike today... but now he couldn't, since I wasn't dressed for it. My gaze flew to his and I narrowed my eyes. His grin deepened, but he quickly dropped the smile and flattened his lips to keep the hardened hitman persona on his face so Justin wouldn't think he'd gone soft.

"I hear you've had some bad luck with Max's group," Uncle Joey said, snapping us out of our silent banter.

"Yes. That's right."

"Tell me what happened."

Surprised by Uncle Joey's intense interest in his predicament, Justin relaxed and explained the story, including Max's deceit of claiming to be a federal agent. "If I'd known he'd want me dead, I never would have told him I was a hacker. Shelby told me that Viper contacted you. I'd like to meet him sometime, if I could."

"I'm sure you would." Uncle Joey glanced my way. "Is there anything Justin left out that we need to know?"

Did he expect me to rat out my brother? "Uh... no. I think that about covers it."

He caught Justin's gaze. "So what do you think about joining forces with me?"

Justin glanced my way before answering. "I think that would be great."

"Good. Then there's something you need to know. I don't like people who grovel, lie, or double-cross me. Is that understood?"

"Uh... yes... completely."

"I consider Shelby part of my family, and under my protection. Since you're her brother, that protection will extend to you, unless you abuse my good faith. That means you don't talk to the police, the press, or anyone with more than a fleeting interest in me or my business. Do I make myself clear?"

"Yes sir."

"Good. Then let's get down to business. Ramos, why don't you tell us what you found."

"My contact at the FBI couldn't find anyone by the name of Max Huszar or Max Fielding, so it doesn't look like he's an agent."

"That's a relief," I said. "What's our next step?"

"We need to find Max," Uncle Joey said. He glanced at Justin. "That's where you come in. We're hoping you can draw him out. But before we do that, we need more information. You have his phone number, right?" At Justin's nod, he continued. "What about an email address?"

"Yeah, I have both."

Uncle Joey's smile widened. He picked up his phone and pushed a number. "We're ready. Come to my office."

A few seconds later, the office door opened, and Forrest came inside. He nodded my way, and his gaze landed on Justin. "Hey Justin, I'm Viper. It's nice to finally meet you."

Justin jumped to his feet and held out his hand. "You too."

"Forrest told me he could hack into Max's phone records to track him down," Uncle Joey said. "He needs your phone and the email address you used to contact him. Why don't you two work on that in Shelby's office?"

"Sure." Justin's relief to get away from Uncle Joey washed over me, and I was glad to see him go. Not that I didn't love him, but his nervous tension was getting to me.

"That went well." I smiled at Uncle Joey. "What's the plan?"

"I think we make ourselves comfortable and see what Forrest can do with the phone number. We should be able to find out where Max is if we're lucky." He was thinking that getting him to pay up should be the easy part, especially if he'd murdered Landon. Holding that over his head would certainly do the job.

That brought a smile to my lips. If Uncle Joey was still the bad guy he'd been in the past, he would have been thinking about beating the crap out of Max before throwing him in the river with a pair of cement shoes. It just reinforced everything I'd told Justin about Uncle Joey changing for the better. He wasn't a bad guy, and neither was Ramos.

"I'm getting some coffee," Uncle Joey said, hoping I hadn't picked up the rest of his plans to make Max disappear permanently. "Jackie brought some pastries if you want any. They're in the conference room."

"Uh... yeah... sounds good to me." Well dang. My theory just got shot to hell. But that didn't mean he'd actually kill Max... he just wanted to. Wanting to do it, and actually doing it, were two different things, right?

As we all left the office, my phone buzzed with a text. I pulled it out to find a message from Dimples, telling me he'd found the ex-boyfriend in the homicide we'd been working on and asking me if I could come in this afternoon to question the guy. I wasn't sure how busy I'd be, but I agreed, telling him I'd try to be there around three. He sent me a thumbs-up, and I put my phone away.

The pastry box sat along the counter space in the back of the room beside the coffee machine, and both Ramos and Uncle Joey had picked out their favorites. After looking the rest over, I found a simple glazed donut and pulled it from the box. It practically melted in my mouth, and I tried not to groan.

"There's a Diet Coke in the apartment if you want one," Ramos said.

I sent him a smile. "You know it. Do either of you want one?"

They both shook their heads like I was nuts to even suggest such a thing. Uncle Joey had begun drinking it a while ago. He liked it okay, but not like I did.

"Okay. I'll be back."

"I'll come with you," Ramos said, surprising me. "There's something I need to get."

I nodded, and we stepped down the hall to the apartment where Ramos spent a lot of his time. While he went into the back room, I opened the fridge and pulled out a can of soda. Besides the soda and a few condiments, the fridge was mostly empty.

Ramos must not be staying here much. Was that because of his neighbor? I knew he had a house somewhere, but I'd never been there. Ramos came out carrying a gym bag, thinking these were the last of the clothes he'd wanted.

"So you're not staying here anymore?" I asked.

"Not at the moment. Manetto offered to let Forrest stay here, since he's from out-of-town."

"Oh. He really trusts him that much?"

Ramos shrugged. "He looks at it as a business arrangement. It isn't the first time he's let an out-of-town guest stay here, and I have my own place, so it's not a big deal."

I nodded. "That makes sense." I popped open my can and took a swig. "So how's your neighbor doing? Did you get her problem taken care of?"

He leaned against the counter with a wry smile. "Yeah. For now." He didn't offer more and my curiosity was killing me, but I wasn't about to ask him. If he wanted to tell me, he would, and I wasn't going to pry.

Ramos was thinking that, while he wanted to help his pretty neighbor, he couldn't be at anyone's beck and call. With the life he lived, he had enough on his plate already.

I nodded, not liking the pretty neighbor part. "If you need my help, just let me know." He gave me that head-nod thing, and I smiled. "Like if you need to go somewhere on your bike... I'm sure I could help with that."

He huffed out a chuckle, thinking *not with that short skirt... unless you want to show off all your assets*? A vision of how he thought I'd look on the back of his bike sent a red stain up my neck.

Before I could smack him, a short knock sounded at the door, and Justin poked his head inside.

"We found him."

Chapter 7

We followed Justin to my office, finding Uncle Joey looking over Forrest's shoulder at the computer. We crowded in next to him, and Forrest glanced our way, his eyes bright with excitement. "I got a bead on him not far from the city."

Forrest kept tapping away on the keyboard until the image of a map popped up with the location he'd found. "There." He pointed at the map. "It looks like it's about forty-five miles southeast of the city, close to the freeway. Do you know where that is?"

"Yes," Ramos said. "But there's not a lot out that way. It's mostly undeveloped land with a lot of open fields and a few houses spread out here and there."

"It sounds like the perfect place for him to hide out." Uncle Joey glanced at Forrest. "Can you pinpoint his exact location?"

Forrest nodded. "I think I can narrow it down. Once we get close, Justin can call Max's number, and I should get a more accurate location then."

"All right," Justin said. "Let's go."

Uncle Joey held up his hands. "Just Shelby and Ramos are going. The rest of us will follow once we have him." He caught Ramos's gaze. "Let us know when you exit the freeway, and we'll make the call. Forrest can direct you from there. And Ramos... keep him alive until I get there."

Ramos nodded and hurried out of the office. After a quick goodbye, I followed him. He waited in front of the elevator, holding the doors open until I stepped inside. On the way down, I picked up his disappointment that we weren't taking the bike. What was I thinking wearing a skirt?

"You're right. I just thought with Justin hanging around I wouldn't get the chance for a bike ride. I'll never make that mistake again."

Ramos smiled and led the way to his car. I glanced at the bike with longing, and stopped to admire it. "It might still work."

"Babe... I don't think so. Your skirt's way too short."

I sighed. "Yeah... probably not."

We hopped into his car, and Ramos took off. He was thinking that his car wasn't such a bad ride, and I had to agree. I wasn't sure of the model, but riding in a black sports car with a black leather interior and sleek lines was pretty sweet too.

Our estimated arrival time was nearly forty-five minutes. With that much time on our hands, I couldn't resist finding out more about Ramos's mysterious neighbor, completely going against what I'd been thinking earlier. But that was his fault since he didn't seem too concerned about it. "So did your neighbor just move in or something?"

His brow rose. I was a lot more interested in her than he'd thought. Why was that?

"I just want to make sure she's a good person, that's all."

He held back a smile. "Honestly, I don't know her that well. A few weeks ago, she had some trouble getting her garbage can out to the street. Since I was putting mine out at the same time, I helped with hers. She brought me some cookies to thank me, and we struck up a conversation."

My brows rose. "You do know she could have contrived the whole thing as a way to meet you, right?"

"Oh, I'm pretty sure she did."

"Oh... uh... okay. So what did she need help with?"

Ramos shook his head, thinking I wasn't going to let it go, so he might as well explain. "After we met, we spoke a few more times, and she asked me what I did for a living."

My eyes bulged. "You told her you worked for a mob boss?"

He snorted. "Of course not. I just told her I worked in security for a large corporation, and my main job was keeping my employer safe from any outside threats. You know... kind of like what I do for Manetto, but without going into details."

If he'd told her that, his bad-ass-ness just shot through the roof. Naturally, it would make him appear even more attractive and mysterious. She probably couldn't resist him.

A sudden desire to meet her washed over me, and I wanted to know exactly what she thought of Ramos. Was she under his spell? Was asking for his help a way to involve him in her life? Was he falling for it?

I could have just asked him that last question out right, but I wasn't sure I wanted to know. I shook my head. What was I thinking? I should stay out of it. I didn't need to know about his love life, and I certainly didn't want to know, either.

Ramos could take care of himself, especially where women were concerned. I'd seen that happen time after time, so I should just let it go.

"Oh... so what did she want?" So much for letting it go.

"I set up a house alarm system for her. She's had a few bad experiences with men, and she wanted to make sure she was safe."

"Oh. That's real nice of you."

"Yeah. Don't worry Shelby, Nico's not interested in me. She's a chemical engineer with a fancy life and lots of fashionable friends. I'm not her type, and she's certainly not mine."

"Got it." I wanted to add that sometimes opposites attract, so he might be wrong about that, but I didn't want to go there. It was his problem to figure out, and I should just stay out of it.

We exited the freeway, and it surprised me that we'd arrived at our destination. "We're here," Ramos said. "Call Manetto."

I put the call through and waited on the line while Justin called Max. "His call went to voicemail," Uncle Joey said. "But it was enough for Forrest to get a better idea of the location. Here... I'm handing the phone over to Forrest."

Forrest came on the line. "Continue west and keep looking for his car. It might be parked in a driveway or in front of a house."

That direction sent us down a lonely stretch of road surrounded by fields and a few trees. We kept going until we caught sight of an old building. "There's a building of some kind just off the road. It's the only one around here."

"It's a barn," Ramos said, pulling off the road beside a stand of trees.

"Oh yeah... we think it's a barn."

"That must be it," Forrest said. "I'll bet he's parked the car inside."

"Do you think he's in there?"

"His phone is... but that's all I can tell you. Just be careful."

"Okay. We'll let you know what we find."

Ramos grabbed a pair of binoculars from his glove box, and we got out of the car. Peering around the trees, Ramos studied the building before lowering the binoculars. "I don't see any windows from here, but let's approach from the back. There's more cover from that direction."

"Okay." I wasn't too thrilled about stomping through the tall weeds in my black ankle boots and bare legs, but I followed behind Ramos anyway. I did my best to push the grass away from my legs, but it brushed against my skin, making it itch.

Nearly there, Ramos stopped. We'd come around to the front of the barn and could see that the doors were held together with a padlock. Several tire tracks were evident in the dirt, but it seemed unlikely that anyone was still there.

Ramos studied the doors and lock. "With it all locked up like this, he may have left the car here and taken a different one."

"Then why is his phone still here?"

Ramos narrowed his eyes. "Maybe to throw us off, or lure us here."

My eyes widened. "You think there's another bomb?"

"No." Ramos didn't think Max would go to the trouble, but there were other unpleasant things he could leave behind. Or, he'd just left his car and taken off. Either way, we needed to open the doors to find out.

He stepped toward the doors and pulled his lock-pick set from his pocket. I stayed where I was, several feet away. He noticed I hadn't moved and lifted his brows. "You're not coming with me?"

"Uh... I think I'll just wait here."

He shook his head, thinking that if I really thought there was a bomb, I should move back at least another fifty feet.

A stab of anxiety tightened my stomach, and I slowly stepped away until I was standing in the middle of all the weeds. They still rubbed against my legs, but right now, that didn't seem so bad. I held completely still while Ramos got to work on the lock.

It seemed to take him a lot longer than normal, and I let out my breath once he was done. Discarding the lock, he unlatched the metal plate and glanced my way, ready to pull the doors open.

Before I could nod that I was ready, I heard a rustling sound near my feet. It was the only warning I got before several sharp stings started at my ankle and rushed up my leg.

The stinging continued up to the back of my thigh, sending panic into my heart. I jumped and screamed, swatting at my leg, but the stinging continued up my bum and into the waist of my skirt where it dug in.

Totally freaked out, I ripped off my skirt to shove the creature off me, only to feel the pricking continue up my bare back. In a frenzy, I pulled my shirt up over my head and flung it off, slapping at my back. Whipping my head back and forth, I reached to the back of my neck to stop it from climbing into my hair.

With my heart racing, I took off running, not caring which direction I went. I only knew I had to get away from there. I ran several feet before Ramos caught up with me. "Shelby! Shelby stop!"

He caught me around the waist, and I slowed down, but I couldn't stop twitching. "Is it still there? On my back?"

He turned me around and brushed his fingers across my skin. "No. You're fine. Nothing's there."

"You're sure?" My breathing came fast, and I kept hopping up and down.

"Yes. I'm sure. Whatever it was is gone."

Gasping for breath, I shook my head. "That was horrible. It just came out of nowhere and ran up my leg." Just thinking about it sent shivers up my spine. I leaned away to brush my hands over my legs and the backs of my thighs, just to make sure it was gone.

"Let me take a look." Ramos pushed my hair over my left shoulder and brushed his fingers over the path the critter had taken. He stopped at the small of my back before sliding his fingers down my bottom.

With a jolt, I stepped away. "What are you doing?"

"I'm just making sure you're okay."

Still shaking with nerves, I heaved out a breath and turned to face him. "What do you mean?"

"You've got these funny little red marks all down your back. I thought I should check them out."

He tried to hold my gaze, but his eyes dipped down to my chest, and I realized my clothes were missing. No shirt. No skirt. Just me... standing there shaking in my bra and panties with Ramos staring at my boobs.

"Holy hell." I crossed my arms over my chest and twisted around. "Where are my clothes?"

"Back there." Ramos nodded toward the field where my clothes had been flung, and it shocked me to see how far I'd run. He was trying not to laugh, but the effort made him sound a little hoarse. "Uh... want me to get them for you?"

His raspy tone held a challenge, and my gaze whipped to his. I didn't want to walk back out there where I'd been attacked, so he needed to do it. "What do you think? Of course I do."

He was thinking it would be more fun if he didn't.

"Ramos. This isn't funny."

A small chuckle burst out of him. "Uh... you're right. It's not funny... it's... hilarious." He couldn't hold back the laughter. "You should have seen yourself... you were screaming... and hopping up and down." He laughed again, only harder. "Then you started throwing off your clothes! I swear I've never seen anyone take their clothes off so fast in my life. Not even for me."

He laughed so hard that no sound came out of his lips. After several long moments, his gaze finally met mine, and he sobered. "Sorry... but, just for the record, I wouldn't have said any of that out loud, but, since you'd hear it anyway, I didn't think it mattered. You know? But hey... it's okay, you didn't mean to get undressed in front of me." He tried to hold back another chuckle, but couldn't do it.

With a low growl, I turned on my heel to march into the field.

Ramos jumped beside me, tugging at my arm. "Stop. You don't want to go back out there. I'll get them."

He was right. I didn't want to step into that field and have the tall grass touch my bare skin, or worry about something running up my leg. Sure, I might be standing here in my underwear, but I had to remember that it wasn't much worse than wearing a two-piece swimming suit. Plus, I had on my best black bra and panty combo. Still, this was about the most embarrassing thing I'd ever done in my life.

Ramos hurried to my clothes and picked up my skirt and shook it out. He took his time, picking off a few of the grasses and seeds. Next, he stepped to my shirt and did the same, taking more time to shake it out and examine it.

I picked up that he was looking for all kinds of bugs, spiders, and dirt, along with a few earwigs, but it didn't fool me. He was dragging this moment out as long as possible. Frustration boiled inside me, and I tried not to clench my teeth. I would have bolted for the car, or gone inside the barn, but who knew what waited in there?

Finally finished, he slipped my clothes over his arm. Then he grabbed my purse and dusted it off before slowly trekking back to my side. This time, his bold gaze raked over me, like he was drinking in every inch of my bare skin.

I swallowed, but I wasn't about to cower under his perusal. I stood straight and tall, even though sudden heat flared in the pit of my stomach and turned my insides to mush. "Hurry up. You're killing me."

His gaze met mine, and a slow smile creased his lips. "Good, because I feel the same way."

I wasn't sure if he'd said that out loud or not. Still, my breath whooshed out of me, and I thought for sure I was going to burst into flames right then and there. "Flames of hell."

"What?" he asked, stepping in close enough that I could feel the heat coming off his body.

I swallowed and closed my eyes, unsure of anything but this moment and the promise of long denied fulfillment. He reached up and gently rubbed his fingers across my collarbone, sending shivers of arousal down my spine. I stood on the edge of a cliff, ready to fling myself at him, but the ringing of a phone broke the spell, and the fog of desire fell away from my brain. My eyes jerked open, and I took a step back. "That's got to be Uncle Joey."

Ramos cursed under his breath before shoving my clothes into my arms. Turning away, he pulled the phone from his pocket and answered. He kept walking until he stood in front of the unopened barn doors.

Knowing I'd just been saved by the ring-tone, I quickly pulled on my clothes. Once my skirt and blouse were in place, I caught my breath and straightened my spine. Ramos finished his call, but kept his eyes glued to the door. "You dressed?"

"Yes." I was still breathless, but managed to put some conviction into my tone.

His shoulders relaxed, but his gaze stayed on the doors. "Good, because I'm opening the doors. If you want to move back, I suggest you do it now."

Swallowing, I marched to his side. "What? And miss all the fun? No way."

That brought his head around. As our gazes met, he sent me a grin. "Okay. Here goes."

He flipped the metal off the lock and pulled the doors open. Thankfully, nothing exploded. With the light coming through the doors, we could see the inside of the barn pretty well. It was filled with junk, making it look more like a shed than a barn. In the center of all that junk was Max's car.

Before stepping inside, I cocked my head and listened, hoping to pick up the thoughts of anyone who might be hiding there. Hearing nothing, I shook my head. "I don't hear anyone. I think we're alone."

Ramos nodded and stepped to Max's car. He tested the driver's side door, and it opened right up. Max's phone sat on the console, and he picked it up. Leaning over, he pulled the trunk release lever and it popped open. I stepped to the back of the car and lifted it the rest of the way.

My breath caught. All kinds of wires and explosive materials were sitting inside a box, but I couldn't see any sign of a switch or a red countdown clock. "Uh... I think you need to come see this."

Ramos came to my side and studied the box. "It's materials for a bomb, but it's not assembled. Could be the leftovers from the bomb he planted at the warehouse. He may have left in a hurry and didn't take the time to make another one. Either way, we're safe enough."

Ramos turned away to examine the rest of the space. He squatted near the other side of the car and examined the dirt. "It looks like there was a motorcycle parked here. He must have taken it to make his escape."

"I wonder how long ago that was?"

"Probably after he spoke to Justin. By now, he's long gone."

"Then what did he do with Uncle Joey's computer? It would have been too big to carry on a bike."

"Not if it was just the hard drive."

"That's too bad. I was hoping we'd find something useful."

Ramos shrugged. "Well, we have his phone, although it's probably a burner phone with nothing on it, but maybe Forrest can use it. I want to do a thorough search of the car in case he left something behind."

"While you do that, I'll take a look around the barn for anything else he might have stolen from the warehouse."

I didn't find anything, but Ramos uncovered the remains of Uncle Joey's computer. Sure enough, the hard drive was missing. Ramos pulled out his phone and reported to Uncle Joey, telling him we had Max's phone and the remains of his computer. "It won't do any good, but we'll bring it back with us."

He disconnected and slipped the phone back into his pocket before meeting my gaze. "Well... we didn't find Max, but I'd say that our little jaunt out here wasn't a total loss." He was thinking about the shock of watching me throw off my clothes. That had certainly been worth it.

I shook my head and widened my eyes. "Stop thinking about that. It was so embarrassing. Can't we just forget it ever happened?"

He snorted. "Not on your life."

I sighed. It was something I'd never forget either, but for totally different reasons. "What do you think ran up my leg anyway?"

"A lizard. Poor thing probably died of fright."

"You're never going to let me forget this are you?"

His answering grin brightened his eyes. "Nope. But don't worry. It will be our little secret."

I ducked my head and covered my face with my hands. This was going to be bad. Every time he thought of it, I'd know and have to keep a straight face. How was I ever going to do that? I was sure he'd milk it for all it was worth and think about it at the most inopportune times. Crap. I was in for it now.

Seeing the misery on my face, he stepped closer. "Come on, Shelby. You have to admit that was pretty funny. Someday soon, you'll look back on this and laugh your head off."

"Ha! I doubt it. In the meantime, please try not to think of it too often."

"And take away all the fun in my life? No way."

I huffed out a breath and rolled my eyes. "Whatever. Let's go."

We closed and locked the barn doors, before taking the road back to the car instead of walking through the field. My legs were still itching from the grass seeds, and I could feel tiny stings from the lizard's claws up my leg and across my back.

Just thinking about it made me twitch, and I couldn't wait to take a shower when I got home. Soon, we were on our way, and I looked forward to changing out of these clothes. As cute as they were, it was a horrible idea to wear them. I'd never make that mistake again.

"So now how are we going to find Max?" I asked Ramos.

He shook his head. "I don't know. I guess we'll just have to wait and hope Max will set up a meeting with your brother."

"Who knows if that will ever happen? Do you think Forrest can still track down the crypto?"

"I have no idea."

We arrived back at Thrasher and gave Max's burner phone, along with the remains of the computer, to Forrest. He didn't think either of them would be of much use, but he took them anyway.

It was after two-thirty and nearly time for me to go, so I came up with a good excuse to talk to the police. "I'll head over to the precinct and see if the detectives found out anything else about Max. Sound good?"

Uncle Joey smiled, thinking that I was finally on board with using the police to help him, and he hadn't even had to ask. "That's a good idea."

Dang... now I felt guilty about lying. I glanced at my brother, who was thinking that there was nothing I wouldn't do for the mob boss, and it made him a little nervous. Good thing I had a lawyer for a husband, because someday I'd need him.

"Great... I'll head over."

"What about me?" Justin asked, alarmed that I'd just leave him there.

"Oh... I guess you can come if you want."

"I was hoping you could just take me home." He didn't want to be anywhere near the police station if I was breaking the law.

Before I could answer, Forrest spoke up. "I can take you. I need a break, and I can get some groceries while I'm out."

"Oh, sure. Is that okay with you, Shelby?"

"Yes, that's perfect."

We left Ramos and Uncle Joey behind and took the elevator down to the parking garage. I said my goodbyes and drove over to the precinct, hopeful that Clue or Williams might have found something helpful on Max that I could tell Uncle Joey; then maybe I wouldn't feel so guilty about lying to him.

Wait... did that mean I was totally on Uncle Joey's side? The only reason I'd lied to him was so I'd be on time to help Dimples interview the ex-boyfriend... but now I was hoping to find out information about Max to help Uncle Joey. My life was so confusing.

I entered the detectives' offices and didn't see Dimples anywhere. I was about fifteen minutes early, so this might be my lucky break of the day. I sure needed one. I spotted Clue coming into the office and hurried to her side.

"Hey Clue, have you found out the identity of the dead person at the warehouse?"

"Yes, we have. His name is Landon Woods. Does that name ring a bell?"

I shook my head. "Uh... no, sorry. How about Max? Do you have any leads on where he might be?"

Her eyes narrowed. "No. Do you?"

"Me? No... sorry. If I did I'd be sure to tell you."

"I certainly hope so." She wasn't sure she believed me, but there was nothing she could do about it. Tracking down information about Landon only led to more questions. He was like a ghost. He supposedly lived in Riverside, California, but he hadn't been there for months. With no good leads, this whole case was so frustrating that it was driving her crazy.

"All right. Well... let me know if you need anything, I'm happy to help out."

"There is something. We searched Max's house and his office. Both of them were a mess. You wouldn't happen to know anything about that, would you?"

My brows rose. She was right, why didn't I know who did that? "No, I don't. The person responsible must have been looking for something. I wonder what it was?"

"Could your premonitions help with that? I'd be happy to go to his office with you now if you have the time."

And run into his neighbor? That wouldn't be good. "Uh... I would, but I'm here to help Dimples with that homicide. We're interviewing a suspect. How about a little later?"

She nodded, but thought I was hiding something. What did I know that I wasn't telling her? Was I protecting Max because he was my husband's client? Did I really know where he was? "Sure." Turning on her heel, she strode back to her desk, convinced I was in on it somehow.

How did she know I had more to do with it? Was I really that bad of a liar? Of course, she was a top-notch detective, so what did I expect?

Dimples arrived, and relief swept over him to see me. For some reason, he wasn't sure I'd come to help him.

I sucked in a breath. What was going on around here? Did everyone think so little of me?

Noticing the crushed look on my face, Dimples smiled real big, hoping his dimples would cheer me up a little.

Naturally, that brought a smile to my lips. "Hey. I made it. How's it going? Did you make any progress with that construction firm?"

"Yeah. It took me some time to track down the job that Kai was working on. They've had some setbacks because the owner, Chuck Walker, had a heart attack and ended up in the hospital. With him cutting back his hours, he turned most of his work over to his son, Eli. I managed to make an appointment with him for first thing in the morning. Will that work for you?"

"Sure."

"Just so you know, I'm hoping we won't have to go."

"So you think the ex did it?"

He shrugged. "He's our best suspect so far, so I guess we'll find out, right?"

"Yup."

"He's in interrogation three. Let's go talk to him."

I followed Dimples inside the room and glanced at the man sitting at the table. He looked pretty harmless, but I knew looks could be deceiving. Mid-to-late twenties, with sandy-brown hair, he shifted in his seat, unable to sit still. There was a slight yellowing along his jawline, like a bruise that was nearly gone.

"I'm Detective Harris, and this is my partner, Shelby Nichols. Do you know why you're here Mr. Navarro?" Dimples asked.

He shrugged like he didn't care, but being asked to come here had freaked him out. "No. I don't."

"Do you know Mikiko Nisogi?"

His lips turned down, and his brows drew together. "What's this got to do with her?"

"Isn't it true that you've been harassing her?"

"What? No." He didn't continue, thinking that he'd just wanted to talk to her and explain things. Had she called the police and reported him? Was that what this was about? "I just wanted to talk to her, that's all. There's nothing wrong with that."

"She broke up with you," Dimples continued. "I don't think showing up at her house at all hours of the night, and basically making a nuisance of yourself, shows you're someone who just wants to talk. She finally got tired of it and told her brother."

Dimples leaned forward and got up close to Navarro's face. "He confronted you, and you argued. He told you to leave her alone, or you'd regret it. It made you so furious that you decided to kill him, so you waited in the park while he was out jogging and you stabbed him, again and again."

Navarro's eyes bulged, and he jerked back. "Are you crazy? I'd never kill anyone. This is nuts. You've got it all wrong."

He was telling the truth. He didn't kill Kai. In fact, he hadn't even thought about it. He'd been upset about the breakup with Mikiko because he'd thought she was the one. He'd hoped that, if she'd just listen to him, she'd understand and come around. He could see now that he'd gone too far, but he'd been desperate. She was the love of his life. How could she not feel the same way? How could she not see that?

"Then prove it. Tell us where you were yesterday morning between six and eight am."

"I was on my way to work. I leave at seven because I have to be there at seven-thirty. I didn't do it."

Dimples glanced my way. Had I picked anything up? I nodded and motioned toward the door. "We'll be back." Dimples straightened and held the door open for me.

Out in the hall, I turned to face him. "He didn't do it."

He let out a breath. "Dammit. That's too bad. I was hoping to catch a break with this case."

"Yeah. I know. Now what?"

He shook his head. "Besides him, there's not a lot to go on. You haven't picked up anything from Kai's... uh... ghost... have you?"

"No. Not a peep." I didn't add that my mind had been so preoccupied with my brother and the crypto problem that I doubted much else could get through. "I'll try to keep an open mind though." I sent Dimples a wink, but he barely acknowledged it.

"Okay... I guess we'll be keeping that appointment tomorrow."

I sighed. "Yeah. Did you get a list of Kai's friends? One of them might know if Kai was involved with something shady."

He nodded. "I did. His sister gave me a list, and Bates and I have already spoken with everyone on it. I've got nothing so far, but maybe if you talked to them, you'd pick something up."

Just thinking about doing all that work made me tired, but I didn't want to let Dimples down. "Sure. If the construction guy doesn't work out, we can do that."

"Good. Thanks Shelby. I'll see you in the morning."

I told him goodbye and headed to my car, grateful to let him finish up with the ex-boyfriend and be done for the day. It was already after five, and the stinging from the lizard's sharp claws was beginning to burn. My legs were still itching, and I couldn't wait to change into something more comfortable.

Thoughts of flinging my clothes off in front of Ramos like a crazy person sent a whole new wave of embarrassment over me. Still, looking at it from his point of view, I knew I'd really missed out on hearing his thoughts. What had he been thinking at that moment? It must have alarmed him a little, but the vain part of me really hoped he liked what he saw.

I cringed and shook my head. What was I thinking? Now I was going to hell for sure. Why did these things always happen to me?

Chapter 8

I didn't make it home until nearly six because rush hour traffic was a mess. At least Josh had volunteered to order a pizza, so dinner was taken care of. Chris texted that he'd be late, so I told the kids to go ahead and eat while I took a shower. I couldn't put it off any longer.

The marks on my leg were barely visible, and I had to twist and arch my back to see the ones along my waist and up my back in the mirror. Some of them had drawn blood, surprising me. No wonder I was throwing off my clothes.

I slipped on a pair of loose sweats and a baggy t-shirt, before heading downstairs for a piece of pizza. To my dismay, there were only two pieces left, so I put them in the fridge for Chris and made myself a piece of toast with a glass of chocolate milk.

As I finished up, my phone rang. The area code was from New York. I'd only given my number to a couple of people who lived there. One of them was Hawk, a detective with the NYPD, and the other was Ella St. John, a nurse I'd met there.

I doubted Hawk would call me unless it was a dire emergency, so I hoped it was Ella, especially since I hadn't heard from her since the poker tournament, and I was curious to know how things were going.

Taking my phone into the living room, I answered. "Hello?"

"Hey Shelby, this is Ella. How are you? It's been a while."

"Ella! It's so good to hear from you. I've been wondering how you were doing. Did you ever make it back to New York?"

"Yeah, I did."

"And what about Creed?"

"Well, that's another story. We're married."

"What?"

She chuckled. "Yeah. It's kind of a long story."

"That's okay. I've got time."

"If you're sure."

"I am totally sure."

"Okay. Here goes." She began with an explanation of why Creed had played poker in the tournament for Sonny in the first place, telling me it was because of his sister, Avery, and her involvement with Sonny's casino. She explained about the murder charges against Sonny, and I had no idea Avery's testimony at his trial was the key to putting Sonny away.

After she told me about her sudden marriage to Creed, I knew there had to be a lot more to it that she'd left out, especially after their move to Los Angeles, which included a second, more formal wedding. Then she dropped a bombshell I didn't expect. "But Dom showed up at the wedding reception and kind of ruined it." Dom Orlandi worked for Sonny, and anytime he showed up, it had to be bad.

"He did? Holy hell. What did he want?"

"That's the reason for my call." She explained that Avery was well enough to testify at Sonny's trial, which was happening now, and that she and Creed were in Las Vegas for the trial. "The worst part of it is that Avery was abducted from the safe-house. At first we were worried that Sonny was behind it, but it turns out that someone else got to her first, and he's the one pulling the strings. His name is Gage Rathmore. Do you know who he is?"

Hearing that man's name threw me for a loop and sent dread into my heart. It took me several seconds to respond. "Uh... I haven't met him, but yeah... I've heard of him. Why does he have Avery?"

"Well, it turns out that Sonny owes Rathmore a lot of money. We know Rathmore took Avery to put pressure on Sonny to sign over his hotel and casino to pay his debt. In return, Rathmore said he'd hand Avery over to Sonny so she wouldn't testify against him. But that didn't work. Sonny refused to sign anything, and now Avery is testifying against Sonny. The trial started today."

"Wait. I don't get it. Rathmore will lose if she testifies. Does he still have her?"

"That's the thing." Ella sighed. "Creed and I went to see him to bargain for Avery's release. He's a powerful man. Besides owning most of the city, he's got his fingers in the police department and probably the state government too.

"It sounded like the charges against Sonny wouldn't stick if he didn't want them to, but he still wouldn't give up Avery. He's holding her hostage for another reason now."

Oh no. Was this why Ella had called me? Foreboding tightened my stomach and I swallowed, barely managing to speak above a whisper. "What does he want?"

Ella let out a breath. "I'm so sorry, Shelby." She paused. "He wants me to set up a meeting with you."

I groaned. Of course he did. How could this be happening? I thought I could avoid him, but now I was in his sights because of Ella. He must have known we had a connection from that night at the poker tournament, and now he was capitalizing on it.

Ella continued in a rush. "I guess he's been trying to work something out with your Uncle, but he hasn't had any luck. Somehow, he found out about our connection, and now he's threatening Avery if I don't set something up."

"Did he say what he wanted?"

"Yes. He was at the poker tournament and saw you play. He promised that he just needed you for a one-time thing, and then you'd be done. It's a meeting of some kind that he wants you to attend with some people. That's all I know."

I huffed out a breath. This was the exact thing I'd hoped to avoid. "Well, damn."

"I'm sorry to ask, but he promised that if you came to this meeting, he'd release Avery to us, and you'd never have to help him again."

I let out a humorless laugh. "Right. I've heard that before."

"I'm so sorry. I had no idea this would involve you. We have until the trial is over to give him an answer, so I can still try to figure out another way to get Avery away from him. But if I can't... I don't know what else to do."

"What's going on with the trial?"

She explained everything that had happened so far, including that the trial could be over tomorrow. That meant the meeting with Rathmore could happen the next day, which didn't give me much time to come up with an excuse for Uncle Joey. But maybe I could just tell him I was sick. As long as he didn't know the truth, it could work.

"I'm not sure if Avery's testimony is enough to convict Sonny," Ella continued. "But I'm sure he's guilty."

"Did Rathmore really say he could get Sonny off?"

"It sure sounded that way."

"Okay... let me see what I can do. Maybe you could tell Rathmore that I'll come, but only if Sonny goes to jail. That way at least something good will come out of it. But I have to be honest. Uncle Joey won't want me to come, even with Avery's life on the line. Rathmore's dangerous. More dangerous than you know, and Uncle Joey won't want me anywhere near him. That means I'll have to go behind his back, and that scares the crap out of me."

"I'll come to the meeting with you. I'll make sure that nothing happens to you. Creed and I can both—"

"No. That's not necessary. I might be able to get Ramos to come with me. You remember him, right? He's great in a fight, and I'm not so bad, either. Besides, it won't come to that. If Rathmore just wants me to use my premonitions in a meeting... that's not such a big deal, right? It will take what... an hour? That's a piece of cake. And then Avery will be fine. It'll all work out." I tried to look on the positive side for both our sakes, but I wasn't sure it was working.

"Look," Ella said, regret in her tone. "We'll see if we can figure something else out. We have until the trial's over. Let me see what I can do before you worry about coming."

"Ella... I know you wouldn't have called if there was any other way. This isn't your fault. Tell Rathmore I'll agree to come, and then let me know what he says. In the meantime, I'll figure things out on my end and see if Ramos will come with me."

She let out a long breath. "I'm so sorry to ask this. I just don't know what else to do."

"I know. It's okay."

"Thanks Shelby. I'll call you soon."

Disconnecting, I leaned back against the couch and closed my eyes. What was that saying? Out of the frying pan and into the fire? Rathmore had me in his sights, and he knew just how to pull my strings to make me play his game.

That meant I had to be smarter than him. Good thing I could read minds. If I was in a meeting with a bunch of people, I was bound to hear something from one of them that I could use to keep him away from me.

It reminded me of the first time Uncle Joey had asked me to a meeting with his people. He'd wanted to know if any of them wanted him dead. Practically all of them did. If Rathmore was as bad as they said, someone was bound to feel the same way. Having information like that could be a game-changer, and the worry in my heart faded from panic to something more manageable.

The back door opened, and Chris came home from work. I hurried into the kitchen and practically jumped into his arms. "Whoa," he said, pulling me tightly against him. "What's that for?"

"I've had a rough day, and I'm glad to see you."

"Umm... that's nice... I mean... I'm glad to see you too. What's going on?"

I followed Chris to our bedroom so he could change his clothes while I filled him in. Since I wasn't sure I should tell him about Rathmore wanting me for a meeting, I started with Justin's meeting with Uncle Joey and explained that Forrest had tracked Max's cell phone to a barn.

Naturally, I left out the part where I threw off my clothes in front of Ramos, and went straight to finding Max's car inside. "He'd left his phone there, so we took it back to Forrest at the office, along with the remains of Uncle Joey's computer. It didn't look like Forrest could do much with it, but you never know.

"After that, I had a meeting with Dimples for the homicide case we're working on." I ended by telling him about the boyfriend angle that didn't pan out.

"Wow... you've been busy."

"Yeah. But I saved you some pizza. Want some?" Mentioning food always got me out of explaining a lot of things I didn't want to, and it was easy to keep Ella's call to myself while I figured out what to do about it. In the end, I decided to wait until Ella actually called to set up the meeting before I said anything. I mean... it might not happen, and I didn't want to borrow trouble.

Later, I finally got to tell everyone about Miguel and Maggie's visit coming up on Friday. Both Josh and Savannah were thrilled, although Savannah was more excited than I'd seen her in a long time.

She tried to play it down, thinking that Miguel hadn't come home earlier in the summer when he'd said he would. She'd worried it was because he didn't like her anymore, and she didn't want to get her hopes up.

I wanted to tell her it was probably because of Uncle Joey's deception, but that might not be true either. He might have just been too busy to come home. Who knew? I guess we'd find out on Friday.

Of course, that was the same day I could be headed to Las Vegas. Damn. Why did everything have to happen at the same time? If Rathmore was anything like Uncle Joey, he'd have a private jet, which meant I could insist that I was back in time for the party or I wouldn't go.

That helped settle my nerves, and I went to bed hoping for the best.

Unfortunately, it was still a long time before I could go to sleep. I tossed and turned, knowing I had to convince Ramos to go to Vegas without telling him where we were going. If he knew, I was sure he'd tell Uncle Joey. If that happened, I'd never be able to board the plane. So how was I going to pull that off? Nothing came to mind, and I finally drifted off into a restless sleep.

I jerked awake with a yelp, slapping at my legs, convinced a critter of some kind was trying to eat me. Realizing it was just a dream, I flopped back down on the bed and stayed there until my racing heart slowed.

Chris was gone, and I could hear voices downstairs in the kitchen. Dragging myself out of bed, I splashed cold water on my face before joining my family. The frantic pace of getting everyone out the door left me with little time to remember my bad dream, or the incident that had caused it.

Once the kids had left for school, Coco barked for his daily walk. I had just enough time before my appointment with Dimples to take him, so I hurried to get dressed. Grateful to find another beautiful fall day, I enjoyed the brisk morning air, which helped clear my head and settle my nerves.

By the time I got home, things didn't look so bad. Who knew? By the end of the day, we might have a lead on finding Max, and the murder case with Dimples could be solved. Two things off my plate in one day.

I shook my head, knowing it would take a miracle for that to happen. Besides that, how could I forget that I might be heading to Las Vegas to meet with Gage Rathmore tomorrow? He was the worst of the worst, and just thinking about him turned my stomach into an aching blob.

Still, things could change... maybe Ella and Creed wouldn't need me after all? I let out a breath. Who was I kidding? I'd just have to focus on the here and now, otherwise I'd go crazy. Today was a beautiful day, and I might even get to go on a motorcycle ride with Ramos.

That was enough to raise my spirits, and I got ready, making sure to wear my black jeans, black boots, a blue top, and my leather motorcycle jacket. Looking good, I climbed into the car and drove to the precinct, determined to solve the case and have one less thing to worry about.

I pulled into the precinct and sent a text to Dimples that I was there. A few minutes later, he came out and motioned me to his car.

"Didn't you want to come inside?" he asked.

"Not really. Yesterday, Clue was thinking that I could help with her case, and I didn't want to turn her down again. She's starting to think I had something to do with it, which I don't."

"That's too bad." Dimples knew they hadn't had any breaks, so I was probably right about Clue wanting my help. Since it probably had something to do with Uncle Joey, he could see my reluctance. "Is Manetto involved?"

"Yeah." Oops. Did I just say that out loud?

His brows rose. He couldn't believe that I'd just admitted that to him.

"I can't believe it either." I let out a breath and blurted it out. "If you must know, Max stole several million dollars' worth of cryptocurrency from Uncle Joey. That's why we're hoping to track him down. I'd tell you more if I could, but it's nothing illegal, so you don't need to worry."

"Really? That's not at all what I expected. You know... that could really be helpful to Clue and Williams."

"How would it help them?"

He shrugged. "I don't know... give them another angle to look into?"

I shook my head. "I don't think so. We're not getting anywhere either, and we know what's going on. It's like he disappeared into thin air. But please don't tell them yet. If I get something that will help, I promise I'll pass it along."

"Okay." He was thinking *whatever*, but refrained from saying that since it was sarcastic.

I shook my head. "You know I heard that anyway."

"Oh... yeah. I guess you did." Hoping to make up for it, he focused on our upcoming meeting. "It will be interesting to see what Eli has to say... or not say... as the case may be." He glanced at me and smiled, thinking I was his ace in the hole, and the advantage it gave him was immeasurable.

Knowing he was using the full force of his flattering charms, I forgave him and smiled back, unable to resist the pull of his swirling dimples, and... if I was being honest, the compliment didn't hurt either.

I asked him how Billie Jo was doing, and we spent the rest of the drive catching up with their family drama. Reaching our destination, we turned down the street in front of the old stadium, where a chain-link fence blocked off access around it for several blocks. Dimples gasped as realization dawned.

"What?"

"We've had it all wrong. This isn't a construction site, this is a demolition. I've seen this in the news. MRP Capital must have hired Pinnacle Engineering to get the permits to bring down the stadium." He caught my gaze. "A project like this is worth millions, and it opens up a lot of possibilities for murder."

"What do you mean?"

"Just think... if something's not right with the permits and the demolition, the consequences could be huge."

I nodded. "I see your point. If Kai had an objection, the project manager might just want it to go away instead of fixing it. Do you know when the demolition is supposed to happen?"

"Yeah... I think it's next week."

"Then, if something's wrong, we haven't got much time."

We pulled into the parking area where several portable offices had been put together. The one in front had *Walker & Sons* on the side, so we headed for that one. A woman sat behind a desk that blocked the front part of the office from the back.

Dimples held up his badge. “Detective Harris and Shelby Nichols to see Eli Walker. He’s expecting us.”

The woman glanced up with narrowed eyes, before changing her expression into a polite smile. “Please have a seat, and I’ll let him know you’re here.” She motioned us toward the chairs perched along the front wall of the trailer.

She was thinking that Eli had enough on his plate without talking to a couple of detectives. What did we want with him anyway? She was sure they’d handled all the paperwork for the job.

It reminded her of the phone call from Chuck, and she knew she’d have to report our visit to him. Hopefully, she’d find out why we were there. Eli hadn’t shared much with her lately, and it was frustrating. His father was counting on her to make sure Eli didn’t mess this job up, but she couldn’t do that if she didn’t know what was going on.

Unable to put the call off any longer, she picked up the receiver and called Eli’s cell. “Your appointment is here to see you.” She nodded. “I’ll let them know.”

She replaced the receiver and glanced our way. “I hope you don’t mind waiting, but he’s on-site, so it will be a few minutes.”

“Not at all,” Dimples answered.

Fifteen minutes later, a man dressed in jeans, work boots, an orange work vest, and a white hard hat rushed into the office. “Sorry to keep you waiting. I’m Eli Walker.” He held out his hand, and Dimples shook it before introducing us.

"Nice to meet you both," he said. "Come on back to my office and we'll talk." He had no idea what we were doing there, but he didn't want Ivy to find out. She was too nosy for her own good, and it pleased him to no end to keep things from her, especially something as juicy as a visit from a couple of detectives.

On the other hand, our visit made him nervous. Ever since his Dad's heart-attack, he'd been in charge, and it seemed like there was just one thing after another that he'd had to take care of. Now we were here, and worry tightened his chest. Couldn't anything go right for a change?

As we followed him to a door at the back of the reception area, I felt kind of bad about the news we had to share.

Eli pulled the door open and motioned us inside. We entered to find a large table in the center of the room taking up most of the space. It was covered with rolls of architectural plans, with one plan in the center propped open, and fastened to the table at the corners.

Eli sat down in a large leather chair behind the table and pulled off his hard hat. With reddish-brown hair and a ruddy complexion, he looked much younger than I'd first thought, and I put him in his mid-twenties.

"Please sit down." He motioned us to a couple of folding chairs. "What can I do for you?"

"We're homicide detectives investigating the murder of Kai Nisogi," Dimples began. "He was murdered two days ago. Because you've worked closely with him, we'd like to ask you a few questions."

All the blood drained from Eli's face, and I was afraid he might faint.

"Eli? You okay?"

He blinked, and his face cleared. "Kai's dead?"

"Yes," I answered.

"He was murdered? What happened?"

Dimples glanced my way, thinking Eli couldn't be faking his shock, so he had to be innocent. I nodded to confirm his suspicion, and he sighed before explaining Kai's death.

"His sister mentioned that he'd had an argument with someone, and his co-workers told us it was with you. Is that right?"

Eli was still trying to process everything, and it took him a moment to reply. "That was weeks ago."

When he didn't continue, Dimples prompted him. "What was it about?"

He took a deep breath, and his eyes suddenly widened. Did we think he had something to do with it? This was horrible. He'd never do anything like that.

Shaking his head, he swallowed. "Kai found a flaw in the plans that took us out of compliance with the demolition permit. It wasn't a game-changer, but it required some extra work that could have set us back a couple of weeks."

He was thinking that the money they would have lost wouldn't have been good either. His dad would have had another heart-attack if that had happened.

"I wasn't real happy about that, because we were already behind by several days. I can admit now that I didn't see it as a big enough problem to fix, but I took it to Steve Mosely, the head of operations at MRP Capital. They're the company that gave us the sub-contract for the demolition."

Eli's mouth had gone dry, and he licked his lips. "Steve took the plans and told me he'd have a different engineer take a look at it."

He skipped the part about how much money the delay would have cost MRP Capital, and continued. "The next day, I got his recommendation for a workable solution. We made the changes they proposed. It ended up only slowing us down a few days rather than a few weeks, so that was positive. I got back to Kai and told him about the changes, and that was the end of it."

He was thinking that Kai hadn't been thrilled about the solution, but he seemed okay with it. Then he showed up at his office three days ago and told Eli that they'd made a big mistake. Eli thought Kai was overreacting, and he gave Kai a copy of the plans Steve had given him to prove it. Kai had taken them, and Eli hadn't heard from him since.

Now Kai was dead? Eli shook his head. There had to be another explanation. It couldn't be related to this. He met my gaze, shock and worry clouding his eyes. "Do you have any leads?"

"We're doing everything we can."

"Good. I hope you find him. Kai was a good person. He didn't deserve to die."

"I agree." I glanced at Dimples, signaling that I picked up everything I'd needed. Dimples handed Kai his card and gave him the usual talk about calling if he remembered anything.

As I followed Dimples to the door, the smell of eucalyptus and mint wafted over me. I turned back to the room and looked for the scented plug-in. Not seeing anything, my gaze caught Eli's. "I love that eucalyptus wallflower scent. I'm going to have to get one for me."

Eli's brows drew together. "Huh?"

"You know... that scented stuff you plug into your walls?"

"Oh... sure." He had no idea what I was talking about. He sniffed the air, but all he could smell was his own sweat. Maybe Ivy had put one in here and he couldn't smell it because he smelled so bad.

I took another glance at the walls. "How many electrical outlets do you have in here?"

"Just one. It's by my chair." We both glanced at the wall, finding the outlets filled, and no sign of a scented plug-in.

I sent Eli a small smile. "It must be coming from somewhere else. Anyway... thanks for your time. We'll be in touch."

Dimples waited at the exit door for me, his brows drawn together, wondering what was taking me so long. Ivy took one look at Eli and knew something bad had happened. As we exited the office, I caught her determination to find out what was going on, even if she had to threaten Eli to do it.

Poor Eli. This just wasn't his day.

The eucalyptus scent lingered until the trailer door shut behind us, and I knew it wasn't a coincidence. Kai was trying to tell me that Eli was connected to his death. I knew Eli hadn't killed Kai, but this job had something to do with it.

As Dimples started the car, he turned my way. He knew I'd gotten something and he couldn't wait to hear it. "What did you get?"

I explained what I'd heard about Kai's second visit to Eli, along with the copy of the plans Eli had given him. "I think we need to pay Steve Mosely a visit."

"Let's do it."

Dimples put MRP Capital Development into his app. The company had its corporate offices on the south side of town in a fairly new development. As we got closer to the development, I realized that I'd been there some time ago—with Uncle Joey.

Trepidation turned my stomach, but I tried to ignore it. I couldn't remember a thing about MRP Capital, so maybe it was a different office in the development. Uncle Joey invested in a lot of properties... so that was probably it.

We parked in front of the building with *MRP Capital Development* on it, and a throb of anxiety seized my chest. This was the building, and I distinctly remembered that Uncle Joey had a business deal with the president of the company. Too bad I hadn't remembered the company name, but I chalked it up to fearing for my life.

I remembered the president's name though, mostly because it was Al, and I'd called him Weird Al in my mind, just for the heck of it. I also remembered that Uncle Joey had wanted me to make sure Al wasn't cheating him, and the entire incident came flooding back.

I'd managed to save Uncle Joey thousands of dollars because I'd discovered that the company planned to cut a few corners on the job Uncle Joey had hired them for, while still charging him the full price. After I pointed out Al's deception, he'd had to scramble to save face.

Instead of exposing him, Uncle Joey had done him a 'favor' and kept the deal quiet. Now Uncle Joey had the upper hand over Al and the company whenever he needed it—a position Al hated. I had a feeling that if Weird Al ever saw me again, he'd probably want to kill me.

Dimples got out of the car and started toward the building. He noticed that I was still sitting in my seat and stopped, turning to glance at me with his brows drawn together. Not wanting to explain my hesitation, I quickly got out of the car.

"You okay?" he asked.

"Of course. I was just putting on some lip gloss." I rubbed my lips together, and hoped he didn't notice how dry they were. It must have worked, because he didn't think anything of it, and we headed inside.

Passing through the entrance, I kept my head down and followed Dimples to the receptionist's desk. He told the young woman that we were detectives there to see Steve Mosely. Her eyes widened a little, since she'd never had a police detective come in before.

She put the call through to Mosely's office and was told he was busy in meetings all day. Hanging up, she told us he wasn't available, but we could schedule a meeting with his secretary.

"Sure," Dimples said. "What floor is he on, and we'll go up to his office."

"Uh... he's on the sixth floor... but... I think—"

"Great. Thanks." Dimples led the way to the bank of elevators, ignoring the sputtering receptionist. I followed, rubbing my forehead to make sure no one in the lobby could see my face. Once we got on the elevator, I relaxed, remembering that I'd been to the top floor and not the sixth, so my chances of running into Weird Al were pretty slim.

Dimples glanced my way. "Do you have a headache or something?"

"Me? No. I'm fine."

He narrowed his eyes, thinking something was going on. I was acting weird. Why was that?

I couldn't help it, and a chuckle burst out of me. "Weird... you're right... the truth is... I may have been here before."

"Okay... so?"

"Uh... with Uncle Joey?"

His eyes bulged. "What?"

"Yeah... it wasn't anything illegal. But it might help our case."

"How?"

I lowered my voice. "Because these guys aren't exactly honest."

Dimples let out a breath, thinking I was just full of surprises. First it was the cryptocurrency revelation, and now this. What else was I up to?

"Nothing else... for now." That was mostly true, since I hadn't heard from Ella yet, and I hoped it stayed that way.

We exited the elevator and found the secretary on her phone talking to the receptionist. As soon as she caught sight of us, she hung up and stood. "You must be the detectives. I can make an appointment for you to meet with Mr. Mosely next Monday at three. Shall I put you down?"

"We'd really like to see him today," Dimples countered. "It will only take a few minutes."

"I'm afraid that's not possible."

"We'll wait." Dimples smiled before stepping towards the couch in the waiting area off to the side of the secretary's desk.

Her mouth opened and closed a few times before she shrugged. She was thinking that Chad wasn't going to be happy, but he needed to know we were there. She put the call through, and I picked up that Chad was their corporate lawyer.

"She's calling their lawyer," I whispered to Dimples. "It sounds like he's coming down to talk to us."

Dimples shook his head. "Great... just what we don't need."

A few minutes later, the elevator doors opened, and two men stepped out. The first had dark blond hair and wore a suit. From the way he looked at us, I knew he was the lawyer. The second man slowed to study us before stepping down the hall. With his intense gaze and hardened features, he put me on full alert, and I was grateful he'd headed away from us. I relaxed a bit, until I realized he had stopped just out of sight to listen to our conversation.

"Hi, I'm Chad Finlay. I understand you want to talk to Steve Mosely. I'm his lawyer. Can I ask what this is about?"

Frowning, Dimples stood, so I followed his lead. "We just have a few questions for him about a homicide. Any help he could give us would be greatly appreciated."

Chad pursed his lips, unhappy to have us snooping around. "Why don't you tell me what this is about? I'm sure

Mr. Mosely would be more than happy to comply if he knows what's going on."

Dimples gave in, knowing this was the only option we had at the moment. "We're investigating the murder of an engineer from Pinnacle Engineering who was sub-contracted for a job Mosely is currently heading up. There seems to have been a problem with the plans for the demolition of the stadium. Are you familiar with the job?"

Chad's brows rose. "Of course. Who was the engineer?"

"Kai Nisogi."

"And you think his death has something to do with our company?"

"Not at all. We just have some questions for Mosely about a disagreement he had with our victim." Dimples kept his tone light, but the lawyer seemed to know there was more to it. Probably because he was familiar with the company's dirty dealings.

"I see. Why don't we set up something for tomorrow? Mr. Mosely and I can come into the police station around four tomorrow afternoon. Will that work?"

Dimples sighed, knowing that was probably the best he'd get. Before he agreed, the elevator doors opened and a man stepped out. Dimples recognized Steve Mosely from the company website and smiled. "I think we'll chat now."

Dimples hurried to Mosely's side and pulled out his badge. "Mr. Mosely, I'm Detective Harris, and this is my partner, Shelby Nichols. We'd like a word with you."

"What's this about?" He glanced at Chad, suddenly worried that he was in trouble.

"Could we speak privately?" Dimples tilted his head toward the receptionist.

Mosely nodded. "I suppose so."

"I'll be joining you." Chad stepped to Mosely's side, wishing he could have prepared Mosely for the meeting. He hoped Mosely was smart enough to keep his mouth shut and let him do the talking.

We followed Mosely down the same hall that the second man had stopped in to listen to our conversation, but there was no sign of him. Mosely couldn't figure out why we were there, and my heart sank. If he were guilty, wouldn't he be worried?

Mosely took a seat behind his desk and motioned us into the chairs in front of him. Chad pulled a chair beside Mosely's to face us, and Dimples began. "We just need to ask you a few questions about your work with Kai Nisogi. He was found murdered two days ago, and we understand that he was working for your company, but we're a little hazy on what he did for you. Could you explain that to us?"

"Kai's dead? What happened?"

"Someone stabbed him while he was out on his morning run."

Mosely's eyes widened. "That's horrible. Was it a mugging?"

Dimples shook his head. "I'm afraid not. Do you know anyone who would want him dead?"

"No."

"Get to the point, detective," Chad said. "You're wasting our time. Mr. Mosely had nothing to do with his death."

"I didn't say he did," Dimples answered. He glanced back at Mosely. "We were told you had a disagreement with Kai over a job he was doing for you. Is that true?"

"You don't have to answer," Chad said.

"No... it's fine. Yes, we did have a disagreement, but we got it all straightened out."

"Can you tell us what it was about?"

He shrugged. "Kai thought he found an error in our plans. It didn't make sense, because we'd already gotten the permits for the demolition from the city, so everything was in order. To be on the safe side, I had another engineer go over the plans, and he made a couple of suggestions, which we followed, and that was the end of it."

He was thinking that, with the demolition happening next week, they couldn't afford another setback. "I don't know what happened to Kai, but you're barking up the wrong tree. All our plans and permits have been approved, so there's nothing about the job that would explain his death. Now, if you'll excuse me, I have work to do."

He stood and motioned toward the door for us to leave. Everything he'd said made perfect sense, and he believed every word. He hadn't killed Kai, at least not that I could pick up. But as we walked out, I got a whiff of the unmistakable smell of eucalyptus, confirming that this job was connected to Kai's murder.

Chad opened the door for us, and we stepped into the hall. Standing at the end of the hall was the same man who'd been listening to our earlier conversation. As he walked toward us, my heart sped up.

The man glanced behind us at Chad, who had followed us out. "Mr. Finlay, you need my help with anything?"

Chad shook his head. "No, Braxton. They're just leaving." Chad was grateful Braxton was doing his job as head of security and that he hadn't missed a thing.

Braxton nodded, but kept his stare focused on Dimples. "Let me know if you need me." Braxton planned to tell the big boss about our visit and have a personal chat with Mosely to find out what he'd told us about the job.

"I will." Chad liked Braxton's show of force, thinking it never hurt to intimidate someone who could be an enemy. As we stepped toward the elevator, he stopped us. "In the future, if you wish to speak with anyone else in the company, you'll need to talk to me first."

Dimples nodded, and Chad walked back to Mosely's office, thinking that he needed Steve to tell him everything he knew about the job. Steve didn't make mistakes, so our visit didn't make sense. Still, if we were suspicious of the company, he needed to get to the bottom of it before it got out of hand.

I almost felt sorry for Steve Mosely, but if he had something to do with Kai's death, he probably deserved whatever they dished out.

As Chad disappeared from view, the elevator doors opened, and we stepped inside. Distracted, I didn't notice anyone else until it was too late. I glanced up to meet the gaze of Weird Al, the president of the company. Surprised, I jerked my gaze away, but not quickly enough.

Recognition flashed across his face. He was thinking that I was Manetto's niece. What the hell was I doing there? Was I spying on him for Manetto?

Damn! Now what? I stepped closer to Dimples, mostly because Al was thinking he'd like to slip his hands around my neck and strangle me. The elevator came to a stop, and I rushed to leave. As I stepped out, Dimples grabbed my arm and yanked me back. "Wrong floor."

He shoved me out of the way so Al could leave. Instead, Al held the doors open and looked Dimples over. His gaze landed on the badge at Dimples's waist, that just 'happened' to be gaping open, and his eyes widened.

"Have a good day, sir," Dimples said, giving him a nod.

Weird Al's lips twisted before he stepped away, allowing the doors to close. I slumped against Dimples's arm and let out a breath.

"Who was that?"

"Weird Al... the president of the company."

Dimples chuckled at the name and shook his head. "He didn't seem to like you much."

"I know. It happens more often than you think. If I wasn't such a positive person, it could really get me down."

"I'll bet." He sent a wry smile my way, thinking that being with me was never dull.

We got into the car, and Dimples glanced my way. "So what was that all about?"

I sighed. "Mosely definitely had something to do with Kai's death, but he didn't do it. And that Braxton guy gave me the creeps. I picked up that he's head of security, so he's like a spy who knows everything."

"So does he know why Kai was killed?"

"I don't know. That part wasn't as clear. All I picked up was that he was going to tell the big boss—Weird Al—that we were there, and then he was going to spend some 'alone' time with Mosely." I threw up my hands. "Who knows what that means, right?"

Dimples nodded, but he was thinking it could mean anything from a simple chat to torture. "Mosely didn't seem to think there was anything wrong with the plans though, right?"

"That's true."

"Then why kill Kai?"

"I have no idea."

Chapter 9

We arrived back at the precinct, and Dimples glanced my way. "Are you coming in?" He was anxious to look into MRP Capital to find out more about the company and thought I might want to help.

"Uh... I think I'd better go, but call me if you get something."

"I will... thanks Shelby, we'll figure this out."

I gave him a smile. "You know it. See ya."

I got into my car and contemplated what to do next. The best thing might be to go home and avoid Uncle Joey all together. I liked that idea, but, before I could act on it, my phone rang. "Hey Justin. What's up?"

"Where are you? I thought you were coming in to Thrasher?"

"Uh... I've been helping the police, but I'm done now. Is that where you are?"

"Yes."

"How did that happen?"

"Never mind that... you need to come to the office."

"Okay, but... can you tell me why?"

"Manetto just got off the phone with somebody, and he's not real happy. He asked me to call and tell you to come in. Did you do something wrong?"

"Uh... maybe, but it wasn't intentional."

He huffed out a breath. "You'd better get over here and explain."

"Okay. I'm on my way."

Weird Al must have called Uncle Joey, and now I was in trouble. But that didn't make sense. If Al thought I was spying on him for Uncle Joey—that could be a plus, right? It wasn't a big deal unless... was Uncle Joey working with Al on something? Hopefully, it wasn't with Steve Mosely and his project. But what if it was? I'd have to warn Uncle Joey to pull out of the deal, and hope it didn't ruin all his plans.

Why did these things always happen to me?

Several minutes later, I pulled into the parking garage of Thrasher Development. On my way to the elevator, I glanced behind the pillar and found Ramos's motorcycle sitting there. Usually, seeing it lightened my spirits. Since that failed to happen, I knew trouble was just around the corner, and my stomach twisted with worry.

The elevator let me out on the twenty-sixth floor, and I took a deep breath before entering Thrasher. Jackie sat at her desk and motioned me over. "Hey Shelby. Don't forget the party tomorrow night. Miguel and Maggie will be arriving later tonight, and they're really looking forward to seeing you guys. We thought we'd keep it simple and cook some steaks on the grill with baked potatoes and a salad."

"That sounds amazing. What time should we come?"

"I thought we'd start around six so the kids could go swimming first, and then we'd eat around seven."

"That should work. Do you want me to bring anything?"

"No. I've got it covered."

"Great. It will be fun to see Miguel and Maggie. It's been a long time."

"Yes it has."

I glanced down the hall. "Where is everyone?"

"In Joe's office."

"Okay... I'd better get down there."

It helped to know Jackie wasn't worried about me, so I knocked with confidence before opening the door. Uncle Joey and Ramos were in the office, but not Forrest or Justin. Ramos was feeling sorry for me, and he hoped Manetto was in a forgiving mood.

Uncle Joey's lips flattened. "Shelby. Come in and sit down. I just got an interesting call from Al over at MRP Capital. Want to explain what were you doing there with the detective?"

"Sure. I'm helping Dimples with a homicide. We found out that the victim was working on a project for Al's company right before his murder, so we were there to talk to the project manager. On the way out, I got on the same elevator as Weird Al. He recognized me and thought you'd sent me to spy on him. Is that what he called about?"

Uncle Joey let out a breath, thinking that my involvement with the police was a pain in the ass. "Yes. I had to make it look like I approved of your connection with the police." He shook his head. "I'd given Al my word that I wouldn't involve the police in that other matter, and he thought I'd changed my mind. Since I don't want to lose the advantage I have over him, I had to convince him it wasn't about that. Can you see why I'd be upset?"

"Sure. I get it, but it was just an unlucky coincidence that he spotted me. I didn't mean to run into him... that was an accident."

He sighed, thinking that I always managed to get into trouble, so he should have expected something like this to happen sooner or later. He just wished it would have been later, since he was working out a deal with Al.

"Wait. Are you investing in the stadium project?"

His eyes narrowed. "We're working on a deal."

"Uh... maybe you should hold off for a few days... just in case we find out that the homicide is tied to them."

He sat back in his chair, thinking that he'd been ready to sign the deal until Al called. He might be able to put him off for a couple of days, or maybe until next week, but that was it. Even then, he might lose out on making a huge amount of money. "Fine. But you'll let me know what's going on?"

"Sure. I promise."

"Good." He was thinking that this might be the break he needed. If MRP was involved in a homicide, he might be able to take over the contract and do the job himself with his own company. This might work out better in the long run.

My breath whooshed out and I relaxed, grateful my inadvertent meeting with Al had a silver lining to it. A knock sounded at the door, and Justin and Forrest came inside. "Max took the bait!"

Uncle Joey and Ramos exchanged glances, while I raised a brow. "What bait?"

"I sent Max an email," Justin began. "I told him that I really needed to see him because I'd uncovered the name of one of the other people involved with the Crypto-Knights. He responded with a time and place to meet."

Shock washed over me. "Really? When?"

"Tonight."

Uncle Joey and Forrest were thrilled with this development.

Me... not so much. "Where?"

Forrest glanced at his computer. "Uh... it says to meet on the lowest parking level of the city center parking garage at the north end by the escalators that exit onto Main Street. Max says to come down the escalators at eleven, and he'll meet Justin there."

Justin caught my gaze. "That's late, but not too late, right?" Belatedly realizing that his life might be in danger, the reality of meeting Max lost its appeal.

I shrugged. "It all depends on what time the shows end for the night. There are usually one or two Broadway plays or other types of concerts going on in the area, and most people use the city center parking garage. We should check."

"Already on it," Forrest said, typing into his laptop. "Yeah... it looks like there's a play at the theatre, so it won't be completely deserted at eleven. Still, we'll have to make sure you're safe."

"Ramos will be in charge of that," Uncle Joey said. "He'll make sure Justin survives and that Max doesn't get away this time."

Ramos nodded. "I can do that, but I'd better get started." He was thinking that he'd need a van parked close by so he could monitor the lot. It might be a good idea if he had a couple of other people watching along the way as well. If this was an ambush, he wanted to know what direction it was coming from.

"What can I do?" I asked him.

"You can help me keep watch in the van where your premonitions might come in handy."

Justin's eyes widened. "That's right. You'd know if something was going to happen, and you could warn me." Knowing I could do that eased some of his worry.

He glanced at Ramos. "Do you have a bullet-proof vest I could wear? I'd feel a lot better with one of those on."

"Yeah. We'll get you suited up. I need to make some phone calls and figure out logistics. Why don't we all meet here tonight at nine-thirty? That should give us enough time to have everything in place."

We all agreed, and Ramos left. Uncle Joey turned to Justin, placing his hand on Justin's shoulder. "Thank you for doing this, Justin. I won't forget it."

Justin swallowed and nodded, but couldn't seem to get any words out of his mouth.

Uncle Joey dropped his hand and turned to include me. "As Shelby knows, I take care of my family, and now that includes you. It will be fine. Ramos knows what he's doing, and we'll all get our money back."

Justin nodded and tried to smile, but he began to rub his sweaty palms on his pants, giving away his sudden case of nerves.

Uncle Joey noticed and glanced between us. "Why don't you two go home? We'll see you back here at nine-thirty sharp."

That was my cue to help Justin deal with this turn of events, and I pulled him towards the door. "Okay. See you then."

We made it all the way to the parking garage without speaking, but I heard plenty from Justin's thoughts. Most of it was swearing, mixed with self-loathing and pity.

"Hey... try not to freak out. I've got your back. I won't let anything happen to you, and neither will Ramos. You'll be fine."

He was thinking I could say that, but I didn't know for sure. Still, if any of my stories were true, I'd managed to survive a few dangerous moments, so maybe it would work. "I never thought I'd say this, but I'm really glad you got shot in the head. You'll know if something's off before it happens, right?"

I raised a brow. "Yup. I will."

"Okay. Good."

"I'll come by at nine tonight to pick you up. What should we tell Mom and Dad?"

He shook his head. "I have no idea."

"Let me think about it, and I'll call you."

"Okay. See you Sis."

I watched him get into his rental car, hearing his thoughts about calling Lindsay and the kids as soon as he got home. He wished they were here so he could give them each a hug and make sure they knew how much he loved them. Then he planned to tell Lindsay how sorry he was for everything, just in case—

His car door shut, and I lost his thoughts. It was probably for the best, since his morose feelings of doom were starting to get on my nerves. Still... I vowed that I'd make sure nothing happened to my brother. Nothing. Whatever it took, I'd make sure he didn't die tonight.

I made it home before the kids got out of school, which was good since I needed some time to unwind. Coco greeted me with warmth and affection, which always brightened my mood.

I kicked off my shoes and got a diet soda out of the fridge, then headed out to the swing in the backyard. After throwing the Frisbee a few times for Coco, I settled down on the swing to relax.

I had a few minutes of peace to enjoy the crisp autumn breeze before my phone rang. I wanted to ignore it, but picked it up instead. The number had a New York area code, and my chest tightened.

"Hello?"

"Shelby. It's Ella. I'm sorry, but we ran out of options. I told Rathmore you'd come, and he wants you here tomorrow. I know it's short notice, but he's sending his private jet to pick you up in the morning, and once the meeting is over, he'll take you straight back. Can you make that work? I can send you a copy of his text with all the details."

The strain in Ella's voice stirred anger in my heart. "Yes. I have a plan. Don't worry, I'll be there tomorrow. Did he say any more about what I can expect?"

"Sorry... no. Do you want me to call him back?"

"No... it's fine. I'll see you tomorrow."

"Thanks, Shelby. See you then."

We disconnected, and, a few seconds later, her text came through with the flight details. Rathmore's plane would be waiting for me at eight-thirty, with the flight leaving at nine the next morning at the same private airport that Uncle Joey used. Once the meeting was over, his driver would take me back to the plane, and I should be home in time for dinner.

At least that was positive, since dinner was with Miguel and Maggie. Plus, that dinner gave me something to look forward to. If I focused on that, this whole business would just be an insignificant blip on my radar.

Now I just needed to make sure Ramos went with me. I'd told Ella I had a plan, but that was mostly wishful thinking. The only plan I'd come up with was to ask Ramos to come with me without telling Uncle Joey, and I wasn't sure he'd do that. I mean... Ramos would come with me, there was no question about that, but getting him to keep it from Uncle Joey was another matter.

Then there was Chris and my kids. They probably didn't need to know, either. Just like I didn't want to tell them about tonight. What did that say about my life?

Of course, ever since I got shot in the head and became a mind-reader, this was pretty much normal for me. So... after everything I'd been through since then, this was just a drop in the bucket. They should be used to stuff like this, so I was probably worrying for nothing.

I let out a breath and got comfortable on my swing. Whatever happened, at least I had this moment of peace. I ruffled Coco's fur, comforted by his steady presence, and took a swig of my ice cold diet soda. Right now, things were fine, and somehow, it would all work out.

After dinner, I reminded everyone that tomorrow was our family dinner with Miguel and Maggie at Uncle Joey's. "Jackie thought you might want to go swimming before dinner, so we're supposed to be there by six, with dinner at seven."

"Isn't it kind of cold to go swimming?" Savannah asked.

"Jackie said they keep the pool warm, so it should be fine."

Savannah nodded, but she was thinking that, even though she was still thirteen, she was in the eighth grade now. She wasn't a little kid anymore, and she hated being treated like one. Plus, she didn't want to ruin her makeup or her hair in the pool.

On the other hand, she wouldn't mind seeing Miguel without his shirt on, so there was that. And her boobs were finally starting to show. Maybe she could put on her suit, but not get her face or hair wet? That could work.

I managed to clear my throat instead of choking, and quickly put up my shields. There were some things I just didn't need to visualize. The kids got busy with their homework, leaving Chris and me to clean up.

As a general rule, I tried not to listen to Chris's thoughts, but I'd picked up enough to know that he was preoccupied with a client and the client's upcoming trial. "How was your day?" I asked him.

He told me about the big trial coming up, and that he still had a lot to do to prepare for it.

"It's fine if you want to work on it tonight. I've got to go into the office myself."

His brows rose. "You do? Why? What's going on?"

"Actually, I'm picking up Justin at nine. He set up a meeting with Max tonight, and we're hoping to catch him. Just think, Justin and Uncle Joey might both have their money back by the time we go to bed."

Chris huffed out a breath. "How is that supposed to happen?"

I shrugged. "I'm not too clear on the details, but Uncle Joey and Ramos have it all figured out. I'm just going along to make sure nothing happens to Justin, you know?"

"Yeah... right." He scratched his head, thinking that this sort of thing happened a lot more than he liked. He should be used to it, but he wasn't sure it would ever get any easier. With worry tightening his lips, he met my gaze. "You'll be okay?"

I couldn't help the wonder that widened my eyes. "Wow. This is amazing! You're not even mad. You're the best." I threw my arms around his neck and laid a big fat kiss on his lips.

He kissed me back before pulling away. Shock at my outburst warred with suspicion. Was I buttering him up? Was there more to this than I'd said out loud?

"No. I'm just glad you're not treating this like it's such a big deal, that's all. It's really nice."

His brows drew together. "Shelby... I'm not unreasonable, but now I'm wondering if this really is a big deal. Is Justin going to be in danger? Do you think Max will try to kill him?"

I sighed. "That's a possibility, but since we're planning for it, he should be fine. And… I'll know. That's why I'm going."

Still holding me, Chris closed his eyes and shook his head. "I really should be used to this by now." He met my gaze. "But I'll still worry. I'll always worry about you. So don't do anything stupid… okay?"

I pursed my lips. "You mean heroic… not stupid, right?"

His eyes widened. "Of course. That's exactly what I meant."

"Okay… it's a deal. And, if you're still awake when I get home, I'll show you just how *heroic* I can be." I waggled my eyebrows and pressed a kiss to his mouth.

Dressed in my all-black ensemble, I left to get Justin. I'd called earlier with the excuse that Chris and I had set up an impromptu get together with a couple of college friends that Justin knew.

Pulling up in front of the house, I honked, and Justin quickly came out.

The drive to Thrasher took no time at all, mostly because I kept Justin distracted by asking all kinds of questions about each of his kids. By the time we pulled into the parking garage at Thrasher, Justin hadn't thought about his impending doom once.

He tensed up right after that though, and he could barely nod at Uncle Joey and Ramos. It surprised me a little that Uncle Joey planned to come, but I should know by now that, in many cases, he was a hands-on type of mob boss.

Forrest came into the office, and disappointment radiated off him in waves. "I'm not sure if this is good or bad," he began. "But I traced Max's IP address from the email he sent all over the place before it ended in Europe. That doesn't mean he's actually in Europe, he's just better at throwing me off his trail than I thought. I was really hoping to find his location."

"So you're saying he might not be here to meet me?" Justin asked.

"I think someone's coming, we just won't know for sure whether it's him, or someone he hired to kill you."

"Oh... that's just great." Justin threw his arms up. "So what am I supposed to do?"

"I've got it covered," Ramos said. "I'll take your place, and you can wait in the van with Shelby."

We all froze for a moment, then I said what everyone was thinking. "But... you don't look anything like him."

He shrugged. "I can hunch over a little, and I've got an oversized hoodie I can wear to cover my head. If it's not Max, they won't know the difference. If it is Max... he won't expect it, because he has no idea we're working together."

Justin nodded. "I have to admit I like that plan." He glanced at each of us. "I mean... I would have done it, but Ramos knows how to handle things like this, and I don't."

Ramos smirked, thinking that this was his plan from the beginning. He hadn't shared it with Justin because he didn't want to let him off the hook so easily.

I coughed to cover my snicker. It relieved me to have Justin out of danger, but that left Ramos to take the heat. Not that it changed anything. I'd still do everything in my power to keep him safe as well.

After Ramos explained the plan, we all piled into our separate vehicles and drove to the parking garage. Uncle Joey, Forrest, and Justin were with me in the van, and Ramos drove to a parking spot near the escalator on Main Street. Ramos had asked Ricky, one of Uncle Joey's men, to watch his back, and Ricky waited in the car with Ramos, planning to follow him into the garage at a distance.

At eleven, Ramos would leave his car and take the escalator all the way down to the bottom floor where we'd be watching from the black van parked in the corner. We didn't have fancy earpieces, but sending texts should work.

Waiting in the van for an hour wasn't too bad. At ten minutes before eleven, I got out of the van and crouched behind the back tire on the far side of the van, next to the back wall. I was out of sight, but could still pick up anyone's thoughts from this distance.

The place was deserted, and I hoped Max didn't notice our black van in the corner and get spooked. There were only a few cars in the lot, and all but one had left while we were there.

A few minutes past eleven, I caught sight of Ramos coming down the escalator. All hunched over, with his hands in his pockets, he didn't seem as big as normal, but I wasn't sure he'd fool anyone.

He exited the escalator and took a few steps away to look around the mostly empty garage. Five minutes passed with nothing happening, so he stepped further out to look toward the other end of the lot. He stayed out in the open, hoping to flush Max out.

No one approached him, and he was about ready to give up. As he turned toward the escalator, I caught sight of someone coming down it and froze. Was it Ricky? Ramos had seen him at the same time as me, and he stood firm while he waited. The man got to the bottom, wearing a similar hoodie that covered his face.

He strode toward Ramos and pulled something from his pocket. At the same time, lights from a car flashed on, catching Ramos in the face. Instead of flinching back like a normal person, Ramos kept his attention on the attacking man, managing to deflect the upward thrust of his knife.

Ramos continued the motion, tightening his grip on the man's wrist and twisting. The knife fell from the man's grasp, and Ramos got in a couple of punches before the man twisted out of reach. As he attacked Ramos again, the car squealed toward them. The attacker managed to roll out of the way, leaving Ramos in the car's sights.

At the last minute, Ramos dove to the side, and the car barely missed him. The driver slammed on his brakes, and the car spun out, hitting a cement column. The driver continued to maneuver around the column, hitting it two more times before clearing the obstacle.

In the meantime, Ramos's attacker managed to get the back car door open and threw himself inside. Getting to his feet, Ramos took off after them, following the ramp up to the next floor. Pursuing them on foot puzzled me until Ramos emerged from behind a cement column on his motorcycle and continued the chase.

In the commotion, I'd left my spot behind the van and had followed after them. Forrest, Justin, and Uncle Joey had done the same. Hearing the roar of the motorcycle continue to the exit, we all ran back to the van and jumped inside.

Uncle Joey got to the van first and took the driver's seat, while the rest of us piled in. He expertly sped upward through the levels until reaching the exit. At this time of night, the exit bars were raised, so we didn't have to stop until we came to the street.

"Do you see any sign of them?" Uncle Joey asked, looking up and down the street.

"No." I'd somehow managed to get into the front passenger seat before the others. "I don't even see any car lights."

Uncle Joey heaved out a breath. "Then we might as well head back to Thrasher."

I nodded, disappointed that we'd lost them, and fastened my seatbelt. Uncle Joey did the same and pulled onto the street, driving the few blocks back to Thrasher. Soon, we were all sitting in his office and waiting for word from Ramos.

After fifteen minutes, the elevator doors opened, and my heart rate spiked to have Ramos back. A second later, Ricky came into view, and I slumped in my seat.

"Any word from Ramos?" he asked.

"Not yet," I replied, disappointed that he wasn't Ramos.

"That's good... it means he might still catch them."

I wasn't so sure that was a good thing. What if they took a shot at him? Ramos was outnumbered and out-gunned, but I knew that wouldn't stop him.

Half an hour later, Uncle Joey was just about to tell Justin and me to go home when his cell phone rang. "Yes?" As he listened, I picked up that it was Ramos, and relief washed over me. "Good... no that's not necessary... just bring the phone back with you... yes... see you soon."

He glanced at us with a grin. "Ramos caught them. Let's just say they won't be bothering us again. He has the phone with Max's current number on it, so I'm hoping Forrest will be able to use it to find him."

"I'll do my best," Forrest said.

Justin sank into a chair, thinking that Ramos had probably killed them, and it made him sick to his stomach. I wanted to tell him that Ramos wouldn't do that, but, since I didn't know for sure, I kept my mouth shut. He might have killed them if they'd tried to kill him, but he probably just beat the crap out of them instead.

"I think we might as well call it a night," Uncle Joey said. He glanced my way. "You and Justin can go if you want. It's up to Forrest now, and that might take a while."

Relieved, Justin stood, but I shook my head, knowing I needed to talk to Ramos about coming with me to Vegas tomorrow. "Thanks, but... if you don't mind, I'd like to make sure Ramos is okay first. He should be here any minute, right?"

Justin's eyes widened, and he opened his mouth to argue, but thought better of it. Sitting back down, he knew he couldn't say anything bad about Ramos now. Still, it bothered him that I cared so much about the hitman.

I tried not to grind my teeth and sat on the couch to wait. Uncle Joey called Jackie, Ricky left, and Forrest began tapping away on his computer. From Uncle Joey, I picked up that Miguel and Maggie had arrived safely, and he was anxious to see them.

The elevator dinged, and I glanced down the hall. This time, Ramos came toward the office. He swaggered a bit for my benefit, and I tried not to roll my eyes. His hoodie was gone, and he'd left his gun in the trunk of his car. A small cut along his brow was the only indication that he'd been in a fight.

"You okay?" I asked.

His brow rose. "Yeah." He handed Forrest the phone. "Here it is. I hope you can find Max with it. That's all they had." He was thinking that it took a little persuading to get that much from them, but once they realized they were dealing with the mob, they sang like canaries.

"Great. Thanks." Forrest took the phone and left.

Justin stood, grateful we could finally leave. "Glad you're back." His gaze met mine. "Can we go now?"

I frowned. That wasn't subtle or anything. "Uh... sure." I turned to Ramos. "Thanks for taking Justin's place."

That brought Justin up short, and his mouth flapped open and closed. "Yeah... thanks." He glanced my way with murder in his eyes. Why was I making him look so bad? Angry, he hurried out of the room and down the hall.

"We'll see you tomorrow," I said, giving Ramos and Uncle Joey a little wave. "Uh... Ramos... can I talk to you for a minute?"

His lips turned down, and his gaze narrowed. What was I up to? "Sure." He followed me into the hallway. Between the exit and Uncle Joey's office, I turned to him and lowered my voice.

"I need a favor." My heart pounded with sudden nerves, but I forced the words out. "Could you meet me somewhere in the morning at about eight-thirty?"

His right brow rose. "Why?"

"I can't explain it right now, but it's really important. I'd tell you more if I could, but right now, it's not something I can talk about. Please? I really need your help."

Ramos studied me, wishing he could read my mind. He thought I looked sincere, and a little nervous, so it had to be important. "And you won't tell me what it's about?"

I swallowed. "Trust me... if I could... I would, but I promise I'll tell you everything in the morning. Until then... can I count on you?"

He shook his head, wondering if it had something to do with the police.

"It has nothing to do with them." I glanced at my feet. "It's personal."

Ramos took a deep breath. It was obvious that I was in trouble, and I didn't want Manetto to know. Why was that? He waited for me to say more, but, when I didn't, he shook his head. "You'll tell me in the morning?"

"I promise."

He sighed. "Okay. Where?"

Relieved, I closed my eyes. "Thank you." Letting out a breath, I met his gaze. "I'll text you the address in the morning." His eyes widened, but I threw my arms around him for a quick hug and then took off down the hall before he could say another word.

That may have kept him from asking any more questions, but it didn't stop me from hearing him swear up a storm, wondering what the hell was going on.

Chapter 10

I caught up to Justin, who waited at the elevator, and we took it to the parking garage. We drove home in silence, each of us consumed by our own thoughts. As I pulled up in front of my parents' house to drop Justin off, he turned to face me. "I'm glad that's over with."

"Yeah. I thought it went well."

He nodded, thinking that his flight was scheduled to leave in the morning, and he planned to be on it. He hadn't told me or Manetto because he was afraid Manetto wouldn't let him go. Now he felt a little guilty that he was going to leave without telling me, but, after putting his life on the line tonight, hadn't he earned it?

He'd done more than enough to help, and now that he didn't have to worry about Max trying to kill him, he was ready to go home. Would that leave me in the lurch with Manetto? Maybe, but if I was part of the 'family' like Manetto claimed, he'd get over it, right?

"Goodnight," he said. "Sleep well."

"Yeah... you too."

He opened the car door, but I grabbed his arm before he could get out. "Were you really going to leave without telling me?"

"What do you mean? I just told you goodnight." He deliberately misunderstood my question to throw me off.

"I know your flight leaves in the morning."

"Oh." His brows scrunched together. "Wait, I don't remember telling you."

I huffed out a breath. "You didn't." I pointed to my head. "Premonitions... remember?"

"Oh... right." He shook his head, not liking my ability when I used it against him. If there was a way to get his money back before all the paperwork went through, maybe he could stay in California. That way he wouldn't have to deal with me or Manetto. Not that I was anything like a mob boss, but still... "I didn't want to say anything, but I really should get back and I wasn't sure Manetto would let me go."

I pursed my lips. "He wouldn't stop you."

His brows rose. "Yes he would."

"Well... maybe before. But not after tonight. He got what he wanted."

"Exactly. Which is why I'm going home. You'll tell him for me, won't you?"

I rolled my eyes. "Yes. I'll tell him."

"Thanks Shelby." He gave me a quick hug. "You're the best sister ever."

"Yeah... yeah." What could I say? I know you're lying about the best sister part, but, after the day we've had, I'll let it go? Nope. I preferred the lie. Who knew... maybe there was a little truth in it? "See ya bro. Say hi to Lindsay and the kids for me."

"I will." He got out of the car and ran up the steps to the front porch where he gave me a quick wave and headed inside. He was right. There wasn't anything else he could do here, so he might as well head home.

I wished I could say the same. I arrived home, totally worn out. It was nearly two in the morning, and Chris had fallen asleep with the light on. I managed to wash my face and brush my teeth before setting the alarm for quarter to seven.

Turning out the light, I crawled into bed and snuggled into Chris's side, partially waking him up.

"S'everything good?" he asked.

"Yeah... everything's fine. I'll fill you in tomorrow."

He didn't respond, already falling back asleep. A few seconds later, I turned on my side and tried to sleep. Unfortunately, my mind wandered to all the things that could possibly go wrong on my little jaunt to Las Vegas. Closing my eyes and breathing deeply, I finally fell into a troubled sleep.

My alarm popped on, jerking me awake.

Chris muttered under his breath, while I turned it off and got up to take a quick shower before he did. I toweled dry and began to dress while Chris went in for his own shower. "You're up early. What's going on?"

"I have an eight-thirty meeting."

"What happened last night?"

"Justin wasn't in any danger because Ramos took his place. The bad guys showed up and Ramos took them out. So it's all good."

"Took them out? You mean he killed them?"

"Probably not... but I don't know for sure. They tried to kill Ramos because they thought he was Justin, so, when that didn't work, they took off. Ramos had his motorcycle stowed nearby and took off after them. Somehow, he caught up to them and managed to take one of their cell phones with Max's number on it. So... the good news is that Forrest is going to use Max's cell phone number to track him down. Hopefully, that will do the trick."

Chris shook his head in awe and turned on the water. While he showered, I knocked on Savannah's door to make sure she was awake, then I hurried down to the kitchen to set out breakfast. Cereal would have to do for the day, but I made some toast to go with it.

Forty minutes later, Chris and the kids had left, and I rushed back to my room to finish getting ready. Knowing that I hadn't told Chris about my little jaunt to Las Vegas sent a pang of guilt through me. But this was one of those times it was better he didn't know beforehand.

I'd dressed in my comfortable jeans and a tee with a fleece jacket, but still needed to pick out something nicer to wear for the meeting with Rathmore. Settling on a professional-looking, navy dress-and-jacket ensemble, I grabbed my navy pumps and looked through my jewelry box. I had a hunch that the dress would go perfectly with the necklace-and-earring set Ramos and Uncle Joey had surprised me with, and pulled them out.

Not long ago, I'd taken a few gold and quartz rocks from a haunted mine. I'd given Ramos and Uncle Joey each a large rock, and kept one for myself. They'd used one of their stones to make me a beautiful golden chain, accented by a polished teardrop of white-and-gold quartz, with matching smaller versions for my ears.

I hoped wearing them would help bolster my courage and remind me that they loved me, even if I was doing something they would never approve of. In the light of day, I knew I was asking a lot of Ramos to back me up without knowing why. When the truth came out, I hoped it wouldn't make him too mad.

I slipped the jewelry into my cosmetics bag, along with my makeup and hair brushes. After finding a garment bag for my dress, I was ready to go. Coco waited for me by the garage door for our usual morning walk, and it broke my heart to disappoint him.

"Sorry... but I can't take you today. I have to go."

He woofed, *no walk*? I shook my head. "I'll make it up to you, I promise. Hey... I know... you can come to the party tonight and meet Miguel. You'd like that, right?"

He let out the dog equivalent of a groan and lay down with his head on his paws. The way he gazed up at me with his big, brown, doleful eyes sent guilt racing through my heart. Why did he have to do that? Letting out a sigh, I went to the cupboard and fished out a doggy bone. Handing it over, I patted him on the head. "I'll see you tonight."

I hurried out and jumped into my car, realizing that I hadn't texted Ramos with the address of our meeting place. I knew waiting until the last minute was cowardly, but it was the only way I figured he'd come. I found the address on the map and texted it instead of telling him to meet me at the private airport. I added a note to bring a nice jacket and pressed send before backing out of my driveway.

A few seconds later, my phone pinged with a text. I managed to glance at his response of *what the hell*? and grimaced. Since I couldn't text and drive, I ignored it until I arrived at the private airfield. I was a few minutes late, but it helped to know the plane wasn't leaving until nine, so I waited in the parking lot for Ramos.

The minutes ticked by, and eight-forty-five passed without him showing up. I got out of the car and began to pace. What if he didn't come? I'd have to go without him. Another two minutes passed, and I couldn't wait any longer.

Taking a deep breath, I grabbed my things from the car and began walking to the building. With a deep sense of dread, I checked in at the desk and started toward the hallway that led outside to Rathmore's plane.

"Shelby. Wait."

Relief filled my chest, and I turned to find Ramos rushing toward me. As he reached my side, I threw my arms around him. "You made it." Pulling back, I took a step toward the hallway, but he grabbed my arm.

"What's going on?"

I swallowed. "We have to go. The plane leaves at nine. I'll tell you everything on the way."

Ramos froze for several seconds before releasing my arm. I picked up his confusion and worry, along with the underlying anger that I was forcing his hand. Out of time, I turned away from him and continued my journey toward the plane, hoping he'd follow.

Reaching the stairs leading into the plane, I heard him behind me, and my knees went weak with relief. The pilot waited at the bottom of the stairs and greeted me. "Shelby Nichols?"

"That's me." I turned toward Ramos. "And this is my bodyguard."

The pilot glanced at Ramos and stood aside to let us pass.

Ramos hesitated, but quickly rallied and followed me up the stairs. Sharp anger rolled off him with every step he took, and he was thinking that no amount of begging was going to get me out of the hot seat with him. I should have told him what was going on. He didn't like being coerced. Didn't I trust him? This time I'd gone too far.

Cringing, I tripped over the last stair, falling onto my hands and knees inside the doorway. Chagrined, Ramos stepped over me to help me up, knowing he'd been the cause of my fall. "Are you okay?"

Before I could answer, the flight attendant rushed to my side. She swore under her breath before asking if I was okay.

"I'm fine... really. I'm okay." Totally embarrassed, I got my feet under me and took Ramos's hand. He pulled me up, and I leaned against him until I caught my balance and could step further into the plane.

My right knee twinged, causing me to limp to the couch where I could sit down.

The flight attendant had picked up my garment bag and followed us. "I'll hang this up and get you some water." She rushed away, taking my garment bag with her.

Hot with mortification, I covered my face with my hands and began to shake with uncontrolled laughter. Tears filled my eyes, but I couldn't stop if my life depended on it.

"Shelby?"

I lowered my hands to look at Ramos's face. Seeing his wide-eyed horror sent a gale of mirth into me. "Oh my gosh! That was the worst."

I laughed until I cried, unable to stop, even when the attendant brought my water. In-between bouts, I managed to thank her before starting up again. Ramos helped me buckle my seat-belt, and that sobered me up enough to catch my breath.

Then the hiccups started, along with another bout of laughter. "Sorry." I repeated that word after every hiccup until Ramos told me to stop. The plane chose that moment to take off down the runway, and the force shoved me into his side.

He slid his arm around me and held me tightly. His warmth and comfort eased my stress, and I closed my eyes, finally gaining the control I sorely needed. The plane leveled out, but neither of us moved.

Ramos kept his thoughts to himself, managing to block most of them. Still, I picked up that he was furious with me, although it was buffered by his protective nature to watch over me, no matter what this was all about. Still, I'd called him my bodyguard. What the hell was going on?

Not ready to face the music, I took in my surroundings. This plane was a lot bigger than Uncle Joey's. Near the front, leather seats along the sides faced each other, with a space for a working table between them.

Ramos and I sat on a cream-colored, leather couch with a large-screen TV mounted on the wall across from us. Four more seats in the back faced the front of the plane, and behind them was a sign for the bathroom.

Taking a deep breath and letting it out, I straightened and turned to face Ramos. I sent him a tremulous smile and caught a glimpse of sympathy that I looked kind of pathetic with red splotches on my cheeks, and swollen eyes.

I gasped. "You think I look pathetic?"

His eyes bulged. "Uh... yeah? But just for the moment."

I huffed out a breath and squeezed my eyes shut. "Reading minds is a curse. A complete and total curse."

I didn't know I'd said that out loud until Ramos placed his warm hand over my clenched fist. His other hand cupped my jaw, and he turned my head toward him so he could meet my gaze. "No it's not. It just feels that way right now, but it's a good thing. You do good things with it. You help a lot of people. You've saved lives. Sure it has a down side, but you can handle it."

I wanted to argue with him, but I was acting childish enough already. I let out a big sigh, and my shoulders relaxed. "You're right. Hey... I'm sorry I went a little crazy back there. I don't know what happened, but I'll do better. I know I can keep it together."

He nodded. "Of course you can. But it's okay to fall apart once in a while. I'm here for you, Shelby... I mean... I came, right? I may be mad about this... but I'm here."

My eyes filled with stupid tears, but I blinked them away. "You're right. You're here, and I can't thank you enough for coming."

He grunted, but it pleased him that I'd agreed, because now I owed him so much that it would take the rest of my life to pay him back. I was in his debt forever... hell... I'd kidnapped him. I'd never be able to make up for that.

I twisted my lips. "I'm going to go freshen up in the bathroom." I unfastened my seatbelt and stepped carefully to the back of the plane. My knee hardly hurt anymore, and I took that as a good sign that I was on the road to recovery.

Inside, I found a nicely appointed toilet with a vanity set and a shower, all beautifully done with gold and silver accents. Finding a washcloth, I started on my face, patting it down with cold water until all signs of my breakdown were gone.

I examined my face, hoping the red splotches would disappear before we landed. Once we got closer to landing, I'd need to come back and put on my makeup and change into the dress I'd brought, but, until then, I planned to take it easy, especially since I still had to explain to Ramos what was going on.

Feeling more like my old self, I left to join Ramos and get my explanation over with.

After sitting beside him, I began with the basics. "This is the deal. We're headed to Las Vegas. Ella and Creed... you know... from the poker tournament? They're in trouble, and, in order to save Creed's sister's life, they had to make a deal with Gage Rathmore."

Ramos drew a quick breath and his eyes narrowed. "What does Rathmore want from you?"

I shrugged. "All Ella could tell me was that I'm invited to a meeting where I'm supposed to use my premonitions to get dirt on everyone there." My lips twisted at the irony. "You know... kind of like what I do for Uncle Joey?"

"Yeah... I get it."

"He promised her when it was done, he'd fly me straight home, and they'd get Creed's sister back." I searched Ramos's gaze for some kind of understanding. "I had to help them. It was either that, or he was going to kill her. But I couldn't tell Uncle Joey... he wouldn't have let me go. You get that, right?"

He shook his head. "Shelby... you can't keep this a secret from him." He was thinking that if I didn't tell him, he'd have to, and it would be ten times worse.

"I know. I'm planning on telling him. I just wanted to wait until afterward. I mean... this is one of those times it's easier to ask for forgiveness than permission."

Ramos glanced away, thinking that I was in more trouble than ever. Manetto would be furious. But I probably had a point. No way would Manetto allow me to help Rathmore, especially after he'd worked so hard to make sure nothing like this ever happened. Manetto was going to be royally pissed, and he didn't look forward to the fallout.

"I know... me either."

"So... how is Creed's sister mixed up with Rathmore?"

I spent the next hour explaining everything that Ella had told me about Sonny, the trial, Avery's kidnapping, and now my meeting with Rathmore. By the end, it sounded like some convoluted plot to overthrow life as we know it.

Ramos was thinking, *only you,* before he shoved that thought to the back of his mind. "When we get there, you need to call Manetto."

"But—"

"No buts. If you don't do it, I will."

He was totally serious. "Okay... fine. After we land, I'll call him."

"Good... and, for the record, I'm glad I'm here." He thought that once Manetto knew the circumstances, he'd be glad too, but if I ever pulled anything like this again, there'd be hell to pay.

I shrugged. "I already know that. It won't happen again."

Unconvinced, Ramos frowned. "I would have come anyway... you know that, right?"

"Yeah... I know. But I was afraid you'd tell Uncle Joey. So I had to play my cards right."

He snickered. "You certainly did that."

The flight attendant approached us with refreshments, which we both accepted. "We will be arriving in about thirty minutes."

"Okay. Thanks. I need to change before the meeting. Can I get my garment bag?"

"Of course. Might I suggest that you wait until after we've landed to change? We're a little early, so you'll have plenty of time."

I agreed and finished up my snack before buckling my seatbelt for the landing. Soon we were on the ground, and I hurried to the bathroom to change. Twenty minutes later, with my hair and makeup all done, I looked like a new person. I left the bathroom with more confidence than I'd felt all day.

Ramos looked me over, and his lips twisted into that sexy half-smile of his. "You look beautiful." He was thinking the necklace was a nice touch, and it reminded him that he'd almost lost me in a mine full of gold. "Ever think about going back for the gold?"

I shrugged. "I'm not sure I'd want to chance it." I didn't tell him that I got the coordinates of the cave-in from Josh. I'd memorized them, but I'd also put them in my special hardback edition of *Pride and Prejudice,* which I'd placed in my closet safe, just in case I ever forgot.

Ramos walked beside me down the stairs to make sure I wouldn't fall on my face. I didn't know if I should be pleased that he cared or dismayed that he thought I was a klutz. Before we reached the limo that awaited us, Ramos's cell phone rang.

He pulled it from his pocket. "It's Manetto."

We stopped beside the limo, and Ramos answered. While he spoke, my heart quivered in my chest, and my palms got sweaty. Ramos glanced my way. "Yes. I'm with her. Here she is."

He handed me the phone, and I tried to compose myself so I wouldn't sound too guilty. "Hey Uncle Joey. How's it going?"

"Shelby. Where are you? I've been trying to reach you for the last hour. What's going on?"

From the tone of his voice, I knew he wasn't happy, and all my composure flew out the window. I rushed to explain. "I coerced Ramos into coming with me, so it's not his fault."

"What's not his fault?"

"We're in Las Vegas." I told him the rest of the story as fast as I could, pacing between the car and the plane the entire time. He didn't say a word until I'd finished.

"Give the phone to Ramos." Wide-eyed, I handed him the phone.

They spoke for a few more minutes before Ramos ended the call and put the phone away, thinking I was in so much trouble. "That went better than I thought."

My brows twisted. "What do you mean? You just thought I was in a lot of trouble."

"He was all business. Which means he's furious with you, but he's taking it in stride. Once the danger is over... that's when you need to worry."

I rolled my eyes. "Oh great... thanks."

His grin didn't reach his eyes, making him look totally dangerous. "Shall we go?"

We climbed into the limo, and rode in silence. Each mile taking me closer to Rathmore sent my nerves into overdrive. Entering the city, the driver took us down the famous Las Vegas Strip, before turning into a high-rise office district.

Soon, we pulled into the circular driveway of an impressive, glass-encased building. Taking a breath for courage, I got out of the car and entered the building. Inside, the walls were painted white, with lovely blue accents, ranging from turquoise to a light, sky-blue color.

Before I could take it all in, Ella appeared before me, smiling with relief. "You made it."

She gave me a quick hug, and I listened real close to her thoughts, hoping I could pick up something. Nope. She was the only person I couldn't hear, and it still drove me crazy.

"I'm so glad to see you. Thanks for doing this." Ella turned her attention to Ramos and sent him a nod before glancing my way. "How did your Uncle take it? Are you in trouble?"

"Let's just say that I will be."

She gasped. "He doesn't know?"

"Oh yeah... he knows. But I kind of put off telling him until we landed, twenty minutes ago."

Ella turned to Ramos. "I'm glad you came with her."

His lips flattened. "Yeah, well... it was a last minute thing for me too."

She glanced my way with wide eyes. "How much trouble are you in?"

I chuckled. "Oh... some... but not too much. We'll see how bad it is when I get back." Ramos was thinking that was an understatement, and I swatted his arm. "It was the only way. You know that."

Creed stepped toward us, looking just as handsome as the last time I'd seen him. "Thanks so much for coming. We're in your debt. If there's ever anything you need from us, we'll do it. No questions asked."

Ramos glanced my way, thinking that his offer would be a good thing to remember when it came to smoothing things over with Manetto. I wanted to swat him again, but thanked Creed for the offer instead.

"Ella St. John?" the receptionist called. "I'll take your group up now."

I followed Ella and Creed to the bank of elevators and found we had to pass through security. They made Ramos go through first, mostly because they thought he looked the most dangerous. Unfortunately, they found the knife he had hidden in the side of his jacket and took it.

Creed and Ella went next, and I followed behind, waiting for the guard to finish manhandling my purse. With a big frown, he pulled out my stun flashlight and examined it. He'd never seen anything like it before and wanted to know how it worked.

"What's this?" He pushed the main button, and an electric charge arced between the two metal points, making a loud sizzling sound that made everyone flinch. He turned his frown my way, thinking I was carrying a dangerous weapon, and he wouldn't stand for it.

I worked hard not to roll my eyes and gave him my best smile instead. "A woman's got to have some protection, right? Especially here... in Las Vegas."

He shook his head and set the flashlight down by Ramos's knife. "You can pick it up on your way out."

I shrugged like it didn't matter, not wanting him to know he'd just shattered all my dreams of using it on Rathmore. As we stepped into the elevator, I leaned toward Ella. "No one's ever done that before. Usually they let me keep it."

Ramos snickered. "No one's ever pushed the button before either. Just hearing the sound of that thing is enough to scare someone off."

"You have a point."

The receptionist stepped onto the elevator with us and swiped her key card to unlock the floors. After she pushed the button for the thirteenth floor, we all waited in silence until the elevator stopped and we could get out.

We followed her down a hall to a set of double doors which she pushed open to reveal the same white-and-blue decor as the main floor. We entered to find another secretary sitting at her desk. She jumped up and motioned toward a couch-and-wingback-chair ensemble off to the side.

"Please take a seat. Mr. Rathmore is running a little late, but he'll be with you shortly."

Now that we were here, I didn't mind the wait, mostly because I could ask Ella what Rathmore was like so I'd be more prepared. Ramos sat beside me on the couch, with Ella on the other side of me and Creed taking the wingback chair closer to Ella.

"So, tell me about Rathmore. What's he like? Older? Like Uncle Joey?"

"No. He's got to be in his late forties or early fifties, but it's hard to tell. He's kind of got this whole intimidation thing going for him, but don't let him get to you."

"I'm not planning on it."

The doors to the office opened, and the receptionist from downstairs ushered three men and a woman inside. Two of the older men wore suits, while the younger man wore a jacket over a dress shirt without a tie. The woman wore a power-red jacket over a white blouse and black pencil skirt, with red pumps on her feet. Her dark hair was pulled tightly back from her face, and she wore square glasses.

Rathmore's secretary quickly took them back to his office, and I knew I'd be listening to them during his meeting. I hadn't picked up much, but all of them were nervous and excited to be meeting with Rathmore. I picked up something about an investment opportunity, but that was all that I got before they disappeared.

The secretary returned, thinking that there was one more person coming before the meeting could start. Knowing that, I turned to Ella. "So... how's the trial going?"

In hushed tones, she told us that Sonny had taken Rathmore's deal and was acquitted. I shook my head. "So he gave up his casino and hotel? I can't say I'm sorry to hear that, but I wish he was going to jail, too. Rathmore must have pulled a lot of strings for that to work."

Ella nodded. "Yeah."

The secretary picked up her phone and glanced our way. Ella got ready to stand, but I put a hand on her arm. "I have a feeling that it's going to be another few minutes. It's possible that not everyone has arrived for the meeting yet."

"Oh... I guess you picked that up with your premonitions. Good thing they're still working, since that's why Rathmore wanted you. Too bad he found out, right?"

"No kidding." I caught sight of her wedding ring. "Oh my gosh! I forgot. Congratulations on your marriage."

"Thanks." Ella glanced at Creed with love shining in her eyes. "We're living in L.A. right now and figuring things out."

"How's that going?"

"I'm working at the hospital, and Creed just got a starring role in a new TV series. We're so excited."

"Oh yeah? That's wonderful. What's it about?"

"He's a detective on a cop show, only with a fun twist." She nodded at Creed. "Tell her."

Before he began, I picked up what the twist was and gasped. It took all my self-control to keep a straight face without choking to death.

"Is something wrong?" Creed asked.

I cleared my throat a few times. "No... not at all. I love twists. What is it?"

Luckily, Creed took my word for it and grinned. "My character is a detective who can read minds. I know it sounds kind of nuts, but I'm hoping it will be a fun twist. In the first few episodes, no one knows... but I keep answering their unspoken thoughts, and the main character, who is my new partner, can't figure it out. I mean... it's this big secret that I have, and no one is supposed to know."

Ramos burst out laughing, giving me the excuse to let my laughter out. Holding it back was about the hardest thing I'd ever done. Holy hell! Who would have thought?

"Wow," Creed said. "I hope everyone likes the idea as much as you guys."

I laughed even harder and could barely catch my breath. Ramos was in a similar state, thinking it was the craziest thing he'd ever heard. His thoughts drifted to how I could be a great resource if the writers needed material. Maybe I could give Creed some pointers?

That brought another bout of laughter, and I covered my face with my hands and tried to calm down. Picking up

Creed's puzzlement at our over-the-top reaction helped curtail my mirth. Poor guy. He thought it was a funny twist, but not that funny, so what was going on?

"Sorry." I waved my hand in front of my face. "I don't know why that hit me so funny." Little bursts of laughter kept popping out, so I took a few deep breaths to tamp them down and wiped the tears from my cheeks. Knowing I was probably ruining my makeup served to calm me even more.

The office doors opened, and the downstairs receptionist showed another man inside. Tall and thin, with dark hair and glasses, he moved like he wasn't in any hurry, and was only there as a favor. He wore a suit and tie like the others, and Rathmore's secretary showed him straight to Rathmore's office, relieved that he'd finally arrived and thinking he was the last one to show up.

Knowing it was time to face the devil instantly sobered me, and I wiped under my eyes one more time to make sure I didn't have any mascara on my skin. The secretary returned and headed straight for me.

"Mr. Rathmore is ready for you Shelby. The rest of you will have to wait."

I got to my feet, but Ramos beat me to it and stepped between us to tower over her. "Where Shelby goes, I go. It's not up for debate."

Fear spiked through her before she covered it with a look of disdain. "I'll have to check. Give me a moment." We waited while she hurried back to her desk and picked up the phone. A few seconds later, she set it down and came toward us. "You may accompany her, but the others must stay here."

Relieved, I nodded and turned to Ella and Creed, who stood behind me. "I'll be fine." From the worry on Ella's face, I wasn't sure she believed me, but she gave me a short nod.

With Ramos at my side, we followed the secretary down a short hall to a double door. She paused to knock before opening the door and motioning us inside. A man with wavy, dark hair stood from behind a beautiful oak-wood desk.

Satisfaction blazed in his deep-set hazel eyes, and his prominent dark brows gave his features a hawk-like quality. With his golden-olive skin tone, he reminded me of an Arabian sheik. Even after Ella's description, I'd expected him to look older, but the silver strands of hair at his temples only accented his high cheekbones and square jaw.

"Shelby Nichols. It's such a pleasure to meet you. Please sit down." He motioned to the chairs in front of his desk. "We'll join the others after I've filled you in on what I expect."

Grateful to have Ramos at my side, I sat down, doing my best to look calm and collected, even though my stomach had twisted into knots.

Rathmore sat as well, blatantly studying me like a specimen in a test tube and completely ignoring Ramos. "I have to admit, I wasn't sure this day would ever happen. Your Uncle was quite determined to keep you away from me. I tried every trick in the book to gain his cooperation, but he refused every single one of my generous offers." Rathmore's lips twisted up into a satisfied smirk. "But now look, here you are. Does he know you're here?"

I listened real close, but couldn't pick up a thing. Was he blocking his thoughts? Instead of answering, I went on the defense. "What do you want?"

His nostrils flared, but otherwise his expression didn't change. "I need some information I'm hoping you can uncover. I'm about to embark on a big commercial enterprise, and I want to know who I can trust. With your premonitions, it shouldn't be hard for you to pick up a few things from the group of people I've brought together.

"I don't know much about your abilities, but, after watching you at the poker tournament, I believe your 'psychic' gift is real. So here's the deal... as long as I'm satisfied with the information you give me, I'll make sure Creed's sister is returned to him unharmed, and you'll be free to go home. Do we have an understanding?"

All hope that I could turn the tables on this power-hungry man evaporated. I'd tried as hard as I could, but it was clear as day that nothing was going to work. I'd pushed and prodded, but come up empty.

He was just like Ella. I couldn't read his mind.

Chapter 11

"Yes. I understand." I didn't elaborate, knowing it was best to keep my opinions to myself. I'd learned that someone like him could easily turn anything I said against me, so it was best to say as little as possible.

"Good. Then let's join the others."

We followed him out of his office and across the hall to a small conference room. All of the people we'd seen come in earlier were sitting at a rectangular table. Rathmore took his place at the head of the table and motioned to a couple of chairs behind him.

Relieved to have some distance between me and his group, I quickly sat behind him with Ramos at my side and took out my notebook. Because we weren't part of the group, Rathmore didn't introduce us, which was okay by me. He made a point of using their names, which was probably for my sake, and I wrote them down as they spoke to keep them straight.

Most of them wondered about us, but their thoughts were quickly focused on Rathmore's proposal. While he spoke of investing in the future of new start-up technology,

I listened to each of the participant's thoughts and wrote down the few things I picked up that seemed relevant.

Money was a big part of the equation, but they'd all come prepared to get in on the ground floor of the start-up company, ready to reap the benefits. The only person that didn't seem as interested was Derek Vaughn, the last man who'd joined the meeting.

I focused on Vaughn's thoughts and picked up that he was suspicious of Rathmore's motives. Rathmore had approached Vaughn before, and he'd always turned Rathmore down, worried that Rathmore was out to steal his technology.

A few months ago, Vaughn might have been more open to joining forces, but, now that he knew he was dying, he had no doubt that Rathmore would acquire the outstanding interest and take over everything, decimating his legacy.

If he was healthy, he'd be around long enough to keep Rathmore in check, but now that would never happen. There had to be another way to make his dream a reality. At least he owed it to himself to try.

I shook my head, knowing Rathmore would be happy to have that information, and now I had to tell him and ruin Vaughn's dream. Sick at heart, I moved onto the next person and wrote a couple of notes about his thoughts on joining, which weren't any different than what he said out loud.

Rathmore began talking about some of the breakthroughs in block-chain technology, and how exciting that was to him. Everyone perked up, especially Vaughn, who was thinking he'd come up with a special technology to make it work in a smart city he'd developed. Did Rathmore know about this? How had he found out?

While he pondered that, the youngest man in the group, Gavin, sat up straight, and excitement coursed through him.

Gavin began asking Rathmore questions about cryptocurrency, and my heart picked up speed. Gavin told Rathmore he'd studied the practicalities of using crypto to pay for goods and services in a smart city, expounding on his experience in developing an ICO for its use.

Rathmore's brow quirked up with interest, and he told Gavin to present a plan to him in the next few days. Gavin nodded, thinking that his group already had an ICO in place, as well as over a hundred million dollars in crypto on the books, which he could use to impress Rathmore.

He itched to get his hands on it, but right now that was impossible. Max had run into some problems and had gone to ground in Budapest. For now, Max was off the grid, and he'd planned to stay that way for a few months until things cooled off.

But an opportunity like this only came once, and Gavin knew he'd have to track Max down and bring him back to the states. Since he knew Max's family owned a restaurant in Budapest along the Danube River, he could probably find him by using Max's last name. It shouldn't be too complicated, especially since there could only be one Huszar who owned a restaurant in Budapest. He could do it, and he'd get started right after this meeting.

My mouth went dry. This was insane. How was it possible that the one person I needed to listen to was sitting right here in this meeting? A shiver ran down my spine, almost like a ghost had touched the back of my neck. Was it Landon, the man Max had murdered? Did Gavin have any idea that Max had killed Landon? Was Gavin part of the Crypto-Knights? Since his name started with a G, he could be Galahad, right?

I knew I wouldn't find the answers unless I cornered Gavin and asked him the right questions, and, right now, that wasn't going to happen. Maybe it didn't matter, although I hated the idea of Landon's ghost haunting me until Max was caught. But now that might actually happen.

Rathmore thanked everyone for coming, telling them to follow through with their assignments, and I knew I'd missed that last part. Hopefully, it wouldn't get me in trouble.

After they left, Rathmore glanced my way, and his gaze lingered on my notebook. "It looks like you have some information for me. Let's go back to my office to discuss it."

Without a word, we followed him across the hall and sat down in the chairs in front of his desk. "What have you got for me?"

I listened real hard, but nothing came through. He was just like Ella. But how? What made them that way? There had to be a connection, right? Or maybe it was just a coincidence?

Rathmore's brows rose, and I realized he was waiting for me. "Oh... sorry. Let me just take a look at my notes." I looked at my writing without really seeing it, worried about how I was going to phrase my responses without giving away my secret. "Um... I'll just go down the list and give you my impressions, since that's how it works."

Rathmore nodded, but his eyes narrowed, like he was suspicious of something I'd said. Ramos was thinking I needed to tell Rathmore what I'd picked up, and quit trying to explain anything, because it looked like I was hiding something.

Panic clutched my chest, and my plan to keep Vaughn's secret went right out the window. "There's something wrong with Derek Vaughn. He's sick... I think it's cancer... and it's bad. He hasn't got much time left to live."

Rathmore's eyes took on a predatory gleam that I'd never seen in anyone before, and it freaked me out.

"Also... uh..." I shuffled my papers and told him a few details about each of the participants, before ending with Gavin.

Knowing he expected more from me, I glanced up and smiled. "Yeah... here it is. Gavin's invested heavily in cryptocurrency. In fact, he already has a start-up ICO, and he's hoping to get his hands on a hundred million dollars in crypto. I mean... I'm not sure of the exact amount, so I'm giving you an estimate, but that feels about right. He's very ambitious and will do just about anything to get in on this deal."

Rathmore's lips curved up and he nodded, so I took that as a good sign. "Thank you, Shelby. Well done. You've exceeded my expectations."

I let out a breath. "Great. Then I guess we're done here." His eyes narrowed slightly, so I quickly continued. "Uncle Joey's not real happy with me, and I don't want to get into more trouble, you know? So we need to get back."

Rathmore pursed his lips. "You've fulfilled your end of the deal, and I'm a man of my word. Please make sure your Uncle knows that, won't you?"

"Sure."

"Good. Let me call my driver to take you to the airport." He put the call through and hung up, then caught my gaze and smiled. "He's waiting in front of the building, so you're all set." Standing, he reached across his desk to shake my hand. "Thanks Shelby. I'll see that Avery is safely reunited with her brother."

I really didn't want to touch him, but I gave his hand a quick shake. After pulling back, I managed to keep from rubbing my palm against my skirt. "Good, since I'll be checking up with Ella on that."

His brows rose. After a long second, he dipped his head. "I'm sure you will."

I tried to walk sedately to the door, but I couldn't get out of there fast enough. As his door closed behind us, I heard the whispered words, *until next time,* and my step faltered. Ramos caught my arm to steady me, and, after taking a quick breath, I continued down the hall with him to the reception area.

Ella and Creed caught sight of us and jumped to their feet. Ella's gaze searched mine, and I tried to give her an assuring smile, but with a snake like Rathmore, nothing was guaranteed. Placing my hand on her arm, I leaned in to warn her. "Be careful. There's something... off... about him."

Her eyes widened. "We will."

I nodded. "Good. Please let me know that this worked."

"I will. I'll call you."

"Thanks." I gave her arm a squeeze and stepped toward the elevator. In full bodyguard mode, Ramos was alert for anything Rathmore might try to pull. It made me even more nervous that he thought something might happen, and I moved closer to him than was probably necessary.

We exited the elevator and stopped by security for my stun flashlight and Ramos's knife. As I slipped the flashlight into my purse, my confidence began to return, and I breathed easier. The driver stood beside the car and opened the back door for us. I slid in first, and Ramos followed.

As the driver went around the car, Ramos cocked an eyebrow. "What happened when we left? It was like you saw a ghost or something."

"Didn't you hear him?"

He shook his head. "Hear what?"

"As we were walking out the door, I heard Rathmore say "until next time." You didn't hear that?"

"No." Ramos dipped his head toward the driver, thinking that we'd better wait to talk until we had more privacy.

I nodded to let him know I'd heard that. He grunted, and we both turned our attention to looking out the windows and watching the people on the Strip. Soon, we were out of the city and driving into the private airfield.

Exiting the limo, I picked up that Ramos wanted to call Uncle Joey before the plane took off. He put the call through, and I waited at his side while he told Uncle Joey that we were on our way home.

With that taken care of, we climbed the steps into the plane. This time, I made it all the way inside without tripping over my feet. We settled on the couch once more, but I couldn't relax until the plane took off, and I was away from Rathmore.

Once the plane leveled off, I headed to the bathroom to change my clothes. It felt good to put my comfy jeans and tee-shirt back on. Ramos took off his jacket, and I sat beside him on the couch. "Do you think it's safe to talk now?"

"I do, as long as we keep our voices low."

"Good, because you're not going to believe this." I filled him in on Gavin's thoughts about Max and the hundred million in cryptocurrency. "Get this... Max is in Budapest." At Ramos's widened eyes, I told him about the restaurant. "I guess his family owns it, so that's where Gavin thinks he is."

"That's insane. Are you sure you heard him right?"

"Yes I'm sure. And... I felt something... like a spirit or a ghost... when Gavin was thinking about Max taking all the crypto and leaving the country. It could have been Landon, or just the fact that learning all of this was kind of trippy. I mean... who would have thought finding Max would happen at a meeting with Gage Rathmore?"

Ramos shook his head, blown away that it had happened at all. "Well, at least this might help you with Manetto." Still shocked, he shook his head, thinking that I should tell him as soon as I got the chance.

"Yeah... I was thinking that too. I mean... how can he be mad about this trip now?"

Ramos's brows rose. "Oh he's not just mad, he's furious. You... flying off to Las Vegas to help Rathmore? The stuff with the crypto will just make it easier to swallow."

He had a point, but I decided to look on the positive side. Once we got home, we could plan our next move, which would probably include a trip to Budapest. I never thought I'd go to that part of the world, and it was exciting and a little scary to think about. Still, as long as Ramos went, I'd be okay with it.

A few hours later, we landed at the private air field and exited the plane. As Ramos strode beside me to the parking lot, my cell phone rang with the song I'd assigned to Uncle Joey. Ramos chuckled, thinking the theme to 'The Godfather' was pretty funny, if a little over the top.

I smirked at him before answering. "Hey Uncle Joey. This was perfect timing. We just got back."

"I know. Ramos texted me when you landed."

"Oh... right."

"He said you have information, so I want you to stop by the office."

"Sure... I'll come right over."

He disconnected without saying another word, and I put my phone away. "How much trouble am I in?"

Ramos shrugged. "I guess you'll find out soon enough. Just remember he doesn't like people who grovel, lie, or double-cross him, so watch it." While he spoke, his eyes twinkled, and I shook my head, remembering the first time he'd told me that.

"I know, I know. See you there."

Ramos easily beat me to Thrasher, but he waited in the parking garage by the elevator for me. Jackie wasn't at her desk, and it reminded me of our dinner tonight with Miguel and Maggie. It was half past four now, so this meeting would have to be quick.

After a short knock, Ramos stepped inside Uncle Joey's office, and I followed behind. Uncle Joey stood at the windows, looking out onto the city, and turned as we entered. His brows dipped, and displeasure rolled off him.

"Shelby. What the hell were you thinking? Rathmore is dangerous, and I've spent a good deal of my time keeping you away from him. Then you go and pull something like this."

I swallowed, knowing I'd let him down. Facing his disappointment was worse than I'd imagined, and guilt tightened my throat. "He forced my hand. I didn't have a choice."

"So I heard. But you should have told me up front instead of going behind my back. That was inexcusable."

"Would you have let me go?"

He gave a mirthless laugh. "Do you think I could have stopped you?"

"Well... to be honest... yes."

His lips twisted. Stopping me would have been hard, but I was right... he would have done everything he could to keep me from going. "You don't know the risk you took going to him on his terms." He shook his head. "I thought for sure he'd call me with a demand... telling me that if I ever wanted to see you again I had to do whatever he wanted. These last few hours have been hell."

My stomach lurched. "Oh... I'm so sorry. I never thought of that."

Uncle Joey let out a breath and sat down. "Luckily, that didn't happen." He thought he may have been exaggerating a bit, but he wouldn't put anything past Rathmore. "I've also spent some time looking into him for any kind of dirt that I could use as leverage."

"Did you find anything?"

"Yes. I've found a few possibilities, but you're the best resource I have to help me out with that. You didn't happen to 'hear' some secret he was keeping, did you?"

My heart fell. "No. I'm afraid I didn't. He's... well... there's something different about him."

"What do you mean?"

"He's like Ella. I couldn't read his mind."

After the initial shock, Uncle Joey swore a blue streak in his mind. I picked up some of the same words coming from Ramos. It lasted for several long seconds before his attention turned back to me. "What does that mean?"

I shook my head. "I have no idea." Seeing Uncle Joey's frustration, I knew he needed some good news. "But there is something good that came from all this."

His eyes narrowed. "Like what?"

I grinned. "I know where Max is."

His shock turned to hope. "You do? Tell me."

"First, let me fill you in on the meeting, since there might be something to it that you can use to your advantage." I told him everything I'd learned about everyone there, ending with Gavin and his thoughts about Max and the cryptocurrency.

"Budapest." Uncle Joey's gaze caught mine. "I bet Forrest can find the restaurant. I wonder if that's where the IP address from Max's email account ended up coming from?

Forrest has been working in your office all day, so this will give him something better to do."

"I'll get him," Ramos said.

He left, and Uncle Joey shook his head. "I found out that Justin went home today. Did you know he planned on leaving?"

Oops. "He mentioned it last night, but I kind of forgot to let you know. It's been a busy day. What did you need Justin for? We both thought he was safe after last night."

Uncle Joey shook his head. "That's not the point. He should have told me he was leaving, but I guess not communicating with people runs in your family."

Ouch… that was harsh, but… he had a point… I just wished it wasn't so obvious. Before I could offer an apology, Forrest came into the office with eager eyes and a butt-load of anticipation, so I explained Gavin's part in the meeting to him. "Gavin must be one of Max's Crypto-Knights."

"I agree," Forrest said. "He's probably Galahad. I might want to cross-reference the IP address we already have with Budapest. If that's where it originated, we'll have him."

Uncle Joey nodded. "Do it."

As he left the office, he glanced back. "It might take me a while, but I should have it by sometime tonight." With a lighter step, he hurried back to my office.

Uncle Joey caught my gaze and shook his head. "What a coincidence."

"I know, right?" I checked my watch and stood, surprised by how much time had passed. "I'd better get going. I have a big dinner I need to get ready for."

"That's right."

"How's Miguel doing?"

"Really good. I didn't think it was possible, but I think he grew another inch or two."

"Really? Wow. It must be all the fun he's having."

Uncle Joey came around his desk and met my gaze. "Shelby... I'm glad you're back. And I'm glad you got Ramos to go with you. But don't you *ever* do anything like that again."

His worry and concern slammed into me, and I flushed with remorse. "I won't."

"Good." He leaned in to give me a quick hug, hoping I'd learned my lesson. Sure, he may have forgiven me, but he wasn't about to let me forget it. He straightened. "Now you can go."

I pursed my lips. He enjoyed ordering me around, but two could play that game. I sent him a playful grin and stepped toward the door. "Yes... I've learned my lesson. From now on, I promise I'll always tell you before I do something like that again." His mouth dropped open, but, before he could respond, I slipped out the door.

Relief swept through me to have that over with, and I hurried to my car. As I buckled my seat belt, a call came through. Ella's name popped up, and I quickly answered. "Ella? Did it work?"

"Yes. We got Avery. How about you? Are you okay?"

"Yes... we made it home."

"I hope your uncle wasn't too mad at you, but I have no doubt that Avery would be dead if you hadn't come. I'll never be able to repay you for that, but if you ever need me for anything, I'll come. That includes my healing touch. Promise me that you'll call if you need me. Okay?"

Her offer warmed my heart, especially considering how much trouble I always seemed to get into. "Thanks. I will. So what's going on? Are you still in Vegas?"

"Yeah, but we're leaving in the morning."

"Good. Get as far away from Rathmore as you can."

"That's the plan."

I sighed, knowing that was much easier said than done. "I have a feeling it's not the end... for either of us. When this is all over, and you're back home, let's talk."

"I'd like that."

"Good. Thanks for letting me know it worked out."

"Of course. And Shelby... if Rathmore ever contacts you again, will you let me know? Maybe we can help each other where he's concerned."

Sharing information when it came to Rathmore would definitely come in handy, and I readily agreed. "Sounds good. Thanks Ella. Don't forget to call me when things settle down."

"I won't. Take care."

"You too."

I got home in time to change into a fresh t-shirt and collect my family. Remembering my promise, I grabbed Coco's leash and his bag of toys, along with his dog food.

"We're taking Coco?" Savannah asked.

"Yeah. I thought you'd like to show him off to Miguel."

Savannah grinned. "That's perfect."

Chris raised a brow. "You sure that's a good idea? Did you tell Manetto?"

"No, but it will be fine. I mean... Coco's part of the family, right?"

"Yes." Savannah clipped Coco's leash on him and took him out to the car.

"Where's Josh?"

"Coming." Josh carried his swimming suit and towel in his arms. "Do you have a bag for this?"

"Oh... yeah. Let me get it."

A few minutes later, we were in the car and headed to Uncle Joey's house. Savannah had fixed her hair with a dramatic side part, and, with the makeup she wore, she could have passed for a couple of years older than thirteen. I didn't like that much. Why couldn't she just be happy to be thirteen? It seemed like we were always trying to be older when we're young and younger when we're old. Wasn't there something wrong with that?

Of course, some people couldn't help it that they looked older. Take Josh for example. At fifteen, he could have easily passed for seventeen. But... that wasn't exactly right. He'd be sixteen in another month, and he was getting ready to take his driver's test. He already had all of his driving hours and had saved up for a car. Yikes! Maybe I was the one with the problem?

"Shelby?" Chris said.

"Yeah?"

"I just asked you how your day was."

"Oh... it was... good. Everything turned out okay."

His brows drew together. "What happened?"

"Oh... not much... well, I mean a lot... but I'll have to tell you later." I tipped my head toward the kids.

He let out a sigh. "Sure." He understood that they couldn't know everything I was involved with, but he also had a sneaking suspicion that I didn't want to tell him because he wouldn't like it. In the not-too-distant future, the kids would both be gone. What would I do then?

I rolled my eyes. "Tell you, of course." Oops... I glanced back at my kids, but they were both looking at their phones, with Coco sitting happily between them. "So how was your day?"

Chris spent the last few minutes of the drive telling me about the round of golf he got in with a client, and one of the great shots he'd made. For some reason, hearing that made me feel better about my trip to Las Vegas. Who knew?

We pulled into Uncle Joey's driveway and parked. Savannah could hardly contain her excitement to see Miguel, and bounded up the steps to ring the doorbell. Josh had taken charge of Coco and kept him on his best behavior.

The door opened, and Miguel stood there with a big grin on his handsome face. He caught Savannah in a hug and stepped out to hug the rest of us, even crouching down to meet Coco. After that, he motioned us all inside, and we followed him out to the back yard where Uncle Joey was grilling up the steaks.

"Shelby! Kids!" Maggie stepped out of the house, and we all gathered around her. I noticed something different about her, but I couldn't place it. After we'd all given her hugs, I pulled her aside.

"You look great. But something's different."

She drew in a breath and slowly let it out. "You're right. I uh... left the order."

My eyes widened. "You did? Why?"

Her lips twisted. "You mean you don't already know?"

I chuckled. "Oh... well... I can guess." Then it hit me. "Syd?"

She nodded. "Yes." I glanced around the yard, but she put her hand on my arm. "He's not here. I thought it best to tell everyone first." I picked up that she hadn't told anyone yet, including Uncle Joey, and she was saving it for after dinner.

"I think they'll be thrilled. I know I am!"

She smiled, and I gave her another hug.

"It's time," Uncle Joey announced. "These steaks are done, so we'd better eat them. Everyone get your plates. You can pick out the one you want."

We spent the next hour eating our food and enjoying one another's company. After everyone had finished up, Maggie told us she had an announcement to make. We all glanced her way, and she got a little tongue-tied. Licking her lips, she began.

"This may come as a shock, but I've left the sisters. I've found something else that I've wanted for a long time. Syd asked me to marry him, and I said yes. We want you all to come to our wedding."

Amid the gasps and words of congratulations, I caught Uncle Joey's complete and utter surprise. After all these years, he never thought his sister would give up her vows. And for Syd? When had that happened?

He shook off his shock and joined the rest of us in congratulating her. "When's the wedding?"

"In a few weeks. At this point in life, we don't want to waste any time. It's a simple church wedding... nothing fancy. Do you think you can come?"

"We wouldn't miss it." He glanced around the table, thinking we'd all better show up or we were toast. I hid a grin and agreed that we'd all be there.

After all the excitement, it was time for dessert. Jackie left to get the apple pie and ice cream, and Maggie and I trailed behind to help. Soon we were eating the best dessert ever. We finished up, and the kids left to feed Coco and show Miguel the cool tricks he could do, while the rest of us began to clear the table.

I picked up that Savannah was in heaven, and was still as enraptured with Miguel as ever. From Miguel I picked up that he had missed her and Josh. As much as he liked his success in the Big Apple, he couldn't imagine living that way for the rest of his life. He wanted a stable home... something he'd never had until he'd met his father. That didn't mean anything had to change for a while. Savannah was only thirteen... and who knew what she'd be like in ten years?

I nearly choked on my spit, but managed to cough a few times while Chris pounded on my back.

"You okay?" he asked.

I caught my breath, managing to nod while stacking the dishes. After a couple of deep breaths, I calmed down enough to think rationally. Sure... Miguel might be thinking about a future with Savannah... but he was still giving it ten years... so, a lot could change in that amount of time, right? I managed to finish clearing the table, even though I felt a little light-headed. Still... what the freak?

With the table cleared, Uncle Joey called Chris and me over to the grill. Stepping to his side, I caught his intentions and froze in my tracks. Chris collided into my back and put his arms around me so we wouldn't fall over.

Uncle Joey raised a brow, thinking that he was giving me the opportunity to tell my husband what I'd done today while he was there. That way I'd tell Chris the whole story, and, with him as a witness, Chris couldn't yell at me like he might at home. Shocked at his manipulation, I wanted to tell him off, but he'd outsmarted me. I picked up that he may have forgiven me, but he was still going to make me pay.

"Shelby has some good news as well. Why don't you tell Chris where you've been and what you found out today?"

Chris's brows rose, but he kept his mouth shut, thinking that I must have pissed off Manetto pretty bad for him to put me on the spot like this. But he couldn't complain since he kind of liked seeing me squirm.

I frowned, but kept from rolling my eyes. "It wasn't like I planned it. I didn't even know I was going for sure until yesterday, and I didn't have a choice." They exchanged glances before fixing their gazes on me, and I caught that they were both enjoying this moment.

I threw my hands up, and turned to Chris. "This morning I flew to Las Vegas for a meeting with... Gage Rathmore. Do you remember him?"

Chris sucked in a breath. Of course he remembered Gage Rathmore, mostly because Uncle Joey didn't want to have anything to do with him. So what had changed? Frowning, he glanced at Uncle Joey. "The debt-collector?"

"Don't look at me... it wasn't my idea."

Chris turned back to me with narrowed eyes. "What happened?"

"Ella St. John needed my help." As I quickly explained what had happened, Chris's eyes got bigger and bigger until I thought they just might pop right out of his head. It alarmed me enough that I just skipped to the end. "So at the meeting I picked up Gavin's thoughts about the cryptocurrency that he and Max had stolen from Uncle Joey."

That might have been the wrong thing to say, since Chris shook his head like he was having a seizure. He looked between me and Uncle Joey several times before he found his voice. "Are you guys pranking me right now? Seriously, it feels like you're pranking me. This can't be real."

"Well... yeah... it's real. But you haven't even heard the best part yet."

"Right... and what's that."

He still didn't believe me, so I shrugged and continued. "We know Max is in Budapest. Gavin was thinking he'd left the country to get off the grid for a while, and he was staying with his extended family. So now... all we have to do is track him down, and we'll get the crypto back."

Chris shook his head and glanced at Uncle Joey. "Did you know about this?"

"No. She didn't tell me until she landed at the airport." He glanced at Chris, wondering if he should tell him that I'd made Ramos go with me. He didn't think Chris would like that much, so naturally he went ahead with it. "But she didn't go alone. She got Ramos to go with her."

Chris's nostrils flared and his lips flattened. Satisfied, Uncle Joey continued. "But, get this... she didn't tell him what was going on either." He shook his head. "It was good Ramos went, or who knows what Rathmore would have done. But Ramos wasn't too happy about it."

My shoulders drooped, and anger tightened my throat. "Are you done?"

Uncle Joey knew he'd probably gone too far, but I'd worried him today, and he didn't like it, especially considering who Rathmore was. Uncle Joey had worked hard to avoid dealing with Rathmore, but I'd messed that up. Now that Rathmore knew how helpful I was, it would be even harder to keep him at bay.

He shook his head, knowing he'd need to do whatever it took to find some kind of leverage over the man, just to keep him in check. Good thing he had a contact in Las Vegas who could handle it.

In the meantime, he'd concentrate on getting his crypto back. That would help put him in a good mood, and balance out the fiasco of my visit to Vegas.

"Yes." He put his arm around my shoulder and pulled me into a tight squeeze. "Shelby... you know if I didn't care about you, this wouldn't have mattered so much. You get that, right?"

"Yeah... I get it."

He turned to Chris. "She really didn't have a choice, so don't be too hard on her."

"I know," he agreed. "It's the story of my life, so I just try to deal with it the best way I can, you know?"

"Yes. I know exactly what you mean."

I shook my head, and took their teasing with a grain of salt. "So, what's the plan?"

Uncle Joey dropped his arm from around me. "I'm sending you with Ramos and Forrest to Budapest tomorrow. I want my crypto back before Max hands it over to Rathmore."

Chris let out a breath. He was afraid of that. But hadn't he just told Manetto he'd learned to deal with my crazy life? He couldn't complain now, especially since Manetto had deftly shoved him into a corner as well. *That manipulative bastard.* "Let's hope it works."

"It will." Uncle Joey smiled. "After all... we've got Shelby on our side."

Chapter 12

I didn't know how Uncle Joey managed it, but the next day, I boarded a plane with Ramos and Forrest for Frankfurt, Germany, with a connecting flight to Budapest.

By the time we arrived in Budapest, I was exhausted. I'd managed to take a couple of naps on the plane, but my internal clock was telling me it was long past time for bed, instead of late afternoon.

We checked into our hotel with a plan to meet in a couple of hours for dinner and go over our plans to catch Max. Ramos's room was next to mine, and Forrest's was across the hall.

I opened the door to enter my room and found a spectacular view of Castle Hill across the Danube River. The imposing building framed by my window was built in a Baroque architectural style. There was a huge dome in the center, and it was adorned with elaborate motifs and decorations.

The sight was truly amazing, and I hoped I'd get a chance to explore the area. Who would have thought I'd be here in

Budapest? It boggled my mind, and I couldn't wait to see more of the city.

After taking a soothing shower, I flopped on the king size bed and fell asleep. I didn't stir until loud knocking roused me. Pushing my hair out of my face, I stumbled to the door and pulled it open.

Ramos stood there, looking fresh and sexy in his black jeans and leather jacket. His clothes weren't even rumpled. How did he do that? "Uh... come in. I need to run a comb through my hair before I'll be ready." I stepped back, and he followed me inside, closing the door behind him.

Taking my time, I splashed cold water on my face to help me wake up. After combing out my tangled hair, I pulled it back into a ponytail and was ready to go. In my black skinny jeans, paired with a tank top and t-shirt, I stepped into the bedroom and slipped on a comfortable sweatshirt before pulling on my black boots.

I wasn't sure what the temperature was here, but it was late fall, so I had to plan on it being a little chilly, especially at night. Ramos had been sitting in a chair and stood once I had my shoes on.

"Where are we eating dinner?" I asked.

"There's a restaurant in the hotel."

"Good, because I'm hungry... get it... Hungary?"

He shook his head, thinking that was bad and I needed more sleep.

"Yeah... I know."

We knocked on Forrest's door, and he joined us in the hall. We took the elevator down to the restaurant and found an outdoor table with a view of the river and Castle Hill. It was a little chilly, but totally worth it.

Once we'd ordered our food, Forrest pulled out a map. "I picked this hotel because it was close to the IP address Max used. I thought we could walk in that general direction after dinner and see what's there."

"Sure," I agreed. "But what if Max sees us?"

"He won't if we're careful," Ramos said. "And it'll be dark soon. If it's a restaurant, we'll know that's where he is. Then we can come back here and figure out a plan."

We finished our dinner and left as the sun went down, strolling through the streets until coming to the address Forrest spoke of. Before us, we found a covered outdoor café, and restaurant with a two-story building behind it. The building looked like it held apartments, but I couldn't tell for sure. "That could be the restaurant that belongs to his family."

"Yeah," Forrest agreed. "You might be right."

"I agree," Ramos said. "Let's head back to our rooms and figure out what to do." He was thinking that we'd have to watch the place until we spotted Max. Once we had him in our sights, we could grab him and make him talk.

I invited them into my room and opened the door to find the spectacular buildings on Castle Hill all lit up with golden light. "Wow... would you look at that?"

We admired the view for several seconds before getting down to business. A small couch with a coffee table sat against the wall next to the window, with a desk and chair on the other side. Forrest pulled up the chair, while Ramos and I shared the couch.

Ramos glanced my way. "Has Max ever seen you?"

I shook my head. "Not unless he knew I was following him, but I never picked up that he'd spotted me, so no... I don't think so."

Ramos nodded. "Then I have a plan. You could get your breakfast at the cafe tomorrow. If you spot him, you could let us know, and we could go from there." He was thinking that he'd need to find a secluded spot to beat the information out of him, but that shouldn't be a problem.

"You're going to beat it out of him?"

He shrugged. "If I need to."

"He might have Manetto's hard drive here somewhere," Forrest said. "If he hasn't hacked into it, we'll need it back. If he has, we're going to have to persuade him to transfer the crypto to a secure place." He was thinking he had a wallet for that, and, if he took it, all that money would belong to him. Of course, that would be a death sentence, so he couldn't keep it. Still... what a rush to have that much money in his possession... even if it was for just for a few minutes. Pure bliss.

I shook my head. "Okay. Well... I can't think of anything better, so I guess we'll go with that plan."

Ramos's brows rose. Anything better? Had I just dissed him.

My eyes widened. "No... that's a great plan. I just wish Max was easier to track down... that's all."

Forrest glanced between the two of us, knowing he'd missed something. "Uh... sure. Let's do it." He stood, ready to go back to his room and sleep off his jet-lag. "What time should we meet up in the morning?"

"Let's say eight." Ramos glanced at me. "Will that work for you?"

"Yeah. It will."

"Okay, see you in the morning." Forrest got to his feet and told us goodnight before heading to his room.

In the silence, Ramos glanced my way. A wave of desire washed over him, and he studied me, thinking we were alone in a room, far away from everyone. If something happened between us, it would be our little secret. No one else would need to know.

My mouth went dry, and I jumped to my feet. "Want to go for a walk? I'd love to see more of the city. I bet it's beautiful with all the lights... I mean... just look at it out there." I motioned to the window.

Ramos's lips curved slightly. "Actually, I was planning to head back outside myself. I need to see if there's a secluded spot where I can take Max... you know... to beat him up."

"Oh... right."

"Goodnight, Shelby. I'll see you in the morning."

As he got up to leave, I swallowed. I was more tempted than he knew, but that was a line I wouldn't cross. Not if I ever wanted to face my husband. I couldn't do that to him or my family.

He opened the door and glanced back at me. "It's okay, Shelby. I was just thinking how easy it would be... but I didn't mean that we should. I don't want things to change between us... and I think they would if we crossed that line." He shook his head. "It's not your fault. I blame that damn lizard."

Thoughts of me throwing off my clothes while I jumped and screamed brought a smile to his lips. He closed the door on a chuckle, and I let out my breath. That was close. Ramos may have thought about it, but at least he didn't do anything... like kiss me. If he had... I probably would have enjoyed it for at least thirty seconds, but after that, I totally would have stopped him.

Relieved that I'd never know if I was kidding myself, I shook my head. I wasn't sure what was worse. Facing someone like Rathmore, or facing the temptation of Ramos. Why did these things always happen to me?

I woke at five in the morning and called Chris. With the time difference, it was around nine pm for him. Since I didn't have a lot to tell him, he did most of the talking, and it was nice to hear his voice and hear how everyone was doing.

Finished, I decided to take another shower and get ready for the day. Ready by seven, I thought it would be nice to take a walk around the city before breakfast. I sent Ramos a text telling him I was going on a walk, and he told me to wait and he'd join me.

A few minutes later, he knocked at my door with Forrest by his side. We spent the next hour and a half taking in the sights and ended up at Max's restaurant. Ramos and Forrest found a spot at an outdoor cafe across the street where they could watch while I went inside to eat.

The restaurant was busier than I imagined, but I was able to get a place along the far wall where I could see who came and went. My server spoke English, so I told him I was visiting Budapest for the first time. He told me I needed to visit Castle Hill and all the sights there, and mentioned that I couldn't leave without visiting the Great Market Hall to buy some Hungarian Paprika.

I told him I would, and he left to get my food. Half an hour passed with no sign of Max. Done with my food, I wasn't sure if this was going to work. The server returned with my bill. Luckily, I had some Hungarian money to pay for it. With no idea how to add up the large sum, I just gave him several of the bills, and he said he'd be back with my change.

His thoughts were mostly Hungarian, but I picked up a few words of English. He was thinking that I was nice, but he thought it strange I was there alone.

Coming back with my change, he told me I needed to visit the famous Széchenyi Thermal Baths. He repeated that it was world famous, and seemed surprised that I'd never heard of it. He was thinking that his American cousin spent a lot of his time there, so I should like it.

My heart raced, and I hoped this was my opening. "That sounds amazing. Can you tell me where it is, or how to get there from here? Or better yet... is there someone who can show me the way?"

His brows dipped, but he shrugged. "Maybe... let me check."

Several minutes later, he returned with a piece of paper. "Sadly, there is no one to take you, but here are the directions." While he explained the map to me, I picked up that I'd just missed Max, who'd already left to spend a few hours there. "You will need a bathing suit, but you can buy towels there. Don't worry about the coolness of the air... the water is nice and hot. Eighteen thermal pools. Very good for you."

"Sounds great. Thanks so much."

I grabbed my purse and left the restaurant. Outside, I waited at the corner for Ramos and Forrest to join me. "Any luck?" Ramos asked, stepping beside me.

"Yes. He's at the thermal baths for the next couple of hours, so we have to buy bathing suits if we're going to catch him there."

Ramos's brow puckered. "Or we could just wait for him to come out."

"What? And miss a chance to visit the world famous thermal baths? They're supposed to be really good for you, so I say we get some bathing suits and get over there before Max leaves."

Ramos smirked, knowing a con when he heard one. But the scowl left his face as the thought that seeing me in a bathing suit would probably be worth it... especially if he helped me pick it out. I did owe him a lot... so it was the least I could do.

I groaned just a little, and we set off to find a store that sold bathing suits. True to his word, Ramos picked out a skimpy, blue, two-piece number that was in my size. I tried it on, just to make sure it fit, knowing most bathing suits in the states ran two sizes too small.

It fit really well, so I gave in and bought it. Still... deep down, I knew the giving-in-part wasn't exactly true. I wanted to wear that suit because I looked good in it, and Ramos had picked it out. That meant I was probably going to hell for sure.

We took our newly purchased suits and followed the map to the Széchenyi Thermal Baths. The building was huge and built in the same Baroque style as most everything in the city. Since it was still early in the day, we opted for the cabin ticket, bought the towels, and got a wristband to our private changing rooms.

We followed the numbers to find our changing rooms and discovered that they were nowhere near each other. I wandered down one hall, while Ramos and Forrest ended up going their separate ways.

I finally found the right number and entered the small room, which reminded me of the dressing rooms at a department store. After changing, I worked my hair into a French braid, using an elastic band to hold it together.

I wasn't real comfortable in my tiny swimsuit, so I wrapped my towel around my waist and left to join the others. I wandered through countless halls, looking for Ramos, and couldn't see him anywhere.

After twenty minutes, I wondered if we were even in the same building. I lost count of the pools I passed, and I was so intent on finding Ramos that I forgot about Max. The three biggest pools were outside. Since I hadn't checked them yet, I found the door leading outside and stopped near the middle pool.

With the temperature in the high fifties, the pools had steam coming off them, making it hard to see into the water. How was I supposed to find anyone now? A breeze blew over me, and I shivered. Maybe I should just get into the hot water and hope for the best?

I found an empty lounger and left my towel on it before stepping into the pool. The hot water felt amazing, and I sank into it with a sigh, finally getting some much-needed warmth. Too bad Ramos wasn't already here, and I still needed to find him, because now that I was in, I didn't think I'd ever get out.

"Babe. What took you so long?" I twisted around to find him behind me.

"I've been looking all over for you. This place is a maze."

"There's a lot of pools." He didn't realize I wouldn't head straight to the outdoor pools, like he and Forrest did. "I guess we didn't make it clear to come here first."

My lips twisted. "Yeah... I guess not." I glanced behind him. "So where's Forrest?"

"While I waited for you, he went to look for Max in the other pools."

"So no luck yet?" He nodded, and I continued. "What are we going to do if we find him?"

"Good question." Ramos was thinking he'd be happy to hold his head under water for a while. "Get him to talk, I guess."

I smiled. "It won't be that hard since you have me. In fact, maybe I should just start listening to people? He'd be thinking in English, so that would set him apart, right?"

"Sure. Go for it. While you're doing that, I'm going to look around the pool. Don't go anywhere."

"I won't."

He disappeared into the mist, and I began my own search, closing my eyes and sweeping the pool with my mental ability. It amazed me that so many people were thinking in English... must be the tourists. I picked up a few other languages, but nothing stood out.

Leaning my head against the edge of the pool, I relaxed, enjoying the water's heat. This was amazing, and I just wanted to enjoy it for a few minutes and forget all about Max. Splashing caught my attention, and I picked up a few frantic thoughts that included some swearing.

A man got out of the pool and stepped toward the doors. With his wet hair, I almost didn't recognize him, but his thoughts about Ramos confirmed it was Max. He was trying not to draw attention, and walked sedately across the distance toward the doors leading inside. Since I was close, I hurried out of the pool to follow him.

Taking a second to grab my towel, I rushed after Max, managing to keep him in sight until he disappeared inside the building. I glanced behind me, but couldn't see Ramos anywhere. He was going to be mad at me for leaving, but I couldn't lose Max after coming all this way.

I managed to keep Max in my sights and followed him down a hall and through a couple of doorways to another indoor pool. He skirted the pool, and I kept on his trail, following him down another hall and coming to a different pool that was smaller.

The exit was on the other side, but, instead of skirting the pool, he got in. Not sure what to do, I stood there for a few seconds before stepping beside the wall, hoping to make myself small and inconspicuous. Now that I was out of the hot water, the cool air sent shivers down my arms.

Max took notice of me and wondered why I was just standing there and not getting into the pool. Not wanting to stand out, I set my towel on the ground and stepped into the water. A relieved breath whooshed out of me to feel the hot water on my skin. As inconspicuously as possible, I made my way to the side of the pool opposite Max to keep an eye on him.

He kept a close watch on the doorway for Ramos and began to relax after several minutes passed with no sight of him. I wondered where he was, too. Focusing on Max, I picked up that he wasn't certain Ramos had seen him. Since Ramos hadn't come through those doors, there was a good chance he was right. But what about the woman? I looked familiar. Had we ever met?

My eyes widened, and, for some stupid reason, I looked right at him. That gave me away, and, before I knew it, he was standing right in front of me. I backed up and hit the side of the pool.

His blue eyes turned to ice, and he leaned in close. "I've seen your picture. You're Shelby. Manetto's niece."

It wasn't a question, but I feigned confusion and stepped away from him. "Uh... no. You must have me confused with someone else."

He moved with me, keeping me hemmed in until I was backed into a corner with nowhere to go. He began to panic, wondering if Manetto had sent Ramos to kill him. He shouldn't have left the hard drive back in the states, but he could still use it as leverage... unless we'd found it.

"Where is the hard drive?" I asked.

His eyes widened before blazing with triumph, and I realized I shouldn't have asked.

He closed in on me, and my heart began to pound. I opened my mouth to scream, but he clamped his hand over my lips. It wasn't until that moment that I realized we were alone in the small pool, and panic seized me. I kneed him in the groin and twisted away, but the water kept my action from doing any damage.

He was bigger and stronger than me, and easily forced me under the surface. I began to flail and kick, but his hold didn't loosen. He shoved me on my back down to the bottom of the pool, and I opened my eyes to find his face and torso under the water as well.

Using his feet and legs to keep his balance, he pushed me tight against the bottom to minimize the splashing noise. I tried in vain to push against the flooring with my arms and feet, but he was too strong. My lungs started to burn, and I knew my time was running out.

With one last, frantic try, I twisted to the side, scraping my back along the cement, and kicked at his leg. His foot slipped, and his grip faltered, giving me just enough leverage to push to the surface.

Breathing huge gasps of air, I tried to get away, but he caught me and shoved my head down. His arm snaked around my waist to hold me against him, pinning my arms to my sides. With his other hand, he pushed my head under the water.

I fought and struggled for all I was worth, but I couldn't get out of his hold. Darkness began to close in, and my limbs went weak. The need to breathe overwhelmed me, and I tried to hold on, but I was losing the battle. Just before losing consciousness, I felt the pressure holding me down lift, and strong arms grabbed me, pulling me up.

"Shelby! Shelby!"

A hard mouth came over mine and forced air into my starved lungs. It was enough to jump-start my reflexes, and I gasped in big gulps of air. Still heaving, I blinked and coughed, taking in as much air as I could manage.

As I continued to cough and shake, Ramos held me close to his chest. After several long seconds, strength slowly returned to my arms and legs. Finally feeling better, I threw my arms around him and cried with relief.

"You... you found me."

"You're safe, Shelby. It's okay. I've got you."

"Where's... Max?"

Ramos glanced away before answering. "He's gone."

I lowered my head and cried harder.

"It's okay Shelby. We'll get him."

"But... it's... my fault."

"No. It's not. Please..." He swallowed to regain his composure. "Don't cry."

I took a shuddering breath and tried to calm down. I'd thought I was going to die, and that helpless feeling overwhelmed me. Concentrating on the here and now, I focused on my breathing.

Ramos had found me in time. I wasn't dead. He'd saved me. Centering my thoughts on that amazing fact, my panic and tears began to slow until my control returned. I was alive, and, right now, I was pressed against a hard, sturdy chest, full of warmth and safety.

Not only that, but I could feel his strong, steady heartbeat against my ear. I closed my eyes and absorbed the weight of his love as he held me tight. He was thinking that he'd almost lost me, and tears flooded his eyes. Mortified, he blinked them away and pulled himself together, knowing he needed to be strong, or I'd never let him live it down.

Now it was my turn to swallow, and I blinked back my tears for a whole different reason until I was back under some semblance of control.

"You ready to get out?" he asked. As much as he didn't want to let go of me, a crowd had gathered, and we needed to move.

"I think so."

"Good." He tucked me against his side, and we walked to the stairs and stepped out of the pool.

A couple of men in uniforms and carrying equipment burst into the room. I had no idea what they were saying, but they rushed toward us and made me sit down. One of them spoke in English, asking me how I felt and telling me they needed to listen to my lungs.

Luckily, I'd kept from inhaling too much water, and my lungs were mostly clear. Still, they insisted that I go to the hospital for some x-rays to make sure I wouldn't develop an infection.

I directed Ramos to my towel and gave him my bracelet so he could get my clothes out of my dressing room. The paramedics insisted on taking me to the waiting ambulance on a gurney. Too weak to fight them, I agreed. After I got situated, Ramos threw my towel over me and held my hand until we got to the ambulance.

Sudden fear that I was in a foreign land and headed to an unknown hospital gripped me, and I didn't want to let go of him. "You'll come find me, right?"

"Of course. I'll be there as soon as I can."

With no choice, I let go of him, keeping my gaze glued to his until the doors shut.

"It will be fine. We take good care of you." The paramedic beside me smiled and patted my arm. I nodded and managed to smile back before resting my head against the cushion. I couldn't understand his thoughts, so I quit trying to listen and closed my eyes.

True to the paramedic's word, the doctors and nurses took good care of me. After taking the x-rays and checking everything over, they declared that I was good to go, warning me that if I developed a fever or a persistent cough, I needed to see a doctor immediately.

After I signed some papers, a nurse came in with my clothes and told me my *kedvesem* was waiting for me. I had no idea what that meant, but I caught a mental image of Ramos and nodded. I quickly dressed and followed her to a waiting room. Ramos caught sight of me and stood. I stepped into his arms and held him close.

"You okay?" he asked, squeezing me tightly.

"I am now." I held him for a few more seconds before dropping my arms. With his arm around my shoulders, we left the hospital and found a waiting cab to take us back to our hotel.

"So what's been happening?" I asked.

Ramos shook his head. "Max is gone. His relatives won't talk, and the police aren't much help. Forrest doesn't think we'll find him now. We might be able to track him down if he reaches out to Gavin in Las Vegas, so I guess that's our next move."

He was thinking Forrest could use his hacking skills to track Gavin down, and then find a way into his email accounts, but it would take time. By then, Max and Manetto's crypto would be long gone.

"Not if we get it first."

Ramos met my gaze. "What do you mean?"

"Max didn't bring the hard drive to Budapest. It's still at home, and I have a good idea where it is."

Ramos let out a breath and smiled. "Tell me."

"He was thinking that he'd hidden it at his office. I know we went through his office and didn't find anything, but I caught an image of something else. Remember the neighbor next to his office? She's some kind of interior designer?"

"Oh... yeah." He was thinking she was the one who'd looked at him like he was good enough to eat, and had given him her number. Too bad he couldn't remember her name. "He gave it to her? How come you didn't pick it up from her thoughts?"

"Because he didn't give it to her. But I think he may have hidden it somewhere in her office. Or at least that's the impression I got. Where he hid it isn't as clear to me, but I'm sure that's where he's headed next."

Chapter 13

The cab let us out in front of our hotel, and we started toward our rooms. "Is Forrest here?"

"Yeah... let's have him meet us in your room, and we can tell him what you found out."

Ramos stopped to knock on Forrest's door while I opened the door to my room. He told Forrest to join us, and they both came inside. I sat on the small couch, leaving room for Ramos to sit beside me, while Forrest took the chair across from us.

"I'm so sorry I wasn't there," Forrest said. "I can't believe Max tried to kill you. I didn't think he knew who you were."

I rested my head back against the cushions. "I didn't think he knew either, but he must have seen a picture of me at some point. He put it together that I'm Uncle Joey's niece."

"I should have stuck closer to you guys, but I thought I saw him in another pool." He was thinking that he'd never met Max in person, so he wasn't as helpful as he could have been. When he got to the pool where Ramos had found me nearly dead, Max was long gone. "I wish I would have been there. I could have caught him." He shook his head. "I guess

Manetto won't be too happy we lost him. Did your premonitions tell you anything about where he might be?"

"Well... not where he is, but I have a good idea where he's going. I picked up where the hard drive is, so it wasn't a total loss."

His eyes widened. "You did?"

"Yeah. I'm pretty sure that Max hid Manetto's hard drive in the office next door to his."

"Really? The interior designer's office?"

My brows rose. "Yeah... how did you know?"

He ducked his head. "I may have gone to his office and searched through his stuff. I didn't find anything."

"That was you? We wondered who had trashed the place. Did you go to his house too?"

"Uh... yeah." He shrugged. "I would have mentioned it before now, but since I didn't find anything, I figured there was no point."

"I'm going to call Manetto," Ramos said, standing. "We need to get the hard drive before Max beats us to it."

Ramos stepped away and put the call through to Uncle Joey, eager to explain what I'd found. Finished, he slipped his phone into his pocket and came back to sit beside me. "Manetto's sending Ricky over to get it." He checked the time. "It's Sunday night there, so he shouldn't have a problem breaking in."

"That's a relief."

Ramos glanced my way, thinking that I used to have a problem with breaking and entering. Now I was all for it.

"What can I say? You're a bad influence on me."

Ramos's eyes widened, and he glanced at Forrest, who was thinking my comment made sense to him. Working for a mob boss definitely changed things, but I was still a good person.

I sent Forrest a big smile of thanks, and he smiled back.

Ramos shook his head. "Manetto said he'd call once he had the hard drive. In the meantime, he wants us to come home, so we need to get our flights booked."

I nodded, a little disappointed that we were leaving so soon. But, I supposed, with our work done, there was no rest for the weary... or in Max's case... the wicked.

We managed to get the next available flight to Amsterdam the following morning, with a connecting flight home. That meant we still had the rest of the day and the evening to do a little sight-seeing, and I wanted to make the most of it.

I talked Ramos and Forrest into taking a tour of the city, and they left so I could take a nice, hot shower. After I dressed in my jeans and comfy shoes, we found a guide to take us on a tour of the Castle District, with a visit to the Buda Castle, Hero's Square, and the Matthias Church.

It was amazing to walk through the medieval streets of this beautiful city. Naturally, I stopped at a tourist shop where I bought some earrings and a t-shirt with an imprint of the massive, baroque style parliament building on the front, and *Budapest, Hungary* written in big letters across the bottom.

We also visited The Fisherman's Bastion, which had amazing views of the Danube river and the Pest side of the city, along with many more towering statues and beautiful gardens.

As fun as that was, it had completely worn me out. We took a taxi back to our hotel and had a wonderful dinner in the outdoor restaurant overlooking the Danube and the Palace of the Buda Castle. As it got dark, the lights came on, showing the palace in all its golden glory, and I knew why they called Budapest "The Pearl of the Danube."

Too tired to stay awake any longer, I told Forrest and Ramos goodnight. Ramos offered to walk me to my room, and I couldn't turn him down. I knew I could trust him, and, after the scare I'd had, I wanted him to make sure Max wasn't hiding in my room.

Using his amazing bodyguard skills, he announced my room safe and asked if I needed anything else. He was thinking that he could stay until I was asleep, if it helped.

My heart melted just a little, and I was tempted to take him up on the offer. Before I could answer, his phone began to ring, and he pulled it out of his pocket. "It's Manetto."

He answered and only spoke for a minute before I knew it was bad news. "But it's got to be there somewhere." Listening, he began to pace. "I don't think Shelby's wrong. You want to talk to her? Sure, here she is."

He handed the phone over, and I took in a breath, preparing to sound more chipper than I felt. "Hey there."

"Shelby... we seem to have a problem. I need you to walk me through everything that happened with Max today. You must have missed something."

"Uh... okay. You want me to start at the beginning? Or from when Max tried to kill me? Or maybe just when he was thinking about the hard drive?"

"What? He tried to kill you? When did this happen?"

"Oh... I guess Ramos left that part out." I met Ramos's gaze, and he rolled his eyes. Oops. "Uh... let me just tell you what I picked up—"

"No... I want to know everything."

"Okay, but first you need to know that I'm fine now. The doctors checked me out at the hospital, and they let me leave. So... I'm really tired, but otherwise, I'm good."

"Shelby—"

"Right. Okay." Knowing this might take a while, I sat down on the couch and tugged the curtain aside so I could enjoy the amazing view. "We tracked Max down to his family's restaurant this morning, but he'd already left for the Thermal Pools." I continued my story and got a little emotional when I came to the part where I thought I was going to die.

"Ramos pulled me out... I think he did mouth-to-mouth..." I met Ramos's gaze, and his lips quirked up into a sexy smile. "I'm sorry I missed that part."

Oops! Did I just say that out loud? "Anyways... while he was saving me, Max got away. Oh... and I picked up that he'd hidden the hard drive in the office. It was while he was drowning me, so it's a little fuzzy."

"In his office? Or his neighbor's office?"

"I'm pretty sure it was the neighbor's office, because I saw the color of her walls in his mind, but if you couldn't find it there, maybe I wasn't thinking straight. I wasn't getting as much oxygen to my brain at that point, so I might have been mistaken about which office he thought about."

"It's fine, Shelby. I'll send some guys over to check his office as well... just in case."

I shrugged. "Yeah... okay. I hope you find it."

"Me too... but either way, I'll be watching for Max. He's bound to show up for the hard drive, and when he does, we'll be ready. We won't miss him this time."

"Oh... that's a good idea."

"Yes, and mark my words, he's going to pay for what he did to you."

I took a deep breath. "Uh... yeah... I'm going to pretend I didn't hear that."

"Good. Plausible deniability... I like that."

"There is one thing I wanted to ask you, though." I licked my lips. "Do you think we could keep my brush with death to ourselves for a bit? I'm not sure Chris would like to hear that part. At least... not yet."

After Uncle Joey had made me tell Chris about going to Las Vegas, I wasn't sure he'd let me keep it a secret. More importantly, I didn't want to add this incident to the list of things that would keep Chris up at night. "I mean... maybe I'll tell him someday... but can we give it some time first?"

It took him a few seconds to reply. "That's probably a good idea."

"Really?"

"Yes."

"Great. Thanks. I guess I'll see you tomorrow."

"Have a safe trip home."

"Will do."

"And Shelby... make sure it's uneventful."

I chuckled. "Sounds good to me."

He disconnected, and I handed Ramos his phone. "I'm sorry he didn't find the hard drive, but he'll be waiting for Max, so he'll get it eventually, right?"

"Of course."

I yawned. "What time do we have to be ready in the morning?"

"Let me check."

As Ramos checked the flight time, my phone began to ring. I'd already spoken to Chris, so it couldn't be him. I pulled out my phone to find Dimples's name and quickly answered. "Hey there... what's up?"

"Shelby? Is Ramos with you?"

Alarm spiked through me. "Uh... actually yes... he is. Why?"

"We've been looking for him since early this morning."

"Why?"

"I just need to ask him a few questions."

I pursed my lips. "Whatever you think he did, he didn't do it."

"You don't know that."

"Yes I do, because he's been with me this whole time." At Dimples's indrawn breath, I rushed to explain. "We're in Budapest looking for someone. You know... as in Budapest, Hungary? We've been here for a couple of days. What's going on?"

He let out a long breath. "Oh... okay. But that's... it doesn't explain what's going on."

"Explain what?"

"You know the case you're helping me with? Kai Nisogi's murder?"

"Sure."

"Well... his sister Mikiko is in the hospital. Someone broke into her house and beat her up pretty bad. We're still trying to figure out what happened, but from the looks of things, she fought them pretty hard. Luckily, the house alarm scared him off, but when the police got there she was barely conscious. She only said one name over and over before she passed out... but the name she gave us was... Ramos."

My eyes widened, and my gaze flew to Ramos. "She must have meant someone else. There are lots of people with that name."

"Is he there?" I didn't answer. "Can I talk to him?"

"Oh... yeah... sure." With my heart in my throat, I held the phone out to him. "It's Dimples. He wants to talk to you."

With narrowed eyes, Ramos took the phone. "Yes." As he listened, the fight went out of him, and he shook his head. "Yes, I know her. She's my neighbor. I installed the security system for her. Is she going to be okay?" Listening, he stared out the window before lowering his head. "Obviously, I had nothing to do with it." He listened for a few seconds longer before huffing out a breath. "We're coming back tomorrow. I'll answer your questions then."

He disconnected the call and handed me the phone. I knew he'd hung up on Dimples, but for some reason, it didn't bother me. "I'm sorry about your neighbor. I thought her name was Nico."

He sat down beside me on the couch and rubbed a hand over his face. "It's the name she told me to use."

"Oh... that makes sense. So how is she?"

"They don't know if she'll make it." He was thinking it shouldn't have happened. He'd installed the system with a failsafe. The only way someone could get inside was if she let them in.

But if the alarm went off, that didn't make sense either, unless... maybe her attacker had waited out of view, and, once she disarmed the system, he had forced his way inside. The failsafe had worked if the alarm went off before she reset it. Since it scared him off, it might have saved her life.

He met my gaze. "She told me about her brother the night I went over to finish setting up her security system." He didn't add that she'd been a mess, and he'd spent a few hours comforting her that night. "What can you tell me about the police investigation?"

"We think it has something to do with a job he was working on, but we don't have anything conclusive." I told him about Kai's job as an environmental engineer and the company who'd hired him to get all the permits.

"MRP Capital?" His brows rose. "Manetto does business with them."

"That's right. He was considering investing in a project, but I told him not to."

"Good. So what happened?"

"We spoke to the project manager, but I didn't get much from him." I shook my head. "But I doubt that this has anything to do with Mikiko's attack. Why did she want you to install a security system anyway?"

"She had an ex-boyfriend who was stalking her. When I came home one night, they were arguing in front of her house. He shoved her pretty hard against the car, and I may have roughed him up a little."

"Oh..." I narrowed my eyes. "So you're the one who gave him that bruise on his jaw. I saw it when we interviewed him. I thought Kai had done it."

"So you spoke to the guy?"

"Yeah. Mikiko told us he might have had a grudge against her brother, so we brought him in for questioning." I let out a heavy breath. "But he didn't have anything to do with it. In fact, by the time we spoke with him, I think he was pretty much over her." I met his gaze. "I think it might have had something to do with her scary neighbor."

A hint of a smile touched his lips. "Then who beat her up? And why?"

I shook my head. "I don't know, but I'd like to visit her in the hospital. Even if she can't talk, I might be able to pick up something from her mind." I sighed. It reminded me of the girl in New York who'd been in a coma. I hadn't been able to help her before she was killed, but maybe it would be different this time.

Ramos stood. "If you're okay, I think I'll go."

"Sure." I followed him to the door. As he moved to open it, I took hold of his arm. "Wait. I never thanked you for saving me today."

"Shelby... you don't need to. I'm just glad I found you in time." He shook his head. "That was close."

"I know... it scared me pretty bad."

"Me too." He pulled me into his arms and kissed the top of my head. I closed my eyes and clung to him, relishing this moment of intimacy.

Before I was ready, he set me away from him. "Goodnight Shelby." Letting out a deep sigh, he pulled the door open and stepped into the hall.

"Goodnight Romeo."

Hearing his answering chuckle, I closed the door.

We got home the next day just after one in the afternoon, but, with the time zone difference, that meant we'd been traveling all night long. Still, I couldn't complain since I'd had a first-class ticket, thanks to Uncle Joey. I'd slept for some of the trip, but my internal clock was so mixed up that I wasn't sure what day it was, let alone the time.

Uncle Joey sent Ricky in the limo to pick us up, and it struck me that I was officially part of the mob. No ifs, ands, or buts about it. Before, I'd always managed to think that I worked for a mob boss, but that wasn't who I was. Now, I was a bona fide member of a crime family.

I'd gotten used to riding in a limo, taking a private jet, and flying first class. None of that would have been part of my life without the mob part as well. Maybe at first I'd only helped Uncle Joey once in a while, but now, here I was, returning from Budapest and riding in a limo. What kind of a crazy life was this?

I glanced at my companions. Forrest was thinking that he could get used to this kind of life and wondered if Uncle Joey needed a hacker on his team.

Ramos sat beside me, perfectly content with this lifestyle. He'd chosen it, and it suited him just fine. He didn't have any of the angst that plagued me. But then, why would he?

He considered himself a bad guy, so there was nothing to feel bad about.

Maybe I should think of myself as a bad guy, too? I huffed out a breath. Nope… I couldn't do that. I wanted to be good, so I was just going to have to deal with it. Besides, I may be part of the mob, but I was the good part, so that should balance things out, right?

Before pulling into traffic, Ricky turned to look at us. "Manetto wants to see you in his office… except for you, Shelby. He wants you to go home and get some rest."

"Oh… isn't that nice." After everything I'd been thinking, why did that hurt my feelings?

Ramos raised a brow, thinking I'd sounded upset that I wasn't included. What was up with that? "I'm sure you can come if you want to."

I shook my head. "No. That's okay. I want to go home and take a nap."

"That's an excellent idea," Forrest said, thinking he was lucky to have the apartment in the office because that meant he might be able to take a nap too. It kind of bugged me that Forrest thought of the apartment as his. It was Ramos's. He should be the one to take a nap there.

I glanced Ramos's way and picked up his yearning to go on a motorcycle ride up the canyon. Getting out on his bike to take in the cool breeze and beautiful surroundings would help relieve the tension.

That sounded pretty good to me, and I had to admit that I was tempted to beg him to take me with him.

He caught me staring, and his lips turned into a knowing smile. Then he ruined it by thinking of me throwing off my clothes and screaming my head off. The vision was so funny that he had to bite his cheek to keep from laughing.

I huffed out a breath and tried not to roll my eyes. Moments later, we pulled up in front of my house. Ricky grabbed my luggage from the trunk, and I got out of the car.

"Have a nice nap," Ramos said.

My lips twisted. "Thanks. You... be safe."

His brows rose, but he sent me a chin lift.

Ricky handed me my luggage, and I watched them drive off before turning toward my house. I went through the side door into the garage and opened my kitchen door. As I closed the door behind me, Coco came bounding in. I dropped my bags and knelt down to hug him. He squirmed against me, so excited to see me that I had to laugh.

Giving me several wet doggy kisses, and more than a few yips of happiness, he followed me up the stairs to my room. After sending a text to Chris that I'd made it home, I changed into black leggings and a long-sleeved tee and snagged a soda from the fridge.

It was the perfect temperature to lounge outside on my patio swing. Armed with a soft pillow, a light blanket, a soda, and my dog, I relaxed onto the cushions, and promptly fell asleep.

The noise of a door closing snapped me awake, and I sat up to find Josh stepping outside onto the patio. "Hey Mom. How was Budapest?"

"It was great. It's an amazing city. Do you want to see my pictures?"

"Sure. Did you find the guy you were looking for?"

"Yeah... but it's not over yet. I'm afraid he got away, but we know where he's headed, so I'm sure Uncle Joey will find him."

Josh was wondering if that meant he'd end up dead somewhere. My breath caught, but I managed to keep from blurting that Uncle Joey would never do such a thing, mostly because I knew it could happen, especially after what Max did to me. Instead, I kept my mouth shut, and changed the subject.

"Here they are." I pulled up the photos on my phone, and we spent the next several minutes looking at them. I picked up that Josh wasn't real interested, but he was happy to look at them with me... as long as there weren't too many.

His luck held out, since I only had about twenty photos.

"Cool," Josh said. "I'm going to get something to eat." As Coco followed him inside, he thought of asking me what we were having for dinner, but held back, knowing it would be a waste of time since I probably had no idea.

He was right about that. Before I could come up with any ideas, Savannah came home with her friend Ashley. "Oh, hey Mom. You're back." She turned to Ashley. "Mom just got back from Budapest. She was there helping my uncle." Her brows drew together. "You were looking for someone, right?" At my nod, she continued. "Did you find him?"

"Yes."

"Wow," Ashley said. "That's so cool."

"Yeah. I have some pictures if you want to see them." They both sat beside me to look at the photos, ooo-ing and ah-ing at all the appropriate times. Savannah was happy to show me off to her friend, since what I did wasn't the usual mom stuff.

"So you work for your uncle... no wait, if he's Savannah's uncle that would make him your brother, right?" Ashley asked, trying to put it together. "I thought you were a consultant or something."

"Mom just got her PI license," Savannah said. "And it's her uncle... so I guess that makes him my great-uncle, but I just call him my uncle because it's lots easier. Anyway... Mom investigates all kinds of things. Right Mom?"

"Yes," I answered. "But it's not as exciting as it sounds." In my case, that was a big, fat lie, but that was mostly because I worked for a mob boss. Still, going with the PI explanation was a lot better than saying I was part of a crime family.

After that, the girls got bored pretty quick and headed up to Savannah's room. Josh came out with Coco and threw the Frisbee for him. I settled back to watch them play together, happy that they'd bonded so well.

I got a text from Chris telling me that he'd gotten off a little early, and he'd be home soon. Knowing it was time to step back into my role as a cook, I headed into the kitchen to find something I could make for dinner.

I spent a lot of time staring into the refrigerator and ended up with another diet soda in hand and no idea what to fix. The kitchen door opened, and Chris came in with a big bouquet of flowers.

"Oh wow. Are those for me?" I knew it was a stupid question, but that had never stopped me before.

"Yes." With a pleased grin, he set them on the table and pulled me into his arms. "Welcome home. I've missed you." He gave me a searing kiss and held me tight. His love washed over me in waves, and I let out a contented sigh.

"So how was the trip?" He pulled back to look me over, noting that my face was a little pale. I looked tired, but overall, I looked okay. Knowing I'd heard that, his eyes widened. "Great... I mean you look great."

"It's okay, honey... and thanks for the flowers. They're beautiful." I turned to admire them. It wasn't that long ago that a crazy stalker had sent me all kinds of flowers, and I wasn't sure I'd ever like them again, but this proved me wrong. I loved that he got them for me.

"I'm glad you like them. I thought maybe we'd take the kids and all go out for dinner. How does that sound?"

"Really? I was just trying to figure out what to make, and I couldn't come up with a single thing."

"Then let's do it."

I cocked my brow. "Why are you being so nice?" A spike of guilt came over him and left so quickly that, if I wasn't a mind reader, I might have missed it. To cover it up, he went on the defense.

"What do you mean? I'm always nice." His gaze met mine, and he opened his mouth to say more, but shook his head instead. "I'm going to go change." As he climbed the stairs to our room, he called over his shoulder. "Think about where you want to go for dinner."

"Okay." A small grin creased my lips. I'd picked up enough to know that the flowers and dinner had been a suggestion from Uncle Joey. Chris had a sneaking suspicion that things may not have gone as expected in Budapest, and some tender loving care was in order.

Deep down, he'd wanted to ask me what the hell had happened, but Uncle Joey had given him strict instructions to wait until I told him, and he was doing his best to give me the space I needed.

I shook my head. As much as I loved Uncle Joey, I really didn't like his involvement in my marriage. I knew he meant well... but this had to stop. Of course, I loved the flowers... and the fact that we were going out to dinner... so maybe it wasn't so bad.

Knowing that Chris was in a tight spot, I headed up the stairs to tell him how grateful I was for him. Having a mind reader for a wife wasn't easy, but he'd learned to handle it. Being part of a crime family, with a head-honcho who liked to be in control of everything, was a little harder. But we'd figure it out.

Dinner was a huge success, and we had a great time. It ended up being just what our family needed. It was just after eight when we got home, and my phone rang as we walked into the house.

"It's Dimples... I'd better take it. Hello?"

"Hey Shelby, did you make it home?"

"Yes, I did. We just got back from dinner. What's up?"

"Do you think you could come to the hospital? Ramos is here, and it would be nice if you were here too."

"Of course. How's Mikiko?"

"She came through surgery, but she's not out of the woods yet."

"Okay... I can leave in a few minutes. Where should I meet you?" He gave me Mikiko's room number, and we disconnected.

"I have to go to the hospital." I explained to Chris that Kai's sister was in the hospital, and Dimples wanted me to see if I could pick up anything. "He thinks it might be the same person who killed Kai, so if I can help, I need to go. I shouldn't be long."

I sort of left out the part that Ramos was involved. I knew I should be more transparent about that, but then I'd have to tell Chris more of the story, and there just wasn't time. I could tell him all about it when I got home and fit it in with everything that had happened in Budapest. It might take all night, but I could do it.

I arrived at the hospital and went straight to Mikiko's room. Dimples waited in the hall, and his shoulders visibly relaxed when he spotted me. "Good. You're here."

I wanted to give him a hug, but he seemed a little standoffish with Ramos there, so I held back. "Of course. How's Mikiko? Is she awake?"

He glanced toward her room. "Her concussion is pretty bad, so she's in and out, but Ramos thought you might be able to pick up something from her anyway."

"I'll do my best." I stepped into the room to see Ramos sitting in a chair beside the bed. It seemed a little strange to find him by her side like that, almost like they were more than just neighbors. I hadn't picked that up from him, but he was good at blocking his thoughts, so what did I know?

He stood as soon as I came in, stepping around the bed to my side. "Thanks for coming. I didn't want to ask you, but Harris insisted." He was thinking that Dimples didn't know about my brush with death, and he hoped it wasn't too much to ask. "How was your nap?"

"It was good. How about you? Did you get to go on that bike ride?"

"Not yet. Manetto..." He glanced behind me at Dimples and pressed his lips together, finishing his sentence by thinking that Manetto had too much for him to do... most of it involved setting a few traps for Max, and finding the hard drive. Manetto had hoped to find the hard drive without my involvement, since I'd nearly died over it once already, but maybe tomorrow I could go with him... and we'd take the bike.

My eyes widened, and I nodded enthusiastically. Dimples cleared his throat, thinking that it was weird to know that Ramos was talking to me without saying a word. Is that what it looked like when I did that with him?

I gave Dimples a tiny shrug before turning my attention to Mikiko. "Hey Mikiko, it's Shelby Nichols. Are you doing okay? Is there anything you need?"

Her eyes were closed, and I couldn't hear a thing. I listened a few seconds longer and shook my head. "She's out." I glanced at Dimples. "Did she tell you any more about what happened?"

"No. She hasn't spoken yet. That's why we wanted you to come. We were hoping to speed things along... with your ability... if we could."

"Yeah... I get that." I listened again, but found nothing in her mind and shook my head.

Dimples sighed, then he motioned us toward the door, and we both followed him out of the room. In the hall, Dimples explained what they'd found at her house.

"We think the guy was hiding outside in wait for her. Once she disarmed the code, he pushed her inside and closed the door. The place was a mess when the police arrived. At first we thought the mess was because she had put up a fight, but now we think he was looking for something."

"Like what?"

"I don't know."

Ramos pursed his lips, wondering if he should tell Dimples about the security camera hidden in the entryway. It would have recorded the incident, and they could access it through the app on her phone. Of course, getting into her phone would take time. Luckily, his security camera had picked it up as well, and he'd already looked at it.

Her attacker had worn all black and had hidden in the bushes until she'd opened the door. With a black ski mask covering his face, he wasn't identifiable, so seeing it probably wouldn't help much, but it would give Dimples something to do.

I widened my eyes at him, but he refused to take the bait. I glanced at Dimples. "Did you look at the security camera footage?"

His brow puckered. "What security camera?"

"The one in the entryway." At his confusion, I turned to Ramos. "Please tell him about the camera."

Ramos folded his arms in front of his chest and glowered at me. I'd given him away, and he didn't like it.

I frowned and turned to Dimples. "There's a surveillance camera near the front door. It's triggered by a motion sensor, so it should have recorded the incident."

Dimples huffed out a breath. Why didn't Ramos start with that? "Is it hooked up to her phone?"

Ramos nodded, knowing he might as well tell Dimples everything. "Yeah. There's an app on her phone if you can get into it. But it won't do you any good. Her attacker wore a ski mask over his face, so you won't be able to identify him."

"How do you know that?"

Ramos shrugged. "I have a camera on my house across the street, and it picked up the incident."

Dimples's jaw jutted out, and if looks could kill, Ramos would be dead.

Ramos hid a smile and pulled out his phone. "I'll show it to you."

He tapped the app and found the correct date and time and hit play. We all watched the attacker shove Mikiko into her house and close the door. It wasn't long before a loud alarm went off, and the attacker bolted from the house, leaving the door open.

"Will you send me a copy of that?" Dimples asked.

"Of course. If you'll do something for me."

His eyes narrowed. "Like what?"

"I'd like to take a look inside her house. I think I might know if something is missing."

Dimples's brows rose. "You've spent a lot of time there?"

"Enough."

That was not the answer Dimples wanted, but it was all Ramos planned to give him.

"And I want Shelby to come." Ramos glanced my way, thinking that I hadn't told him if I'd picked up anything from her dead brother, but, if I had, maybe I'd hear him at her house.

"Oh... yeah." I glanced at Dimples. "I think I should go... you know... in case there's something for me to pick up."

Dimples huffed out a breath. "You mean from the dead brother?" He was thinking we should just talk in front of him like normal people. He glanced at Ramos. "You know that I know what Shelby can do, right?"

"I couldn't remember for sure."

Dimples shook his head and rolled his eyes. "Whatever. Let's go."

Dimples turned on his heel and started down the hall. I shook my head at Ramos, and he shrugged, thinking *what did you expect... I'm a bad guy.*

Now it was my turn to roll my eyes. He grinned and tugged me down the hall after Dimples.

Chapter 14

We all drove separately to Mikiko's house. Since Ramos was her neighbor, I was curious to see where he lived. We came to a sub-division in an older neighborhood where most of the homes were small and cozy and built in the Craftsman style, with low-pitched roofs, protruding gables, and overhanging eaves.

In this tree-lined neighborhood, the homes all seemed more private and less pretentious than the newer areas, but they also displayed a timeless quality that would never go out of style.

Ramos pulled his motorcycle into the driveway of his house, and I pulled to a stop in front of it, admiring the wide, open front porch held up by two thick, tapered columns, which were covered in beautiful stonework.

Large windows with wooden frames stood on both sides of the heavy wooden door, and the wood siding was painted in green earth tones and cream colored accents. Softly rounded shrubs, with colorful perennials, along with small accent trees, complimented the charm of the house, and a stone paver walkway to the front door tied it all together.

It was lovely and masculine, all at the same time.

I got out of my car and waited for Ramos to join me. "Your house is really nice. It looks like you've done some work on it."

"Yeah. It's a work in progress, but I don't spend as much time on it as I'd like. I hire out the yard work, but I've done a lot of the interior work myself." He shrugged. "I like building things."

He was thinking of the beautiful table he'd made, and wished he could show it to me. But inviting me inside his house was not a good idea... at least not for now.

He caught my gaze and raised a brow.

"Yeah... you're probably right, now's not a good time. In fact, Dimples is waiting." I knew that wasn't what Ramos was implying, but I chose to ignore that part and started across the street.

Dimples wondered why we were taking so long, but he managed to keep his frustration in check. It wasn't easy since I seemed more on Ramos's side than his, and he didn't like it.

What? There were sides? Good grief. Still, deep down, I knew he had a point, Ramos could be nicer, and, in this case, I was caught between two worlds. It was up to me to be the bridge between them, so I stopped in front of Dimples and smiled at both of them. "Ready to solve the case?" They thought I was nuts, but I plunged ahead. "Let's do this."

As I marched to the front door, Dimples wondered if I was trying to make up for Ramos's surliness. Ramos thought I was jet-lagged and a little loopy... you know... normal. Now... if I started throwing off my clothes, he'd be worried.

Stopping to let Dimples go ahead of me, I sent Ramos a pointed stare, with my brows drawn together and my lips pressed into a flat line. It was my killer look, but he just grinned. Dropping my shoulders, I shook my head, knowing that intimidating him was a lost cause.

Luckily, Dimples had missed the whole thing. With crime scene tape fluttering across the front door, Dimples got out the key to the house and unlocked it. He pulled the yellow tape down and flipped on the lights before ushering us inside. "We've already gone over everything for fingerprints."

"You'll probably find mine then," Ramos said. "Since I've been here a few times installing the security system."

"Yeah... we did. It's lucky you have an airtight alibi."

Ramos frowned. He didn't like Harris's attitude, but what could he expect? He had a reputation to live up to, so he took it in stride. "Yes... I'm very lucky." Glancing at me, he winked.

With Dimples watching, I did my best to keep from rolling my eyes, but that was too much to ask and I did it anyway. "I think I'll walk through the place and see if I can pick up anything."

"Sure," Dimples said, annoyed with the easy banter between Ramos and me. "Take your time."

I stepped down the hall to the master bedroom and flipped on the lights. Drawers and clothes lay strewn on the floor in heaps, and the bedding had been pulled off the mattress. The attacker had done a thorough job of making a mess. Had he found what he was looking for?

He'd skipped the bathroom, so I went inside and took a look around. Nothing seemed disturbed or out of the ordinary. I searched her closet as well, but found nothing there either.

I closed my eyes and waited to hear or smell something from Kai, but came up empty. After searching through the rest of the rooms, I had nothing to show for it, and joined

Dimples in the living room. "You have any ideas of what the attacker was looking for?"

"No. The only thing that comes to mind would be building plans. Kai worked on them all the time. If he found something wrong on one of them, he may have made a copy and stashed it somewhere. The killer must have thought it could be here."

"That makes the most sense."

Ramos joined us. "Nothing's gone that I can see."

Dimples nodded. "Okay, thanks for looking." He glanced my way, thinking that it would be helpful if I let him know whether or not Ramos had taken anything while we were there. He and Mikiko must have had a relationship of some kind. Even if it was something personal that Ramos wouldn't want us to see, it might be helpful to the case.

I widened my eyes to give him the stare of death. Was he really asking me to spy on Ramos? He had the good sense to look away, knowing it didn't sit well with me. Still... he knew Ramos was a bad guy... and I shouldn't be so trusting.

I shook my head and held in a groan. Being in the middle of these two was pure torture. Maybe it was time to go home.

Ramos glanced at the coffee table lying upside down and picked it up, moving it into place. After setting it upright, he noticed something. "Her mail's gone. She always left it on the coffee table." His eyes sparked with excitement, and he caught my gaze. "We need to go to my house. I think I might have what they were looking for."

"What is it?" The sudden smell of eucalyptus and mint filled the air, and I knew Ramos was onto something.

"She asked me to get her mail the other day. We left for Budapest before I had a chance to give it to her, so it's still at my house."

With surging excitement, we followed him to his house. He took us around to the back entrance, and my mouth dropped open. The tall fence surrounding his back yard gave him total privacy, and the trees and garden, featuring a small stream, made it seem like I'd been transported into a different world.

The back of his house was more modern than the front. A set of French doors that came from the master bedroom opened directly onto a beautiful, wooden deck covered with green vines.

A stone path from the deck led to a stunning stone patio near the stream. The patio featured a lovely gas fireplace and comfortable furniture. Beside the furniture, the highlight of the patio was a ground-level Jacuzzi hot tub.

Sheesh... I thought the front of the house was nice, but this was amazing.

Ramos disarmed his security system before ushering us inside. After re-setting the code, he led us into the kitchen and dining room area. It was easy to see that a few walls had come down, leaving the space open and airy.

With a high beam ceiling and medium tone hardwood floors, the kitchen sported a farmhouse sink, light wood cabinets, a stone tile backsplash, stainless steel appliances, and white countertops. It fit the house and the man perfectly.

The kitchen table caught my attention, and I stepped closer to run my fingers over the wooden top. It had some kind of an epoxy finish covering the beautiful wooden surface, and the design was amazing. He'd made this? It must have taken a long time.

Ramos found Mikiko's mail on his kitchen counter and handed it to Dimples. Stuffed between the regular junk mail, a small, bubble-cushioned envelope had her name on it, with Kai's name in the return address.

I gasped. "That must be it. Open it."

Dimples hesitated. He was thinking the search warrant should cover it, but that meant he couldn't open it until he was back at the station.

"You're not going to open it?"

"I can't risk it. Once it's logged into evidence, we can open it and use whatever's inside to build the case. If we open it now, I won't be able to use it as evidence. I have to do this the right way to make it stick."

My shoulders drooped. "Really?" Disappointment washed over me. We'd come this far, and now he couldn't open the package? "Okay. At least tell us what it feels like."

He rubbed his thumb and fingers over the package. "It feels like a thumb-drive."

"That's got to be what the killer was looking for."

He nodded. "I agree. I've got to get this to the tech lab. I'll let you know what I find out."

"Okay."

He turned to Ramos. "Thanks man... this is the break we needed."

"Sure."

As Ramos disarmed his security system, Dimples hurried toward the door. I glanced at Ramos and panicked. As much as I wanted to see the rest of his house, I knew it was a bad idea. "Uh... I'd better go too. I'll see you tomorrow. Okay?"

Ramos shook his head, thinking I was a chicken, and I nodded. "You know it."

I waved before rushing out the door to catch up with Dimples. He paused to wait for me, pleased that I hadn't stayed. There was something going on between Ramos and me that was just asking for trouble, and he didn't want to see my life ruined.

"Thanks for your help, Shelby. I'll let you know what's going on tomorrow. Think you can help me?"

"Of course. I can't wait to find out what's on that thumb-drive. Be sure and call me once you know."

"I will." He crossed the street and hopped into his car. As he drove away, I glanced back at Ramos's house. I couldn't see if he watched from any of the windows, but I gave him a quick wave anyway... then, feeling more bold... I blew him a kiss. Chuckling, I jumped into my car and sped off.

With the jaunt to Ramos's house, this had taken much longer than I'd planned, but at least we'd made some progress. It still boggled my mind that Ramos's neighbor had turned out to be Kai's sister, and he'd been involved all along. Now it was just a matter of time before we found out what information was on the thumb-drive, and we could solve the case.

Still, I wouldn't find out anything until tomorrow, and my excitement cooled off, making my lack of sleep more evident. All at once, I couldn't wait to get home and sleep in my own bed. I pulled into the garage, and stepped into the kitchen. The beautiful bouquet of flowers greeted me, and I leaned over to smell them.

"I thought I heard you come in," Chris said, coming to my side.

"Yeah." I smiled up at him. "I'm back, and I'm not going anywhere else tonight."

"Good. You keep disappearing on me. So how did it go?"

"We found a clue that could break this case wide open."

"Nice."

"Yeah, you'll never believe this, but the neighbor who was helping Mikiko turned out to be Ramos."

His brows drew together. "What neighbor? I think I missed that part."

"You know... I think there's a lot you've missed. Why don't we get ready for bed, and I'll fill you in."

"You'll tell me everything?" He was thinking about the part Manetto was worried about.

"Maybe... it depends... how mad will you be?"

"Shelby..."

"Hey... I can't help it if things happen to me. You know that, right? I'm not trying to get into trouble."

He wasn't sure that was true, and my mouth dropped open. "What?"

"Maybe it's like a self-fulfilling prophecy?"

"No... that's not what you meant. Tell the truth. If you don't I'll just pick it up from your mind anyway."

He growled. "Never-mind. I don't want you to feel bad because of my thoughts."

My lips turned down. "You mean the ones where you're thinking I bring some of this on myself because I make stupid choices?"

"That's not fair." With his brows drawn together, he was thinking that he would never say that... out loud. And he loved me enough to know it wasn't always the case... just some of the time.

All the fight went out of me. "Okay... maybe you're right. But after I explain what happened, you'll see that this wasn't one of those times."

"Fine. Then tell me what happened."

Damn... I'd decided not to tell him I'd nearly been killed, but now I had no choice. Maybe I did bring this stuff on myself. "Uh... let's wait until the kids have gone to bed and we don't have to worry about getting interrupted."

He shook his head, knowing I was making excuses. "All right, but you're not getting out of this."

"I'm not trying to... geeze."

It didn't take near as long as I would have liked to have everything settled for the night. After saying goodnight to our kids, I got ready for bed and climbed under the covers.

Jet lag had caught up to me, and I could hardly keep my eyes open.

Chris climbed in beside me and I snuggled against him, hoping he'd give me a break and let me sleep. He was thinking, *here we go again... another night of not telling me anything.*

Guilt that he was right jolted me awake, and I sat up beside him. "Sorry... I'm just a little jet lagged. Let's see... why don't I start my story after we got to Budapest?"

"Sounds good to me."

I began with my visit to the restaurant Max's relatives owned, and moved on to finding out he was at the thermal pools. When I got to the part where I saw Max leave the outdoor pool and followed after him, Chris's eyes narrowed. Just thinking about how much trouble that choice probably got me into tightened his chest, and I couldn't finish.

"Go on," he said. I didn't respond right away, and he got even more suspicious. "Shelby... what happened?"

I shook my head, knowing I had to spill it. "He tried to kill me."

"What?"

"He took me by surprise. I didn't think he knew who I was, otherwise, it would have been fine."

"So what did he do?"

"I followed him into one of the other pools and he confronted me. I asked him where he'd hidden Uncle Joey's hard drive, and he tried to drown me. But, on the positive side, I heard where the hard drive is... so that's good."

Chris clenched his teeth so hard I thought they might fall out, so I told him the rest of the story as fast as I could. "Ramos saved me, and I had to go to the hospital, but they declared me fit as a fiddle, and we came home. While we were on our way home, Uncle Joey sent some people to Max's office to find the hard drive, but they couldn't find it.

I thought it was at his neighbor's office, but now I'm not sure if it's there or at his office."

I shook my head. "But either way, Uncle Joey's keeping an eye on both offices since they're right next to each other. When Max comes looking for the hard drive, Uncle Joey will catch him and get the hard drive, so it should all work out."

While Chris worked on loosening his clenched jaw, I pushed my point. "So... see? What happened was not because I made a stupid choice. Right?"

Chris closed his eyes. He knew I was mostly right, but what the hell? Sometimes being married to me was almost more than he could handle. Within the last week, I'd nearly been blown up at a warehouse, I'd flown to Las Vegas to meet with a crime lord who made Manetto look like an angel, and then I'd nearly been killed in a thermal pool while visiting Budapest. How was this happening? You couldn't make this stuff up.

Working hard to calm down, he let out a long breath and slid his arm around me to pull me close. Once the shock had worn off, he kissed the top of my head, thinking that it was a good thing I was so sexy and beautiful, otherwise, he'd have second thoughts about sticking around.

I jabbed my elbow into his ribs. "Right back at ya."

His answering chuckle warmed my heart. Then he pulled me beneath the covers, and I forgot about everything else.

The next morning, I woke refreshed and ready for the day. After Chris and the kids left, I took Coco on his morning walk. On our way home, my cell phone rang, and excitement bubbled inside me to hear from Dimples.

"Hey Shelby, you ready to come help me solve the case?"

"Yes! Did you see what was on the thumb drive?"

"Yeah, we did, but it's not as straightforward as I'd hoped. It looks like two different architectural plans of the stadium. I can't tell what's so special about them, but I called Kai's office and spoke with his co-worker, Tina Danson. She said she'd be happy to take a look at them for us."

"Sounds good. I'll be there as soon as I can."

I arrived exactly one hour later and hurried inside the police station. Dimples sat at his desk, and, catching sight of me, he jumped up with barely contained excitement. "Good. You're here... let's go."

As Dimples threw on his jacket, Clue spotted me and hurried over. "Shelby... do you have a minute?"

I glanced between her and Dimples. "Uh... we're just leaving, but I can spare a minute." I caught Dimples's gaze. "Is that okay?"

"Sure. I'll wait."

"Thanks," Clue said, hoping I had some information I could give her, since they'd hit a snag in the case. "We found a record of Max boarding a plane for Europe, so we know he left the country, but we don't know where he went."

"Yeah? You know... that makes sense now that I think of it. His last name is Huszar. I think it's Hungarian. Maybe he went to Budapest?"

Her eyes widened. "Oh... that's interesting." She wondered how I could be so specific about where he'd gone, even right down to the city.

Before she could think about checking it out, I continued. "But I have a feeling he might be coming back... or that he's already here. Maybe you should check with customs? They'd have a record of his arrival. If he's back, you might be able to track him down."

"Okay... that's a good idea. Thanks, Shelby."

"Of course." I wished I could do more, but right now, I needed to catch Kai's killer. I followed Dimples out, and we took his car to see Tina Danson at Pinnacle Engineering. "So there wasn't anything else on the thumb-drive? No clues or explanations from Kai?"

"I'm afraid not. We'll just have to see what Tina can tell us."

A few minutes later, we stepped into the office and asked to see Tina. She came to the front desk and greeted us with enthusiasm. "Come back to my desk and I'll take a look at those plans. How did you find them?"

We explained that they'd been mailed to Kai's sister, and we'd just discovered them. "Wow," Tina said. "Pretty cloak and dagger of him, right?"

"Yup," I agreed.

She took the thumb-drive and plugged it into her computer. "It looks like there are two files here." She opened them one at a time and split her screen to compare them. After studying them, she pointed out the differences.

"This file contains the plans for the stadium demolition. It has all the levels of the building with radius blast zones. You can see here..." she pointed to different places on the screen. "...are where the charges are set to bring it down."

She pulled up the other file. "This one looks like the stadium building plans from thirty years ago. They're roughly the same plans, but this one shows more details for the foundation. Wait a minute... there's another file here."

She clicked on a folder icon at the bottom of the page, and another set of plans popped up. This one showed something completely different, and we all leaned forward to see what it was.

"These are specs of an oil refinery. Look at that... it was built in eighteen-ninety, and the date here..." she pointed in the corner, "...is the year nineteen-seventy-one. This plan must be from seventy-one, and it shows all kinds of underground pipes and tanks."

She pressed on several keys until she manipulated the plans to lay the current demolition plans over the oil refinery plans. They matched up perfectly. "It looks like the stadium was built over the oil refinery."

"What does that mean?" I asked.

"It means Kai might have found out that all that stuff under the stadium was never cleaned up. I've seen things like that before. If the pipes and tanks were never removed, they'd pose a threat to the workers, especially if the stadium comes down. All that toxic chemical waste could be released into the air. Most of those old pipes were covered in asbestos, and, back in the day, a lot of the waste was routinely dumped into the soil."

"If that's the case, how did they get the permits from the city for the demolition?" I asked.

Tina shrugged. "It happens. If the tailings were covered up for this long, they might not think it's a problem. But, more than that... it would cost millions to clean it up, much more than a new stadium is worth. They probably figured it was best to let it slide."

"Yeah," Dimples agreed. "Until Kai threatened to go public with it."

"We need to talk to Steve Mosely," I said. "He's got to know what's going on. He might be part of the cover-up."

"Thanks, Tina," Dimples said.

"Sure." She closed down the files and disconnected the thumb-drive before handing it back to Dimples. "I hope you get it figured out."

We thanked her and headed out of the building. A few minutes later, we stood in the lobby of MRP Capital Development. Dimples flashed his badge. "We need to speak with Steve Mosely."

The receptionist typed in his name and shook her head. "He's not here. It looks like he's out of the office until two o'clock."

"Do you know where he is?"

She glanced at her screen and nodded. "Yeah... with just about everyone else. They're at the demolition site."

My stomach tightened. "What do you mean?"

"The old stadium's coming down in an hour and ten minutes."

Dimples swore under his breath and pulled me to the exit. "We've got to stop it."

"How?"

As we continued to the car, he shook his head. "I don't know. If I can get a judge to look at the thumb-drive, I might be able to get a court order. But getting it in time will be the hard part." He'd gotten search warrants in a short amount time, but this was different.

"Let's just go over there and tell Mosely about the thumb-drive. He's got to know something about it. If we threaten to go public with it, he could end up in jail, and his company could lose millions. That should motivate him to pull the plug."

Dimples let out a breath and nodded. "Sure. Let's try it."

On the drive over there, my phone rang. The caller ID said it was Justin, so I quickly answered. "Hello."

"Hey Sis, I was just wondering how things went in Budapest. Did you find Max and get the hard drive back?"

"Oh... well... we found Max, but he got away before we could catch him."

"Really? Dammit! That sucks."

"Yeah... but I got a lead on the hard drive. Get this... he left it here, so he hasn't taken the crypto yet. We're hoping to find the hard drive before he does, but that's been a bit of a problem."

"What do you mean? Where do you think it is?"

I sighed. "We know it's in his office building, we just don't know exactly where he stashed it. But don't worry, Uncle Joey's got people watching the place. When Max shows up, we'll..." I glanced at Dimples, realizing he was listening to the whole thing. "Uh... get it back."

"So what you're saying is... you've searched his office and you haven't found it?"

"Yeah... basically." I didn't want to go into the details with Dimples sitting there.

"Okay." He sighed. "Well... Chris has the paperwork ready for my signature, so I'm just getting ready to board the plane to meet with him and my new partner. I should be there in a couple of hours. My appointment's at three. Maybe I can help you look for the hard drive after we're done?"

"Yeah. Why don't you call me then, and we'll work things out."

"Sounds good. Talk to you then."

I slipped my phone back into my purse and caught Dimples's thoughts about my trip to Budapest. He'd wondered if it was about finding Max and the cryptocurrency he'd stolen. Too bad Max had gotten away. But it sounded like he'd be coming back here. If Manetto got his hands on Max, would Max end up dead? If they found Max's body somewhere, he'd know it was Manetto, and it gave him a sour taste in his mouth.

I let out a breath. "I'll do my best to make sure that doesn't happen, but I can't promise anything."

"I know." He knew my power was limited when it came to stopping a mob boss, even if he treated me like part of the family. "I just wish you weren't so involved with him. When stuff like this goes down, it puts you in danger with the law." He shook his head. "Especially with the ongoing investigation into Landon's murder at the warehouse. Max is a suspect based on your eyewitness account. If he ends up dead, it will look bad for you."

He was thinking it might be the tie they needed to bind me to Manetto. He had no doubt they'd want me to turn on Manetto in some kind of a sting operation, so they could send him to jail where he belonged.

It was bound to put me in a tough spot, and if I refused, I might have to quit helping the police all together. He'd hate that, but it might be for the best. Still, it would put a target on my back, and the police wouldn't forget that I'd let them down. Even worse, I could end up in jail too, and he hated the possibility that it could happen.

"Let's just hope it never comes to that, okay?" I knew how it sounded, and his negativity wasn't helpful. "Besides, we've got bigger fish to fry right now."

"That's true." He glanced my way and managed to smile. "And you're the best partner for the job."

I smiled back. "That's right."

A few minutes later, we arrived at the stadium lot. Balloons and big banners were strewn across the chain-link fence, and we pulled into the lot designated for the media and special guests.

It looked like all the people involved in the company, along with their families, were arriving, including the mayor and his staff. Several news outlets had also taken up prominent positions to record the event, and my stomach tightened. This was not going to go well.

"Let's see if we can find Steve Mosely," Dimples said, stepping toward the crowd.

We split up and began our search. I recognized a few people from the MRP office and asked if they'd seen him. All of them said he had to be around somewhere, but no one had seen him for a while.

People were still arriving, so I hurried to the side of the area that had been roped off for spectators and walked slowly toward the platform, hoping to spot him. I took my time, but couldn't find him anywhere.

Nearing the platform, I noticed both the mayor and Al Clawson talking beside the podium with several other dignitaries. Steve wasn't among them, but maybe Al would know where he was, especially if he'd sent him off on an errand.

After pausing to bolster my courage, I took a step toward them, but someone grabbed my arm and pulled me back.

"What are you doing here?" The attorney, Chad Finlay, held my arm in a tight grip.

I met his gaze and jerked my arm from his grasp. "I'm looking for Steve Mosely. Have you seen him?"

He huffed out a breath before taking a look around. "No... I haven't. He should be here somewhere."

My lips twisted. "That's what everyone says, but I can't find him anywhere."

His gaze flicked over me and he smirked. "What do you want him for?"

"Do you know who killed Kai?"

His brows rose. "Of course not. I don't even know who the guy is."

He was telling me the truth, and I sighed. "Fine... but I need to talk to the president of your company. There's something he needs to know."

"Mr. Clawson?" He shook his head. "I don't think so." He grabbed my arm and tugged me away. "I think you need to leave."

"Let go of me." I tried to pull away from him, but his hold was too strong, and he began to drag me toward the outside edge of the crowd. At that point my Aikido training kicked in, and, instead of fighting his pull, I moved with him. Raising my elbow loosened his hold, and I twisted toward him. With my next step, I shoved his chin up with my palm, pushing his head back and throwing him to the ground.

People scattered and gasped. Standing across from me, Dimples had seen the whole thing and he was thinking, *you don't mess with Shelby Nichols.* That brought a smile to my face, until Chad growled and surged to his feet.

Dimples rushed to my side and gave Chad a steely-eyed stare, his body tense and ready to cuff him if he tried to come after me.

Humiliated, Chad straightened his suit coat and smoothed his angry face into one of mild boredom. He didn't want me bothering the big boss, so he stalked off, deciding to get Braxton to keep an eye on me.

"Did he threaten you?"

I met Dimples's gaze. "He was trying to make me leave before I spoke with the big boss. What time is it?"

"Twelve-fifteen. We haven't got much time, and there's no sign of Mosely anywhere."

"I think it's too late for that... you need to stop the demolition. Is there time to get a court order from a judge, or do you think the mayor will listen to you?"

He shook his head. "There's not enough time for a court order unless I get Bates to help. He might get to a judge in time. Let me call him."

It took an extra five minutes to explain what was on the thumb-drive to Bates so he could begin the process. "Okay," Dimples said, disconnecting the call. "He's on it, but I think I need to talk to the mayor."

"I think you do too. I'll keep looking for Mosely while you do that."

Dimples sent me a nod of thanks before straightening his suit coat. Ready, he pushed through the crowd to reach the mayor, who had moved to stand on top of a wooden platform next to the podium with Al Clawson and a few others by his side.

A man with the security detail stopped him, so Dimples brought out his badge and explained that he needed to speak with the mayor about a threat. That got the agent's attention and he told Dimples to wait while he cleared it with the mayor.

While Dimples waited, I searched the crowd another time for Mosely, knowing something must have happened to him. As the project manager, there was no way he'd miss this.

Maybe Eli Walker would know where Mosely had gone. Before I could look for him, a familiar face caught my attention. As our gazes met, his undisguised irritation sent a chill down my spine. Chad must have found the head of security for MRP Capital and sent him in my direction. Braxton quickly strode to my side, stopping my departure, so I went on the defense.

"I'm surprised you're not standing on the podium with your boss. Aren't you head of security for the company?"

His gaze flicked from me to the stand. "The mayor's got enough security to cover it." He spotted Dimples and frowned. "What's he doing up there?"

"You mean my partner? He's hoping to stop the demolition. Did you know the stadium was built over an old oil refinery that was never cleaned up?"

He straightened. How did I know about that? "What?"

"Yeah. Apparently, it poses a risk to the environment. Now that your boss owns it, I guess he'll have to clean it up. It's going to cost him millions."

He was thinking that I must have found Kai's evidence, but how? He'd looked for it everywhere and had come up empty-handed. He'd thought with Mosely out of the way, this problem would end, but not if we managed to stop the demolition.

"Where's Mosely anyway? Shouldn't he be here?"

He blinked, not expecting that question. "What makes you think I know?"

Listening intently, I caught exactly where Braxton had left him, and my blood went cold. Not only had Braxton killed Kai, but he'd managed to leave Mosely in the stadium to die when it came down.

"Excuse me, folks," the mayor said, speaking into the microphone. "Sorry for the interruption, but due to extenuating circumstances, we're postponing the demolition for an hour."

The crowd began to grumble, and the mayor lifted his arms to silence them. "Something's come to my attention, but I hope to resolve it as soon as possible. For now, please be patient."

Braxton forgot about me and pushed his way through the crowd toward the stand, hoping to convince Al Clawson to continue the demolition as planned. Dimples stayed near the mayor, and I picked up that he'd told the mayor about the oil refinery and the hazardous waste it contained.

The mayor hadn't been completely swayed. This deal was highly lucrative, and all the permits had been met, so he hated to stop it. But if he was wrong, the repercussions concerned him enough to halt the demolition for an hour to gather more information on the problem.

With all of that going on, I knew it was up to me to find Steve Mosely. Steve must have figured things out, and Braxton had decided that blowing him up in the demolition was a good way to get rid of him.

I turned my attention to the crowd, hoping to spot Eli Walker. Finding him on the other side of the yellow tape, I hurried in his direction. He wore an orange vest and white hard hat, and he stood beside a small platform of equipment.

Slipping under the tape, I hurried to his side before someone could stop me. "Hey Eli... I need your help. Steve Mosely is missing, and I know where he is."

"Oh yeah? Where?"

"Someone left him tied up inside the stadium."

Chapter 15

"What? That's not possible."

"Yes it is. The head of security for MRP Capital tied him up and left him there."

"Why?"

I shook my head. "I don't know everything, but I know it has something to do with Kai's death."

"You're sure he's in there?"

"Yes."

He huffed out a breath. "Well shit. We can't go in there now. Everything's cleared for demolition."

"But you heard the mayor. They've postponed it."

"That place is a maze. It would take hours to find him. There's not enough time unless they call it off."

"They might call it off if they know Mosely's still in there." I glanced toward the stand, relieved that Braxton wasn't there. "Why don't you tell Al Clawson that Mosely's inside the stadium, and I'll start looking for him. I know he's somewhere on the lowest level... and there's a bunch of pipes in the room."

Eli thought there were several areas with pipes, but the main room was in the middle of the stadium on the lowest floor. "I'll tell him, but I'm going with you. Wait here for me."

He made his way onto the platform and pulled Al aside, pointing my way and telling him that Mosely was tied up somewhere inside the stadium. Al asked him how he knew that, and Eli pointed at me, telling him that I'd figured it out.

Al frowned, shaking his head and wondering if this was a plot to shut him down. Had Manetto put me up to it? Eli spoke again, telling him it had something to do with his head of security.

Al's eyes widened in shock. Braxton? Was that why he'd wanted Al to push so hard for the demolition to go forward? What had Braxton done? First Kai, and now this? He glanced my way, wondering how much I knew. It was uncanny, almost like I had a sixth sense about things even he didn't know.

Heaving a sigh, he nodded and stepped toward the mayor, hoping to salvage as much of this as he could.

Eli joined me. "He said he'd put everything on hold until he heard from me. Are you sure you know where Mosely is?"

I nodded. "Yeah... pretty sure."

"Okay. Let's go."

Eli told his foreman that he was headed back in for a missing person and to make sure the detonation device was secure. "And Kurt... whatever you do, don't let anyone near it. I'll keep in touch with the two-way radio. Let me know what's going on up here, okay?"

"Sure boss," Kurt nodded. "And you keep me posted as well."

"I will."

We hurried toward the stadium. The distance was a lot further than it looked, and several minutes passed before we made it to the entrance. Inside the outer ring of the stadium, the outside sunlight that came through was minimal, leaving us to search in semi-darkness.

Eli led the way to the main staircase and pulled the door open. He flipped the light switch before remembering that the power had been cut. Reaching up to his hard hat, he flicked on the light before letting the door close behind us.

Luckily, I had my trusty stun-flashlight in my purse, and I pulled it out, grateful to have my own light. Eli started down the stairs, and I followed. There were a lot more levels than I expected before we hit the bottom floor. The cold and damp sent chills down my spine, but that was nothing compared to seeing all the charges around the pillars holding up the massive concrete stadium.

The blinking red lights on each charge of C4 were like red beacons in the dark, reminding me that this whole place could go up at any moment. My heart raced, and regret that I'd ever agreed to come down here, stole the strength from my legs.

At the bottom, Eli led me into a corridor with pipes running along the length as far as our lights could reach. We followed it for a while, before Eli turned down another hallway and we entered a large furnace-type room.

In the dark, with the massive concrete structure looming above my head, fear reached into my heart, and I suddenly wanted to get out of there.

"Let's spread out," Eli said. "You go to the left, and I'll go to the right."

Swallowing my dread, I did a quick search, but something about this place wasn't right. In Braxton's mind, Steve Mosely was stuffed behind a pipe in a smaller space. The pipes here were too exposed.

"I don't see him," Eli said, coming to my side. "Are you sure this is the right place?"

"Not anymore. He's by some pipes, but the space is smaller. Do you have any ideas where that could be?"

Eli shook his head, thinking this level was a maze of pipes, and finding the right one would take hours. We'd have to start at one end of the stadium and search through every single corridor until we came to the other end.

Even with a lot of people searching, it would take hours. "I'm calling it in." He pushed on the radio and spoke to his foreman, telling him we needed more time and men to do a thorough search. The foreman told him he'd let the big boss know and get back to us.

Eli slipped the radio into a pouch on his vest and glanced my way, thinking this job was jinxed. First Kai and now Mosely. What was going on? Before he could ask me, his radio crackled, and he took it out.

"Yeah?"

"Boss, you need to come back. They're telling me they're going ahead with the demolition."

"What? They can't do that. We haven't found the guy yet."

"They're saying they found him. So you need to get out of there."

Eli pursed his lips, thinking something wasn't right. "Fine. But something's going on, and I don't like it. Pull the plug on the detonation device. I don't want anyone near it."

"You got it."

"Thanks. See you soon."

I followed him out of the room and back to the corridor, shocked that they were going ahead with the demolition. What had changed? Maybe Braxton or Al had told them they'd found Steve?

Letting out a cleansing breath, I stopped and closed my eyes. If Mosely was down here, I should be able to pick up his thoughts. Ahead of me, Eli stopped and glanced back. "What are you doing?"

"I know this might sound strange, but I think Mosely might still be down here. Do you mind if I call his name... just in case?"

"That would mean they're lying about finding him. Why would they do that?"

"You already said this job was jinxed. Something's going on, and I just want to double-check. It won't hurt to call his name."

Eli's lips turned down. He'd thought the job was jinxed, but he'd never say that out loud, because that would jinx it. Now I'd jinxed it anyway. "Uh... fine. Go ahead."

I nodded. "Steve! Steve! Can you hear me? We're looking for you. Where are you?"

Thick silence answered us. Then I heard it... *help... help me.*

"Where are you?"

I'm not sure.

"Is it dark?"

I'm behind a big pipe, but that's all I know.

"Okay... we'll keep looking. I'm using a flashlight. Let me know if you see a light."

I will. Please don't leave me here.

"We're coming."

I glanced at Eli. "Steve's down here and he can't be too far. He's behind a pipe of some kind. Are there any small rooms off this corridor?"

Eli's mouth opened, and his eyes widened. "What are you talking about? I didn't hear anything."

Oops. "I'm a psychic... sometimes I can hear things. Just go with it, okay?"

"But we need to get out of here."

I started walking down the corridor in the opposite direction of the way we'd come in. Either Eli would follow me or not. I held my breath and soon felt his presence behind me. The corridor seemed to stretch on forever, with no rooms that branched off. Was I going the wrong way? "Steve? Can you still hear me?"

I listened real close, but heard no response. "We must have passed him. Let's go back."

Eli shook his head and we turned around. As we came to the place I'd first heard Steve, Eli's radio crackled on. "Boss? You there?"

"Yeah. We're here. What's going on?"

"Some guy got to the detonation button. Luckily, I'd disarmed it, or the whole stadium would have come down."

"Shit. Did you catch him?"

"Sorry... no. He got away. He was wearing a vest and a hard hat, so we didn't notice him right away. A bunch of guys are looking for him now. Are you just about out? I'm getting a little nervous here."

Eli took his time to answer. "Yes... we'll be there soon." He thumbed off the radio and caught my gaze. "We've got to go."

"Yeah. You're right." Hearing that someone had tried to blow us up sent shock waves down my spine. What the heck was going on out there?

I swallowed. "Let me try Steve again. Steve? Can you hear me now?"

Yes. I thought you were coming.

"We are... will you keep talking? I think I lost you before."

Uh... sure.

He went silent, so I prodded him. "Tell me about your favorite vacation."

Okay... it was the time we took our family to...

I tuned out his story and just listened to his voice, unsure if this would even work. I knew I could only hear thoughts when I wasn't too far away, so if he started to cut out again, at least I'd know I'd gone too far. Still, it felt like I was on the wrong side of the wall or something.

His voice started to fade, so I turned back around. "Is there a parallel corridor around here somewhere? I feel like we're missing something."

Eli shook his head. "I don't know." He turned his head so his light shone on the ceiling, but there weren't any gaps that he could see. I kept walking, and Steve's voice came back into range. I took my time, studying the pipes as we passed. The sudden smell of eucalyptus halted me in my tracks, and I turned to study the lower two-foot-round pipe.

There was just enough room to crawl between that pipe and the one above. The wall behind this area seemed darker, and I pointed my flashlight between the pipes.

Is that you?

"Can you see my flashlight?"

Yes. Oh God. I see it. Please get me out of here.

"We're coming." I glanced at Eli. "He's in there. Will you help me get him out?"

Eli shivered, spooked that I'd actually found him. "Sure."

"I'll go first." I slipped between the pipes and crawled into the opening. The space was only about five feet high and twenty feet in width. I shone my flashlight, and the beam played over a body lying in the corner. While Eli came in behind me, I hurried to Steve, finding him completely immobilized with duct tape.

I pulled the piece covering his mouth off first, and he gasped in a couple of deep breaths. "You're... that detective, right?"

"Yeah... Shelby Nichols. How long have you been down here?"

"Since early this morning." Tears oozed out of his eyes, and he worked hard to keep them back. "It was Braxton. I overheard him telling Al that he'd killed Kai to shut him up. I didn't think Braxton knew I'd overheard him until we were down here checking the site. He used a Taser on me, and I woke up in here."

I nodded, noticing the blood from a cut across his brow where he must have hit his head. Eli pulled out a knife and began cutting through the tape. It took us several minutes to get Steve loose and help him out of the hole.

He moved stiffly, and it took him a few steps before he could continue without trouble. We came to the furnace room, and relief washed over me to be heading out. From here, it wasn't far to the end of the corridor.

Eli's headlamp died, and we all froze. Eli swore and turned to me. "I guess you need to go first."

"Sure." I stepped in front of him, and a sudden urgency to leave washed over me. "Let's move faster."

Leading the way, I began to jog. For someone who'd been tied up most of the day, Steve managed to keep up. As we came out of the corridor, Eli pointed the way to the staircase door. Pulling it open, we all filed in and started up the stairs.

The complete darkness reminded me of the damp cave I'd been stranded in, and panic tightened my chest. As we passed each level, I flashed my beam of light on the numbers to give me courage. By the time we reached the ground level, I was breathless, but we'd almost made it out, and my fear began to recede. Eli pulled the door open, and we stepped into the semi-darkness of the ground level.

"This way," Eli said, taking the lead into the main thoroughfare of the stadium. We could see well enough without my flashlight, so I switched it off and put it back in my purse.

As we walked, Eli took out his radio and thumbed it on. "Kurt it's Eli, we found the missing man and we're coming out." He waited a few seconds before repeating the message, but got no response. "Kurt, what's going on out there?"

"Eli," Kurt finally answered. "Are you coming out?"

"Yes, we found the missing person, and we've just come out of the staircase."

"I suggest you hurry. Things are crazy out here."

"We're on our way."

Eli picked up the pace, and we followed behind. The walk seemed to take forever, but we finally saw the stadium entrance ahead of us, with the outside sunshine a welcome sight. Just before reaching it, a man stepped into view. With the sunlight streaming in behind him, we couldn't make out his face, but the menace of his thoughts sent a chill down my spine.

"That's far enough," Braxton said, aiming his gun in our direction. "Put the radio on the ground and kick it to me."

Still holding the radio, Eli flipped it on, but he didn't want to let it go without a fight. "What's this about?"

Braxton pulled the trigger, sending a bullet into a concrete pillar beside us. We all ducked, and Eli held his hands up. "Stop! You might hit an explosive!"

"I'm shooting you next. So set the radio down on the ground. Now!"

With shaking fingers, Eli slowly lowered it to the ground. "Why do you want the radio? Are you planning to kill us?"

"Shut up, and kick it to me."

Eli did as he was told, kicking it hard enough that it went past Braxton. Scowling, Braxton stepped toward the radio to pick it up. He was thinking that after we were dead, he'd give them the all-clear to go ahead with the detonation. It was the only way out of this mess. If they refused to detonate, he'd head out the back way and use a bullet to trigger the C4. There wouldn't be enough of our bodies left for anyone to figure out that we'd been killed before the blast, and his secret would die with us.

Now he just had to shoot us.

"Run!" I yelled.

The first shot went off, and Steve yelped before falling to the ground. I dove to the side as another shot sounded. I crawled on my hands and knees before lurching to my feet. I took a few steps before Braxton caught up to me, and shoved me against the wall.

Hitting it with my shoulder and arm, I cried out in pain and slid to the ground.

Braxton stepped back and aimed his gun at me. He hesitated, taking in my frightened, pleading eyes. Shaking his head, he licked his lips, and cursed me and this stupid job.

"Police! Drop it."

Braxton froze, shocked that the police had gotten here so fast. Had someone followed him? He couldn't get caught, but there might still be a chance. Slowly turning toward Dimples, he raised his arms, still holding the gun in his hand.

"Put the gun on the ground. Now!"

With his jaw clenched, he slowly lowered his gun to the ground. As Dimples started toward him, he turned and ran. Dimples took off after him, and caught up, managing to tackle him to the ground.

Braxton kicked at Dimples and got free. Jumping to his feet, he tried to get away, but Dimples rose as well, and threw a punch at Braxton's head, connecting with his chin. Braxton stumbled back but managed to stay on his feet. He faced Dimples, ready to fight.

A low growl came from Dimples, and I picked up his desire to beat Braxton to a bloody pulp. They clashed together, throwing punches and taking hits. Braxton clipped Dimples in the temple. Dimples shook it off and began sending quick one-two punches into Braxton's stomach.

With Braxton doubled over, Dimples sent a hard uppercut into his jaw, and Braxton went down. Before he could get up, Dimples snapped his cuffs onto Braxton's wrists and told him it was over.

Rubbing my sore shoulder, I managed to get my feet under me and stepped toward the others. More people had arrived, including Detective Bates and several police officers. Paramedics, who'd been on stand-by for the demolition, rushed to Steve's prone form, and I hurried to his side.

Blood oozed from his right upper chest, and the paramedics took out a gauze pad to stanch the bleeding. As they applied pressure to the wound, he let out a groan. After slipping an oxygen mask over his face, they moved him onto a gurney.

Before he was taken away, his eyes fluttered open and he focused on me, thinking that I'd saved him. Somehow I'd heard him down there in the dark, even though he'd only spoken in his mind.

"Hang in there Steve. You can get through this."

He was thinking that he'd do his best, so I nodded and smiled. "You'd better."

As they carted him away, he was thinking that maybe I was his guardian angel. *A real live guardian angel. How about that?*

Eli caught sight of me and hurried over. "Are you okay?"

I moved my shoulder, amazed that it still worked. "I think so. I'm going to have a big bruise though. How about you?"

He nodded, thinking that was close, and he might be dead if Braxton had gone after him instead of me. He felt bad for Mosely, especially after he'd been tied up all day. Losing all that blood couldn't be good, either.

"I think he'll be okay. He was hit closer to his shoulder, and they got to him pretty quick. He should pull through."

"Oh... yeah... good." Eli studied me, thinking there was definitely something to my psychic powers.

"Good move turning on the radio. That must have been what brought the police to help us."

He nodded, thinking that facing Braxton was the scariest thing he'd ever been through.

Bates and two police officers escorted Braxton out of the stadium, and Dimples came to my side. I gave him a one-armed hug, grateful he'd saved me. He held me tight, thinking I'd taken ten years off his life, and he didn't know if he could ever forgive me.

He pulled away to look me over. "Are you okay? I saw him throw you into the wall."

I moved my shoulder again, finding it a little sore, but nothing serious. "I think it's just bruised. I'm sure glad you showed up, though. That was too close. What happened out there? We kept getting weird messages from Eli's foreman."

He motioned toward the exit, eager to leave the stadium behind and hoping to get a paramedic to look at my arm. He didn't like the way I was cradling it against my chest.

"It's not serious, I promise."

Letting out a huff, he wrapped his arm around my waist to steady me, and we began the trek back to the staging area. Wanting to hear what happened, Eli walked with us, and we followed the remaining officers into the sunlight.

Dimples shook his head. "I think it was after you both left that Braxton pulled Al away to talk to him. I couldn't hear what they said, but Al came back pretty upset. Al went to the mayor, and I could have sworn he was threatening him. The mayor spoke to a few of his people before telling your guys to re-start the countdown."

He motioned to Eli. "Your men protested that you'd gone into the stadium to find a missing person. That stopped him, but after speaking to Al again, he told them it was a misunderstanding, and the missing person had been found."

"Yeah," Eli said. "I believed them. But Shelby didn't. She called Steve's name a few times and then said she could hear him. It was strange because I couldn't hear a thing, and it was quiet down there. I should have heard him, too."

Eli stared at me, waiting for a response. I shrugged. "I told you down there that I'm a psychic. It means that sometimes I hear things that others don't. I can't explain it, but it happens to me a lot. I would appreciate it if you didn't tell anyone about it though. Would you mind?"

Eli's mouth opened and closed a few times before he shook his head. "I guess." He shrugged. "Who would believe me anyway?"

I nodded and smiled. "You got that right."

He wasn't satisfied with my answer, mostly because he wanted to know more. Before he could ask me if I'd always been that way, I turned to Dimples. "So what happened after that?"

"I guess Braxton got his hands on a vest and hard hat. He made it past your workers and pushed the detonation button. Your guy... Kurt, came unglued. He started yelling at Braxton and shoved him away." He shook his head. "Somehow Braxton disappeared into the crowd."

I glanced at Eli. "I'm sure glad you told Kurt to disable the button."

"No kidding. I hadn't realized it was such a close call."

Dimples nodded. "Right after that, Bates showed up with the order from the judge to stop the demolition. After the mayor announced the postponement, the crowd got a little angry, but, with the extra police officers Bates brought, they calmed down pretty fast."

He glanced my way, thinking that I'd forgotten to tell him I was heading inside the stadium to look for Steve. He hadn't known I was inside until Eli's foreman had told him. Right after that, Braxton had tried to detonate the charges. He'd just about fainted right then and there. When nothing happened, he'd never been so relieved in his life.

He caught my gaze and thought, *don't ever scare me like that again.*

I smiled back at him and nodded. I would have answered out loud, but Eli was right there, and I was done explaining my ability.

Dimples glanced at Eli. "We heard Braxton threaten you over the radio. That's when we knew you were in trouble, especially after the gunshots."

He'd run the long distance at full speed and had barely managed to stop Braxton from shooting me. Shaking his head, he flexed his swollen knuckles, thinking it was satisfying to let loose on the bastard.

With all the excitement, the crowd of people were still there, including a couple of TV crews. One reporter stood in front of a camera, and the cameraman caught Bates and the other officer leading Braxton away.

Luckily, we were far enough from the attention that we avoided getting caught in the spotlight. Dimples debated dragging me to the paramedics and insisting that I go with them, but, with Steve already inside, it was too late.

"I'm okay. If it gets worse, I'll go to the doctor."

"Drew! Shelby!" Billie Jo stood next to the barricade and waved at us. She was Dimples's wife, but also a reporter for the newspaper. "Are you guys okay? What happened in there?"

This was a tough spot for Dimples, since he was a detective and not allowed to speak to the press unless given the go-ahead by the chief. But Billie was his wife, so he had to tell her something.

"Officially, I have no comment because it's an ongoing investigation. Unofficially, we're both fine and... that's all I can say." Dimples shrugged. "But I'll tell you more when I can. How's that?"

She sighed and looked at me, hoping I'd be more forthcoming. "We found some old records about an oil refinery that was built here. It doesn't look like the mess was cleaned up before the stadium was built on top of it. Now, with it coming down, it's a huge problem, with all kinds of environmental risks. You might want to look into that angle."

She grinned. "Thanks Shelby. You're the best." Leaning over the barricade, she gave Dimples a kiss. "See you at home." With a wave, she quickly left.

A police officer caught Dimples's attention, and Dimples left to talk to him. I picked up that this had become a crime scene, and Dimples might be here for a while.

My phone began to ring, and I pulled it out of my purse. "Hey, honey."

"Shelby? Are you okay? I just saw you on the news. It looked like you were coming out of the stadium. They're saying there was a gunman who tried to kill some people. What happened?"

While giving him the short version, I wandered over to a concrete barricade and sat down. A few minutes later, I finished my story. "We found Steve, and Dimples arrested Braxton, so it all turned out okay."

"Good. I'm glad you're all right. You looked a little rough on TV, so I was worried."

"Rough?"

"Yeah... and Harris had his arm around you like you were hurt. Did you get hurt?"

"Oh... my shoulder is bruised, but other than that, I'm fine."

He sighed. "Okay. I've got to go, but you can fill me in later. Did I tell you I was meeting with Justin today?"

"No, but he called to ask about Budapest and told me he was flying in."

"Oh good. He should be here soon, so I'll see you in a bit. Love you."

"Love you too."

During our conversation, my phone had buzzed with two other calls, but I'd let them go to voicemail. Checking them, I found one was from Ramos and the other from Uncle Joey. Naturally, I called Ramos first.

"Babe. Are you okay?"

"Yeah. My shoulder hurts, but other than that, I'm good."

"I saw the news." His voice held an edge I didn't like hearing. "I'm a little disappointed you went to the stadium without me."

"Oh... well... after we found out what was on the thumb-drive, we tried to talk to Steve Mosely, but he was here at the stadium, so we had to hurry over and stop the demolition before it blew up and contaminated everything with toxic chemicals."

"Hmmm."

"Hey... it looks like Dimples is going to be here for a while. Can you come and get me?"

"On the bike?"

"Yes."

"I'll be there in a minute."

He disconnected, and I let out a big sigh. Next, I sent a text to Uncle Joey that Ramos was picking me up, and I'd be there soon. I hoped a text was good enough for now, because I just didn't want to go into all the details again. That way I'd only have to tell the story once and hope they didn't get too mad at me.

I sat for a few more minutes, watching Dimples organize the scene and talk things over with Eli. They had to figure out what to do with the explosives that were planted all over the stadium and go through all the red tape that shutting down the demolition required.

Grateful I didn't have to deal with that, I slowly stood, feeling twinges of pain in my hips, back and legs. I gritted my teeth and took a few steps, managing to make it all the way over to Dimples without too much trouble.

"Hey... I'm going to take off. I hope that's okay."

"Oh... of course. I'm sorry I can't leave yet, but I can have one of my officers take you back to the station. "

I waved him off. "It's fine. I've got a ride."

His brows rose. "You do?"

"Yup. Let me know if you need anything." He wondered who I'd called, so I played on his sympathy. "I'm going home to put some ice on my shoulder, and maybe soak in the tub."

"That's a good idea."

We all heard the motorcycle before we saw it, and everyone watched as Ramos pulled up on his Harley. Dimples's sympathy went out the window, but several members of Eli's crew, and even a few police officers, watched Ramos arrive with undisguised admiration.

Ramos handed me my helmet, and I slipped it on my head, snapping the strap under my chin like an expert. With Dimples watching, I couldn't crawl onto the bike, but I wasn't sure I could throw my leg over it either.

Ramos held out his arm to steady me, and I grabbed it while stepping onto the back peg. Standing up a little higher, it was easy to swing my leg over the seat and settle down behind him. Grateful I'd made it onto the bike, I gave Dimples and the rest of the crew a quick wave before pulling down the dark visor and wrapping my good arm around Ramos's middle.

With my injured arm, I grabbed onto the side of his jacket and hoped a one-armed hold would be enough to keep me from falling off. In one fluid motion, Ramos eased the bike away from the parking lot, and I relaxed into my seat. As the stadium receded behind us, the knot in my stomach finally loosened, and I could breathe again.

Chapter 16

Ramos took the side streets from the stadium to Thrasher, giving me a little more time on the bike. Still, it didn't seem like enough. I could have ridden all day, and it still wouldn't be enough. But maybe that was okay, since it gave me something to look forward to when my arm didn't throb.

We pulled into the parking garage behind the pillar by the elevator. Ramos held out his arm so I could hold onto him and get off without falling. I managed to swing my leg around and step away with only a slight wobble. Go me.

I unfastened my helmet and pulled it off my head to hand it over. He stashed it in the trunk of his car and glanced my way, raising a brow. "You might want to fix your hair before you see Manetto." He was thinking it was poking up in a few places, and there was a smudge of dirt on my chin he wanted to rub off.

I automatically brushed at my chin and ran my fingers through my hair, finding a few knots here and there. "Is that better?"

His eyes twinkled, and he raised his hand to my face and rubbed the dirt off my chin with his thumb. I did my best not to lean into his touch, or moan, or close my eyes. I must have failed at one of them because he dropped his hand and wrapped his arms around me in a soft embrace, like he thought I might break.

I rested my cheek against his chest and inhaled his woodsy scent before pulling away. I smiled up at him. "Thanks. That was just what I needed."

He pursed his lips. "You're welcome." He hadn't meant to be so nice to me since he was mad that I'd gotten myself into trouble again. Only this time he hadn't been there to save me. That meant that I was using up my nine lives way too fast. At this rate, I probably only had one or two left, and that was unacceptable.

His declaration softened my heart, and my tiny grin stayed in place until we walked into Uncle Joey's office. His frosty stare would have frozen me in place a year ago, but now I knew it was only there because he cared about me.

"What the hell, Shelby?" He frowned, realizing he'd said that a lot lately. "I just got a phone call from Al. He accused me of ruining him. Is that true?"

I nodded. "If he's talking about me, it's definitely a possibility. You didn't invest in the stadium project, did you?" I took my regular seat in front of Uncle Joey's desk and sank onto it with a sigh.

"No. You never told me it was all right, and we've been a little busy around here."

"That's good, because I'm pretty sure that whole deal is going down the drain. There was an old oil refinery on that site, and the stadium was built on top of it without cleaning it up. Once that stadium comes down, cleaning up the site will cost millions."

Uncle Joey's eyes narrowed, and he nodded. "The city gave Al the permits, so he doesn't bear all the responsibility, but this whole fiasco will uncover a host of dirty business dealings."

I nodded. "I think it might involve the mayor too. At least it looked like Al was threatening him, and he was actually going along with it for a while."

"That's too bad. I liked working with our mayor." He was thinking that the next mayor might not be so open to... he glanced my way and amended his thoughts from "bribes" to "gifts."

"There is that."

"So what stopped him?"

"Al's head of security killed the environmental engineer who brought the oil refinery to his attention. They were still going to go ahead with it. Unfortunately for Braxton, Steve Mosely, the project manager, overheard Braxton telling Al about the murder. That meant Braxton had to get rid of Steve, so he tied him up and left him in the basement of the stadium to get buried under all the rubble.

"Unfortunately for Braxton, I came along and figured it out... with Dimples's help, of course."

"Of course." Uncle Joey smirked. "So what did you do?"

I told them about finding Steve in the basement, and how Braxton tried to blow us up. "That's when Braxton decided to shoot us all and leave our bodies in the stadium to be buried. He didn't know that we'd found out about the oil refinery and had used that evidence to stop the demolition. If Dimples hadn't stopped him, I think he would have tried to set it off another way. But, as you can see, he failed, because I'm still here."

I grinned at them, hoping they'd look on the bright side. They just frowned at me instead.

"What's wrong with your arm?" Uncle Joey asked.

Until he'd said that, I didn't realize I'd been holding it against my chest. "Oh... Braxton shoved me against a wall. I think my shoulder's bruised."

"Let me take a look," Ramos said.

"I'm not taking my shirt off."

His eyes widened, and he shook his head. "I just want to see how far you can move your shoulder without pain."

"Oh... okay."

Uncle Joey glanced between us; pretty sure he'd missed something. Had I taken my shirt off in front of Ramos recently?

My eyes widened, and I felt a flush stain my cheeks. Damn it all. Why did he have to think that?

Ramos held out his hands, and I focused on him, letting him move my arm back and forth. "Tell me if you feel any sharp pains."

He rotated my shoulder and moved my arm up and down.

"It hurts a little, but there's not a sharp pain."

"What about here?" He felt along my collarbone, thinking that sometimes a shoulder injury caused the collarbone to snap.

I shook my head. "Nope. No pain there either. I think it's just bruised."

"Good. You might want to put some ice on that."

"Yeah... I'll do that when I get home." Wanting to change the subject, I asked about the missing hard drive. "Have you heard anything from Max?"

"No," Uncle Joey said. "Ramos has the place booby-trapped, and we've got our people watching the premises, but Max hasn't shown his face. Are you sure that's where it is?" He hated to ask, but it didn't make sense.

I shook my head. "I guess I need to talk to him again. That's the only way I'll know for sure."

Even as Uncle Joey considered using me as bait, Ramos put his foot down. "That's not going to happen. We'll find it. Maybe you just need to see his office again, and you'll figure it out?"

"Hey... yeah. That might work." I sighed, suddenly drained. "But you know what? I'm done for today. I'll help you out tomorrow if you still need me. Right now, I'm going home. I need a nap... and maybe some pain reliever and an ice pack."

Uncle Joey blew out a breath, thinking he hated putting it off, but he had everything in place to catch Max. There was no way Max could get near his office without his knowledge, so it should be fine. Besides, he used to do this sort of thing long before I joined the family. "Of course. Tomorrow's soon enough."

"Great. I'll plan on it." I slowly got to my feet with only a few twinges of pain and turned to Ramos. "Uh... I left my car at the police station. Do you mind dropping me off?"

"Not at all. But I think we should take the car instead of the bike."

Pursing my lips, I had to agree. "Sure. I don't like it, but you're right." I said goodbye to Uncle Joey and followed Ramos down the hall to stop at Jackie's desk.

"Wait here." He continued to the apartment, and I glanced at her desk. It was tidy and neat, so she'd probably left for the day. A few minutes later, Ramos returned with a zip-lock bag full of ice. "Here. This should help."

"Oh... thanks." I held the bag against my shoulder and let out a groan. "This is just what I needed. Thanks."

"Sure."

"So where's Forrest? Last I heard, he was wondering if Uncle Joey wanted to hire a hacker."

Ramos snorted. "I'm not surprised. He's good at what he does, but I don't think we need him on a permanent basis."

"Yeah, probably not. But he's still here, right?"

"Yes. He'll be here until we get Max. He wants his finder's fee as much as Manetto wants his money."

"Makes sense."

Ramos let me out in the parking lot of the police station, and I went straight to my car. As soon as I got home, I took a couple of pain pills and changed into my comfy clothes. Black and blue bruises covered my left hip as well as my shoulder, but at least I'd escaped with my life. What were a few bruises compared to that?

I settled onto my patio swing with a soda and Coco at my side. Totally relaxed, I closed my eyes and began to doze off. On the edge of sleep, my phone rang, jerking me awake, and I fumbled to pick it up. "Hello?"

"Honey... have you heard from Justin?"

"What? No. Why?"

"He never made it to our meeting, and it was over an hour ago."

Blinking the sleep away, I sat up. "Did his plane land okay?"

"Yes. I had my secretary check with the airline, just to make sure. It got in a couple of hours ago. I thought Justin was coming straight from the airport."

"And you've tried his phone?"

"Yes. He's not answering. I've left messages on his voicemail, and I've texted him, but so far, he hasn't responded. I'm worried. What do you think is going on?"

Ice cold dread sent chills down my spine. "I don't know unless... do you think it might have something to do with Max?"

Chris hesitated. "But... that doesn't make sense. I know Max wanted him dead at one point, but not anymore, right?"

I swallowed against the fear tightening my throat. "I thought so. We all thought he was safe. I'd better call Uncle Joey."

"Yeah… that's a good idea. Let me know what he says."

"I will." I disconnected and took a couple of deep breaths to calm down. That helped, but the panic wasn't too far away. Just to make sure it was true, I called Justin's cell phone.

It rang and rang before going to voice mail. I disconnected and tried again, hoping he may have been too far away to answer. For the second time it went to voicemail. Still, I had to try one more time, but after it went to voicemail again, I had to admit that it was true. This time I left a message, telling him I was worried and to please call me back.

With my heart racing, I called Uncle Joey. He picked right up. "Shelby? I thought you'd be taking a nap by now."

"It's Justin. He's missing."

"What?"

I explained the circumstances and managed to hold back my panic. "Do you think Max has something to do with it?"

"That would be my guess. But why now? He's dealing with me, and after the incident in the parking garage, he should know that Justin is under my protection."

"Maybe that's it. If he wants to bargain for the crypto, he could use Justin as leverage."

Uncle Joey hesitated. "Yes. It makes sense. But I'd feel better if we had the hard drive."

"You've made it impossible for him to get it, right? I need to talk to Max. It's the only way we'll know what's going on."

"I agree. But that's going to be hard unless he contacts us first." He paused. "But why would he go after Justin now?"

"Well... if he knows I'm your niece, and he knows that Justin's my brother, he'd say that Justin was your nephew. So it's a way to get to you, right?"

"Yes. It looks that way."

"What do we do now?"

"We need to find that hard drive. Without it, we don't have a lot of bargaining power."

"You're right." I gulped down my fear. I had to save my brother, no matter what it took. "I'll head over to Max's office. Maybe once I see the place, something will line up with what Max was thinking, and I'll figure out where he hid it."

"Fine. My men are there, but I'll send Ramos to meet you."

"Okay." I hung up and hurried to get ready, barely feeling my aches and pains.

I pulled into the parking lot of Max's office building and hurried into the lobby. A security guard sat behind a narrow desk by the door. That was new. He nodded at me, and I picked up that he recognized me as the boss's niece.

So that was one way Uncle Joey had kept an eye out for Max. I smiled and turned toward his desk. "Is Ramos here?" I hadn't looked for his bike in the parking lot, so I didn't know.

"Yes, ma'am."

"Thanks."

I got out of the elevator on Max's floor, but there was no sign of Ramos in the hall. Sounds of a woman's laughter reached me, and I stepped down the hall to the neighbor's office. As I tried to remember her name, the familiar cadence of a low voice caught me by surprise. Was that Ramos?

Without knocking, I opened the door and found him talking to... Celeste... that was her name. They both glanced in my direction, and Ramos straightened from his position of leaning toward her.

"Shelby, you made it." He gave me a quick wink that Celeste couldn't see, and tried to act guilty that I'd caught him doing something naughty. "I was just talking to Celeste about helping us with our remodel. She totally gets that I don't want any lacy frilly stuff, but she said there's plenty of other things we can do that I shouldn't have a problem with."

My brows rose. "Really?" I glanced at Celeste. "Did he tell you I want lacy, frilly stuff?"

"Uh... something like that." She didn't want to alienate me, but she totally understood why Ramos would hate that. She wondered why on earth I would encroach on his manly perfection. It was downright criminal to insist on ruffles and lace. Just the thought nearly made her gag.

Holy hell. He'd said that about me? I gave him my killer look. This time, he bit his lip and wouldn't meet my gaze, totally pulling off the act of a guilty man.

Using all my willpower to keep from rolling my eyes, I sat beside him and placed my hand over his. "Babe... whatever gave you that idea? The only lacy, frilly stuff I want will be on me... not decorating the house."

Ramos's eyes actually bulged for a whole second. I'd never seen that happen before. He swallowed before his eyes narrowed with menace, and I couldn't help the chuckle that burst out of me. Now it was his turn to roll his eyes.

I glanced at Celeste who was thinking that seeing us together certainly cemented the fact that we were a couple, and all her hopes were dashed. I tried not to let that bother me too much. Who was I kidding... it didn't bother me at all, but mostly because Ramos had said she wasn't his type.

I glanced at Ramos. "Did you ask her if she'd seen Max?"

He nodded, thinking that he'd done that first before asking if she had some tips about decorating his house.

"He did," Celeste answered. "Max hasn't been back that I know of... at least not in the last few days." She glanced at the clock, thinking it was time to call it a day. "Do you want me to come up with some ideas for your house?"

"Sure," I said. "Let's start with some artwork first. I'd like something to add color to the walls. Ramos has this thing for wood. He's got hardwood floors and exposed beams in the ceilings, so it's kind of dark. I mean... it's great... but I think it just needs something to brighten it up, you know?"

"Of course." That was exactly what she'd been thinking. Maybe I wasn't so clueless after all? "I'll find some things and call you."

"Great. Here's my card." I pulled out my business card and handed it over. She'd meant to call Ramos, and I'd thwarted her again.

A twinge of remorse hit me. I was a terrible person. Instead of examining her office for the hard-drive, I was flirting with Ramos... all while Justin was missing and probably in Max's clutches. I was going to hell for sure.

Doing what I'd come here for, I studied the office and noticed the large green plant in the corner. I'd had one like that when Chris and I were first married. I'd loved it, but it got so big that I didn't have room for it, so I gave it to my mom.

"I love your plant. Did you say that Max gave it to you?"

She glanced at it. "Yeah. It's so big that it must have cost him a small fortune, but I think it looks good in that corner." She caught Ramos's gaze. "Do you have any plants? That might be just what your place needs."

While they spoke, I tried to remember the image in Max's mind when he thought about the hard-drive. It was somewhere in this room... I just knew it. I came back to the plant. Could he have put it in there?

The pot was probably big enough. In fact, sometimes plants were in two pots; one for the dirt, and the other for decoration. If he'd waterproofed the packaging, it was a great hiding place, and he could have slipped it inside before he took off.

Ramos cleared his throat. "Shelby?"

"Huh?"

"You ready to go?"

"Oh... yeah. Sorry. Thanks again."

Celeste told us she'd call, and we hurried out. After the door closed, I turned to him. "I think I know where it is, but we'll have to wait until she leaves to find out for sure."

"We can't wait in Max's office, but the bathroom is down the hall." Ramos thought that we should wait in the men's bathroom, so I followed him inside, grateful to find no one else there.

Ramos pulled the door slightly ajar, watching for her to leave. After she got on the elevator, we hurried back to her office, and he used his lock-pick set to get the door open.

Slipping inside, I led him to the plant. "Max gave this plant to her. I think he might have put it in there." I pushed the plant leaves out of the way to study the pot.

"We need to take the inside pot out." I wrapped my hands around the plant and lifted. It barely moved. "Wow... that thing's heavy. You might have to do it."

Ramos traded me spots and easily lifted the inner pot from the outer pot. He set it down and we both looked inside. A package sat at the bottom of the pot, and my heart picked up speed. Ramos reached in and pulled it out.

"It's the right size." My heart thumped. "Open it up."

Layers of plastic covered the package, making it difficult to open. Ramos took out his knife to cut through the wrapping, being careful not to damage the inside. After pulling off the plastic, we found dark wrapping paper underneath.

Ramos carefully pulled the paper off, exposing a glint of silver. He finished the job, revealing the hard-drive in all it's glory. It kind of boggled my mind to think that it held the keys to a hundred million dollars.

I caught his gaze. "We found it."

"No… you found it," Ramos said. "Good job." He re-wrapped the paper, and handed it to me. I stuffed it into the bottom my purse where it would be safe. Next, we put the plant back into the pot and cleaned everything up.

After closing and locking the door, we took the elevator down to the lobby. Ramos spoke to Uncle Joey's 'security guard,' asking him if he'd seen anyone out of the ordinary. The guard replied that it was just the regulars, and Ramos told him he'd be in touch with an update soon.

We parted ways in the parking lot, and Ramos followed me to Thrasher. Having the hard-drive relieved some of my anxiety about Justin. At least now we had something to bargain with, but it still puzzled me how Max knew about Justin's relationship to me in the first place.

Of course, he'd figured out that I was Uncle Joey's niece. Maybe Justin had mentioned that he had a sister living here? After Ramos had beaten up the people Max sent to kill Justin in the parking garage, they'd probably told Max, and he'd put it all together, tying everything back to Uncle Joey. Could it have been as simple as that?

Ramos joined me at the elevator, and we soon stepped into Thrasher, eager to tell Uncle Joey the good news.

Forrest sat in front of Uncle Joey's desk, his fingers moving restlessly on top of his legs. Excitement rushed through him, and he jumped to his feet. "Did you get it?"

"Yes."

"Sweet." His excitement seemed a little extreme, but then I remembered the bargain he'd struck with Uncle Joey to get a nice finder's fee. I wanted to tell him that I'd found the hard-drive, so I should get the fee, but he'd made the deal, not me.

He turned to Uncle Joey. "I can put it in your computer right now, and you can get your codes and all your money back." Before Uncle Joey answered, he held his hand toward me for the hard-drive.

I glanced at Uncle Joey, who seemed a little taken aback by Forrest's enthusiasm. He certainly didn't need Forrest to install the hard drive in a computer for him, so what was he thinking?

Pulling the hard drive from my purse, I handed it to Uncle Joey. "I think Uncle Joey might want to do that. It's his hard-drive, you know?"

"Oh. Right." Forrest deflated right in front of us. He'd been too obvious, and now it would cost him.

"Were you planning to steal it yourself?" I asked.

He jerked liked he'd been slapped. "No. Not at all." He took in our wary gazes, and his eyes widened. "I'm just worried that Max may have hacked into the hard drive and already taken the codes."

Uncle Joey glanced at me and I nodded. "He's telling the truth."

"I think that's something we'd all like to know." Uncle Joey glanced at Ramos. "So let's find out. Take the hard drive and put it in a computer that's not hooked up to the Internet. You know the passwords."

Ramos took the hard-drive from Uncle Joey and nodded.

Uncle Joey glanced at Forrest. "You're going to help me with something else."

"What's that?"

"Justin is missing, and I want to know where he is."

Forrest swore under his breath. "You think Max took him?"

Uncle Joey nodded. "We do, but we haven't heard from Max or Justin, so we don't know for sure. Justin flew in today and never made it to his three o'clock meeting. Maybe you can hack into the airport surveillance cameras and see what happened to him."

Forrest nodded. "Of course, I'll start looking right now."

After he left, I sat down in front of Uncle Joey's desk. "It's kind of nice having a hacker on the team, right?"

He huffed. "It does give us an advantage."

My phone rang, causing my heart to skip a beat. Pulling it out, I found Chris's name, and tried not to sound disappointed. "Hey Chris."

"Have you heard anything?"

"Not yet."

"Damn. I wonder what happened to him."

"I know. I'm at Thrasher, and I'm probably going to stay here for a while. Are you on your way home?"

"Yes. I'm just leaving the office. I'll take care of dinner and the kids. Just call me as soon as you hear anything."

"Thanks, Chris. I will."

We disconnected, and I glanced at Uncle Joey. "What happens now?"

"Let's see if I have any crypto codes."

We left the office and found Ramos on one of the computers in the security room. He'd found Uncle Joey's crypto codes, so at least that had gone right. After linking to the Internet, Uncle Joey had him exchange the crypto for real money and send it to an off-shore account.

After that was done, we checked on Forrest in my office and gave him the good news. He'd managed to hack into the surveillance videos, but had yet to find Justin on any of them. As he checked another camera, my cell phone rang.

I pulled it out, and my heart raced. "It's him!" With shaking fingers, I answered. "Justin? Is that you? Are you okay?"

"Shelby... you have to do what I tell you, or he'll kill me."

"You mean Max? Max has you?"

"Yes. He wants the hard-drive. Do you have it?"

"Uh... yes."

Justin let out a shaky breath. "Good. He wants to trade me for the crypto codes."

"Okay... sure. I can give him the hard drive, as long as he lets you go."

"No... he doesn't want the hard drive anymore. He just wants the codes."

"Okay... but how am I supposed to do that?"

"You just send them to his phone. Once the exchange has gone through, he'll release me."

"No... I'm not going to do it that way. He could kill you long before the exchange goes through. There has to be another way. I want to talk to him... face-to-face."

"Uh. Let me ask him."

I heard his muffled voice before the sound of a chair scraping across the floor, along with a thud, came through. "Justin? Justin? You there?"

"Shelby," Max said. "I'm afraid your brother just had an accident."

"What do you mean? If he's hurt, you're never getting any of this money. Do you hear me? I swear I'll kill you myself."

"Calm down. He's fine, and you'll get him back safe and sound as long as you do what I say. Understand?"

Frustration boiled up inside of me, but I knew if I wanted to have any advantage at all, we had to meet in person. "Sure. I'll do whatever you want, as long as we do it face-to-face. You can even choose the place and time."

"I want the crypto... all one hundred million of it."

"So... by crypto, you mean the codes, right? So how do I give you the codes if it's all digital?"

He let out a long-suffering sigh. "You bring your phone, I'll bring mine. You send me the codes. I send the codes to my crypto wallet and we're done. It's simple."

"Okay, but what about Justin? Where will he be?"

"I'll bring him to the meeting. Once I have the codes, I'll let you have him."

There was so much that could go wrong with this that it boggled my mind, and I was already exhausted. "It's okay with me, but I have to ask Uncle Joey. Can I call you back?"

"Don't take too long."

He disconnected, and I told Uncle Joey his demands. "I don't know how to save Justin and the crypto. Do you have any ideas?"

"If we can beat him at his own game... that would be best." He glanced at Forrest. "You're the hacker. Is there a way to do that?"

Forrest considered it and nodded, thinking this was his best chance at earning his finder's fee. "Yes... there might be a way. If he's using his phone for the transaction, I can clone his number and get into his crypto wallet and empty it into your account before he puts it in his. It's called Sim Hacking. There's a few steps I have to take, but I could do it pretty fast, especially if he's kept busy."

"How fast?"

"Within ten to fifteen minutes of the transaction."

Uncle Joey's lips twisted. Fifteen minutes to keep Max busy could work, but it was still a risk. Of course, it was for my brother, so he'd do it... for me.

I let out a breath, surprised that I'd been worried. I should have had more faith in Uncle Joey. Even if we weren't really related, we were still bound by ties that were deeper than blood. I sent him a grateful smile, and he nodded.

Then he ruined it by thinking I wasn't a very good negotiator. "I wish you hadn't been so willing to let him set the time and place, but I guess you were too worried about Justin. That said... before you call him, let's go over some ground rules. Our goal is to get Justin back, so we need to ensure that he is someplace where we can see him, preferably close to Max and his phone.

"I'd also like to have plenty of time to look over the area, so make sure we have a two-to-three hour window before this transaction takes place." He glanced at Forrest. "Anything else she needs to know that would help you out?"

"Yes." His gaze met mine. "Once you get the phone number, you need to stall for at least two minutes. Longer if you can. I need that much time to clone his number. After you've sent the crypto and he downloads it into his wallet, I should have access to it, but I might have to bypass his security. That's why I need a little more time, but, once that's done, I can empty his wallet pretty quick."

"Okay... got it. Anything else? What kind of diversion are you thinking of?"

Everyone glanced at Ramos, since that was his area of expertise. "Once you're safely away, I'll take care of it, but I'll know more after he picks the place."

I sighed. "Okay. I guess it's time to call him back." Uncle Joey nodded, so I called Justin's phone.

Max picked right up. "Do we have a deal?"

"Yes. I'll bring the codes, you bring Justin, but he has to be in plain sight. I have to see him and make sure he's alive before I give you anything. I also want him close, so he can walk to me after it's done."

"Of course. But if you try anything, I'll shoot him."

"So you're bringing a gun? If that's the case, then I'm bringing one too."

He huffed out a breath. "Fine, but you need to come alone."

"And you're going to be alone? Just you and Justin?"

"Of course."

I didn't believe that for a second. "Fine... so where are we meeting?"

"There's a bar just outside of town with a secluded parking lot in the back. It's called The Cotton Bottom. I'll bring Justin and meet you there at two... in the morning."

He disconnected before I could say a word, but I couldn't help the grin that spread over my face. I'd been to The Cotton Bottom before, and there were plenty of places for Ramos and Forrest to hide. This could actually work out.

"Why are you smiling?" Ramos asked the question they were all thinking.

"Because he wants to meet in the parking lot of The Cotton Bottom Bar. I've been there before, and so have you.

Ramos nodded. "That's right. You were helping your detective solve a case, and you barged into a meeting I had there with your suspect."

"I didn't barge in. You kept me out, remember?"

He nodded, remembering pinning me against the wall so the killer wouldn't see me. "Didn't I save your life?"

I huffed out a breath. "Probably, but honestly, I can't remember many of the details."

"What time is the meeting tonight?" Uncle Joey asked.

"Oh... he said two in the morning. Do you know why he'd wait until then?"

"Yeah... I think the place closes at one on weekdays," Ramos answered. "There won't be anyone there at two." He was thinking he'd been there a couple of weeks ago with a... he glanced my way and didn't finish the thought... on purpose.

Was he going to say a date... or a friend? Ugh.

"But the best thing about it..." Ramos continued. "Is that I know the owner. I think he'll let us inside, and we can set up shop for the meeting." He glanced at Uncle Joey. "For a small fee."

"Naturally."

"I can see why Max would want the meeting there," Ramos continued. "They have a few cameras around the building, but nothing in the parking lot. And the only lighting is on the back of the building, so the parking lot is pretty dark."

"It sounds like a good place for an ambush," Uncle Joey said.

"That's true," I agreed. "If I remember right, there's a park with a lot of tall trees behind the lot, and across the street are a few small businesses. They'll be closed by then, so it's an isolated spot."

"That won't matter," Ramos said. "We'll have the upper hand, and Max won't know what hit him."

On that happy note, we spent the next hour going over strategies and timing. Forrest would set up shop inside the bar and be ready to go after Max's phone. Ramos planned to set up a special video camera so that he and Uncle Joey could keep track of everything.

Ramos also had a few surprises up his sleeve to make sure Max was distracted long enough for Forrest to steal the crypto. Once I had Justin, the fun would begin.

"Is there a back-up plan?" I asked. "Not that I think we'll need it, but you never know."

"Yes," Ramos answered. "If Max tries anything, I'll shoot him."

"Oh... well, okay."

After going over the plan a few times, I left, hoping I remembered everything I needed to do, and knowing it was going to be a long night.

Chapter 17

I made it home in time for dinner, but with everything going on, I couldn't eat more than a few bites. The biggest hitch came when my mom called and asked if I knew where Justin was. I had to lie to her, telling her that he was at our house and would probably stay the night with us.

I told Chris the whole story, and he didn't like it one bit. In fact, he almost insisted that he come with me, but I talked him out of it. "I'll be fine. This is actually the best scenario we could have since we'll have access to the bar. I just hope Justin is okay."

"But what about Max? What's going to keep him from shooting you both once he has the crypto?"

I thought that was a good question, since it worried me as well. "He's not going to do that. Covering up one murder was hard enough, and he's still in the hot seat for that one. Hey... that gives me an idea. Do you have a digital recorder?

"Yes... I do. What are you thinking?"

I told him my idea, and he had to admit it was a good one. As long as I didn't push my luck.

"I'll be careful."

He wondered how many times he'd heard that? Was it over twenty? It was probably closer to fifty by now.

"Hey... I'm still alive."

"Yeah... but all it takes is once."

"I know... but this time it's my brother. I have to do this."

He nodded, knowing I was right. "I have to admit that Manetto took me by surprise. I didn't think he'd give up a hundred million dollars for Justin."

"Yeah, it worried me a little too, but he wanted to do it."

"It probably didn't hurt that Forrest has a way to get it back. I know you explained it to me, but I don't have any idea how stuff like that works. Remind me not to buy any crypto."

"No kidding. There's just too much that can go wrong with it."

"That's for sure." He shook his head. Times like this made him realize how drastically our lives had changed. All because I'd stopped at the grocery store for some carrots. Sometimes it made sense, but most of the time it didn't. Now I was off to bargain for my brother's life. "Are you sure I can't come?"

"I can ask Uncle Joey, but I don't think he'll want you there. Sorry..." Knowing this was hard for him, I rubbed my hand across his chest. "There is one thing you can do for me. We have a couple of hours before I need to leave, and I wouldn't mind a back rub."

His brows rose. "I thought you were too bruised for something like that?"

"Only my shoulder and hip are bruised."

"Is that right?"

"Yeah." I continued caressing him, before leaning in for a kiss. "Besides, facing danger makes me realize my priorities, and making sure you know how much I love you is at the top of the list."

A low growl sounded in his throat. "Oh baby, oh baby."

I left home at one-thirty, dressed in all black, which I realized had become my standard work outfit. It reminded me of the early days when Uncle Joey had insisted I wear black all the time, and I'd been unhappy about that. I shook my head. Things had certainly changed.

I slid my cross-body purse, holding my stun-flashlight and a few other necessities, over my shoulder and grabbed a black cap to cover my braided, blond hair, so I wouldn't stand out as a target.

The plan to meet Max on my own would have terrified me if not for knowing that I had back-up inside the bar. I sent a text to Ramos, telling him I was on my way, and began the drive. With Justin's life on the line, fear turned my stomach into a hollow knot.

So much could go wrong, so I concentrated on driving and tried not to think about it. The drive took no time at all, and I pulled into the parking lot and turned off the car. After rubbing my sweaty palms on my jeans, I sent a text to Ramos that I was there. At one-fifty, I was early, so I stayed in the car and tried to be patient.

The seconds ticked by, turning into long, never-ending minutes. At two, with no sign of Max, worry clawed my insides. Five more minutes passed with no sign of him, and I had to take a few deep, calming breaths to keep from freaking out.

Those five minutes stretched to ten, and I picked up my phone to call Justin's cell. As I brought up his number, a car pulled into the lot behind me. It continued to the other side of the parking lot, close to the exit, and stopped.

The driver's side door opened, and Max stepped out. In the back seat, another man got out before reaching inside and tugging on Justin's arm. His hands had been tied behind his back, and he moved slowly. Once Justin had his feet under him, the man pulled him beside Max to face me.

In the dim light, it was hard to see Justin's face clearly, but the shiny strip of gray duct tape across his mouth, and the line of blood across his temple, sent anger surging through my chest. I got out of my car and moved close enough to pick up their thoughts.

Wearing an over-sized jacket, with the zipper closed all the way up to his chin, Justin stood stiffly, like he was in pain. I listened to his thoughts, picking up his anger and frustration, as well as his worry and fear. He'd hoped I wouldn't come, and now I was going to die.

I straightened, shocked that he thought that.

"As you can see, we're ready for the trade," Max began.

"You said you'd come alone, and you've already broken our agreement."

He sneered. "And you don't think I know that Ramos is here somewhere? I think we're even, unless you don't care if Justin dies."

The man holding Justin's arm lifted a gun and pointed it at his head.

My breath caught, and I took a step back. How was this supposed to work now? I took out my phone and opened a screen. "You've made your point. Just give me your phone number."

Max took out his phone and told me his number. I sent the number in a text to Ramos, and flipped my screen to a new text message and entered his number. "Okay. I have it. But before I send the codes, I'd like to talk to Justin and make sure he's all right."

"You can see him... you don't need to talk to him." Max chafed at the delay, determined to leave the tape covering his mouth.

"But—"

"No. Now send me the codes, or my friend here will be happy to put a bullet in his head."

"Fine... but while I'm at it, I'd like to know why you killed Landon. Wasn't he part of your group or something?" This was part of my delaying tactic, and I made sure the digital recorder was on so I could give it to the detectives. One way or another, Max was going down.

Shock rippled over him, and his mouth dropped open. "That has nothing to do with this."

"Yes it does. I found him in the warehouse with his throat slit. I thought he was on your side, so it doesn't make sense. He's the one who stole Justin's crypto, so what happened? Did he want the hard drive for himself so you killed him?"

Exasperated, Max shook his head. "He was part of the group, but he got greedy. After he got his hands on the hard drive, he tried to kill me. I had no choice. Now, send me the codes, or Justin dies."

The man holding Justin pushed the gun hard against Justin's head, causing him to flinch away. I held up a hand. "Okay... geeze... give me a minute."

Justin kept thinking *don't do it, don't do it, we're both dead if you do. If he shoots me, at least you won't die.*

Holy hell. That made no sense. I swallowed and began to type the text message. "I'm almost done... uh... Justin? ... You okay? Is there something you need to tell me?"

I heard him clearly. *He's got a bomb attached to my chest. He's planning on blowing us up once they leave.*

My legs turned to jelly. What the hell?

"I'm not seeing any codes," Max said. "What's taking you so long?"

I pinned Max with my flinty, narrow-eyed stare. "This is unbelievable."

"What?"

I threw my hands up and huffed out a breath. "You've put me in a no-win situation." I motioned toward Justin. "You've got a bomb strapped around his chest. If I give you the money, you'll kill him. If I don't give you the money, you'll kill him." I shook my head. "So, I guess if you really want the money, you're going to have to take the bomb off him. It's the only way I'll give you what you want, and we both win."

"How did you—" He huffed out a breath wondering how in the hell I'd figured it out. Glancing at Justin, he couldn't see any evidence of the bomb. This was insane. Now all his careful planning was for nothing. He wanted revenge so bad he could almost taste it.

He glanced my way, and I held up my phone. "I have the codes right here if you want them."

With a frustrated growl, he brushed his fingers through his hair. "Fine." Stepping toward Justin, he unzipped the jacket, exposing the bomb. In order to take it off, he had to free Justin's hands and slip the jacket off his shoulders.

Opening a knife, he cut through the duct tape and pushed the jacket off. It fell to the ground, but he ignored it. With careful and precise movements, he disarmed the bomb. Finished, he cut through the makeshift vest and carefully pulled it away from Justin's chest.

"Keep the gun on him," he ordered his accomplice. Holding the vest at arm's length, he stepped to his car and carefully laid it across the back seat. After closing the door, he returned to stand beside Justin. "Satisfied?"

"Yes." I pulled up my phone and copy-pasted the codes into the text, then pushed 'send.' "I just sent them, now send Justin over here."

"Just a minute." Max watched his phone for my text to come through. A few seconds later, relief and triumph washed over him. He copied all the codes and transferred them into his crypto wallet before glancing my way. "He's all yours."

His accomplice shoved Justin toward me, making him fall onto his hands and knees. I ran to help him up, while Max and his accomplice jumped into their car. As they drove away, I pulled the tape off of Justin's mouth, and he caught me up in a hug.

"Shelby. You did it. I wasn't sure we'd get out of this alive. You're amazing... you knew about the bomb." He shook his head. "I'll never doubt you again."

I pulled away. "I'm just glad it all worked out. Uncle Joey's inside the bar with Ramos and Forrest. Let's go inside and see if our plan worked."

"What plan?"

"Our plan to get the crypto back by hacking into Max's crypto wallet. It was Forrest's idea."

We stepped through the back entrance and followed a short hall to the bar, finding Ramos and Uncle Joey at a table, watching Forrest work on his computer.

"I got it!" Forrest raised both arms in the air and whooped.

Uncle Joey patted Forrest on the shoulder and turned toward us with a big grin on his face. "Good to see you Justin."

"You too. I don't know how to thank you for saving me." He swallowed. "That was a lot of money you put on the line."

"Yes... it was." Uncle Joey placed a hand on Justin's shoulder. "But you're family now, and Shelby would never forgive me if anything happened to you." He squeezed Justin's shoulder hard enough to make him flinch. "Luckily, we managed to get it all back, so it worked out." He dropped his hand, and Justin automatically rubbed his shoulder.

"The bomb was unexpected though." He turned to me and gave me a side hug, careful of my bruised shoulder. "But you handled it perfectly." He was thinking that I'd come a long way from the early days, and he was proud of me.

"Thanks Uncle Joey."

He smiled and turned to Forrest. "Is the crypto securely back where it belongs?"

"Yes sir. I sent it through the exchange, and it's back in your off-shore account." He closed his computer and stuffed it into his bag.

"Good. On the way back, let's talk. I might have a proposal for you, if you're interested?"

"Yes... I'm very interested."

Ramos pounded Justin on the back. "Glad you made it. Shelby was worried."

"I'll bet... I—"

The sound of a car screeching to a stop cut him off, and we all froze. The back door to the bar flew open, and steps pounded toward us. Max stopped at the end of the hallway, his face red and full of anger. He swore at us before flinging the vest with the bomb still attached toward the bar. "I hope you all burn in hell!"

As the bomb hit the bar, Max took off out the back.

"Run!" Ramos grabbed my arm and pulled me toward the front door. Uncle Joey and Forrest were already there, and they rushed out with Justin following right on their heels.

Ramos and I came next. We made it several yards before the roar of the blast ripped through the building, sending a concussive wave that threw us off our feet.

We hit the ground hard, and darkness enveloped me. As debris rained down around me, Ramos grabbed me under my arms to drag me away, saying something that I couldn't make out above the roar in my ears.

I managed to get my feet under me, and we stumbled forward until we were out of the blast range. Crumpling onto a dried patch of grass, I felt something wet trickle into my eye and rubbed the moisture away. Red blood coated my fingers, and I closed my eyes against the sudden queasiness that hit my stomach.

After taking several deep breaths, the roaring in my ears began to subside, and the fuzziness in my head cleared. Ramos lay beside me, his eyes closed and his chest heaving. Justin and Forrest knelt beside Uncle Joey, who wasn't moving.

Alarmed, I twisted to sit up and had to take a few breaths to quell a dizzy spell. I heard Uncle Joey complaining that he wasn't hurt and telling the boys that he was fine and to let him be for a minute.

Relieved he was okay, I turned to Ramos and placed my hand over his chest. His heart beat was strong, but I knew something wasn't right. He normally didn't take so long to get up. "Ramos. What's wrong? Where does it hurt?"

His eyes opened, and he turned his head toward me. "You're bleeding." He was thinking that I looked terrible with blood running down my face and dripping onto my shirt. Why was I sitting up? I should lie down.

"I don't think it's so bad. You know that head wounds bleed a lot."

He frowned. "Right, but maybe you'd better lie back down anyway."

"Not until I know you're okay."

"I'm okay... my leg is hurting, but I can still move it, so it's not broken." He closed his eyes.

I glanced at both of his legs, but nothing stood out. "Which one?"

"My left." He moved his hand to the back of his thigh where a splinter of wood was poking out.

"Oh no." My hands flew to my mouth. "Don't touch it!"

He frowned at me and glanced at his leg. With a quick movement, he pulled the wood out.

I gasped. "What the hell?"

"It wasn't in that deep."

Examining his wound, I shook my head. For something that wasn't deep, it sure bled a lot. "Uh... I might need your shirt to staunch the bleeding."

He pushed to a sitting position. "Something about this sounds vaguely familiar." He met my gaze and sent me his sexy half smile. Naturally, I couldn't keep from grinning back. "But this time, I think it's your turn." His left brow quirked up in a challenge.

My lips twisted, and I glanced at his wound again. "Uhh... I don't know. Maybe it's not so bad."

The sound of sirens drew closer, and soon, a huge firetruck pulled into the parking lot. As the firemen got started on the blaze, a couple more emergency response vehicles joined them. The paramedics pulled beside us and quickly came to our aid. Luckily, both Ramos and I had been wearing our leather motorcycle jackets, and that had kept our injuries to a minimum.

Several police officers arrived, along with Detectives Williams and Clue. Uncle Joey didn't want to talk to them, so he pointed them in my direction. Since we hadn't done anything wrong, I was willing to tell them the whole story, starting from when Max kidnapped Justin to make Uncle Joey pay him off.

After I got to the part where Max threw the bomb inside the building, I pulled out my digital recorder. "I even got this." I turned it on, playing Max's confession to killing Landon Woods.

"That's enough to arrest him," Clue said, excited to finally have a lead. "Too bad we don't know where he is."

"I might be able to help with that," Forrest said. "I'm still hooked up to his phone. Let me see if I can get a location." He pulled out his laptop, grateful it had survived the blast, and managed to tap in to Max's phone. "It's right there." He pointed to a house on the west side. "Just so you're aware, they have guns, and Max made that bomb," he told Clue. "So you might want to be careful."

The detectives jumped at the chance to arrest Max and scrambled to put a team together. As they left, I smiled with satisfaction. It did my heart good to know that Max would be behind bars in a few hours, and I was glad my plan to get his confession had worked.

The paramedics finished patching us up, telling us that we all needed to get a few stitches at the hospital. My car was in the back parking lot between two firetrucks, so Justin and I went with Uncle Joey and Forrest, while Ramos took his bike.

It must have been a slow night, because we were all patched up pretty quick. Ramos needed the most stitches, probably because he'd shielded me from the blast... again. How many times did this make? I would have felt bad, but he was thinking that he should have expected something like that from Max, and he was glad we'd all survived.

In between everything, I gave Chris a call, prepared to leave a message that we were okay. He surprised me by picking up, so I briefly explained what had happened and told him we'd be home in an hour or two.

Sometime later, we drove back to the bar in the early light of dawn. Seeing the damage gave me a healthy appreciation that we'd made it out alive. I felt bad for the owner, but I was sure Uncle Joey would work something out... after all... he had his hundred million back.

Uncle Joey dropped us off in the back parking lot, telling me to give him a call if anything came up, but to take the next few days off. I wasn't about to argue with that.

Justin and I made it home near six in the morning. Justin had no idea what had happened to his carry-on bag, so I grabbed some of Chris's clothes for him.

"Do you think the police caught Max?" he asked me.

"I sure hope so. But... if he managed to get away, I doubt that he'll get far. I think he messed with the wrong mob boss."

Justin huffed out a breath. "No kidding." But he was thinking that Max shouldn't have messed with me. In the end, I was the one who brought him down. "I'm exhausted, so I'm going to bed. Thanks for everything, Sis."

He gave me a quick hug and went straight to the guest bedroom, thinking he'd take a shower after he'd slept for a couple of hours. I knew just how he felt.

Bruised, dirty, and tired, I stepped out of my clothes and into the shower, making sure to keep the side of my head with the stitches out of the water. Feeling better, I toweled off and slipped on my pajamas.

As Chris's alarm went off, I crawled into bed.

He glanced my way. "Are you just getting home?"

"Yeah." I snuggled into the crook of his arm, and he held me close. A few minutes later, he got up and said something about getting the kids off to school so I could sleep a little longer. At least that's what I hoped he'd said, because, after that, I was out like a light.

A noise woke me up at noon. I sat up and gasped with pain. Every muscle in my body had tightened, sending a painful reminder of what had happened in the last few days. Moving slowly, I managed to make it downstairs and found Justin eating a bowl of cereal.

He'd showered and looked pretty good for being kidnapped. Of course, he didn't have all the bruises from the day before yesterday like I did. Was it only two days ago that I'd been threatened by a murderer in a stadium set for demolition? I shook my head... my life was not normal.

"Hey Sis," he said, his mouth full and dribbling milk. It was crazy to think that his cereal-eating habits hadn't changed in all these years.

"You know that's gross. It was gross when we were kids, and it's still gross now."

"Hey... I'm starving, give me a break."

Since he wasn't used to all these near-death experiences like me, I let it slide. "Fine. So... how did you sleep?"

This time, he swallowed before speaking. "Like the dead. I don't think I've ever been so worn out. I've got black and blue bruises all over me; you should see them." He was thinking he looked like he'd been in a car accident.

Taking in my pale face, and the stitches along my hairline, he wondered how I kept my sanity if things like yesterday happened to me very often. They probably didn't, or I'd be a mess. And... since I was basically the same bossy person he remembered, it hadn't affected me at all.

And here I was feeling all mushy about him still being alive.

"Max took my phone, so I've been using yours. I hope that's okay."

"Sure. Use away." I got a cereal bowl from the cupboard and joined him. Coco came in through the doggy door and rushed to my side with yips of excitement. After smothering him with kisses and praise, and getting several wet doggie kisses in return, I ate my cereal.

"Do you think the police got Max?" Justin hoped they had, because a part of him was still worried that Max would find a way to retaliate.

"I'll give Dimples a call and find out."

"Dimples? Who's that?"

"He's the detective I work with. His name is Drew Harris, but he has these big dimples in his cheeks. They're huge... so the name stuck."

"Right." He felt sorry for the detective. The guy probably hated it. Then he remembered his friend from grade school with the big dimples, and that I'd had a gigantic crush on the kid. Hadn't I followed him around the playground, just to get a look at them?

Oh my gosh! He was right. I'd forgotten all about that kid.

"So... you'll call *Dimples* and find out?" Now he wanted to meet the detective, just to see his dimples.

"Uh... yeah. I'll call him as soon as you're done with my phone."

Since he'd already called Lindsay and Mom, he handed it over. "Here you go."

I was still eating, but I took it from him anyway and set it on the table.

He finished his cereal, draining the milk from his bowl. "I still can't believe Max came back to the bar with that bomb."

"I know. I can't believe he put it on you in the first place."

"But you figured it out." He shook his head and began talking about everything that had happened to him. I told him about Budapest, and that the hard drive had been in Max's neighbor's office the whole time. As we spoke, I realized that the shared experience had brought us closer together.

My only regret was that he had a mob boss to answer to. Of course, that wasn't all bad, since Uncle Joey had saved his life. And... in a way, it was nice to know I didn't have to lie about that part of my life... just the reading minds part. But at least he believed I had premonitions, so maybe he'd listen to me and my 'bossy' ways once in a while.

After that, I called Dimples, and he relayed the news that Max was indeed behind bars. A couple of hours later, Justin got his wish to meet Dimples, since we had to go to the police station and give our statements of last night's events. Justin even got his phone back, so it all worked out.

Two days later, I'd mostly recovered. My bruises were now green and yellow, and the cut along my hairline was hardly noticeable. I could move without cringing, and I didn't jump every time I heard a loud noise.

Justin had re-scheduled his meeting with his new partner and had signed the papers to open a new dental practice here in the city. Uncle Joey had even offered to pay off Justin's debt with the crypto money, telling him he'd earned it. With a smidge of misgiving, Justin had accepted the money, mostly because it meant he wouldn't have to live with his in-laws for the next few months.

Dimples called, telling me that Mikiko had checked out of the hospital and was recovering at home. She'd asked him to relay the news and wanted to know if I'd come visit her. Since I knew right where she lived, I'd agreed, and was now pulling to a stop in front of her house.

It was mid-afternoon, and filtered sunlight shone down through the fall foliage, turning the light into a golden hue. Against the crisp blue sky, the light seemed almost magical, and I was grateful I was alive to enjoy it.

I got out of the car and glanced across the street to Ramos's house. I hadn't seen him since the blast, and I wondered what errand he was running for Uncle Joey today. It had been nice to have a few days to recover, but now I was ready to jump back into things.

But, in all honesty... I'd have to say that what I really wanted to jump back into... was a motorcycle ride. This was the perfect fall day for that, and I knew there weren't too many days left like this before it got too cold for a ride.

Sighing, I headed to Mikiko's front door and rang the bell. An older woman, who looked just like Mikiko, answered the door. "You must be Shelby. I'm Chiyoko Nisogi, Mikiko's mom. Please come in."

She took me into the living room where Mikiko was propped up on the couch. To my surprise, Ramos sat on the chair beside her. "Shelby," Mikiko said. "Thank you for coming. Ramos was just telling me that you work together. Please sit down."

She motioned to a space on the couch, wondering what kind of work I did with her mysterious neighbor. There was a touch of mystery and danger about him that should have made her nervous. Instead, she felt safe. It didn't make any sense.

"I'm glad you're here. I just wanted to thank you for finding the person who..." she swallowed, still having a hard time admitting that her brother was dead. "...killed my brother."

"Of course. Did the detectives fill you in on what we believe happened?"

She nodded. "Yes. I know it was about the stadium demolition. Now that Kai's findings are out, they've postponed the demolition until they can figure out how to do it safely." She was thinking that at least he'd made a difference to the community, even though he'd never be around to see it. Tears threatened to fall, bringing on a sudden headache.

"Tell me about your brother," I asked. "From what I've seen, it sounds like he cared about taking care of the world."

"Oh... he did." She talked about Kai with pride and enthusiasm, relating a few stories that only she knew because they'd grown up together. While she spoke, the scent of eucalyptus and mint wafted through the air, reminding me of green spaces and blue sky.

It lingered while she spoke, bringing a feeling of peace and comfort into the room. She finished her tale and smiled at the memory, thinking that it almost smelled like he was there. The anger in her heart lifted, giving way to the love she'd felt for him.

She blinked, surprised her headache was gone, and glanced my way. "Thanks for coming." Her gaze found Ramos. "Both of you."

I stood. "Of course. I hope you feel better soon." She nodded and thanked me, her troubled spirit calm. Ramos and I left together, but the fresh eucalyptus scent stayed behind, and I hoped it helped Mikiko and her mother through the pain.

She'd lost her brother, and I'd almost lost mine. It made me realize how fragile life could be, and I was darn lucky to still be around to enjoy it with the people I loved.

Ramos followed me to my car. "That was... interesting." He wanted to ask me what had happened, but another part of him didn't want to know. Still... something had changed, and he'd felt... good. What was it? Of course, since it involved me, anything was possible. "It's a beautiful day. Do you have time for a ride?"

My heart did a little flip-flop, and I grinned. "You know it! I even wore my jacket."

He smiled, taking in the rough patches and the holes in the sleeves and thinking that my jacket had seen better days. After a couple of explosions, it might be time to get a new one.

I shook my head. "No way. You gave it to me. Besides, this jacket has character. I can tell you how each of these marks got there, and I wouldn't trade it for anything."

His grin widened, and he knew it was my way of telling him that I loved him, so he wouldn't argue. Someday, he'd just buy me a new one, and he was sure I'd love it just as much, since it came from him.

My breath caught, but what could I say? He was right. Ramos opened his garage door and stepped to a side table with a big shopping bag sitting on top. Opening it, he took out a box with a brand new motorcycle helmet inside. He pulled out the full-face helmet and handed it to me.

"Wow. That is so cool!" Naturally it was black, but it had a pink rose on the side and a few pink designs across the back, making it look super sexy.

He also handed me a pair of black motorcycle gloves. "Now that it's getting colder, I thought you could use them."

“These are great. Thank you!” Without waiting, I slipped the helmet on. Ramos helped me adjust it before handing me the gloves. I pulled them on while he closed the garage and put on his own helmet and gloves.

Ready for a ride, I straddled the bike behind him and we rode through the streets, taking in the sights of the beautiful, fall day. I didn’t know what crazy adventures the future would bring, but, with my family and friends beside me, I would treasure every second.

Thank you for reading **Ties That Bind: A Shelby Nichols Adventure.** I am currently hard at work on Shelby's next adventure and promise to do my best for another thrilling ride!

If you enjoyed this book, please consider leaving a review on Amazon. It's a great way to thank an author and keep her writing! **Ties That Bind** is also available on Kindle and Audible!

Want to know more about Ella St. John? Get **Angel Falls: Sand and Shadows Book 1** and find out how Ella, the nurse Shelby meets in Ghostly Serenade, ended up in Las Vegas with Aiden Creed. It is available in ebook, paperback, hardback, and audible. Don't miss this exciting adventure and the sequel, **Desert Devil: Sand and Shadows Book 2**!

Ramos has his own book! **Devil in a Black Suit,** is about Ramos and his mysterious past from his point of view. It's available in paperback, ebook, and audible formats. Get your copy today!

NEWSLETTER SIGNUP For news, updates, and special offers, please sign up for my newsletter on my website: www.colleenhelme.com. To thank you for subscribing you will receive a FREE ebook.

SHELBY NICHOLS CONSULTING Don't miss Shelby's blog posts about her everyday life! Be sure to visit shelbynicholsconsulting.com.

ABOUT THE AUTHOR

USA TODAY AND WALL STREET JOURNAL BESTSLLING AUTHOR

Colleen Helme is the author of the bestselling Shelby Nichols Adventure Series, a wildly entertaining and highly humorous series about Shelby Nichols, a woman with the ability to read minds.

She is also the author of the Sand and Shadow Series, a spin-off from the Shelby Nichols Series featuring Ella St. John, a woman with a special 'healing' touch. Between writing about these two friends, Colleen has her hands full, but is enjoying every minute of it, especially when they appear in books together.

When not writing, Colleen spends most of her time thinking about new ways to get her characters in and out of trouble. She loves to connect with readers and admits that fans of her books keep her writing.

Connect with Colleen at www.colleenhelme.com

Printed in Great Britain
by Amazon

25994926R00199